OCEAN
PREY

Praise for the novels of John Sandford

'Sleek and nasty . . . A big scary, suspenseful read, and
I loved every minute of it'
Stephen King on *Rules of Prey*

'Sandford knows all there is about detonating the gut- level
shocks of a good thriller'
New York Times

'That rare beast – a series writer who reads like
a breath of fresh air'
Daily Mirror

'*Rules of Prey* is so chilling that you're almost afraid to turn
the pages. So mesmerising that you cannot stop . . .
a crackle of surprises'
Carl Hiaasen on *Rules of Prey*

'Terrifying . . . Sandford has crafted the kind of trimmed-to-
the- bone thriller that is hard to put down'
Chicago Tribune on Rules of Prey

'This gripping thriller is over too soon'
People on Rules of Prey

'Few do it better than Sandford'

John Sandford is the pseudonym for the Pulitzer Prize-winning journalist John Camp. He is the author of thirty other Prey novels, most recently *Masked Prey*; four Kidd novels, twelve Virgil Flowers novels, and six other books, including three YA novels co-authored with his wife, Michele Cook.

Visit johnsandford.org or find him on Facebook.

ALSO BY JOHN SANDFORD

JOHN SANDFORD
OCEAN PREY

**SIMON &
SCHUSTER**

London · New York · Sydney · Toronto · New Delhi

First published in the United States by G. P. Putnam's Sons, 2021
An imprint of Penguin Random House LLC

First published in Great Britain by Simon & Schuster UK Ltd, 2021
This paperback edition published 2021

1 3 5 7 9 10 8 6 4 2

Simon & Schuster UK Ltd
1st Floor
222 Gray's Inn Road
London WC1X 8HB

Simon & Schuster Australia, Sydney
Simon & Schuster India, New Delhi

www.simonandschuster.co.uk
www.simonandschuster.com.au
www.simonandschuster.co.in

A CIP catalogue record for this book is available from the British Library

Paperback ISBN: 978-1-3985-0553-7
eBook ISBN: 978-1-3985-0552-0

Printed and bound in Great Britain by CPI Group (UK) Ltd, Croydon, CR0 4YY

For Michele, again

THE MUGGERS

LUCAS DAVENPORT USED his phone's flashlight to illuminate the cut through the knee-high wall, and from there, to the path that led down to Fort Lauderdale Beach. Early-morning traffic down Beach Boulevard was quiet, the subdued hum of small SUVs and sedans. The cars turning left off Sunrise Boulevard played their headlights across his back as he walked, throwing his shadow on the white sand.

Out on the Atlantic, he could see a bare hint of the coming dawn. Lucas walked across the sand until he was a dozen feet from the water, where the smell of seaweed pressed against his face like a hand. He sat down, took off his shoes and socks. He sat there for a while, as the eastern horizon grew brighter. Not much was going through his head—the light, the smell of the seaweed, the sound of salt water breaking up the beach.

A breeze sprang up with the dawn, but was barely strong enough to push the six-inch rollers ashore. After a while, he noticed that the world was beginning to light up. His phone rang. He dug it out of his jacket pocket and turned it off without answering, or even looking at it.

At some point, the rim of the sun broke the edge of the horizon, a brilliant arc throwing rippling orange slashes across the water. A sportfishing boat went by, a half mile out.

Then the muggers showed up.

Two men, one Anglo, one Hispanic, both thin, dark-haired, wearing worn dark clothing, their faces weathered from life on the street, like driftwood boards. Lucas knew they were muggers by the way they approached, a certain crablike walk, a phony confidence, an attitude that could turn in a moment from friendliness to naked aggression and then possibly to retreat, if Lucas should turn out to be something unexpected.

They checked him out, a guy in a sport coat barefoot on the sand, maybe shaking off a drunk? A gold watch on the left wrist, right hand in his lap. He looked at them and said, "Hey, guys."

The Anglo said, "Nice watch you got."

Lucas: "Got it from my wife for my birthday. A Patek Philippe. Twenty-eight thousand dollars, if you can believe that. I told her we should have sponsored some hungry kids somewhere. She said that we already did that and I should have some nice things."

The guy in back stopped and hooked his friend's elbow to slow down his approach; the feral sense that something was not right.

"You okay?" the lead mugger asked.

Lucas said, "No."

He slipped his right hand out of his lap, and held it straight up in front of his nose; he was gripping a black Walther PPQ.

One of the muggers said, "Whoa."

"Why were you guys going to mug me? Don't bullshit me, tell me the truth," Lucas said. "You gonna stick something in your arm? Stick something up your nose? Or what?"

They stuttered around for a moment, looking like they might run, but there was no place to hide on the empty beach and running through the sand would be slow. Much slower than a bullet. The Anglo guy said, "Mostly looking for something to eat. Ain't had nothing to eat since yesterday morning."

"Okay." Lucas sat motionless for a few seconds, the muzzle of the gun straight up to the sky, between his hands, as though he were praying, and then he fished in his jacket pocket for his wallet, extracted a bill, folded it into quarters, and tossed it across the sand. "Pick it up," he said.

The Anglo looked at his friend, then eased carefully forward, stopped, and picked up the bill. "Fifty bucks."

"Fifty bucks," Lucas said. "Go get something to eat."

They backed away, watching him, then turned and moved away more quickly. Before they were out of earshot, Lucas called, "Hey. Guys."

They stopped and looked back.

"When I get up from here and walk down the beach, if I see you jumping someone, I'll fuckin' kill both of you. You understand?"

The Hispanic guy said, "Yes, sir." And the two of them hot-footed it down the beach path to the street and out of sight.

Lucas looked back out at the ocean. The sun was halfway above the horizon now, the orange burning off, going to yellow.

Another day.

Wasn't going to be a good one.

JULY

CHAPTER

ONE

FIVE YEARS EARLIER, the high school guidance counselor sat Barney Hall down and said, "Barney, you're bright enough, but you're not college material. Not yet." He was looking over Hall's standard test scores and other accumulated records from thirteen years in the Lower Cape May Regional School District. "You're not mature for your age. If you hadn't been sent to detention once a week, you wouldn't have done any studying at all."

Hall was a cheerful, good-looking, middle-sized kid with broad shoulders and bright white teeth, who must have said a hundred times in his life, "Watch this—and hey, hold my beer, willya?"

He had a girlfriend named Sue, whom he'd known since fourth grade, who was happy to hold his beer, most of the time, and then apply the bandages afterward. Hall worked after school and all summers as a mechanic in his dad's yacht salvage yard, or junkyard, depending on who was doing the talking.

"I'm trying to do better, sir," he told the counselor.

"Don't bullshit me, son. Would I be correct in believing that you were drinking beer at Toby Jones's wedding last weekend and got drunk and fell off the dock and damn near drowned?"

"I'm a good swimmer, sir. There was no danger."

"That's not the point, Barney. Anyway, if you want to do anything in life, you need to get serious, and right quick. Knowing you, looking at these records, I'm thinking your best course would be the military. The military would give you responsibility from day one. If you don't come through, they'll slap your ass in the brig. You need that discipline. Mind, I'm not saying the Marine Corps. You're way too smart for that."

"I wasn't thinking college, not right away," Hall said. "I've been talking with Sue, and . . . How about the Coast Guard, sir? There're some Coasties that hang out at my dad's place and I like listening to them talk. I've been on the water and working on boats all my life."

The counselor poked a finger at him: "That's the smartest thing I ever heard you say, Barney. You do a few years in the Coast Guard, get yourself some rank and responsibility and they'll even send you to college when you're ready. God help me, you could wind up an officer."

"Whoa. That'd be awesome, sir."

"And do me a favor, son. Get rid of that T-shirt." The T-shirt featured a basketball-sized, full-color image of a bantam rooster, with the legend, EVERYTHING'S BIGGER IN TEXAS.

Hall looked down at the T-shirt. "It's just a chicken, sir."

"It's a cock," the counselor said. "You know it and I know it. I don't want to see it in this school again."

HALL MARRIED SUE the June after high school graduation, joined the Coast Guard at the end of a glorious summer, and after boot camp and advanced training, was stationed in Fort Lauderdale.

Sue Hall went to Broward College and became a registered nurse and started working on a bachelor's degree in nursing. Hall found the boatyards of Marina Mile to be the most amazing places he'd ever been. When Sue got pregnant with their first one, he got off-duty work rebuilding diesel engines in one of the Marina Mile engine shops. The extra work would get them childcare money so Sue could finish her BS degree.

At night, they'd drink PBR under palm trees in their trailer park, until Sue got pregnant, when they switched to ginger ale, and she'd say, "Barnes, we're gonna do good in life. I can feel it coming on."

The owner of the engine shop had a pile of old boats out back, which he couldn't sell, and Hall kept looking at a 1999 Boston Whaler 260 Outrage that had been stripped of the twin outboards and had a hole in the hull, and now sat derelict atop a tandem trailer with two flat tires on each side, overgrown with weeds. After some talk, the owner agreed to give Hall the boat along with two badly abused, but salvageable, Merc 225s and the trailer—all Hall had to do was work five additional unpaid hours a week, in the evenings and on weekends, on top of his regular weekend shift, for two years, and the boat was his.

Plus, he could use the shop and its tools to rehab the trailer and the Mercs and do whatever fiberglass work the boat needed. The boat was solid, except for the hole, which could be fixed.

THAT'S THE ENTIRE backstory as to why Hall, Sue, and their first boy, Lance, almost a one-year-old, were trolling down the debris line on the outer reef south of Pompano Beach, Florida, looking for dorado—mahi-mahi—when Hall spotted something unusual happening with a snazzy-looking Mako center console a half mile ahead of them. He said, "Sue, hand me the glasses."

The Mako had two white outboards hanging off the back, which Hall recognized as big 350s, giving the boat seven hundred horses with which to get across the ocean.

"What's out there, Barnes?" Sue asked. She was a rangy young woman, would have been a cowgirl in Texas, sunburnt, fighter-pilot blue eyes, her rose-blond hair frizzy from salt water.

"Something strange going on, babe. I've been watching him, 'cause that's a sharp boat. All of a sudden it slowed down and stopped and it looks like it picked up a diver in the middle of the ocean. I mean, who was already in the middle of the ocean before they got there. Went right to him."

"You don't see that every day," Sue said.

Hall was still on the glasses. "He's, uh, looks like they've got some lift bags coming over the side . . . in the middle of the ocean."

"Maybe picking up some bugs?" She was referring to spiny lobsters.

"From a guy they left in the middle of the ocean?"

Sue said, with a sudden urgency, "Barnes, I've got a bad feeling about this. Let's turn around. Bring the boat back north."

"Yeah." That seemed like a good idea.

Hall turned the boat in a wide fisherman's semicircle and headed back north, but kept watching the Mako through the glasses. He was careful to be standing behind the center console when he used the binoculars, because he'd learned early in his Coast Guard training that if you saw somebody whose arms, head, and chest formed an equilateral triangle, they were looking at you through binoculars—and every few minutes, one of the men on the Mako would check them out with binoculars.

Twenty minutes after it stopped, the sleek-looking craft lurched forward and headed south. Hall got his cell phone, called in to the watch officer at the Coast Guard station at Fort Lauderdale.

"Sir, this is Barney Hall. I'm south of Pompano Beach in my own boat, but I saw something strange out here. There's a black-and-white Mako 284 heading toward Port Everglades. We saw him picking up something from the middle of the ocean. He was running fast, then stopped, and there was a diver waiting for him right there in the water. There were no other boats around, no dive flag. They were using lift bags . . ."

"Can you stay with him, Hall?"

"No, sir, not entirely, he's running fast. I can keep him in sight until he makes the turn. I'll be a mile back of him by then."

"He looked suspicious?"

"Yes, he did, sir. If I was on duty, I'd stop him, for sure."

"We'll do that, then. We'll have somebody waiting for him inside."

HALL TOLD SUE to put on her life jacket and bring in the fishing lines; the baby was already wrapped in a fat orange PFD. He turned the boat and they tracked the Mako until it made the turn into the Port Everglades cut. Hall got back on his phone and called the watch officer and said, "It's Hall, sir, he's making the turn."

"We're on it, Hall. Good job."

◆◆◆

THE MAKO WAS ambushed by a Coast Guard RIB—rigid inflatable boat—which had orange inflatable tubes wrapped around a hardshell hull. The petty officer second class who was running the boat got on channel 16 and called, "Mako 284 *Chevere,* this is the United States Coast Guard coming up behind to make a courtesy inspection. Cut your speed to five knots and hold your course. We'll board you from the starboard side."

Coast Guard inspection boats were usually larger RIBs with pilothouses; the boat that had been scrambled to intercept the Mako was smaller, three men aboard, no pilothouse. The Coast Guard boat pulled up behind the Mako and the petty officer in the bow saw two men waiting in the stern—bulky guys, dressed like sport fishermen, bright-colored shirts and shorts, sunglasses, and billed hats.

Then, as they were a few feet off, ready to board, one of the men on the stern of the Mako lifted up a heavy long-nosed black rifle with a red-dot sight. With a motion that was practiced and almost graceful, he shot the two Coast Guardsmen in the bow, and then twice shot the PO2 who was running the boat. The four shots together took no more than two seconds. The gun barked, rather than banged, a flat noise because of the suppressor on the barrel; the gunshots were loud, but not especially audible over the sound of the boat engines.

The PO2 had killed the boat's speed for the boarding and when he saw the rifle come up he reached forward to hit the accelerator, but a bullet took him in the throat and then another in the chest, and the slugs turned him away and he fell into the bottom of the boat, dying, blood spreading around him on the wet floor, a purple flood. The Coast Guard boat turned into a slow circle across the wide port and the Mako accelerated away.

As the Mako left, Hall, Sue, and the baby nosed through the cut in their rehabbed Whaler and saw the Coast Guard boat turning away from it.

Hall watched for a moment, then said, "There's something wrong, Sue."

"Get over there," Sue said. "That Mako's running like a thief in the night. I'll get the gun." They kept a .38 Special in a waterproof can down an equipment hatch.

Hall pushed the boat as hard as he could, but they were a full minute away from the Coast Guard RIB. He couldn't see anybody aboard as he approached. He slipped his cell phone out of his pocket, but when he got alongside, he saw the three bodies in the bottom of the boat and he dropped the cell phone and grabbed the VHF and screamed, "Mayday, Mayday, Mayday, Port Everglades, three Coast Guards shot in boat chasing black-and-white Mako . . ."

The Coast Guard came back instantly: "Mayday caller, identify yourself!"

"This is Coast Guard Petty Officer Two Barney Hall. We have three men shot inside the Port Everglades entrance. They look bad, man, they look really bad."

Then the watch officer: "Hall, can you help them? We're on the way, but you gotta do what you can . . ."

"My wife's a nurse, I'm putting her on board, sir. Should I go with her or go after the Mako?"

There were several seconds of silence—Sue had handed him the .38, and was already clambering into the Coast Guard boat with the baby and their first aid kit—and then the officer came back: "Your call, Hall. Chopper's coming, but it'll be a few minutes."

Hall looked down at his wife, who had checked one man quickly and then moved to the bow. She'd done two years in emergency rooms and she knew what she was seeing. She looked back at him and shook her head and Hall shouted into the radio, "I'm going after the sonsofbitches, sir."

He dropped the hammer on the Whaler. The Mako was most of a half mile ahead of him, moving fast down the Intracoastal Waterway, and there was no way Hall would have caught the other boat if the Mako hadn't swerved to a pier, where three men jumped off. One ran to a parked SUV, opened it, and backed it to the edge of the pier. Two others ran what looked like black buckets to the white SUV. A fourth man was still on the boat, carrying more black buckets to the bow. They were in a frantic hurry: radios automatically monitored channel 16, so they'd heard Hall's Mayday and the Coast Guard's response.

After moving more buckets to the bow of the boat, the fourth man hoisted a five-gallon gas can out of a hatch on the Mako's stern and began spraying the boat with gasoline and then, as Hall roared toward them, stepped off the boat, lit what looked like a piece of newspaper, and threw it toward the Mako. The boat exploded in flame.

The three men who'd been loading the black buckets into the SUV jumped into the car and the fourth man ran up to the back door and yanked it open. Hall had the .38 in his hand—he was close enough to feel the heat from the flames—and fired three wild shots at the car, no hope of hitting anything because the careening Whaler was pounding the deck against his feet, making any kind of an accurate shot almost impossible.

Impossibly, one of his shots hit the fourth man in the head.

The man dropped flat on the concrete pier, stone-cold dead. The driver of the car jumped out, grabbed the man by his shirt, looked at him, dropped him, looked for a moment at Hall, his face unreadable behind dark glasses, then leaped back into the car and spun it out of sight.

The Mako was burning like a torch.

The watch officer was shouting, "Hall, Hall, where are you?"

"Look for the fire, sir; I'm south of the cut where the fire's at."

FOR HIS ACTIONS, Hall was given the Coast Guard Medal. Other than the man killed by Hall, none of the men on the Mako or in the car were caught or even identified. The dead man was a minor hoodlum from Miami Beach, whom the feds called a "known associate," though he appeared to be an associate of every piece of scum on the Beach, which was a lot of scum.

The Mako's Florida registration was real enough; the owner wasn't. The fire, which sank the boat, wiped out fingerprints and DNA. The SUV was never identified or found. No gun was found on the sunken boat or in the area around it.

Hall was presented the medal by the rear admiral who commanded the Coast Guard's District Seven. When the admiral asked him his plans, Hall said, "My hitch is almost up, sir. I'm going to college at FIU. If I go full time, I'll be out in three years. Then I might be back, if I can get into OCS. I really like what we do."

The admiral patted him on the shoulder with some affection. "You'll get in. With your history, I can guarantee it. Get a degree in something useful."

"I'm thinking crime science," Hall said.

"That'll work," the admiral said.

"Sir, if you don't mind. I do have a question."

"Go ahead."

"Nobody's been caught for killing our guys," Hall said. "Where's the FBI?"

"I asked that exact same question, a couple of weeks ago, but I wasn't as polite as you are," the admiral said. "I asked, 'Where the fuck is the FBI?' The answer was, 'Nowhere,' and you can quote me on that."

NOVEMBER

CHAPTER

TWO

VIRGIL FLOWERS LEFT the courtroom and caught an elevator going down. He turned as the doors began to close and a dark-haired hatchet-faced woman in an old blue floral dress, carrying an antique white woven handbag, standing outside in the hallway, looked straight into his eyes and held them. She was only a foot or two from the elevator doors, but made no effort to step inside.

When the elevator doors closed, a woman next to Virgil said, "Well, that was weird. I thought she was going to shoot you."

"Couldn't get a gun in the courthouse," Virgil said. A couple of people behind him laughed, more nervously than heartily.

Virgil worked his way down to the Hennepin Government Center's basement cafeteria, where he spotted Lucas Davenport sitting at a table to one side, legs crossed, reading a free newspaper. Davenport saw him at the same time and waved. He'd walked to the courthouse from the federal building.

Virgil went over and shook hands and asked, "You eat?"

"Not yet. I wasn't sure when you'd get out." Davenport was a tall man, but thin, weathered, athletic, dark hair shot with gray, crystalline blue eyes; he was fifty-two, and looked his age. He was wearing a blue woolen jacket, a white dress shirt, black woolen slacks, and cap-toed dress shoes; a light cashmere coat was draped over the back of his chair. He might have been a prosperous attorney, but he wasn't.

"What's that?" Virgil asked, nodding at a two-inch-thick brown file envelope sitting by Davenport's right hand.

"Maybe a case," Lucas said. "I'm thinking about it." He stuck a hand in a jacket pocket, pulled out a twenty-dollar bill and handed it to Virgil. "Get me a cheeseburger, fries, and a Diet Coke."

"What, I'm a waitress now?"

"I'm saving the table," Lucas said. "Or would you rather eat standing up?"

VIRGIL CAME BACK a few minutes later with a tray, scraped out a chair, put the food down, and said in a quiet voice, "There's a woman sitting behind me . . . Don't look right away, be casual about it. She's wearing an old blue dress with flowers and has a white handbag sitting on the table."

He sat down and Lucas looked casually past his shoulder and checked the woman. He turned back to Virgil and picked up his cheeseburger and asked, "Who is she?"

"She's the wife of the guy I testified against. He's going to prison for ten years or so."

"What'd he do?"

"Robbed credit unions. One every three or four months, down in southern Minnesota and northern Iowa. I caught him a couple of months ago, in Blue Earth. He was the family's sole support."

"She does look mean. I'd be worried, if I were you," Lucas said. "Did you get mustard?"

"Only ketchup. I don't think she's armed, but . . ." Virgil picked up a piece of silverware and waggled it at Lucas. ". . . I'd rather not have a fork stuck in my eye."

"Not to worry. If she rushes you, I'll put three Hydra-Shoks through her belly button."

"Thank you, I'd appreciate it," Virgil said. Davenport got up, went to the cafeteria line, and came back with three packets of mustard. Through a forkful of hot macaroni and cheese, Virgil said, "Frankie says hello."

"How are the twins?"

"Loud. Very loud. Relentless," Virgil said. The twins, one of each, were two months old. "Frankie would need about six tits to keep them happy—don't ever tell her I said that. My mother's down there with them. I get two hours of sleep a night."

"I thought you were keeping your mother away?"

"That would be like keeping gravity away," Virgil said. "Not gonna happen. She still staring at me?"

"Still staring," Lucas said, watching Virgil's stalker from the corner of his eye.

"I can feel her eyes burning a hole in the back of my neck," Virgil said.

Lucas asked, "What happened with your novel?"

Virgil had been writing wildlife magazine articles for years, but since the previous winter had been working on a thriller novel. Lucas was one of the few people who knew about it. Virgil said, "Didn't fly. Not good enough."

"You gonna give up?"

"No. I've got this agent in New York. She told me that I could make a living at it, but I didn't know what I was doing yet. She gave me some ideas, and I'm starting over."

"You can do it," Lucas said. "I'll be bragging to people that I know you."

VIRGIL WAS AS tall as Lucas, but with blond hair worn too long for an agent of the Minnesota Department of Criminal Apprehension. He was wearing his court clothes, a gray suit, white shirt, and blue necktie, an ensemble unsettled by his cowboy boots, though the snakeskin was well polished. He poked his fork at the brown file envelope next to Lucas's hand. "What's the case?"

"Three Coast Guardsmen got shot to death a few months ago, down in Fort Lauderdale," Lucas said. "Broad daylight. Nothing's happened on that. Nothing."

"I remember reading about it."

"The FBI has been investigating, but haven't been getting anywhere," Lucas said. "The thought was floated by a U.S. senator from Florida that maybe the Marshals Service could take a look."

"Was the senator one of your political godfathers?"

"No, but people talk," Lucas said. "He called me directly."

"So when he suggested the Marshals Service might take a look, he meant you. Personally," Virgil said.

"Yes. That didn't go over real well—it implied that the FBI wasn't getting anywhere," Lucas said.

"Which they weren't."

"True, but the implication was resented. The FBI has a lot more clout in the Justice Department than the Marshals Service and they've been peeing on our shoes. Actually, my shoes," Lucas said. "The longer the case stretches out, with no progress, the more pressure . . . Uh, the woman with the handbag got up, she's . . ." Virgil pulled his head down. ". . . going to the cafeteria line."

"Check what she orders. I've seen a woman get burned bad by a slice of hot pizza. Red hot, stuck to her face, couldn't get it off," Virgil said, resisting the urge to look at the woman. "Anyway, you're tangled up in a bureaucratic feud. What are you going to do?"

"I've been reading the files," Lucas said. "They keep coming, but they never have much in them. Lots of paperwork. The feeling is, we're dealing with drug smugglers and the drug is most likely heroin, and it may be coming in from Colombia, but nobody knows for sure."

"That's it? That's all they got?"

"The Coast Guard says that a freighter probably dumped a bunch of heroin in watertight containers on a reef off Lauderdale. It was being recovered by a diver from a fishing boat, and when the Coast Guard tried to stop the boat, three Coast Guardsmen got shot and killed and the boat was burned to get rid of biologic evidence. A Coast Guardsman killed one of the smugglers, but the rest got away. The Coast Guard has been watching the general area of the dump, but they haven't seen any more recovery efforts. Maybe it's all gone. Then again, the Broward County sheriff has picked up rumors that it's still sitting out there."

"Has anybody been looking for the stuff? Navy divers?" Virgil asked.

"Yeah, that's mentioned in the files, but the search area is large, the water is really deep for divers, and the visibility isn't all that good," Lucas said. "They had one of those remote-control submarines looking for a while, but didn't find anything."

"Then how are the smugglers finding it?"

"They've probably got precise GPS coordinates that'll put them right on top of the containers," Lucas said. "The Coast Guard thinks the containers may have some kind of proximity device— push a button on a transceiver and it sends out a locator beep. That's what they tell me, anyway."

"Huh. What do you think you could do? You're not a diver, you don't know shit about submarines or GPS. If the feds . . ."

Lucas said, "Your friend bought two slices of pizza."

Virgil: "When I went by there, the pizza was so hot the cheese was bubbling . . . What's she doing now?"

"Staring at you. Carrying the pizza to her table . . . Okay, she's sitting down. She's eating the pizza. Still staring."

"It's creeping me out," Virgil said.

"It's creeping me out and I'm not even you," Lucas said.

Virgil wrenched the conversation back to the heroin dump. "What could you do down in Lauderdale? Other than get out of Minnesota in November?"

"What could I do? That's what I've been thinking about," Lucas said. "The FBI doesn't do confrontation. We need some confrontation to shake things up. Push people around. Deal some get-out-of-jail cards in return for information. Street-cop stuff. Find out who gets upset."

"You're gonna do it?"

"I dunno. Those meatheads at the FBI . . ." Lucas stroked his chin with a thumb and forefinger, staring past Virgil, not at the woman, but at the blank wall to one side. Virgil let him stare, un-interrupted. Then, abruptly, Lucas looked back at Virgil and said, "Yeah. I'm gonna do it."

"Good. Nice to see an older guy have a hobby . . . What's she doing now?"

"Finishing the pizza," Lucas said. "She's still staring, though. She looks really tense. She's fumbling in her purse . . ." Lucas backed his chair up a few inches, so he could clear his gun if need be. "She's got a . . ."

"What?"

". . . ChapStick."

"ChapStick?"

"Yeah, you know, for chapped lips," Lucas said.

Virgil leaned back in his chair. "Wait: I gotta change my underwear for a ChapStick?"

THAT EVENING, LUCAS's wife, Weather, took their two children-at-home to the Mall of America. When they got home, carrying shopping bags and wearing pleased expressions, Lucas had spread the FBI files around the den and was looking at U.S. Senator Christopher Colles of Florida on his iMac screen, a FaceTime call.

"My daughter's husband is a commander in the Coast Guard and these boys were like family to them," Colles said. "Elmer and Porter say you're my best shot." Elmer was Elmer Henderson, Porter was Porter Smalls, both U.S. senators from Minnesota.

"I've looked at the files and I'm interested, Senator," Lucas said. "Would you know the U.S. attorney for the Southern District of Florida?"

"Sure do, she's one of my crew. Anna Rubio. Can she help you out?"

"When I go in on something like this, maybe with a couple other marshals, we don't have the investigative abilities of the FBI . . . the research abilities, the surveillance teams, the personnel. What we do is we go in and kick things over, make some offers that some bad people can't refuse. The FBI doesn't do that. We won't do anything illegal, you understand, but I might need backup from the U.S. attorney. Or an assistant U.S. attorney, who carries the water for the boss."

"Give me an example of what you're talking about."

"Maybe a get-out-of-jail card for a relative," Lucas said. "Not for murder, but for like a mid-level drug deal. Maybe somebody's got two more years to serve on a ten-year sentence, they get an early parole. Maybe we catch somebody with an ounce of cocaine and instead of waving him off, the U.S. attorney talks tough to him and his attorney . . ."

"Sounds fine to me," Colles said. "I'll call up Anna and tell her you'll be in touch. Give me a call once in a while and tell me how you're doing."

"I will do that," Lucas said.

WHEN HE GOT off the call, he saw Weather standing in the doorway with crossed arms. "So you're going?"

"Looks like it. Are you going to give me a hard time?"

"No. It's what you do, but you've got to be here for Thanksgiving," she said. "Letty's coming and there'll be some parties that weekend. You should plan to be back that whole Thanksgiving week." Letty was their adult adoptive daughter, about to graduate from Stanford University with a master's degree in economics.

"I can do that," Lucas said. Thanksgiving was almost a month away. "By then I should have a handle on the situation."

AFTER TALKING WITH Weather, Lucas called Bob Matees, a marshal with the service's Special Operations Group.

"Taken you a while to get back," Bob said. "We sent that stuff to you a month ago. More than a month."

"Homeland Security and the Justice Department have been arm wrestling over jurisdiction and decided to split the difference," Lucas said. "We're allowed to monitor and assist the investigation, but the FBI keeps the lead."

Bob said, "I don't know what that means."

"It means we're in, if we want to be. We might have to go to some meetings, but basically, we'll be on our own."

"You and me?"

"And Rae."

"Rae's out for the time being," Bob said. "Her mom was diagnosed with breast cancer last week and Rae's taken leave and gone home. She'll be there until the docs figure out a treatment program."

"Her mom gonna die?" Lucas asked.

"That's not what the docs are saying, but it's serious. The treatment is gonna be tough. She's at MD Anderson in Houston, so that's good."

"All right. Let's stay in touch with her," Lucas said. "I'm thinking we get down to Fort Lauderdale in the next few days . . . the task force is working out of a hotel off I-95."

"How many guys?" Bob asked.

"A dozen FBI agents, representatives from the Miami-Dade cops, Broward sheriff's department, Fort Lauderdale cops, and Homeland Security—Homeland Security is the Coast Guard. We'll be the last guys through the door."

"Ah, man." Bob was pre-discouraged.

"It is what it is. You want in?" Lucas asked.

"Of course. I'm already packing my Jockey shorts."

"Girlfriend's okay with it?"

"I told her it might be happening," Bob said. "She worries, but she knows what's what."

"I've got to do some more diplomacy here, but Weather's on board. I'll talk to Russell and get your airline tickets going."

"See you in Lauderdale, man."

THE NEXT MORNING, a woman named Elsie M. Sweat called from Miami and introduced herself as an assistant U.S. attorney. "I've been briefed by Anna and Senator Colles's assistant. We won't do anything . . . ethically . . . challenging, but we can help you in your discussions with possible informants."

"That sounds fine," Lucas said.

"When do you expect to start?" she asked.

"Monday. I'm not sure we'll need your help, but it's a possibility. I wanted to have it lined up in advance."

"We're here. This Coast Guard thing has been a constant irritant and the FBI doesn't seem to be making measurable progress," Sweat said. "We'd love to get rid of the whole problem—so good luck and keep your asses down."

"We'll do that."

Keep your asses down.

Lucas had been told that by other cops, and had even used the phrase himself a few times, but had never been told that by a prosecutor. Maybe there was something about the culture of South Florida that would make the reminder relevant?

"I guess we'll find out," he said aloud, that night in bed, in the dark.

Weather was nearly asleep: "What?"

"Just . . . ruminating."

THREE

LUCAS WALKED OUT of the Fort Lauderdale airport's Terminal Three into a sweaty night that smelled of ocean, even though the airport was a couple of miles from salt water.

He got lost trying to find a shuttle bus ride to Terminal One, where the car rental services were located. He finally walked there, cutting across a parking structure, dragging his roller bag. He rented a Nissan Pathfinder, drove north up I-95 and checked into the TRYP Hotel, with a room overlooking a complex of on- and off-ramps.

Bob was already at the hotel and when Lucas called his room, Bob said, "I've spotted what looks like a decent seafood restaurant that we can walk to. From the satellite photo, it looks like they'll have a nice view of a marina."

"Give me a half hour. I want to wash the airplane off and knock on the task force leader's door and say hello . . ."

Lucas spent five minutes in the shower, pulled on jeans, a T-shirt, and a sport coat, then went up a floor and knocked on Dale Weaver's door. They'd talked on the phone and Weaver seemed like a congenial guy, for an FBI supervisory agent, anyway, and Lucas had told him that he'd stop up when he got to the hotel.

Weaver came to the door, a stocky man with a square face, lined by years and maybe tobacco, balding, showing white in what was left of his originally reddish hair. He was wearing a T-shirt and gray sweatpants. The run-up to *Monday Night Football* was playing on a TV behind him. He smiled and said, "Davenport—you look just like your picture on the internet."

"Well, hell. I thought I looked like George Clooney in real life."

"He could be a distant relative," Weaver agreed, as they shook hands. "Very distant. Fourth or fifth cousin. C'mon in."

Weaver sat on his bed and Lucas took the desk chair and they spent twenty minutes getting acquainted, talking about the task force and the problems it faced. Weaver didn't try to disguise the fact that they hadn't accomplished much.

"We didn't have a place to start. We know where the boat was kept, which was on the New River, next to a house. Down here, as you get closer to the coast, it's like Venice, the New River and all these canals running up through the neighborhoods. The space was rented from an absentee homeowner based on an advertisement he'd put up on the net and he'd never actually met the boat owner."

"Pretty convenient for the boat owner, given what they were doing with the boat," Lucas said.

"Good piece of research by the assholes, is what I think," Weaver said. "The homeowner, the guy with rights to the dock space, is one of those super-rich investment honchos. He has about six houses, up in Manhattan and the Hamptons and a ranch in Wyoming and another place down in the Islands. He's here about three or four weeks a year. He has a management service to take care of cleaning and maintenance, and it was actually the service that put up notice for the dock space rental. Those people didn't see the boat owner, either. They said the whole deal was handled by mail, they got a money order to pay six months' rent, and one day the boat was parked there. They clean the house twice a month and they only saw the boat twice, so it probably wasn't parked there for more than a month and a half. The last time they saw it was a week before it burned and sank."

"And the homeowner looks straight?"

"We now know the color of his undershorts. I mean, however much junk got dumped in the ocean, he could buy all of it, and a hundred times more with the money he earned last year. I got the feeling he's a crook, but not a dope crook, a financial services crook."

"All right. Well, my partner and I—I think you've heard from him . . ."

"I have . . ."

"We've read all your research paper and we'll be reading it again, and then we'll go kick over some garbage cans. You've been around for a while, what do you think about that whole idea?"

Weaver shrugged: "Nothing else has worked. Might as well try some marshal stuff. I know about your record, so . . . glad to have you."

That, Lucas thought, was the first time an FBI agent had actually said that to him.

BOB WAS WAITING in the lobby. "Good talk?"

"Yeah, we'll get along. Weaver will take anyone who can help. Any scrap he can get."

They left the hotel and walked down a narrow dark lane to a

place called the Rendezvous, got a table outside overlooking a marina crowded with half-million-dollar boats—those were the ordinary ones, the big ones were parked around the edges—ordered sea bass for Bob and chicken tenders for Lucas.

Bob was a large man, with a square face, small battered ears, short hair, and an easy smile. He was neither fat nor tall. He'd killed a cannibal earlier that year, more by accident than by intention, but nobody grieved for the dead man. Bob had finished third in the NCAA's heavyweight wrestling division in his senior year at Oklahoma and could do a hundred good pushups in three minutes with his girlfriend, who weighed a hundred and thirty pounds, sitting on his shoulders. He was wearing a double-extra-large golf shirt, khaki shorts, and cross-trainers. He could have sold billboard space on his back.

He said to Lucas, over margaritas, "I've seen a couple of FBI spooks. I went up the elevator with two of them. They had those plastic cards around their necks, you know the kind? It's not like they're hiding. I said hello and one of them was tempted to nod at me, but he didn't."

"Sounds about right," Lucas said. A good-looking waitress came over to make sure the drinks were okay, complimented Bob on his shoulders, and leaned in as she refreshed their glasses of water. When she left, Lucas looked back to Bob and asked, "How's Rae doing?"

"She was in town yesterday to get more clothes. Her mom's starting chemo right away. Gonna lose her hair. Rae wants her to shave her head before it starts coming out."

"Ah, boy . . . Is Rae still pissed at me?" Lucas had shot to death a man on a case the three had worked together.

"She was never pissed. She just would have given that guy a chance," Bob said. "She thinks you went there intending to kill him and that's what you did. Her brain doesn't work like that. Neither does mine, come to think of it."

"Even though you saw the dead kid in the schoolyard?"

"Even though. I'm a lawman," Bob said. "You're looking for justice. Those are two different things. We know that, me'n Rae, and we're willing to live with it."

"Yeah, well . . ."

"I'll still kiss you on the lips if you want," Bob said.

"Not necessary."

THEY SPENT THE meal talking about this and that, a one-man band in the corner playing vintage soft rock over the conversation, the rumble from I-95 providing the thumping bass notes. When they were ambling back to the hotel through the dark, Lucas said, "This is boat show week. It's over by the ocean. We need to start there tomorrow morning."

"What's there?"

"The Coast Guardsman who killed that dope runner. He's out of the Coast Guard now, he's going to college down here, and he's working the boat show for extra cash. We need to talk to him. Before that, there's an eight o'clock status meeting with the task force in one of the hotel meeting rooms. That should be done by nine."

"I'm looking forward to it," Bob said, and he yawned.

"Wear shorts," Lucas said. "Gonna be hot."

"All right."

"And maybe you should bring your gear bag with you. Leave it partly unzipped with your M4 on top."

Bob brightened. "That wouldn't have occurred to me, but I can already see it in my mind's eye."

THE HOTEL HAD a breakfast spread in the morning, twelve dollars. Bob ate some of everything in sight, Lucas focused on pancakes, with a bottle of Diet Coke from the gift shop. Four men who looked like FBI agents were there, clustered in a quiet group bent over their food, all in suits but none wearing neckties; there must have been a special tropical dispensation, Lucas thought.

They glanced at Bob and Lucas from time to time, but made no move to talk to them. The daytime temps were supposed to reach 84 and Lucas and Bob were going to a boat show, so they were wearing guayabera shirts loose over their guns, khaki cargo shorts, and athletic shoes. Bob added a blue baseball cap that said NIMBUS on the front.

"What's a Nimbus?" Lucas had asked.

"A rain cloud. Or, could be a halo, but in this case, I think a rain cloud, since we're gonna rain on the FBI's parade," Bob said.

"Good-looking hat."

"Thank you. I got it for free from some guy who had a box full of them in the lobby," Bob said. "I think it's the name of a boat he's trying to sell. Guy looked like a country singer, but I can't remember which one."

On the way to the elevators, Lucas, trailing Bob, realized that their shirts and shoes almost matched, and their shorts did match.

In the elevator, he asked, "The way we're dressed . . . you think we look like aging gay guys?"

"I'm not aging," Bob said.

THE MEETING ROOM was a long rectangle meant to look like a corporate boardroom, pale plastic wall coverings and a table that resembled wood. The room had a row of windows, but the shades had been drawn; a box of donuts and a tank of coffee sat on a side table with packs of sugar and creamer. Weaver was hovering over a stack of files and computer printouts on the boardroom table when Lucas and Bob arrived, five minutes early, and he nodded at them.

Eight other men and one woman were chatting or finding chairs, opening laptops. They were all in their twenties or thirties, dressed in either suits or sport coats with coordinated slacks. Neckties had reappeared: some wore ties knotted at the throat, others had slung their ties over their shoulders, like ribbons, to be tied when they went public. They stopped chatting to check out the guayabera shirts and shorts on the marshals.

One of the agents looked at Bob's knees, and then Lucas's, and said, "You're the marshals."

Bob said, cheerfully, "Yup," and pulled out a chair, sat down. He didn't have his gear bag, but he winced and said, "Ouch, goddamnit." He reached under his shirt, pulled out his .40-caliber Glock and dropped it on the table with a clunk. "Hate it when it pokes me in the gut, know what I mean?"

Lucas bit his lip and sat down himself, turned toward Weaver, and said, "We're heading to the boat show right after the briefing. We thought shorts would be the way to go."

"What's over there?" one of the agents asked.

"Boats," Bob said. "And the Coast Guard guy who shot the smuggler. We wanted to start at the beginning."

Weaver nodded and said, "If you want, go ahead. If you read our interviews with him . . ."

"We both have," Lucas said. "Good interviews, but I want to hear him talk."

Weaver finished with the stack of papers he'd been sorting and said, "Let's everybody sit down." When everybody was seated, Weaver poked a pencil at Lucas and said, "The dark-haired gentleman is Lucas Davenport, the bruiser over here is Bob Matees. I have bios for both of them, if anyone is interested. Don't let the stupid shirts and shorts fool you: Davenport closed out eighty murders over twenty-five years with the Minneapolis Police Department, the Minnesota Bureau of Criminal Apprehension, and the Marshals Service. In September, he killed the 1919 sniper. Matees is assigned to the Service's SOG and he's the guy who took down the New Orleans cannibal in that firefight in Nevada last summer. Davenport was there for that one, too."

"Shooters," one of the men said, with a skeptical tone.

Lucas might have curled a lip as he nodded. "Somebody's got to do the heavy lifting."

"Okaaaay . . ." Weaver said. To Lucas and Bob: "You weren't here Saturday for our end-of-week round-up session, but if you've read our latest info packets, you're up to date, because last week and the week before that, we got jack shit. The Miami-Dade cops and Lauderdale cops have mostly pulled out of the task force, we've got one guy from the Broward sheriff's department who for some reason is still with us, maybe for the donuts, although he seems to be running late today, and over here . . ." He pointed his pencil at the woman. ". . . We have Kelly Taylor, a warrant officer from the Coast Guard's Investigative Service. She represents Homeland Security."

His pencil did a 180-degree sweep of the remainder of the table: "The rest are FBI. You'll learn their names quickly enough. Now: let's figure out what we're all doing."

THE ANSWER TO that question, Lucas thought, a half hour into the meeting, was, not much. The task force seemed to be operating on hope, looking for a break from increasingly unlikely sources.

"Our problem," Weaver explained to Lucas and Bob, "is that the group doing the drug import is small and tight, and may not have lit up any law enforcement screens before now."

"I read that the guy who was killed was some minor Miami hoodlum," Lucas said.

"Yeah, he was. He took money from anyone who wanted some rough work done, he wasn't part of any specific organization. His main qualification is that he liked boats. In fact, he usually worked the boat show you're going to, and the Miami Boat Show, which is in a couple of months. We think he was hired to run the boat. Like the diver, we think he had that one special ability, but nothing to do with the purchase and resale of the heroin. If it is heroin we're talking about."

"And the diver . . ."

"We thought that would be a weak point. If this gang is doing what we think they're doing, they need professional divers to work with them. Or they need well-trained divers, anyway. Guys who can go deep," Weaver said. "We worked that hard for the first month after the shootings and came up dry. We think it's possible that the divers involved were brought in from the outside for this one specific job and kept their heads down while they were here. No hanging out at diver bars. Now they may have gone back to wherever they came from."

"How do you know that they're not done with this?" Lucas asked. "The dope guys. That they might not have walked away from it, or have finished picking it up?"

Weaver pointed his pencil at one of the suits, one with a knotted tie, who said, "We've talked to half the goons in South Florida, in jail and out, and there's a persistent rumor that most of the product is still out there. Millions of dollars' worth. Tens of millions. But, it's rumor."

Bob: "Nobody can find where the dope was dumped?"

Weaver's pencil went to the Coast Guard. Taylor said, "Our enlisted man, the one who spotted the activity . . ."

Bob: "The one we're going to talk to."

"Yes. He was in his own boat, a private boat, south of Pompano Beach . . . if you know where that is . . ."

"I looked at it on a map, so I have an idea," Lucas said. "Up north of here, not too far."

"Yes. His fish-finding gear has GPS, but was an old unit and didn't have the ability to record his track. We would kill for that. He believes, but he's not sure, that the other boat was southeast of him, but he's not positive of that, because the coastline isn't exactly north and south. The other boat could have been dead south or a bit southwest. He's also unsure of the distance between them, because it was always changing. Less than a mile, but at least a quarter mile. With two moving boats on the water without landmarks, sometimes moving in opposite directions and at different speeds, it's hard to tell. Altogether, we think the diver was somewhere in an arc a half mile wide, but as much as two or even three miles north to south, covering a series of reefs off the coast, from fairly shallow and easily dived, to depths that would be at the extreme limit of what a scuba diver might want to do."

"Doesn't sound like that huge an area," Bob ventured.

"There're almost forty-two million square feet in one and a half square miles," the woman said. "From Petty Officer Barney Hall's description, the men were loading dark-colored, gray or black, bucket-sized containers off their boat before it burned. We suspect that they may have been twelve-inch or fourteen-inch PVC pipes sealed at the ends, each probably eighteen inches long. We have seen those kind of containers before. Lying on their sides, each pipe would show an area of about one and a half square feet. Trying to find a dark object that small in an area of forty-two million square feet is . . . difficult, to say the least. We'd have to be very lucky to find one."

"Are you still trying?" Lucas asked.

She shook her head. "No. We had a submersible looking for two months and never found a single pipe. If they're even down there. There are currents, there's rough terrain, and the bottom gets churned up and visibility can be down to almost nothing. The pipes may very well be covered with sediment, so we could roll right over one and never see it."

"All of which is somewhat beside the point," Weaver said. "We know that something may be down there, or maybe there isn't, but we're interested in the men who did the shooting, not so much the dope itself. We'll take the dope if we can get it, but what we really want are the killers."

Lucas: "If we can find somebody who knows how to get to the dope, we'll have somebody who can take us to the killers."

Weaver said, "Yes. Of course. The Coast Guard is doing surveillance of the area. We have cameras mounted in beachside condos that scan the area for suspicious activity—boats that may be putting down divers in the target area."

"Are there legitimate divers going out there?" Lucas asked.

Taylor said, "We contacted all the local dive boats and told the owners that anyone diving in the search area will get inspected right down to the screws in the hull. They'll stay away."

Another agent—Lucas could see his plastic name card and it said, BRUCE, DAVID C.—said, "Unless we want them out there. The divers."

Yet another agent groaned and said, "Do we have to talk about that again?"

Weaver pointed his pencil at Bruce and said, "The marshals haven't heard this yet—so talk."

Bruce, a thin, boyish man with careful brown hair and narrow-rimmed, rectangular glasses, cleared his throat and said, "I suggested that we sponsor a kind of . . . Easter egg hunt. That instead of forbidding the dive boats from going there, we offer a substantial reward for one of the pipes. A lot of divers like the idea of treasure hunts. If we offered say, a fifty-thousand-dollar reward for one of those pipes, and outlined the area that we thought they might be in . . . I bet we'd have a dozen boats out there every day, with expert divers. At no cost to us."

"Plus a few amateurs who'd probably die," somebody else said.

Bruce shrugged. "It may be distasteful to some, but . . . not our problem. We could have the Coast Guard check each boat and make sure everybody was properly certified. I don't think deaths would actually be likely."

He looked directly at Lucas: "The other benefit, of course, is that it might stir up talk between the killers and we might hear about it. Sort of what *you're* here to do."

Weaver jumped in, speaking to Lucas and Bob: "It's in the paper you read, but we believe each . . . dope container, each *can* . . . probably carries a location beeper of some kind. You dive down close with your own sonar unit, put out a specific low-power code, maybe a complicated code because it'd be all mechanical, so why not? Then, when the can's unit picks up the code, it beeps back. You use your sonar unit to track right into the capsule. All we need is one of those cans and we'll have the code and then we could find the rest."

Bob asked, "What's wrong with that idea? The Easter egg hunt? That's the best thing I've heard so far . . . not counting the dead amateur diver thing."

"It's a weird way to operate," the objecting agent said. "We'd have to run it through Washington, the whole fifty-grand thing . . ."

Bruce, annoyed, cut him off and said to Weaver, "Dale, we're probably spending twenty thousand dollars a week here, counting salaries and everything else. We're spending that to get, as you said, jack shit. Ask Washington for the money."

"It'd be a waste of time," said the agent who hadn't wanted to talk about it.

After a little more snarling and chipping, Weaver sighed and said, "I already asked for the money. I could hear back today or tomorrow."

There were a couple of groans and Bruce leaned back in his chair, looking pleased. "Good move," he said.

THE MEETING WENT on for the full hour, the agents assigned to contact and recontact various underworld characters working between the Keys and Palm Beach, but from the desultory response, Lucas didn't expect much to come from it.

To Lucas, Weaver looked like a man in the twilight of his career, assigned to run the task force because he had the experience to do it, but without great expectations from anyone higher up. The case was most likely to be resolved by accident, Lucas thought—a cop somewhere arrests a guy who really needs to walk away, and who has a piece of information, and who voluntarily rolls on the killers. Or, he thought, it'd be solved by him and Bob.

When the meeting broke up, Weaver said, "Is there anything I can do for you guys?"

"We'd like to talk to some of the local narcs, here and down in Miami, if that can be fixed," Lucas said. "Guys who could put us onto some of the longer-time dealers."

"Sure. How about this afternoon? Three o'clock?"

"Where at?"

"The best place would be at the Miami-Dade North police station," Weaver said. "They've got a bunch of conference rooms down there. I'm sure we could get one. We could pull in people from both Miami-Dade and Broward. And city of Miami and Lauderdale."

"That'd be great," Lucas said. "Sure you can fix it?"

"Fairly sure," Weaver said. "They've all been cooperative. I mean, they get federal grants."

"Ah."

"Want some DEA agents?"

LUCAS AND BOB took the elevator down to the ground floor with Kelly Taylor, the Coast Guard cop, who asked, "Did you get anything out of that?" She was one of those women who could lift one eyebrow at a time, and she did that.

Lucas said, "Not much new." He had some sympathy for Weaver, running the task force to nowhere; he'd been on a few of those.

"They've given up," Taylor said. "A couple of more weeks and Dale will write a report suggesting that we continue to monitor the possible dive site and arrests of drug-related persons, but that the task force be closed down."

"Do you think they should do that?" Bob asked.

"I think we should try David Bruce's idea of the reward. If nobody finds a dope can, we're no worse off than we are now. At least we've got an iron in the fire." Then she shrugged: "Right now, we have nothing. Unless you two are law enforcement geniuses, that won't improve. I'm ready to go home."

Bob smiled at her: "But we *are* law enforcement geniuses. At least I am. Lucas is more like my assistant, he carries my gun and so on, does my PR. We'll break it in a week or two."

"I'm holding my breath," Taylor said. "Waiting to see you two at work. I know Dale is impressed, and I mean, I could *learn* so much."

Lucas said to Bob, "A cynic. She doesn't believe you."

Bob shook his head. "It makes me sad to think about that."

"I have to confess," Taylor said to Bob, reaching out to touch his arm. "I loved that part where you dropped your Glock on the conference table. That was the most electrifying thing that happened in that room in two months. Well, aside from your shorts."

FOUR

THE NISSAN'S AIR conditioning produced a breeze that was cold and damp, almost wet, so they drove across Fort Lauderdale with the windows down and their elbows out, Queen doing "We Are the Champions" on the satellite radio.

"This fuckin' place is like a monument to the concrete block," Bob said, watching Marina Mile stream by.

"And mobile homes," Lucas said. "Ever been here before?"

"I went on a cruise, once, with an old girlfriend, but I never saw the city. Never been to Miami."

"It's concrete blocks from top to bottom, Palm Beach to Key West," Lucas said. "Same on the West Coast."

"Plus the mobile homes," Bob said.

"Yeah. They're like the architectonic spice to illuminate the stucco," Lucas said.

"I wish I'd said that."

THEY FOLLOWED BOB'S telephone navigation app across Fort Lauderdale and over the Intracoastal Waterway to A1A where they immediately got jammed up in traffic; they grabbed a lucky park-ing space a half mile from the show, and walked along A1A to the show's entrance.

The show was a cross between a state fair, the Daytona 500, and the Sturgis Motorcycle Rally, done on the water, with boats, some of them the size of skyscrapers laid on their sides. "They say there are four billion bucks' worth of yachts," Bob said, gawking. "I be-lieve that."

The line at the entrance was a block long, but they pushed past reluctant ticket-takers with their marshal IDs. A hundred yards in-side the gates, they were stopped by cops in military-style uni-forms wearing wraparound sunglasses and bulletproof vests and carrying semiautomatic black rifles. Their pistols must be printing on their guayabera shirts, Lucas thought. The lead cop said, his gun barrel slightly raised toward them, "You two . . ."

"Federal marshals . . ." Bob said, before the cop finished talking.

"You have IDs?"

"Of course. We're working with the joint services task force on the Coast Guard murders," Lucas said. "I'm going to get my ID out."

He dug his ID out of his pants pocket and Bob did the same. The cops looked them over and then the lead cop asked, in a tone just short of curt: "What are you doing here?"

"Looking for the Coast Guardsman who shot one of the guys on the killers' boat," Lucas said. "He's working out here. You got a problem with that?"

"I got a problem with people with guns," the cop said.

Lucas nodded. "So do I. Especially rifles that might be fired in a crowd. You sure as shit will kill some innocent people if you fire those things."

"That's not the way we see it," one of the other cops said.

"I understand that," Lucas said. "But I'll tell you what. You shoot some innocent citizen with that rifle and I'll testify against you at a murder trial."

The cop opened his mouth to reply, but Bob jumped in: "Have a nice day," he said.

As he and Lucas walked away, Bob muttered, "Always good to have the local cops on your side."

"Whoever sent them out here with rifles is a fuckin' moron," Lucas said. "If they're really worried about a terror attack, they ought to put twenty patrol cops in plain clothes and have them walking every dock." He waved at the megayachts. "Maybe put a couple snipers up on top of those ocean liners with spotters."

"Maybe they've done that," Bob said.

"Then why do they have guys down here in the crowd with the rifles? C'mon, Bob . . ."

"When you're right, you're right," Bob said. Two nearly naked young women, wearing thongs, tops the size of bottle caps, sunglasses, and skates, rolled out of an exhibition hall ahead of them and they stopped talking for a moment. When they started again, Bob said, "Talk about flawless assets."

"Assets," Lucas agreed.

Another young woman walked by, wearing what appeared to be a knee-length white T-shirt imprinted with it's not gonna lick itself.

"I got nothin'," Bob said.

◆◆◆

THOUGH IT WAS still early, the sun was pounding down like a laser and they were beginning to sweat; the whole crowd smelled of SPF 50 banana-scented sunscreen and boiled hot dogs. A man in a captain's hat and a Fountaine Pajot catamaran T-shirt pointed them to a line of exhibition halls where, after wandering around for a while, they found Barney Hall, working in an equipment booth that sold a brand of line-cutters that attached to boat props. He and another salesman were standing next to a video screen that showed a rope being chopped to pieces by the whirling cutter, rather than entangling the prop itself. When Lucas and Bob identified themselves, Barney nodded and said, "There's a food court out back, we could talk there."

HALL LED THE way past a hundred boat-equipment displays and out the back of the building to a line of food booths where they bought Cokes and found a table where they could sit in the shade. Bob was already sweating heavily: "This place is as humid as New Orleans," he said.

"Record heat today," Hall said, as they sat down. "Been hot since April." Hall was dressed like Lucas and Bob: loose shirt, shorts, athletic shoes. He said, "I've been interviewed a whole bunch of times . . ."

"We read them all," Lucas said. "A lot of the questions were about what you did, rather than what the killers did when they were jumping off the boat."

Hall leaned forward, put his elbows on the tabletop. "That part, I mean, what *they* did, only lasted maybe a minute. I keep seeing it over and over in my mind . . . I'm told I don't have PTSD, but that traumatic events tend to stick with you, and I guess this was sorta traumatic. The Coast Guard made me talk to a shrink about it, and the doc said that sometimes you even make up some parts to . . . embellish . . . your real memories. I don't think that's happened with me. It's all like a movie that I see sometimes before I go to sleep, and it hasn't changed."

"What I'd like you to do is rerun the dream for us, if you can," Lucas said. "Close your eyes, see it. I don't care about the parts before you closed in on the Mako. I only care about the people you saw on the boat—and maybe a little about the boat handling."

"You guys know anything about boats?" Hall asked.

Bob said, "Bass boat," and Lucas added, "I've got a twenty-one-foot aluminum Lund with a Yamaha 250 on the back, strictly for fishing, in Wisconsin. I don't know anything about saltwater boats."

"Okay . . . well, big boats and small boats are roughly the same, up to a point. If you can run two hundred and fifty horses, you could run the Mako with a couple hours on the water. You got a little more inertia to deal with . . . So anyway, it was tearing down the Intracoastal Waterway, which is right over there, on the other side of the boat basin."

He pointed toward one of the superyachts, hulking over the equipment sales building. "I was chasing after him in my own boat, which is slower than the Mako. This was after . . . well, I knew the guys in the Coast Guard boat were dead. So I'm chasing him . . ."

"Go ahead," Lucas said.

Hall leaned back and closed his eyes. "He was flyin'. Then all of a sudden, he cut right. There's part of Port Everglades over there, a terminal. There was a white SUV already parked there. Maybe a Toyota. The Mako cuts over there . . ."

He paused in the story, his eyelids fluttering, then he continued: "Four guys got off the bow of the boat. No, three guys, at first. One guy ran ahead to get the car and back it up, two guys were carrying these things that looked like black buckets, but the Coast Guard thinks they were PVC pipes, which is probably right. They looked like buckets to me. They threw them in the back of the SUV. The two guys made three trips, so maybe six buckets."

He sat back and opened his eyes. "Hell, I don't know how many buckets there were, but I think six is a good guess. With the buckets the size I was seeing, I'm told they could get ten kilograms of heroin in each, and ten kilos would be worth maybe three hundred thousand dollars, wholesale. If there were six buckets, that's almost two million bucks."

"Let's go back to the chase," Lucas said. "You see four guys. The fourth guy was spraying gasoline around?"

"Yeah. The guy I shot." Hall closed his eyes again. "The Mako went into the pier . . . let me see, the fourth guy tied it off, real quick, like he was a boat guy. Then he got the gas . . . He had a five-gallon can, but not the kind you'd have on a boat. It was plastic, it was more the kind you'd use for a lawn tractor or something. They recovered it from the boat when they brought it off the bottom. It was melted, but they could see what it was. I told the FBI guys I think they had it there for exactly how they used it—in case they had to burn the boat. That boat was probably worth a couple hundred thousand and they burned it without thinking twice."

Lucas: "So you're closing in. What did the guys look like?"

"Three of them were big guys, including the guy I shot. The fourth one was quite a bit smaller, he was the guy who got the car. Ten kilos is about twenty-two pounds, plus there was the weight of the buckets, or pipes, and these guys were climbing out of the boat onto the pier and running to the car carrying two buckets, so maybe . . . fifty pounds? They had to be a little strong."

"Hair color, or anything like that?" Bob asked.

"The small guy had black hair, I want to say, maybe Latino. The other three guys look like these snowbirds we get down here in the winter, from New York and New Jersey. Kinda burned-looking. I don't know about their hair, but on those guys, it's usually black."

Lucas: "Clothes?"

"Shorts, and you know, tropical-like shirts, like New York guys buy when they get down here. They go to a Tommy Bahama store, first thing. Get parrots on their shirts. Orange and bright yellow, neon stuff. Except the small guy, he was wearing black pants and a dark-colored shirt. Yeah. Dark-colored."

Bob: "New York and New Jersey."

Hall, who'd closed his eyes again, opened them now, and said, "Yeah. Those guys have a look. You see it all the time down here. Wraparound sunglasses, short hair, big guys, square faces, chewing gum, making it snap. They had the look."

"The small guy . . . how small? Let's say the other guys were six feet. How big was the small guy compared to them?"

"Oh, I don't . . . Jeez, now that you ask it that way, about half their size," Hall said. "Skinny. I don't think he came up to their shoulders. I guess that's why I'm thinking Latino."

They talked a while about the recovery of the sunken Mako.

The Coast Guard and Lauderdale cops sent divers down to recover what they could, before the remains of the boat were brought up with a crane. Among the recovered items were two scuba tanks, a badly burned buoyancy control vest, and other scuba gear.

"They found the diver's wet suit, but it got melted into a lump," Hall said. "I guess the guy peeled it off as soon as he got on board the Mako."

"Any fishing gear on board?" Bob asked.

"Yes. They found rods and reels, ordinary stuff, cheap for a boat like that," Hall said. "The FBI tried to trace it to a specific outlet, but . . . nothing came of it. There wasn't much on board the boat. It's like they used it for this one thing, and maybe fishing."

"Maybe kept the personal stuff down to make it harder to identify them, if they got stopped and weren't able to burn the boat," Lucas said. "Even the fishing gear might have been stage dressing, so they'd look like they were doing something legitimate out there."

"Don't know about that," Hall said.

THEY TALKED FOR a while longer, until Hall ran out of things to say. Bob asked, "You feel bad about shooting that guy?"

Hall shook his head. "Nope. They killed three of our guys. I thought maybe I would feel bad, but . . . you know, it's back there in the past now. I don't feel it much anymore. I don't get all moody."

"You'll be okay, maybe you're already okay," Lucas said. "It's a lot easier to live with killing somebody when you did the right thing and when good people agree that it was the right thing to do."

"I think so," Hall said. "My wife's okay with it, and that helps.

Then, I asked one of the FBI guys if they thought these dope guys might come after us, and he said these guys were just criminals, not the CIA. How would they even find us? We live in a trailer park, we don't even have an address on our trailer, only on the mailbox out by the street."

WHEN THEY GOT up to go, Hall asked, "What're you going to do now?"

Lucas said, "The FBI has identified some people that might know something, even if they don't know much. We'll find them, step on their toes. See what they have to say."

"Good. I want them caught. Our guys never had a chance, they just mowed them down."

"We'll get them," Bob said.

"Listen, long as you're here, you oughta go look at the boat show, if you haven't seen it yet," Hall said as they walked back to the equipment-sales pavilion. "I live down here and I've been every year for the last four. Can't get enough of it."

HALL WENT BACK to work and Lucas and Bob spent an hour wandering through the maze of docks, looking at the boats. The megayachts had garage-door type openings on their sterns, open so passersby could have a look. Nestled inside one was a submarine; another had a "skiff" that was twice as big as Lucas's fishing boat; in a third, five women danced and lip-synced to a Rihanna song, like fake-blond Supremes.

Bob: "Wonder if the women come with the boat?"

"Wouldn't be surprised if it was an option," Lucas said.

One of the yachts had fuel tanks with a forty-thousand-gallon capacity. At Lauderdale prices, a single fill-up would cost a hundred and sixty thousand dollars, another gawker told them.

Lucas: "I'm a long way from being a commie, but . . . I mean, Jesus H. Christ. A hundred and sixty thousand for one fuckin' fill-up?"

As they walked back to the car, three fruit-colored Lamborghinis—banana, cherry, and green apple—lurched by, one after the other. Average traffic speed was perhaps a mile an hour.

"That was nice," Bob said. "Now, where do we find the guys whose toes we're going to step on?"

"We need to talk to Weaver some more, without all the other people around," Lucas said, referring to the head of the task force. "I don't want a lot of . . . you know . . . pushback from the Millennials."

"You're going to get us in trouble, aren't you?"

"Bob: you gotta relax, man. They're just a bunch of feds."

Weaver was sitting at the hotel bar, talking to the bartender when they showed up. He tipped his gin-and-tonic glass at them and said, "Tonic water and lime, no gin."

Bob: "That sounds good." He asked the bartender for the same thing; Lucas ordered a Diet Coke.

"You boys ain't gonna bring Lauderdale to its knees, are you?" the bartender asked, as he went to get the drinks. When they came, the three of them took the drinks to a table and Weaver asked, "Anything new? I'm praying you'll say yes."

Lucas said, "No new information, but some new thoughts, maybe."

"I'll take anything."

"Where's the stuff recovered from the yacht? I understand you found a wet suit."

"Locked up in an evidence room down in Miami," Weaver said. "But the wet suit . . . it's a lump of melted neoprene. No way to get anything from it."

"Did anyone weigh it?"

Weaver hunched his shoulders. "I don't know, honestly. I doubt it. I could ask."

"Could you ask, and if they haven't, get them to do it?" Lucas asked. "Quick as they can?"

"Sure, I can do that."

Lucas: "Another thing. When Barney Hall shot the guy, you immediately went around and jacked up a couple of dozen people based on their relationships with the dead man. Were any of those guys dealing dope?"

Weaver shook his head: "Not as far as we know. I'm sure some were users, but it wasn't their big thing. Most of them worked in bars or marinas, or lifting heavy stuff. We're not talking about business geniuses. Dealing? Nothing big-time, if they did it at all."

"What about the meeting with the narcs?" Lucas asked.

"You're set to go at three o'clock."

"That's great."

"No problem. It's nice to have you guys hustling," Weaver said.

"The rest of us have slacked off, I'm afraid. Been a frustrating investigation, banging our heads against brick walls."

"Concrete block walls," Bob said.

Weaver nodded: "Okay."

"What happened with the idea of offering a reward for the dope buckets?" Lucas asked.

Weaver brightened. "I talked to my boss, he thinks it's going to fly. Not a done deal yet, but I'll know before the end of the day. They're hot to get something. Anything."

AFTER TALKING WITH Weaver, Bob and Lucas went back to their rooms, collected their separate files of FBI reports, carried them down to the now-empty conference room and began pulling the interviews with a variety of crime-connected street operators in Miami and Fort Lauderdale, looking for drug hustlers, and found none.

They were still at it when they got a call from a crime scene tech in Miami. Lucas put it on speakerphone. "I pulled that wet suit and weighed it," the tech said. "It came in a tich under six pounds."

"Did much of it get burned up?" Lucas asked.

"No. It's melted, but intact. It's all stuck together, which is why we couldn't get anything out of it," she said. "We could tell it's a seven millimeter, which probably means the diver was going deep and cold. It was somewhat protected from the fire because that boat has a head . . . a toilet . . . and that's where we found the wet suit."

Bob: "Wait—there's a cabin? We thought it was an open fishing boat."

"No cabin, just a head under the center console. Big enough to stand up in, there's a toilet and even a tiny sink, but it's tight."

Lucas: "The wet suit was where? On the floor?"

"Yes. The diver had peeled it off and left it. We assume he was changing when the chase started and he was in a hurry."

"Now. That *is* interesting," Bob said, when they were off the phone.

They spent a half hour calling wet suit manufacturers and talking to the owner of a Lauderdale dive shop. When they were done, Bob said, "It all fits with the wet suit in the toilet stall."

"The head," Lucas said.

"Yeah, the head."

WEAVER HAD LOOKED in on them a couple of times, to see if they'd actually learned anything. He showed up again as Bob made his comment about it all fitting with the toilet stall.

"What fits?" He looked from Lucas to Bob and back to Lucas.

Lucas said, "We got the weight on that wet suit—a little under six pounds, which is consistent with a size small in a seven-millimeter suit. We called a dive shop and asked how much trouble it was to get out of a dive suit. Turns out, they're made to fit really tight and it's a struggle to get both in and out of one. The suit was found in the head, where it would have been even more of a struggle, because the head on that boat is tiny. Hardly room to turn around."

"All right, I believe you. So what?" Weaver asked.

"Hall says the diver was short and thin . . . quite short. About five-six, or even shorter, we think. The diver went into the head to change. Why was that?"

Weaver shook his head. "I don't know. You tell me."

"Because she wanted some privacy, away from the men on the boat."

Weaver stared, then then put up both hands to fend them off: "Oh, no. No, nope, you're shitting me now."

Lucas said, "We're not a hundred percent on it, of course. But that suit was right for an average-sized athletic woman."

"Fuck me."

Bob to Weaver: "Did you look at any women divers?"

"I don't think so. It never occurred to anyone that . . . aw, hell." Weaver agreed that the FBI task force agents would try to track down an average-sized, athletic, professional or semipro female diver.

Lucas asked, "Where would they get their tanks refilled?"

"We checked all those, but we'll recheck, asking about women," Weaver said. "The thing is, you can buy a scuba compressor for two or three grand. If you're willing to torch a quarter-million-dollar boat, you're probably willing to spend three grand on your own compressor. We did check compressor shipments into the three-county area here and tracked them down. Nothing happening there."

Bob: "Anything on the reward idea?"

Weaver shook his head: "Not yet." He looked at his watch: "It takes a while to get to Miami. You guys should get going. I'll get started on this female diver. If she's local, she should be identifiable."

FIVE

BECAUSE THEY'D BE on the street, Lucas and Bob traded their shorts for jeans but stayed with the guayabera shirts and the cross-training shoes, and headed south to Miami. The Northside Miami-Dade District's police station had the South Florida look that was almost an architectural style, a boxy red-and-white concrete building with useless pillars out front and a clutch of flagpoles by the street.

They were taken to a conference room populated by eight plainclothes cops, a bunch of soda cans, and a couple of cups of coffee. The cops stopped talking when the marshals were shown in, and somebody said, "See, I told you: they're not FBI."

"You're right, we're not," Lucas said, as he and Bob pulled out chairs and sat down. The narcs, Lucas thought, looked like a collection of postal clerks or shoe salesmen with added facial hair, as did narcs in most places. "We're marshals. We're looking for the guys who killed the Coast Guardsmen last summer. We're new on the case and we work differently than the FBI guys." Long pause. "Good as they are."

There were a number of snorts and a little laughter, and a guy with a beard held up a hand and said, "I'm DEA and for official re-porting purposes, I'm not laughing."

"You looked like you were laughing," somebody said.

The DEA agent ignored that and asked, "What do you want?"

"Names and locations of a few long-term dealers who might hear things and who might talk to cops if they're put under enough pressure," Bob said. "We're hoping that one of them can point us at the specific organization that brought the heroin up the coast."

"That could get you dinged up," somebody said.

"We've been dinged up before and we're still here," Lucas said.

Another cop: "Yeah, we looked you up. You do have a few dings."

Yet another one: "If we give you names, you'll be fucking with our sources."

"We lie a lot," Lucas said. "They won't know it comes from you. In fact, they may be calling you for help."

"Exactly what are you going to do?" the DEA agent asked.

Lucas told them.

Some of the narcs were skeptical and walked; others gave them names.

Like Tobin Cain's.

Tobin Cain was known on the street as Foot-Long, not because of any personal measurement, but because he dealt his dope out of a back booth at a Subway franchise near downtown Miami. The Subway was located on a hot, shabby, black-tar street with weeds growing up through the cracks. Cain's business was basically okay with the franchisee, because nothing boosted traffic like dopers with the munchies.

Cain liked the place for the free refills and the Wi-Fi; a

sloppy-fat black guy, he was sitting in a back booth, wearing an aqua-and-orange Miami Dolphins jersey and hat, the hat worn forward. He was poking at an iPad. The DEA agent, whose name was Ramon Herrera, and who smelled strongly of tobacco, pointed him out from behind the red-rock steps of a closed, life-battered Jesus the Savior Church, across the street from the Subway.

"Make sure you keep his hands where you can see them," Herrera said. "He doesn't carry a gun anymore, because of the felonies, but he still carries a screwdriver. Those can hurt, especially if he sticks it in your heart."

"Will he have some dope on him?" Bob asked.

"He usually phones out to an assistant, but one reason I suggested Foot-Long is that he fired his guy last week. A kid named Dope."

"Dope?"

"Sort of a giveaway, huh? He'd sit here on the church steps, where he could see Foot-Long. He kept the dope right here off the side of the steps, where we're standing, in these weeds." He kicked a weed, which ignored the attack. "Foot-Long would call him with the specs on what he wanted delivered. Heroin or meth or weed, and how much. Then, the way I heard it, Dope started clipping the meth and reselling it on his own."

"That's the kind of entrepreneurial enterprise that made this country great," Bob said.

Herrera blinked, considered the comment, shrugged. "Anyway, the word is that Foot-Long fired Dope and since there's nobody else out here at the church, he's probably sitting on some dope himself."

"Any particular way we should handle this?" Lucas asked.

"The bathroom's at the back. If he smells cop, he's gonna get back there in a hurry and the door has a lock. He'll shove it in the toilet and flush. I think the one of you who looks least like a cop . . ." He surveyed the two of them, then said, "Okay, you both look like cops. So, if I were you, one of you ought to go through the whole sandwich-ordering routine and by the time you get to the cash register, he might be a little less interested. Then get a table and sit down for a minute or two, take a couple bites, let him relax, and then rush him."

Bob: "How about if I unbutton my shirt and let him see some skin, going in. A construction-worker vibe."

"Could help," Herrera said.

"Then let's do that," Bob said. "I've done it before." He pulled the gun from his belt and handed it to Lucas. "Hold this for me. Better if I go without."

Herrera: "Really?"

"Bob was an NCAA wrestling champ," Lucas said.

"Third place," Bob said. "If it comes to a fight, I'd rather not have a gun flying around. Lucas, I'd want you in there one second after I hit him."

"Yup. Let's set it up."

LUCAS GOT A marshal's vest out of the Pathfinder and walked around the block to get sideways to the front door of the Subway, which was in an anonymous yellow-painted concrete block commercial building, with what looked like apartments on the second floor. Bob walked down the block out of sight from Foot-Long's booth and Herrera stayed where he was, behind the church steps, standing in the weeds, where he could watch the action.

When Lucas was in position, he called Bob, who shambled into view from the Subway windows, bare-bellied with his open shirt. He paused across the street from the Subway and gave his belly a scratch, may have picked something out of his navel, smelled it, flicked it away, whatever it was, and crossed the street.

Inside the door, he carefully didn't look at Foot-Long, but focused on the sandwich board, eventually ordering an Italian BMT, no mayonnaise. He continued shambling and scratching, got a cup for a Diet Coke, paid the cute Hispanic woman behind the cash register, shambled down the aisle to an empty booth with his back to Foot-Long, sat down, took a few bites of the sandwich, then pulled out his phone, called Lucas, and said, "Five seconds. Four, three . . ."

He went on one, pushing out of the booth, leaving the phone behind, charging down the aisle like a linebacker going after a quarterback and Foot-Long had only begun to scramble when Bob slammed into him, pinning him in the booth.

Bob snarled, "Pull that fuckin' screwdriver on me and you'll be pulling it out of your rectum."

There were six customers trying to get out of other booths, but Lucas pushed through, a badge in his hand, shouting, "U.S. Marshals, U.S. Marshals!"

Foot-Long, still pinned against the back of the booth, said, "Aw, shit."

Bob said, "Lucas, grab my phone, will you? I don't want it to disappear."

FOOT-LONG WAS WEARING cargo shorts, from which Lucas pulled four ounces of what looked like heroin and another four ounces of what looked like meth, all neatly packed in tiny Ziploc bags, along with a short but very sharp flat-blade screwdriver. Bob bent him over the Subway table and cuffed him and they walked him across the street to the church steps.

Herrera had disappeared. "I heard you fired Dope," Lucas said.

"Lawyer."

"You're on probation for domestic assault," Bob said. "Lawyer ain't gonna save you from getting your probation pulled."

"Lawyer," Foot-Long repeated.

"It's possible we could work out something right here," Lucas said. "We're basically looking for information."

"Fuck you. Lawyer."

"Trying to figure out who might have killed those Coast Guard guys last summer. They were heroin dealers like you, shot three guys in cold blood. If you . . ."

"Lawyer."

That's all he said. Bob finally called in the Miami cops, and when a squad car arrived, explained that they'd gone after Tobin Cain looking for information on the Coast Guard murders, and found him holding the dope. "We'll testify if you need us, but it'd help us out if you guys could take the arrest," Lucas told the cops. "He's on probation on a domestic assault charge, pled down from rape, so . . ."

"We'll take him, though he'll probably be back out tomorrow," the Miami sergeant said. He took Foot-Long by the arm. "Let's go, Footie."

"Lawyer."

As they watched the cops haul Foot-Long away, Bob said, "We're hearing that 'lawyer' stuff all the time now. Hell, every time. The assholes are getting better trained. Keep their mouths shut, except for that one word: 'lawyer.'"

"Which is why I prefer to shoot them," Lucas said. "It unclutters the process."

"Don't let anybody hear you say that," Bob said, looking around. "Seriously, you could get your process all cluttered up, if anyone heard you say that."

THAT WAS THE day's only wrestling match.

With more help from Herrera and a Miami narc named Dan Colson, Lucas and Bob hit four dealers that afternoon and evening, three men and a woman. The dealers were willing to chat; they had no idea who dumped the dope. They were convincing.

They were all holding dope. The woman, who had hair the color of a winter haystack, also had a Smith & Wesson snub-nose .38 revolver in her purse and had a felony in her history. They all took cards from Lucas.

"Here's the deal," Lucas told them. "We want you to tell your friends, your suppliers, that we're out here and we're coming for them. We got get-out-of-jail cards for good information on the Coast Guard shootings. But it better be good."

Bob took the dope and scattered it in the streets, like cinnamon sugar. The woman said she needed the gun for self-protection because she worked in a bad area, so they let her keep it after unloading the weapon. Bob put the cartridges in his pocket as they walked away, and later threw them one at a time out the window of the Pathfinder.

Then, later that night: the man with the worst sheet and the best drug connections was a louche redheaded dude named Axel Morris, a former high school teacher who dealt weed, coke, heroin, and methamphetamine out of a booth in a nude-dancer club called Bandit's.

A Miami narc, Walker Weeks, had suggested Morris as a target during the meeting, and that evening he met Lucas and Bob in a McDonald's parking lot on 163rd Street in northern Miami-Dade County.

Weeks looked like a wide receiver, a lanky black guy wearing a black T-shirt under a black sport coat, with black jeans and black sport shoes and a diamond in one earlobe. He had a wide smile and big white teeth. "You feds have been a little backward about going after the assholes who killed the Coasties. What changed?"

"We did," Lucas said.

"I thought marshals mostly shuffled prisoners around," Weeks said.

Bob: "Not all of us."

"WHAT'RE YOU PLANNING to do?" Weeks asked, as they shook hands under the Golden Arches.

"Put a dog collar on him," Lucas said. "We know he wasn't on the boat, he doesn't match what we know about them. They were sorta porky. In the mug shot you gave us, Morris looks like a rake."

"Yes, he is."

"What's his story?" Bob asked.

Weeks shrugged: "He was a music teacher down at Hialeah High School. Supposedly, one of his students was dealing weed to him and he figured the kid was making more than he was, so . . . One summer he went into business himself and quit teaching. Also had a taste for those high school girls, and that can get you put in prison if you're a teacher. Handsome guy when he was young. I guess he still is handsome, for his age. Likes to have a girl on his lap."

"How's this gonna work?" Lucas asked.

"Axel has a personal back booth at Bandit's," Weeks said. "When you go inside, point your noses at the back room; you'll see it. The bouncer inside the door will check you out and he'll smell pork. He'll give a look to the bartender and then push you outside and the bartender will wave off Axel. He'll slide out the back door to his Cadillac. That's where I'll be, leaning against it. You don't even have to talk to the bouncer. As soon as he gets you outside, walk around the back and that's where we'll be, me'n Axel."

"Morris knows you personally?"

"Sure. We don't bust him anymore because, what's the point?" Weeks said. "We don't prosecute less than twenty grams of weed and he doesn't keep any of the other shit on himself. If a buyer wants that stuff, Axel'll have somebody in a car close by and he won't call the car unless he knows the buyer personally, or somebody he trusts vouches for the buyer."

"But he'll have something? Weed, coke, meth?" Lucas asked. "Any amount will work."

"He'll have weed," Weeks said. "He gives it away to guys inside the bar, priming the pump. He won't ditch it because he won't know for sure you're there for him, and it'll be less than twenty grams. He knows he won't be prosecuted for that."

Bob smiled: "Not by you, anyway. Don't arrest him. We'll do it."

"If you can worry Axel, you'll be doing a public service. At least move his ass across the line to Broward County. I hate him shifting that smack around my territory."

"We'll worry him," Lucas said.

Bob added, "I don't want to freak you out, because I'm actually a puppy dog in real life, but I'm gonna do my bad-guy act with Morris. I'm gonna come on hard. Mean."

"Let's get it on," Weeks said with a grin. "Puppy dog . . ."

BANDIT'S WAS A cuboid, plain and simple, a three-dimensional concrete block rectangle painted clitoral pink, set squarely in a potholed parking lot, with fluorescing purple paint around the blacked-out front doors and the rain gutter. To the right of the door was the fluorescing image of a mostly naked, winking woman with a top hat on her head, her back turned to the parking lot. Across her bare legs was the club's name, BANDIT'S.

"Ass bandits," Bob said, as they got out of the car.

"I got it," Lucas said. "We're dealing with people with good taste."

There were thirty cars and pickups in the lot, many of the cars newer, undented and unscratched compacts, probably rentals, men down for the boat show.

"The bouncer's gonna see the guns," Bob said, as they walked up to the door. "Might even have a metal detector on the door."

"We're the heat," Lucas said. "We get to carry guns. Even into a shithole like this one."

"I'm just hoping he doesn't shoot first and ask questions later,"

Bob said. "You want to step in ahead of me?" They looked at the front door, which was as crappy as the rest of the exterior, a black sheet of steel that might even be bulletproof.

Lucas said, "Hey, it could be nice inside."

No.

When Lucas and Bob stepped inside, the unidentifiable rock music was so deafening that real conversation would be impossible. The bar vibrated with red and blue LED laser lights; it smelled like a car deodorizer tree, as if it had to be hosed down every night, and maybe it did, with overtones of beer and whiskey and cigarettes and a whiff of weed.

The customers were all male, as far as they could see, defensively boisterous, jammed into red vinyl booths along the walls and on a motley bunch of barstools. A couple of naked tattooed women gamboled around a small stage with a brass pole. The waitresses wore some clothes, but were also young and tattooed.

A back-bar mirror was covered with so many bumper stickers— IT'S NOT CHEATING IF MY HUSBAND WATCHES, FREE THE BOOBS, I LOVE LIPSTICK ON MY DIPSTICK, BANDIT'S T-SHIRTS $10—that only slivers of the mirror were visible. The ceiling above the bar was plastered with one-dollar bills, for no obvious reason.

The bartender was a large man whose nose pushed out over a heavily waxed handlebar mustache. He had an inch-wide steel ring in his left ear. The bouncer was shouting at four guys in a booth halfway down the floor, friendly shouting. He was an even bigger man with a gallon-sized head and steroid muscles in his arms, shown off by a sleeveless sweatshirt.

When he saw movement at the door, he turned and did an eye-check on Bob and Lucas, as Weeks had said he would. He walked toward them, glancing at the bartender and calling, "Rick," as he did. The bartender looked over at Bob and Lucas and the bouncer jabbed a finger at the door and shouted over the noise, "We need to talk. Outside." They all went outside and the bouncer asked, "Are you . . ."

"Let's go," Lucas said. He and Bob broke away from the bouncer, leaving him standing by the door, and walked around the building toward the back. There, they found Weeks talking with Axel Morris. Morris was standing at the back door, crutches under his arms, a black medical boot on his left foot.

When they came up, Lucas asked, "He holding?"

Weeks held up a baggie of weed. "Yeah. Gave it up without a fight."

Morris looked like an Army officer in a British war film, skinny, big-nosed, slant-eyed. Women would like him, Lucas thought. Morris frowned at them: "Who are these people?" he asked Weeks.

Weeks said, "Federal marshals."

"What?"

The bouncer came around the corner. "What the fuck is going on here?"

"Federal marshals," Bob said. "You should go back in the club."

"How do I know you're marshals?"

"Because we said so," Lucas said. "Go back in the club."

"What if I don't?"

"Then we'll arrest you as an accessory to narcotics distribution and put you in prison," Bob said. "And listen, I'm trying to be nice about this."

The bouncer puffed up and opened his mouth, and Bob added, "And if you take us on, I'll break your arms and legs and kick your balls off and then arrest you for assault on federal officers and accessory to narcotics dealing. And put you in prison."

Weeks winced and said, "Jesus, take it easy, man. Kick his balls off?"

"I have no tolerance for being attacked and I thought he might be inclined that way," Bob said, staring down the bouncer.

The bouncer looked him over and something in Bob's eyes warned him off. He unpuffed and said, "I'm getting the manager," and he pulled open the door behind Morris and disappeared into the club.

MORRIS ASKED WEEKS, "What the hell are the feds doing here? It's only fifteen grams."

"We don't have the Miami law," Lucas said. "Marijuana is a Schedule 1 drug . . ."

"That's bullshit, man," Morris said. He looked to Weeks for support, and Weeks smiled.

"A Schedule 1 drug, same as cocaine and heroin," Lucas continued. "The president decided we needed to take you off the street and you know what? I checked your sheet and you qualify for the federal three-strikes law."

Bob pulled handcuffs out of his pants pocket. "So, let's get the cuffs on. Listen, don't worry about federal prison, Axel. Can I call you Axel? Turn around here, Axel. They've got really good medical care in the federal prison system, especially for you older guys."

"I'm not older . . ." Morris said, as he turned to the cuffs. "I'm not even forty."

"You will be older, with a three-strike conviction," Bob said. "In fact . . ." He turned to Lucas. "With a three-strikes, will he ever get out?"

"Don't believe he will," Lucas said. To Weeks: "We'll stay in touch, Walker. We'll need you to testify about the weed."

"Absolutely. Happy to do it," Weeks said. "Glad to scrape this piece of shit off my shoe."

LUCAS SAID TO Morris, "Like Bob was saying, being in prison is not really much different than, you know, hanging out all day in any crappy building. Like a high school. Or this club, for instance. Of course, there's no pussy inside . . . unless you're the pussy."

Bob had Morris hooked up, his hands shackled behind his back, and Morris exhaled in exasperation and asked, "Okay, what do you want?"

"I don't think we're dealing, are we?" Lucas asked Bob.

"I'd be reluctant to deal," Bob said. "Axel is sorta a big wheel. Get it? Axel, wheel?"

Morris said, "I've heard that joke a thousand times. And you guys *are* dealing. You wouldn't even talk to me if you weren't."

"If we gonna deal, it'd have to be on something large," Bob said. "In the meantime, you have the right to remain silent . . ."

"Yeah, yeah, yeah, I know it by heart," Morris said.

"I got to say it," Bob said. "So shut up or I'll smack you in the head."

The club manager came around the corner at the front of the building, followed by the bouncer, who had an iPhone in his hand, holding it above his head, a bright light shining at them, apparently making a movie of the arrest.

"Smile, we're on video," Lucas said to Bob.

"Fuck 'em," Bob said. To the bouncer: "You keep shining that light on me, I'm gonna shove that phone where Find My Phone won't find it."

Weeks looked from Bob to Lucas and said, "You guys really aren't the FBI, are you?"

THEY LEFT WEEKS talking to the club manager, put Morris in the back of the SUV with hands cuffed behind him and Bob sitting next to him. Morris said, without prompting, "I'll tell you everything I know about everything if you drop me off and we forget this goofy drug shit. I got work to do tonight."

"Everything you know? Smart guy like you, that could take years, which we ain't got," Bob said. He said over Lucas's shoulder, "You want to take him to the federal lockup now, and then go to McDonald's, or McDonald's first?"

"Well, we know where that McDonald's is, and I'm hungry," Lucas said.

"I could use a Whopper," Bob said.

"You guys . . . where the fuck are you from? You from Arkansas or some fuckin' place?" Morris asked. "Whopper is Burger King. McDonald's is Quarter Pounder."

"You're lucky you didn't say Oklahoma, I'd punch you in the kidneys by accident," Bob said. And to Lucas: "Let's hit the Mc-

Donald's. Maybe Axel can tell us about something more interesting than he is."

THERE WEREN'T MANY patrons in the McDonald's and they got three Quarter Pounders with Cheese, large fries for everybody, and two shakes, and one Diet Coke. Bob took the cuffs off Morris and said, "Don't try to climb over me and run. You wouldn't get anywhere with that boot on your foot and it'd piss me off and I'd beat the shit out of you."

"What's this violence thing you keep rockin', man? Whacking people in the head? Kicking their balls off? Punching them in the kidneys? I mean, Jesus, you ever hear of Xanax?"

Lucas: "So you're not gonna run?"

"I'm not running, I'm dealing," Morris said. "What do you want?"

They had wedged him into the farthest back booth, Bob sitting next to him on the outside, Lucas across, and Lucas said, "The president—we talked to him before we came down—he said, 'Get that fuckin' Axel Morris off the street . . .'"

"You know, you're not funny. This isn't funny," Morris fumed.

"'. . . and find out who killed those Coast Guard guys. I don't want to hear any excuses.'"

"You can tell your president to kiss my rosy red rectum," Morris said. "Tell me what you want. Like I said, I got things to do tonight." He looked at his Quarter Pounder. "You got another one of those ketchups?"

Bob pushed a ketchup packet across the table and Lucas said, "If you've got anything on those shootings, anything we can use, we'll leave you here with that sandwich. If you don't, we'll lock you up so the president won't be totally pissed with us."

Morris stopped fiddling with his sandwich, looking first at Bob and then at Lucas, and said, "I might be able to help. If anyone hears I've been talking to you . . ."

"Nobody will hear anything from us," Lucas said. "You know who was involved?"

"No. I don't know any names or anything like that." Morris popped the top on the Quarter Pounder and squeezed the ketchup packet on the meat patty. "But . . . I do know *some* stuff."

"Tell us," Lucas said.

Weed, cocaine, heroin, and methamphetamine, Morris said, came in from Yucatan for local distribution, with boats crossing the Gulf of Mexico and landing on Florida's Gulf Coast or in the Keys. "That's been set up for a long time, and it's smooth, and fuck the DEA," Morris said. "I don't personally know the big guys in that business, or anything about them, except what I see on TV. They're all Mexicans, both sides of the Gulf. They're over in Naples or Fort Myers. I'm about five steps down the line, but that's where my goods come from—Mexico."

He'd heard, though, that there was now a second group operating in South Florida, that did no local distribution. "All I know is these rumors. The rumor is, they bring the goods in from Venezuela or Colombia, but it's not sold here. They don't want to fight the locals. They move it up to New York and New Jersey. The rumor is, it's the Mafia and they made arrangements with the Mexicans not to mess with each other. Maybe the wops even buy a little from the pepperbellies."

"Ah, Jesus," Bob said, rolling his eyes. "The Mafia."

"It still exists, sorta," Lucas said.

"And that's what I heard," Morris said.

"Where are they down here? The Mafias?"

"They aren't any one place. I mean, they've got condos, like everybody else," Morris said. He peered at the side of the Quarter Pounder, then took a bite.

"So basically, you don't know anything," Lucas said. "It's the Mafia, they live in condos." Lucas looked at Bob. "Don't put the cuffs away."

"Wait, wait, wait," Morris said. "I've heard that they hang out together, down on Miami Beach. There's a hotel called the Angelus, it's right on the beach. Nice place. I've been there. Supermodels showing their tits around the swimming pool. About a hundred Porsches parked outside. The manager of the place is supposedly connected, so the Mafia guys feel welcome."

"The Angelus."

"You can't tell anyone you heard it from me," Morris said.

"Do your suppliers know who these people are?" Lucas asked. "Specifically? If they have this arrangement . . . I mean, there are all kinds of Mafia groups."

Morris looked out the window, as though he was thinking about jumping through it. "C'mon, man, you're gonna get me hurt."

"Axel . . . you've gone this far," Bob said.

Morris hunched forward on the table. "I'm willing to take a chance pissin' on those Mafia motherfuckers, 'cause they don't know who I am or where I am. But my boys here . . . they *do* know, and they'll know you picked me up with that fuckin' Weeks. You give me a choice between life in prison and them, well, at least I'm alive in prison. If I give you a name of one of my boys, and if they know it came from me, they'll kill my ass. They're as mean as any Mafia dude. Meaner, even."

Lucas asked, "Does Weeks know the name you're gonna give us?"

Morris narrowed his eyes, thinking, then said, "Probably heard of him. Some of the narcs know him. Or they've heard of him."

"Then we'll blame it on the narcs. We'll blame it on Weeks," Bob said. "You can even call up your man and warn him off. Tell him that we wanted the names of the Mafias and you said you didn't know them and we turned you loose, but that Weeks might be bringing us around. Tell him that Weeks gave us a list, and he's on it, and you know that because we asked if you knew the names on it."

It took a while, but eventually, Morris caved: "There's a guy named Magnus Elliot, he lives over on 27th Avenue. He's on papers, five years of probation after eight in Raiford. He must be three or four years out, now, so there's a probation officer who'll know exactly where he lives. If I'm like five steps down from the top, he's like two. If there's a deal with the goombahs, he might know some exact names."

Lucas nodded. "Okay. That's two things. The Angelus Hotel, which isn't much; and Magnus Elliot, which isn't anything, yet. We need a third thing, a bigger thing, or the cuffs go back on."

Morris sighed and stuck a French fry in his mouth and snapped it off. "Rumor is, these guys, whoever they are, dropped a ton of smack in the water off the coast and they got almost none of it out before the shooting. They're going back for it, sooner or later.

Maybe there'll be more than one bunch of assholes out there. We got any number of redneck diver guys who'd like some of that action. They got guns, too. Could turn into a free-for-all. Mafia, the diver guys, maybe some Mexicans, the Coast Guard . . . and you."

"When you say a ton, you mean a lot," Lucas said.

Morris pointed another French fry at Lucas. "No. The rumor isn't a lot, the rumor is a *ton*. You know? Like two thousand pounds. Except they use the metric system, so a ton is actually more than two thousand pounds. Supposedly sealed up in pipes, dropped off a freighter. That's what the rumor is."

Lucas did some numbers in his head: "Thirty million, wholesale."

"I don't do wholesale," Morris said. "If somebody got it to me, it'd be a whole lot more than thirty million dollars, stepped on five times and street prices. Of course, I couldn't move that much, but somebody could. You'd need a big organization."

"Okay, I'm not going for this rumor-has-it bullshit, I need to know something real," Lucas said. "You got anything? Or . . . ?"

Morris said, "Okay, one more thing. Not a rumor. There's this old guy who lives down in Coconut Grove." He looked from Lucas to Bob, and added, "That's down in Miami."

"Okay."

"Back in the day, he was a big-time smuggler, bringing in weed from the Bahamas," Morris said. "He got caught, got out of it, somehow, and retired. I bumped into him, I don't know, last summer, a hotel down in Miami Beach. We got to talking about the shooting, which was still a big deal down here. And he told me the diver was a woman."

Bob: "A woman? That's something. What's this guy's name?"

"John."

Lucas and Bob looked at each other, and Lucas said, *"John?* That's what you got?"

Morris shrugged. "I don't know him that well, but I do know that way back when he was busted, he was part of what the newspapers called the Blue Tuna Gang. There were five or six of them and he was the only one named John. You should be able to look him up."

Lucas nodded, and asked, "You got anything else we should know, now that we're best friends?"

"Nope." Morris said, "But you lucked out talking to Weeks. As far as I know, he's straight. There are a lot of crooked cops involved in the dope action down here, so if you go asking around about Magnus, he'll know you're coming. I wouldn't even ask the probo. If I were you, I'd try to look at his files online, without him knowing."

Lucas said, "Huh. You really think things are that shaky down here? Cop-wise?"

"Look. A cop busts Magnus, and he says, 'I'll give you a million bucks to go away. In cash. In an hour.' The average cop salary down here is making maybe 70k, before taxes. I mean . . ."

"All right," Lucas said.

"I CAN'T SAY it's been a pleasure talking to you," Bob said, "Weeks told us you're dealing heroin and meth. Is that right?"

"Gotta make a living. I don't recommend that people use the stuff. I'm a sales guy, a middleman," Morris said. "They're gonna get it one way or another."

Bob: "Heroin and meth. You're really a low-life piece of scum, Axel."

Morris said, "Hey, I thought we were best friends now." He flashed his charming smile back at Bob and ate another French fry. "You guys gonna give me a ride back to Bandit's? I don't do Uber. What? C'mon, don't be little federal bitches about it."

CHAPTER

SIX

AT THE HOTEL the next morning, Lucas and Bob were walking down a hallway toward the conference room, past a woman in a do-rag running a floor polisher. They were a few minutes early, and saw Weaver step out of an elevator alone, carrying a briefcase. Bob called out to him, and when they caught up, asked, "Are you doing the reward?"

Weaver nodded: "Yeah. They added up all the possibilities in Washington and figured they couldn't lose. If we get nothing, they pay nothing, no change. If they do have to put up the fifty thousand, we've got a bucket of heroin to show for it and probably even more buckets. It pays for itself in PR."

"That's important," Bob said, with an eye-roll.

"Maybe not for you, but it is for me," Weaver said. "If I don't get something, I'll be wearing a 'Fucked it up' sign around my neck. I'd rather not retire for another ten years or so." He checked them out—they were wearing jeans, knit shirts, and sport coats—and asked, "What happened to the Hawaiian shirts and shorts?"

Bob shrugged. "Got cold overnight. We're gonna be on the street, some."

Lucas: "Let me embarrass myself with a question. You're sure of the guys on this task force? We won't get any leaks?"

Weaver didn't answer directly. Instead, he asked, "You get anything last night?"

"A couple things," Lucas said. "If somebody leaks for any reason . . . even something bureaucratic, like trying to one-up the Marshals Service, we could have a tragedy. We're talking about people who shot down three Coast Guardsmen in cold blood. A guy we talked to said the whole Miami narc community leaks like a sieve."

"I'll say a few words before we start," Weaver said. "I'm very confident of these people, but I'll say a few words."

He led the way down the hall, and when he stepped into the conference room, Lucas hooked Bob's arm and muttered, "We never heard of anyone called Magnus Elliot. Or John."

Bob nodded: "Gotcha."

WHEN ALL THE agents and the Coast Guard cop had settled into the conference room, joined by the Lauderdale cop who'd been missing the day before, Weaver looked around and said, "The marshals here have been scuffing around, talking to people. We'll hear from them in a minute, but I want to warn everybody: if anyone talks about what is said in this room, and I find out, I'll run you out of the FBI, I'll run you out of the law enforcement profession, and, if I can, I'll put you in jail. I don't want you talking to anybody, including spouses, girlfriends, dead uncles. Nothing gets out. Is that clear?"

Everybody nodded and there was a shuffling of feet and annoyed glances passed around the room, and then Weaver said, "Good," and he turned to one of the senior agents and asked, "What do we have on the diver?"

The task force had contacted twenty-one female professional and semipro divers in the three-county South Florida area. Sixteen of them had provided superficially convincing alibis for the day of the shootings, which still had to be checked, but none of them looked really good for the diver being sought. Given Barney Hall's description, many of them were simply too heavy, and that included three of the five who couldn't provide solid alibis.

"We're not seeing a lot of really, mmm, lithe female divers," the lead agent said.

"That's not what you see on YouTube," the Lauderdale cop said.

"You spend a lot of time watching women divers on YouTube?" asked Taylor, the female Coastie.

"I do it some," the cop admitted with a grin.

"YouTube divers are a whole different reality," another agent said. "Anyway, we're not feeling real good about the prospects with the ones we've checked. One of them told us something I guess we knew, which I'm not sure helps at all—the water out there where the dope is, runs anywhere from a hundred to two hundred and fifty feet deep. You can get training to dive down to a hundred and thirty feet in two weeks, starting from nothing. Going deeper than that, especially for novice divers, gets risky, but for the kind of money we're talking about . . ."

"How long would it take to train to go down deeper?" Lucas asked. "Go down to a hundred and fifty or two hundred feet?"

"A lot of places wouldn't do it for liability reasons. What you'd do is get some experience. Take the training to get down to a hundred and thirty, which is routine, learn something about nitrogen narcosis and really how to manage your decompression problems, then start dipping deeper. Take technical courses. Learn to really use your dive computer and your lights and whatever kind of direction finder you have."

"Are you a diver?" Bob asked.

"Yeah."

"What's a decompression problem?"

The agent explained that nitrogen in air, under high pressure, as found in deeper scuba diving, is forced into the bloodstream. When the diver surfaces, the nitrogen can come out of the bloodstream as bubbles that lodge in the joints and internal organs, and cause painful, sometimes crippling, and sometimes deadly effects.

"It's called the bends," the diving agent said. "You don't want the bends. You prevent them by stopping on the way back to the surface, when you're still under pressure, to let the nitrogen work its way out of your body through the lungs . . . you exhale it as a gas."

"I've heard of the bends," Bob said. "Note to self: don't get them."

Lucas asked him, "How deep would you dive? On air, like the diver on the boat?"

The agent said, "A hundred and fifty feet wouldn't bother me too much, but two hundred would be a problem. I wouldn't do two hundred unless it was an emergency, and I sure as hell wouldn't stay long. I wouldn't be picking up any heroin cans."

Another agent suggested, "Maybe . . . Trimix?" He looked at Lucas and Bob and added, "I'm a diver, too."

"What's Trimix?" Bob asked.

"A mixture of gases that'll help you go deeper . . . but we checked that," said the first diving agent. "The gas in the scuba tanks on the boat was straight air."

The agent with all the certifications said, "The Coast Guardsman who shot the guy off the dock. Didn't he say six cans were off-loaded from that Mako?"

Lucas said, "Yeah, six, but he's not absolutely sure of that."

"If the diver brought up six cans, we think that'd be a hundred and thirty pounds of dope, plus the weight of the cans—maybe a hundred and fifty pounds altogether. She probably had to manage at least three small lift bags or two bigger ones, which means she was probably down there for quite a while, finding the cans, loading them, managing the bags, then resurfacing. I doubt she'd be down two hundred feet. She'd have too much decompression time, hanging out halfway to surface and trying to manage those bags and the cargo bags, all at the same time. I'd bet she wasn't down much more than a hundred and thirty or so."

"That's all wonderful, but is it relevant?" Weaver asked.

"Kind of suggests where you don't need to look," the diving agent said. "If we're really going to look."

"Okay." Weaver dipped into his briefcase and came up with a stack of paper. "Now, you all know about our reward program. I want some volunteers to take the reward posters around to the dive shops and boating and fishing shops."

He patted the stack of paper and said, "If I don't get volunteers, I'll make appointments. Volunteers are allowed to wear shorts and shirts, if you wish, even though it's a little chilly out there now. If you're willing to do this, see me when we break up."

◆ ◆ ◆

LUCAS REPORTED ON the meeting with the local narcs, the arrest of Foot-Long and the aborted arrest of Axel Morris, and the chats with the other dealers. He left out Magnus Elliot, the name Morris had given up. He did mention the possibility that Morris believed the Mafia was involved and that they might be staying at the Ange-lus Hotel, which raised some eyebrows and even the level of en-thusiasm.

"That could be something," Weaver said. "We could plug one of our Mafia specialists into the hotel, see who shows up."

"Four hundred dollars a night," Bob said. "I looked it up."

Weaver winced, but said, "Won't come out of our budget. Washington will have to pay for it. I'll make some calls."

He asked Lucas, "What's up next?"

"We got more names from Weeks and we plan to work them. Morris said that if we push the cops in Miami-Dade, word is going to get out and some of the targets could disappear. We do want word to get out that we're making offers, but we want to hit our targets, too. We need to look through FBI online files without tip-ping anyone off . . . if we can do that."

One of the agents leaned into the discussion: "You said that Weeks and Morris put you onto people who got their drugs from Mexico. Where's it gonna get us to keep hitting on the Mexico guys if the dope is really from Colombia and going to New York or New Jersey?"

"Don't know," Lucas said. "But that's what we've got. Morris thought that maybe the higher-up guys on the Mexican side might have cut a deal with the Mafia people not to interfere with their action down here. Maybe even give them a little rent money, to keep things peaceful. If we can get a solid name, one of the Mafia's, we can leave it to you to squeeze him. What we're basically trying to do here is stir things up. Get some people worried."

The agent leaned back with a skeptical, "Huh," and Weaver jabbed a finger at him: "It's more than we did."

"If you guys could get a lead on that diver . . ." Bob said. "The diver could take us to everybody."

AFTER THE MEETING, Weaver asked Lucas when they wanted to look at the FBI files.

"Soon as we can. If we could get online and look at some names," Lucas suggested. "That'd be a big help."

"I'll hook you up to God's own VPN network," Weaver said. "If we've got it in our routine files, you can see it—and that includes most routine reports from local police departments."

"What wouldn't be routine?" Bob asked.

"You know . . . spy stuff. Terrorism stuff. What you want, criminal records, probation reports, that kind of thing, that's all routine."

"That's what we need," Lucas said. "When can we get in?"

Weaver looked at his watch: "Maybe five minutes?"

WEAVER HOOKED THEM up to the FBI database and after a few minutes' instruction, left them alone to work the records. Weeks had given them a half dozen possible targets in addition to Morris, and they checked them all, looking at mug shots, histories of violence, and taking down relevant location information. Finally, they pulled up Magnus Elliot's file. Lucas had assumed he'd be black or Hispanic, because of the way Morris had talked about him. Elliot looked like he'd just gotten off the boat from Sweden.

"Won't be hard to pick out," Lucas said. "Looks like the lead singer in one of those hair bands back in olden times."

"Twisted Sister," Bob said. "My brother still has their albums."

That done, they looked up the Blue Tuna Gang. The FBI had nothing under that name, but the *Miami Herald* did. One of the defendants was named John Gentry. They found a John Gentry in Miami with a Florida driver's license and a boat registration. The address, when they looked it up, was in the Coconut Grove neighborhood of Miami, so Axel Morris had gotten it right.

The *Herald* also referred several times to a DEA agent named Mac Campbell, who'd led the investigation into Gentry. The FBI files kicked out a recent cell phone number for Campbell, with a note that he'd recently retired from government service.

"We can call him on the way down to the Coconut place," Bob said. "Maybe get lucky."

"You ready to do it?" Lucas asked.

"Sure. On the edge of impatient," Bob said. "We're running hot."

They put all the names, addresses, and mug shots on Bob's iPad. They'd go after Gentry first, because he apparently knew something specific: that the diver was female. Magnus Elliot they'd pick up later.

SEVEN

THE DAY BEFORE had been hot, but a cool front had come through, driving the temperatures into the low sixties, and the natives were wearing coats. On the way down I-95 to Miami, Bob synced his phone with the truck so Lucas could participate in the call, and punched in the number for Campbell, the DEA agent who'd led the investigation into the Blue Tunas.

Campbell, as it turned out, was behind the wheel of his RV, headed south from Pennsylvania to Florida's west coast, where he planned to spend the winter. They introduced themselves, and asked him what he remembered about Gentry.

"You can probably get the files, but the whole thing was an evidentiary mess," Campbell said, the growl of the RV's engine a steady background to his voice. "We knew they were bringing it in, but we couldn't catch them red-handed. We finally got tired of chasing them around and got them indicted on the basis of testimony from people who worked for them. Boat unloaders, a wholesaler, like that," Campbell said.

"Didn't fly?" Bob asked.

"Never had a chance. We'd put witnesses up there and the

defense attorneys would drag them through every single crime they'd committed since fifth grade," Campbell said. "They'd ask the jury, how can you trust any of them? They were all asked why they were testifying against their supposed bosses and they all admitted they were getting deals. What the defense called bribes. Besides, the Blue Tunas never brought in the heavy stuff—only marijuana. Half the goddamn jury arrived stoned in the morning—there was no way they were going to convict on the basis of marijuana. Not in the nineties."

"So they walked."

"Yeah. I kept telling the U.S. attorney that they really needed to investigate these guys based on their lifestyles—they all had nice houses and cars. Not real flashy, but good. I asked, where's the money coming from? I said, let's look at their income taxes. That's what I said. I bored everyone. That was just too big a pain in the ass for pot dealers. If they'd been living in beach mansions and driving Mercedes-Benzes, then maybe. But they weren't. They were living in Coral Springs and driving Pontiacs."

"I don't know where Coral Springs is," Bob said.

"Way out by the Everglades," Campbell said. "Nice, but not the beach."

"Maybe they weren't making that much, then," Lucas suggested.

"Oh, they were making it," Campbell said. "They were smart. I was told that they agreed before they started smuggling that they'd do it for five years, and then get out. They put the money in some companies in the British Virgin Islands and you know what the BVI will tell you about that? Not a single fuckin' thing. Their defense attorneys claimed that they took the Blue Tuna cases pro bono. Out of the goodness of their evil little legal hearts. Bullshit. They were paid in cash, under the table."

"Pretty smart for dopers," Lucas said.

"About as smart as they came, at the time. Like I said, not flashy, kept their heads down, spent a lot of time down in the Islands, moving around, so we really didn't have access to them. They'd been operating for four years when we jumped them—and in that four years, I bet they hadn't brought in more than eight to twelve loads . . . only one every four to six months. Very good stuff, though. High-quality Colombian. And when they moved, they brought in a lot. Five tons at a time. More."

"That's nuts," Bob said. "Five tons at a time?"

"Carried it around in moving vans," Campbell said. "That's what we heard, anyway. Every time they brought in a load, they'd clear between five and seven million, after expenses. That was serious money back in the nineties."

"Maybe fifty to seventy million free and clear," Lucas said. "And they stashed it offshore."

"Exactly. Living on it to this day. There were five principals in the group, so maybe . . . ten million each, after expenses? Twelve million? One of the guys was an attorney and another one was an accountant. Gentry had run a construction company before he got into the dope business. I looked him up once, a few years after the case, and he was building homes again. I think just enough to give himself a cover for the money he was spending."

THE DRIVE TO Coconut Grove ate up most of an hour. Gentry lived in a tall, two-story yellow-painted stucco house with a red-tile roof on Gifford Lane. The house had an attached garage with a five-foot-tall steel-bar gate across the driveway, and another steel-bar gate across the sidewalk leading to the front door. The small yard was crowded with palm trees, including one with coconuts.

They parked on the street and walked back to the house. Bob looked up at it and said, "If I owned this place, I'd tell the Marshals Service to kiss my ass and send the pension checks to Coconut Grove."

The sidewalk gate was unlatched. They went through, up to the front porch, and pushed the doorbell. A dog barked—a small dog from the sound of it—and a moment later, Gentry pulled the door open and frowned at them. "Cops? What'd I do?"

Lucas said, "Nothing, as far as we know. Mac Campbell said to say 'Hi.'"

Gentry laughed and said, "I wouldn't mind talking to him someday, maybe buy him a beer, when enough time's passed. Maybe it already has. Anyway, what do you want?"

Gentry was a solidly built balding man in his middle sixties, wearing white shorts and a pale blue golf shirt. He had a white brush mustache, a short pink scar below his left eye, and a cleft chin. He had smile lines on his face, and to Lucas looked like he might laugh a lot.

"We need to talk for a couple of minutes," Lucas said. "We're not here to arrest you, we've got no warrants or anything. We can talk out here if you like, but it'd be friendlier inside."

Gentry hesitated, then said, "Well, what the hell. Come on in. Watch that first step, there's a crack . . ."

Gentry took them through the house, across a burnt-orange shag carpet to what he called a Florida room, a screened-in porch that looked out over a narrow strip of grass to the near-identical Florida room on the house on the street behind them. A knee-high refrigerator was set under a countertop, and Gentry asked, "Beer, Diet Coke, lemonade?"

Lucas, keeping it congenial, took a Diet Coke and Bob went for the lemonade. Gentry popped open a beer for himself, and he asked, again, when they were all sitting down, "What'd I do?"

"Is there a wife around somewhere? A girlfriend?" Bob asked.

"Wife. She's down at Dinner Key—that's a marina—with a couple of friends."

Lucas said, "What you did, is, you stopped in at the Baily Hotel in Miami Beach a few months back to have a beer. You had a little talk with a dope dealer . . ."

Gentry held up a hand. "Nothing illegal about a beer," he said. "I don't deal dope, no way, shape, or form. I'm well out of all that. The bad old days."

Lucas said, "Okay, but this guy knew you, and you got to talking about that Coast Guard shooting up in Lauderdale. You told him the diver on the boat was a woman. We'd like to know where you heard that."

Gentry was sitting on an old-fashioned glider that creaked, *eek-eek, eek-eek*, as he rocked it with his toes. He leaned back into a cushion and closed his eyes, and after a moment he said, "That fuckin' Morris."

"Who?" Lucas asked. In his own ears, he sounded less than convincing.

"You know who," Gentry said, opening his eyes. "I don't expect you to admit it, but the only guy I talked to about that shooting was Morris. I didn't talk to anyone else at the Baily about it."

"What's Morris's first name?" Bob asked, taking a notebook out of his pocket.

Gentry shook his head. "What'd you do, get his ass in a crack? Squeeze him?"

"We don't know a Morris, but we'd like to," Lucas lied. "That's not really the point. The point is, where'd you hear about a woman diver? Where'd she come from?"

Gentry leaned back and closed his eyes again, while Lucas and Bob waited. Then he said, "Before we got busted by the DEA, back in the nineties—we were totally innocent, by the way . . ."

"Of course you were," Bob said.

". . . I did two things. I built custom homes and I ran boats. I liked building homes okay, but you know, they were custom and the wives would get on me like a hair shirt. Bitch and moan, it never stopped. What I really loved was the boats. I had a lot of friends in that community. Still do. Sport fishermen, dive guys, people who live out on the water. Even a couple of Coast Guard and Marine Patrol guys, back when we had a Florida Marine Patrol."

Bob: "We buy that; we've read your file."

"I've still got a boat, a little center console fisherman," Gentry said. "Doesn't have a head on it. Sometimes my wife and I go for a run up the Intracoastal. She likes to look at houses. We've been as far north as Vero Beach, which is a long-ass haul from here. The boat's not big enough to sleep on; we stay in motels.

"Anyway, there's this crazy old fucker named Roger Quinn, a left-over hippie. He might have run a few loads himself. He has a pontoon boat that he takes out to the Intracoastal. He sells hamburgers off a grill and he's got a Porta Potty on the back where girls can take a leak. He charges two bucks a pee, probably takes in a hundred bucks a day in the summer. The boat's called *Big Mac's You're-In-and-Out.* That's sort of a pun . . ."

Lucas frowned. "What's the pun?"

"It's where women go to pee. You're in and out. Urine-and-out." He peered at them. "Urine. Because of the Porta Potty."

Lucas and Bob caught on simultaneously, and they both said, "Ah."

"I've known Roger forever," Gentry continued. "My wife wanted to go up to Lauderdale one day, hot day, smooth water, take a run down the New River and look at houses. We got up there and she had to take a leak, so we stopped at this guy's boat and Roger and I got to talking. This was a month or so after that Mako burned, around Labor Day, in there.

"Roger said he'd seen that Mako. That one day it came over and the guys bought burgers and fries. He said they'd been out diving, there was a black chick on board, and she was the diver. Said the guys were New Yorkers, from their accents, and said that from the look of them, he could believe they shot the Coast Guard guys because . . . they were that kind of New Yorker."

"A black chick? The diver?"

"Yeah."

"Nobody told anyone?" Lucas asked.

Gentry shrugged: "There were cops all over the place, every kind of cop there was, including those fucks from the DEA. I wasn't gonna stick my hand up, not with my history. Not when it involves cops getting shot because of dope. Besides, Roger smokes more weed than the rest of South Florida put together, which is a lot of weed. Who knows what he really saw? And he's a bullshitter. He knows everything on the water, but about a third of it is lies and bullshit."

He hesitated, then added, "With wall-to-wall cops, you'd think they would have discovered that much, huh? The black girl? The New York guys? Roger was right there, every day, all day, not more than a mile from where the shooting happened. You'd think somebody would have talked to him. Some cop."

"You'd think," Bob said.

Lucas asked, "Would he be out there today? It's kinda cold."

"He's out there every day. He's out there on Thanksgiving, Christmas, and New Year's. Doesn't have anything else to do. Even on a bad day, he'll attract some traffic, even if it's just some woman who needs to pee. I gotta say, his hamburgers are good, the fries are great. There'll be a certain amount of dirt and gasoline in them . . . and when I think about it, maybe that's what makes them so good."

"You keep saying 'women' need to pee," Bob said. "I'm a little curious . . ."

Gentry shrugged. "With their plumbing, it's hard to take a whiz off the back of a boat."

Lucas: "So . . . how would we get out there? Where Roger is?"

Gentry said, "You're cops, you could call the Broward Marine Patrol, but . . . actually, if I were you, I'd go up to the Lauderdale Yacht Club. Roger is usually about two minutes from there. Show them your badges at the club, somebody would take you out in a tender."

"Okay. You got anything else?" Lucas asked.

"Nope. I really don't. Listen, don't tell Roger I brought up his name, huh? He's a friend," Gentry said. "I only told you about him because I hated the idea of those Coasties getting shot. I really did. They're water folks like me. And I'm not really getting him in trouble, because he wouldn't have anything to do with those ass-holes on the Mako. He's not a dope guy. He works hard and he's a straight arrow."

"Except for smoking more weed than everyone else in South Florida put together," Bob said.

"That's not even a traffic ticket anymore," Gentry said.

"As we've found out," Lucas said.

Gentry nodded. "Here, I'll sweeten it up for you. You don't tell Roger and I won't give that fuckin' Morris a hard time about giving me up."

"We don't know any Morris," Lucas said. "We'd like to."

"Have it your way," Gentry said, rolling his eyes.

Bob: "What'd you do with your ten million?"

Gentry waved his arm around, taking in the house. "Does this look like ten million?" He shook his head. "There never was any ten million. I was completely, totally innocent."

Bob: "You're sure you don't have a yacht tucked away some-where? Maybe under a BVI corporate name? Maybe over in St. Pete, or Naples, or Lauderdale? Or two blocks from here? At the marina where your wife is?"

"You guys are so *suspicious*," Gentry said. He looked sad, think-ing about it, then ruined it with a sly smile.

They heard the front door open and Gentry turned and shouted, "We're back here, Helen."

He asked Lucas, "Can we be done now? She knows all about Blue Tuna, but she'd freak out if she thought I was still being watched by cops."

"We're done," Lucas said. "We won't tell Roger Quinn where

we got his name. If anything bad happens to this Morris guy—we're gonna look him up—we'll be back."

"Yeah. You're gonna find a Morris in Miami without knowing his first name? Good luck with that," Gentry said. "Oh, wait, I forgot: you don't need any luck, you got him on speed dial. Tell him, 'Hello from John, you fuck,' next time you see him."

Neither Lucas or Bob bothered to deny it.

THEY WERE ALL on their feet when Gentry's wife came through, a thin, sunburned woman in a white golf shirt, slacks, and white visor, pretty, maybe seventeen years younger than Gentry. She looked at Lucas and Bob, then at Gentry and asked, tension in her voice, "What's going on?"

Lucas said, "We're federal marshals and we're investigating a man named Morris, who your husband knew years ago. We thought he might be able to help us." He shrugged. "It was too long ago, I guess. Nothing really to do with your husband, if you're worried about that."

Gentry said to his wife, "The last time I saw Morris was about two hours before Hurricane Andrew, back in 'ninety-two. I never heard of him after that. He's probably dead."

Lucas said, "Thanks for your help, John. We'll get out of your hair."

Helen Gentry stayed in the house, watching from the door, as Gentry walked them out to the truck.

"Thanks for that, but there's gonna be some serious drama tonight," Gentry said.

Lucas asked, "You never heard another single thing about that Mako?"

"I didn't. I'd tell you," Gentry said, shaking his head.

Lucas walked around the truck and got in the driver's seat and Gentry said to Bob, as he was getting in, "You look like the kind of guy who'd be on the water."

"I am, but small water, in Louisiana," Bob said. "I share a bass boat with a friend."

"Shoot, you gotta try the Islands," Gentry said, with a toothy grin. "You go down there once and you'll go down there all the time."

"Like you and your yacht?"

"Maybe see you there," Gentry said, and he pushed the door shut. "Down in the Islands, it's all willing women and the chicken dance."

"Things usually come down to that," Lucas said, as he buckled in. "One way or another."

"Yeah, they do," Gentry said. "Hey—good luck, guys."

As they drove out to the freeway, Bob asked, "What do you think about Gentry? You think we got it all?"

"Campbell was probably right. Gentry's got a bundle salted away somewhere. I don't care about that," Lucas said. "He sounded sincere about the Coasties getting shot . . . so . . . I think we got what he had."

Bob: "Magnus Elliot or Roger Quinn?"

"Quinn. Sounds like he actually laid eyes on the killers."

EIGHT

THE LAUDERDALE YACHT Club was a big white building with water on three sides and oversized yachts tied up on their docks. They went inside, found a manager, who looked at their badges, said, "Cool, no problem." He found a man named Javier to run them out in a little outboard; as Gentry said, *Big Mac's You're-In-and-Out* was about two minutes off the Yacht Club.

Big Mac's was as advertised, a tri-tube pontoon with a sea-green fiberglass Porta Potty on the stern, a barbeque shack on the bow, and tie-up cleats on all four sides.

Roger Quinn, the owner, had an eye patch on his left eye and brown precancerous spots sprinkled across his face; something had been done surgically to one side of his bulbous nose, because it didn't match the other side. He was a short man with shoulder-blade-length gray hair and ragged cutoffs. He was wearing a sleeveless shirt and was barefoot, despite the cool weather.

Javier tossed him a line and Quinn tied off the boat front and back, looked at Lucas and Bob and asked, "What'd I do?"

"Jesus," Bob said to Lucas. "We can't even walk around without people asking us that."

Javier said, "Roger, these two people are U.S. Marshals, Tony told me to ride them out here . . ."

Quinn looked at them with a single watery eye and no visible enthusiasm. "Yeah?"

Lucas explained the mission and when he was done, Quinn asked, "This gonna get me killed?"

"No reason it should," Lucas said. "We don't talk about this kind of thing."

"What if I gotta testify?"

"You won't have to testify—whatever you give us, we'll figure out a different way to get it."

"Might want you to look at some mug shots," Bob said. "See if you recognize anybody."

Quinn said, "Yeah. I seen them close up, but I ain't lookin' at any mug shots. I'm no fool. You're lyin' to me. If I saw them in a mug shot book, you'd make me look at a lineup, and then I'd have to testify in court. So, you know, basically, fuck that."

Bob started, "Look, Mr. Quinn . . ."

Quinn said, "I ain't doing it. If you'll leave me alone, I'll give you something better than me."

Lucas: "What's that?"

"I can give you somebody who *knows* them," Quinn said.

Lucas and Bob glanced at each other, and then Bob asked, "Who?"

Quinn asked Javier, "You know that guy Beddy who runs the *Down East*?"

"I know him a little," Javier said. And to Lucas and Bob: "Captain Buddy runs a party boat called the *Down East*, out of Aventura, which is just down the way."

Quinn said, "That's him, but his name is Beddy, not Buddy. When that Mako was here, the *Down East* come in."

Lucas asked, "What about it?"

"Beddy was doing a party and the boat was full of hairdresser girls. Young girls. They graduated from hairdresser school somewhere and they were celebratin'. Didn't have to pee, not one of them, must be at least two or three heads on Beddy's boat. They came in because they said I looked neat and they wanted burgers and fries. Ran around my boat, like to tipped it over. Had a fry fight, threw most of the fries in the water. Tipped me a hundred dollars. They was all wearing their teeny bikinis, tits and ass all over the place. They started talking to the guys on the Mako and the Mako guys liked that a lot. They were all here for an hour and the way they were talking, I think some of them girls got together with the Mako guys that night, at a hotel."

Bob: "You mean . . ."

"It looked like that to me, some of them girls was gonna get their legs up in the air," Quinn said. "I know they were talking about a hotel."

"You know what hotel?" Bob asked.

"Nope. Didn't pay much attention to that part of it. Do remember, it was down in Miami Beach."

"Where do we find this Beddy guy?" Lucas asked.

Quinn said, "Down to Aventura. It's a big boat basin south of here."

"Anything else?" Lucas asked. "Did you see the diver?"

Quinn scratched his neck. "The diver. She was Bahamian, I think. Black chick. The way she talked, her accent. I'll tell you boys something—if she's gone back to the Bahamas, you'll have a tough time digging her out of there. People in the Bahamas, if they don't want to be found, you won't find them. Too many islands, about six cops between them."

"How do you know she was a diver?" Bob asked.

"I don't—but there were tanks on board the boat and her hair looked like she'd been in the water."

"Okay," Lucas said. "You got a good memory."

"I wouldn't have remembered any of this, if they hadn't burned up that boat a couple days later."

Quinn said he didn't know how to get in touch with Beddy, or precisely where the *Down East* was, but he'd be on the internet, because that's how he got his customers.

Bob asked him why his boat was called *Big Mac's You're-In-and-Out* instead of *Quinn's You're-In-and-Out,* and Quinn said, "I'm selling hamburgers. So . . . Big Macs."

"Ah."

"Don't tell McDonald's."

THEY THANKED HIM for his help and Javier ran them back to the Yacht Club. Half an hour later, guided by Bob's iPad, they rolled into the Aventura marina, found the office, and eventually got pointed at the *Down East.*

The *Down East* looked like a floating condo. They parked and walked down to it, where they found Beddy working in the engine compartment below the back deck. Lucas knocked on the hull and Beddy's head popped up and he said, "You're not Carlos."

"Nope. I'm a U.S. Marshal. Who's Carlos?"

"He's the guy who's going to tell me why the port engine's been running hot. So . . . what's up with you guys?"

Beddy was a stocky man in a white golf shirt that had DOWN EAST embroidered on the chest; he had white hair under a captain's hat, a white bristly mustache and ample stomach, with skinny legs sticking out of his white shorts. He looked, Lucas thought, like a party boat captain. When he got out of the engine compartment, he poured some Engine Off on his hands, and cleaned off a smear of diesel fuel.

Beddy had no trouble remembering the hairdressers. Thumbing through a charter register, he found the boat had been rented by the Zizzorz Wizzardz hairdressers' school in Hollywood.

"Not that Hollywood," he said to Bob and Lucas. "This Hollywood is the first big town south of here."

Bob nodded. "I saw an exit."

"There were these two girls who organized the party. Real live wires," Beddy said, flipping a page in the register. "They were wary of the guys on the boat, those two. A couple of the other girls were all over them. Maybe because of the Mako, which says money. One of the girls offered to cut one of the guys' hair, right here on my boat. They didn't, but they were getting along good."

Lucas prompted him: "Do you have their names? The live wires?"

"Sure do." He held the book away from his face, squinted at it and said, "Alicia Snow did most of the talking and arranging. The other one was Meredith Duffy." He put the book down. "Alicia used to be a waitress, but she wanted something more professional, so she went to school to get into hairdressing. I remember

that: she's a cutie. The Meredith girl was quieter, she was an ath-
lete of some kind before she went into hairdressing. Hell of a
dancer, some old rock 'n' roll tune came up on the radio and she
danced her ass off with the other girls."

"Anything else?"

"I got their phone numbers . . ."

LUCAS TECHNICALLY WORKED for a supervisor in the Marshals
Service's Washington office named Russell Forte. Forte's secretary
did a good portion of her boss's work. As they were walking back
to the Pathfinder, Lucas called her and got her to run down the
billing addresses for the two cell phones. She called back fifteen
minutes later, as they were finding their way out of the marina.
Both phones were on AT&T, and the bills went to the same address, but different apartments.

"WHAT DO YOU want to do?" Bob asked.

"Go talk to these two women," Lucas said.

"Two is fine, but if we wind up having to talk to a bunch of
them, the FBI guys could do it a lot quicker than we can. They
could do all of them at the same time, if we give them the names."

"True. But . . . I'd like to be the one who cracked the case. If we
don't get something solid from the two names we've got, we call
Weaver and sic the FBI on the rest of the women, while we go
down to Miami and find Magnus Elliot."

"That's a plan."

The case was beginning to turn: Lucas could smell it.

Bob could, too; he chatted happily away as they headed west and north from Hollywood.

SNOW AND DUFFY lived in the town of Sunrise, which butted up against the Everglades, in a six-story white apartment building with exterior walkways. From the walkway on the fifth floor, they could see the green/tan sawgrass plain of the 'glades, stretching away to the horizon, on the other side of an expressway that paralleled a levee that kept the water out of the town. A lone hawk hung over the sawgrass, hunting.

"Doesn't look like much, does it?" Bob asked. "Doesn't even look like a swamp."

"But it does look sorta neat," Lucas said. "If we get time, I'd like to go on one of those airboat rides. Scare up some gators."

"And some of those giant yellow snakes they got out there, those Burmese pythons, twenty feet long," Bob said. And he laughed, knowing Lucas's attitude toward snakes.

"Yeah, fuck that," Lucas said. "Gators good, snakes bad."

Lucas led the way down the walkway to Snow's apartment, knocked, got no answer, and then to Duffy's, which was equally silent. He didn't like to call interview subjects ahead of time because it gave them a chance to disappear. The two women were probably at work, but since they had no idea where, Lucas finally called Alicia Snow.

Snow answered and after a bit of back-and-forth about the investigation, admitted that she was working in a shop in the town of Plantation, south of the apartment building, called Salon de Elegance. Duffy, she said, worked in a different salon, but also in

Plantation, called the Bombshell. "I've got a break before my last client, but if you could get here quick, before four o'clock, I could squeeze out a few minutes."

"We're on the way."

The Salon de Elegance was located in a largely vacant strip shopping center with a payday loan office and a dog grooming center the only open stores, other than the salon. They parked and walked across the crumbling parking lot, and Bob said, "You know, this whole place, houses and apartment buildings and shopping centers, looks like it was built to last about twenty years. After that, good luck."

The salon had a half dozen hairdresser stations, two of them occupied by older women, when Lucas and Bob pushed through the door. A Springsteen song was playing softly in the background, and a young blonde hurried over to them and asked, "You're the marshals?"

"Yes." Lucas nodded at her, tried out a smile, which she seemed to miss.

"Come on around in back; I'm Alicia. The owner's out right now, we can use her office."

The owner's office was a beige cubicle with concrete floors, small metal desk, four file cabinets and three chairs, including the chair at the desk, taken by Snow. Lucas and Bob sat down and Snow took out her telephone, punched up her phone list and copied a name, address, and telephone number on a piece of notepaper.

As she was doing that, she said, "Now, I have to tell you. I never knew any of the guys on that boat. I was getting burgers from that burger guy and I never talked to them. I sure didn't know they were involved in those murders. All I know about that Coast Guard thing was what I saw on television and that was only like one or two nights on the news. People get murdered here all the time and I didn't pay attention. I'm sorry. I feel awful about it. I feel really awful now because of Patty."

Bob: "Who's Patty?"

Snow: "Patty Pittman."

She pushed the note toward Lucas, who turned it around so he could read it. Patty Pittman had an address in the town of Islamorada.

Snow said, "Patty . . . disappeared. A couple of months ago, I think, like in September. Her mother called some of us who knew her—not me, because we weren't close—but a couple of the other girls. I heard about it from these other girls. The police say it looks like she moved away with a boyfriend, maybe to get away from her mother. Her mother thinks she's been kidnapped. Or worse."

"She knew the guys on the boat?"

"That's what I heard . . . another rumor from the other girls in our class," Snow said. "That she'd dated one of them. Then she vanished. It was in the newspapers in the Keys, I guess. Some of the girls saw it. I didn't connect her disappearance to the boat guys, though. I don't think the cops did, either. I mean, this was a couple of months after the boat party."

"You know where her mother is?"

Snow shrugged, but said, "I assumed she'd be down around Islamorada. I don't really know."

"Do you think your friend Meredith might know? Ms. Duffy?"

"Oh. Nooo . . . She and Patty weren't friends at all, hardly. Patty was ditsy. *Is* ditsy. Meredith is like the last thing from ditsy. Patty was friendly with a couple of other girls . . . Let me write down their names and numbers . . ."

She punched up her phone again, got her note back from Lucas, copied out phone numbers of Sandra Klink and Karen Loftus. "I know they've moved around, so I don't have addresses for them and we weren't close anyway . . . But I bet they kept their phone numbers."

She pushed the note back to Lucas.

Lucas asked, "You saw the guys on the boat close up . . . Could you pick them out if we showed you some mug shots?"

Her forehead wrinkled and her eyes slid away from his, then she said, "Maybe. If you didn't tell anybody that I did it."

"Good. We appreciate it," Lucas said. "We'll have a couple of FBI agents come around to talk with you."

"They do the clerical part of our investigation," Bob told her. "The paper stuff, instead of the street investigation."

She bobbed her head: "Okay."

THEY TALKED FOR a few more minutes, but Snow had nothing more of interest. As they stood to leave, Lucas asked, "Where's this Islamorada place? Somewhere by Miami?"

"Oh, no, it's like these islands, it's probably halfway down the Keys. Maybe . . . a hundred miles from here? Maybe more. It takes quite a while to get there."

"Okay." Lucas thanked her, gave her his card and asked her to call if she remembered anything more. He told her to expect a call from the FBI.

Outside the salon, Bob asked, "We're not going after this Patty?"

"Not if the cops are looking for her and haven't been able to find her and it's a hundred miles from here. Sounds like a fine task for our friends in the conservative suits," Lucas said. "I'll call Weaver and unload this on him. They'll need to talk to whoever runs the hairdresser school, plus all the classmates, plus Pittman's mother and whatever local cops have been looking for her. Take us a week, it'll take the feds a day."

THEY SAT IN the car and Lucas called Weaver, told him what they'd done and gave him the names and phone numbers they'd gotten from Snow. "If you have your boys get on this, they'll probably be able to dig up some women who could identify the shooters, if you've got mug shots of them, and you probably do, if they're really in the Mafia."

"Lucas, this is terrific," Weaver said. He'd been in the FBI too long to actually sound excited, but he was. "We'll get all over it, starting tonight. What are you doing?"

"We'll talk to one more of these hairdressers, named Meredith Duffy, then . . . mmm . . . we got another guy we want to talk to, but I don't think we'll make it today. He's down in Miami."

"Okay. Thanks again," Weaver said. For the first time, he seemed to have a little hope in his voice.

When Lucas rang off, Bob said, "I feel kind of bad about that. They'll find something good and guess who gets the credit?"

"Life sucks and then you die," Lucas said. He looked both ways as they rolled out of the shopping center into heavy traffic. "Get on your phone and find the fastest way to this Bombshell place."

Bob started tapping on his phone but said, "Life sucks and then you die, so you better take the credit where you can. You know the feds. When it comes to credit, they're always the first in line. Look what happened with that 1919 guy you killed. I never even saw your name in the newspapers."

"There's still newspapers?"

"You know what I mean."

"Yeah. Nobody knows I was involved but a bunch of U.S. senators," Lucas said. "Who would you rather have on your side? Some bureaucrat halfway up the ranks of the FBI? Or a U.S. senator who sits on the Finance Committee and can fund a new machine gun for you?"

"You got a point," Bob said. "Let me get this address."

THE BOMBSHELL WAS in another crumbling mall and apparently aimed at a younger crowd. What Lucas thought of as soft rap was playing in the background, for the half dozen customers and hairdressers.

Lucas showed his badge to a woman at the reception desk, who said, "Yes, Meredith is here, she's working at the moment . . ."

"We only need to talk to her for a few minutes . . ."

"I'll see what I can do." She walked down the line of hairdresser chairs and spoke to a tall dark-haired woman who looked over at Lucas and Bob, then said something to the receptionist, who came back and said, "She's finishing a color touch-up, but she can't stop now. Give her ten minutes."

◆◆◆

MEREDITH DUFFY LOOKED like she knocked off a 10K road race every morning before work; dark hair close-cut, no fat anywhere, long legs, her arms showing some gym muscle. As she left her chair and walked toward them, Bob muttered, "She moves like Rae."

Duffy took them to the salon's back room, a narrow rectangle with shelves on both sides filled with bottles and pieces of hairdressing equipment, and which smelled like vinegar. A small square window penetrated the wall at the far end, letting in some light; the window had two bars across it.

"I didn't interact with those men," she said, when Lucas explained that they were looking for witnesses who might recognize the men on the Mako. "They were not my type. At all. They were sort of porky and red-faced, like they might drop dead of a heart attack five minutes from now. Like they live on surf 'n' turf and tequila. I don't think any of them could have run a block."

"There was a girl named Patty Pittman . . ."

"I heard rumors about her from a friend," Duffy said. "She disappeared, but this was way after the boat thing."

"You heard about her from Alicia?" Lucas asked.

"Yes, have you talked to her?"

"A while ago," Lucas said. "She couldn't identify anyone, either. We need to get to somebody who spent some time with these guys. We heard that some of the women from the boat may have dated them."

Duffy's eyebrows went up and she said, "Uh, you, uh, I . . . Um, I really haven't stayed much in touch with the class, except for Alicia. I'd be perfectly happy to look at photos, if I thought I might help, but . . . I don't think I can. I didn't care about those guys. I was socializing with the other girls. I haven't seen any of them since then—the girls, I mean."

"Except Alicia."

"Yes, except Alicia."

They pushed her on exactly what she'd seen on the boat, and how she'd avoided the men from the Mako. She stubbornly insisted that she simply hadn't paid attention to them. When they'd hit a dead end, Lucas gave her his card. "If you think of anything that might help, call us. These are bad people and they need to be taken out of circulation."

"If I think of anything . . ."

As they were walking out to the car, Bob asked, "When do you think she started lying?"

"When I told her that Snow said she couldn't identify anyone," Lucas said. "Duffy thinks she can."

"I got the feeling that Duffy is *sure* she can. You want to go back and jack up Snow?"

Lucas scraped his lower lip with his upper teeth, then looked at his watch. "It's almost five, it's getting dark, and Snow said she was about to start on her last customer an hour ago. She won't be there. Besides, it might be better to let her stew on it overnight. The fact that she lied. We'll hit her again tomorrow."

"I looked up Magnus Elliot's house on the iPad, the satellite view. That's a place we might not want to go walking around in the dark."

"Okay . . . we got a lot done," Lucas said. He yawned. "Let's find a new place to eat. Maybe the feds will run some of these women down tonight. We'll find out in the morning."

"There's this street over in Fort Lauderdale, Los Feliz or something, supposed to have some good food."

"Let's go," Lucas said. "I'm hungrier than hell."

Turned out that the street was Las Olas, not Los Feliz. Parking was a nightmare, but they lucked into a slot a few blocks from the restaurant they'd picked and walked back. Bob was talking about palm trees and houses when Lucas interrupted: "Did we just make a mistake? Should we have hit Snow again? Or hit Elliot?"

"This investigation has been going on for months," Bob said. "One more day . . ."

"That's not what I asked," Lucas said. He was strolling along with his hands in the sport coat pockets. "I asked, did we make a mistake?"

Bob considered, pursed lips, staring down at the sidewalk.

Then, "I don't know. Maybe."

NINE

ALICIA SNOW WATCHED through the front window as Lucas and Bob rolled out of the parking lot in the Pathfinder. They'd frightened her. They seemed smart and mean, a bad combination. She mentioned Patty Pittman's disappearance because Pittman's disappearance had nothing to do with the boating party, and if the marshals started investigating Pittman, they wouldn't be pushing on her.

She walked back to the office and got on her phone. A man answered after five rings and she said, "This is Al. Where are you?"

"At my place." His voice down low; she could hear a television in the background. "What'd I tell you about calling? My wife is out in the living room, if she . . ."

"Listen to me! Two U.S. Marshals were here, questioning me," Snow said, the fear leaking into her voice. "They asked about the party on the boat. About who could pick you guys out, if they saw pictures. They know about all the girls."

"Shit! I heard about those guys. They're going around hitting on people. How'd they get to you?"

"I don't know, they didn't say. When I told you about Patty

Pittman disappearing, you said it didn't have anything to do with you guys, so I told the marshals about her. I figured that if they're investigating Patty, they won't be questioning me. They really scared me; these marshals are *mean*. What are we going to do?"

After a silence, Jack Cattaneo said, "We're going to take it easy—or you are. Nobody will know about you, about the two of us. I mean, if my wife heard about us, I'd wake up with a knife in my chest. So: you take it easy, play it cool, relax. They . . . didn't try to pressure you? They didn't know anything?"

"No, nothing like that. They were polite, they were going around trying to find people who'd seen your faces. And the girls did. I told them I remembered some guys on the boat coming up while we were getting hamburgers, but I didn't talk to you. I told them I really couldn't pick anyone out from a picture."

"But they got a list of the girls."

"I guess."

"All right. I'll talk to some guys. You stay cool. Here comes Belinda."

He clicked off.

BELINDA WASN'T ACTUALLY coming. Cattaneo's wife was rattling around the family room with her acrylic paints and an oversized canvas she was calling *Moonrise, Big Cypress*. Satisfied that she hadn't overheard the phone call, he put the phone in his pocket, sat on a kitchen chair, and closed his eyes.

He had, indeed, told Snow that nobody on the boat had anything to do with Patty Pittman's disappearance, but he'd been lying. In fact, the men on the boat had everything to do with Patty

Pittman, and now, if Snow had put the feds on the Pittman case, it could be coming back to bite them on the ass, not that they'd had any choice with Pittman.

He chewed on a thumbnail for a moment, sighed, and wandered back to the family room and asked, "Belinda: late lunch?"

"Can't right now, honey. I'm right in the middle of a passage and these paints dry so fast . . ." She was a thin woman with tight black hair and a silver ring on one side of her nose; she was wrapped in a canvas apron.

She freaked her friends out—other housewives bought paint sets and canvases and made bad pictures of their cats and pots of geraniums that wound up in boxes somewhere. Belinda painted Florida and South Jersey landscapes that sold for thirty to fifty thousand dollars each, out of galleries in Miami and Manhattan. They couldn't get enough of them.

"Okay. Well, I'm gonna go walk around," Cattaneo said.

"Why don't you go over to the deli and get a salad?" she asked. "Don't eat any of those fishy things, they make you burp."

She meant fart, but he left it at that. "I'll see you in an hour," he said. "Why don't you call the McKinleys and see if they want to go out to the Cat's Cradle for dinner. I'll buy."

"If you're buying, they'll go," she said.

CATTANEO WENT BACK to the bedroom for his sunglasses, straw hat, and burner phone. He took the elevator down and walked out of the condo onto Collins Avenue, found a piece of shade next to a parked U-Haul truck, and poked in a number.

The phone was picked up on the second ring. "Yeah?"

"This is me. I need to talk to the guy."

"Hang on."

There was a moment of silence, then "Hey."

"Hey. You know those two guys we were talking about? They got in touch with my barber and they were asking about the rest of the girls."

"Goddamnit! Where'd you hear this?"

"Barber called," Cattaneo said.

"They're bringing pressure. They've been all over town, the way we hear it," the guy said.

"They're something new, and they're asking about Patty Pittman," Cattaneo said.

Down the sidewalk, a disheveled street woman had been pushing a shopping cart along, and now she stepped next to a hedge, pulled down her pants, and took a dump. A half block from his condo, for Christ's sakes. Neighborhood was going to shit, literally; maybe they should sell the place.

"That's . . . not good, but I don't think we have any exposure there, not after this long. I'll figure something out," said the guy on the phone. "Have a nice day."

Cattaneo clicked off, put his cell phone in his pocket, walked down the street to the woman, who'd finished and pulled up her pants. He could smell what she'd left behind, and he said to her, "You ever do that again, I'll break your fuckin' arm."

"Kiss my ass, shitbag," she said. She was radically thin, her face seemed to be mostly nose and cheekbones, and gray with dirt.

Cattaneo grabbed her by the arm with one hand—she seemed no heavier than a bird—and with the other, balled into a fist, hit her hard under the armpit and felt the ribs crack. The woman gasped and whimpered and he pushed her behind the hedge where she fell on her back, crying, and he walked away.

Fuckin' trash, he thought. Where were the cops when you needed one?

Cattaneo continued on to the deli, where he had a corned beef sandwich with a ton of mustard and red onions, and a small salad, so that he would, he hoped, smell like a fuckin' lettuce leaf when he got back home. He was licking his fingers when the burner rang and the guy asked, "You at home?"

"Down at Brill's."

"Good. You need to come on over here."

"Give me fifteen minutes? I'm walking."

"See ya."

The caller's name, God bless him, was Michael Behan, as Irish American as ever was, because if one thing was true about the new Mafia, Jersey version, they might be assholes, but they weren't bigots; well, except when it came to black guys.

Cattaneo put on his sunglasses and hat and ambled back out on the sidewalk, looked both ways, as if he were undecided where to go next, then turned left and took his time walking eight blocks down A1A. Halfway to Behan's, he stopped at an ice cream stand next to a hotel walkway to the ocean and bought a double-dip strawberry cone.

Behan lived in a two-million-dollar condo that he'd bought when the buying was good, back in 2009. The condo had two floors, the top being a living room, an entertainment area with a wet bar and a wall-sized television, and a kitchen.

The lower floor, where Cattaneo had never been, comprised bedrooms and a private office, or so he'd heard. Though Behan was an excellent criminal, he was not so good with fashion and furnishings—Cattaneo thought he might be color-blind, though he'd never asked, and worse, he wore white athletic socks with sandals. He'd equipped his two-million-dollar condo with furniture from an online furniture store, guided by two low-rent designers from Lighthouse Point. The furniture had all arrived two weeks later in a truck from North Carolina, had been installed in two hours, and had never been changed or even moved around.

Cattaneo got off the elevator on the thirty-second floor, stepped out into a hallway, where there were only two doors, and pressed the bell for the door on the right. A guy he knew opened the door and said, "C'mon in, big guy."

"Matt, how you doin'?"

Behan was occupying a love seat in a conversation pit that looked out over the Atlantic. He called, "Jack: did you bring me a fuckin' cone?"

"It would have dripped to death by the time I got here," Cattaneo said, finishing the last of it.

There were three other men sitting in the conversation pit. Cattaneo said, "Marc, Jimmy, Greg, you're all looking good. Greg: how's the foot?"

"I can play nine out of a cart," the man said. "Probably make it back to eighteen in a month or so. Not going to be walking for a while, though."

The six men didn't exactly look alike, but there was a general similarity: they were all a little heavy, with guts, but also heavy in the shoulders. Short hair, a couple of them with teeth that were too white, like implants. Red noses, from alcohol or golf. Forties and fifties. If someone were to guess their jobs, the guess would involve trucks in some way, and the things that fell off them. The guess would be correct.

Cattaneo took a chair and looked at Behan. "So."

"We need to do something, right now," Behan said. "These guys, these marshals, they'll eventually trip over somebody who'll know about us. Gonna happen soon. We can't have someone looking at us too close while we're trying to get that shit out of the ocean."

"When's that going to happen, anyway?" asked the man named Marc.

Cattaneo shook his head: "The Coast Guard is sitting on it. The good thing is, they don't know exactly where it is. They're too far north and too far west. I don't think they'll find it, but we can't go out there and dive, either."

"We can handle all that later," Behan said. He heaved himself off the sofa, went to the bar, opened a bottle of lemon tonic water and poured it into a glass with a couple of ice cubes—he had a well-stocked bar but didn't drink himself—and walked over to the windows looking out at the ocean. "What we need to do now is come up with a consensus on the marshals. I talked to Doug, and he thinks we need to . . . lose them . . . and at the same time, give the other feds a rag to chew on."

"What are you thinking?" asked the man named Jimmy. "You thinking you might be leaning on me?"

Behan turned and pointed at the man with his drink hand. "Yeah, I am, Jimmy. We gotta be way careful. You told me once about those brothers, that you could get to with remote control."

"Yeah. The brothers. They're still out there. Crazier than a couple of bedbugs, but they get shit done."

"We'd have to be completely clean . . ."

"We would be. The brothers got no idea who I am. But: we kill a couple of marshals, there's gonna be a stink. There're gonna be marshals and FBI on every fuckin' block."

"Which isn't *necessarily* bad," Behan said. "Dougie said he keeps running into the Romano people up on the Island. He'd like to be done with them. And Don Romano happens to live here, down in South Dade."

"This is sounding more complicated now," said the man named Jimmy.

"Complicated, but not *too* complicated," Behan said. "Dougie and I were talking about it, and this is what we're going to do. If it works, we're in great shape. If it doesn't, we're no further back than we are now."

"Tell us about it," Cattaneo said.

Behan told them about it.

ON THE WAY back to his condo, Cattaneo found two cop cars and three cops standing on the sidewalk. As he went by, he asked one of the cops, "What happened?"

"Somebody beat up an old lady," the cop said. "You live around here?"

"Up in the condo," Cattaneo said, pointing. "An old lady? That's terrible."

"You didn't see anything like that?"

Cattaneo shook his head. "No. I was down at Brill's and

then over at the ice cream wagon by Carmody's. When did this happen?"

"Couple hours ago. They took her in an ambulance," the cop said.

"She say what the guy looked like?"

"She told me it was a tall black guy," said the cop, who was a tall black guy. "Anyway, if you hear anything . . ."

"Sure. I haven't seen anybody like that, though. Except you." The cop laughed and Cattaneo went on his way. At the condo door, he looked at his reflection in the glass and thought, "Tall black guy? I'm nothing but pink."

Made himself laugh.

CHAPTER

TEN

AT THE TEAM meeting the next morning, Weaver said, "We interviewed four of those girls. They're being difficult."

"They're scared," said one of the agents. "They've been talking to each other about the guys who might be in the Mafia, and how this Patty Pittman disappeared."

"You have to push," Weaver said. "These girls could break this for us."

Weaver reported that the $50,000 heroin-can reward notices had gone up in every dive shop in South Florida, from Palm Beach to Key West. Taylor, the Coast Guard cop, said they'd gotten some hits, divers who wanted to go out and look for the dope.

Lucas: "What if somebody decides that three million in heroin is worth more than a fifty-thousand-dollar reward?"

Taylor said, "Everybody's on notice that we'll be right there with them, that we'll be boarding them a couple of times a day, that nobody will leave the search area without being boarded. If they try to run with heroin, they go to prison."

Lucas nodded. "Sounds good."

The plan to put an organized crime expert in the Angelus Hotel was also on schedule, Weaver said. "It turns out that one of our DC organized crime guys is dating a model. A fairly well-known model. She's been on the cover of that American Express *Departures* magazine, and some other ones, too. They approached her and she said she'd be happy to spend a week at the Angelus as long as she didn't have to do anything dangerous. She said she's got a lot of stuff she can do. Her agent is setting up contacts with fashion people on Miami Beach, so they'll look legit. They'll be in there tonight."

Weaver asked Lucas what he and Bob would be doing, and Lucas said, "We've got another guy to talk to in Miami. Don't know what will come out of it, but he's bigger than the dealers we've been hitting so far. We've heard that he might actually be able to tell us something and that he could really use our . . . affection. He has a couple years of probation hanging over his head."

"If anyone busts him, he's going back to Atlanta. Not exactly a garden spot," Bob added.

WITH WEAVER'S BLESSING, they headed south, again on I-95, the only way they knew. On the way, Bob took a call from Rae Givens, his partner, who was still with her cancer-stricken mother in Houston. They talked for a few minutes about her mother's condition and about the Miami investigation.

"We're kicking ass," Bob told her. "We got the only break the feds have gotten so far. We fed it to them. We could get another one in the next couple of hours."

He listened for a moment, glanced at Lucas and then said, "Don't worry about me. I'm taking care . . . I won't. It's just fine."

When he rang off, Lucas said, "She's still pissed at me."

"Naw. She's . . . worried about you."

"Sounded more like she was worried about you and what I might get you into."

Bob wiggled in his seat, then said, "Well . . . you know, what we do is a lot cleaner than what you do. The people we chase have already been in court, one way or another. They're guilty, or they're on the run because they know they're screwed and they're headed for prison. We spot them, plan everything out, and then grab them. With you . . ."

"Yeah?"

Bob was looking out the window at all the passing concrete: "With you . . . it's always kinda fuzzy, more free-form. Sometimes we're not sure who did what, or why. Sometimes things get done for political reasons. Not court reasons."

"You didn't have to come along," Lucas said.

"No, no, I find it interesting. Rae does, too. Every once in a while, though, you go full Schwarzenegger. We've only been hanging out for what, three years? I've been shot and you've been shot and your FBI girlfriend Jane Chase got shot . . ."

Lucas half-smiled: "Jane has signaled that there might be a change in our relationship."

"Because she got shot?"

"No, because I shot the 1919 guy. She wanted a show trial with all the fixin's."

"I'd prefer that myself, to be honest," Bob said. "But, if that's not the way it is, it's still intense. I like intense."

◆◆◆

THEY FOLLOWED THE concrete channel to 103rd Street in Miami, turned west to 27th Avenue, then back north to 131st Street and then east, and Lucas said, "What are we doing? We're driving in circles."

"The streets get all tangled up," Bob said, looking at the map on his phone. "This was the quickest way. Turn here."

They turned south again and after a few hundred yards, again back west on Country Club Lane. The houses were small, flat, concrete block boxes generally separated from the street with chain-link or steel-bar fences. The narrow, blacktopped streets were potholed and cracked, all set in a flat landscape of palms and slick-leaved tropical-looking trees, along with a few cedars and rubber trees. Bob said, "Banana tree! Bananas grow upside down. See?"

"I knew that," Lucas said.

"Bullshit you knew that . . . Magnus is around the corner. There's a canal . . . It's the green one."

Elliot's house looked across the narrow street and a canal toward the back of an apartment complex. They cruised the house, which was a sour chemical green with a tar roof, the yard surrounded by a chest-high steel-bar fence; each of the bars had a sharp arrow point at the top. The yard, like the neighboring yards, had ankle-deep grass, unmown for weeks. The driveway was gated, and a single pedestrian gate would open toward the street, if it hadn't been chained shut.

"A little fort," Lucas said, as they drove past. "You're wearing Nikes, right?"

"Yeah. I can't vault that fence, if that's what you're thinking. I'd wind up getting one of those arrowheads right in the nuts."

"That's not what I'm thinking. What I'm thinking is that there's no curb, so I drive right up to the fence, nose in, we climb on the hood of the truck and jump down. Don't want to dent the hood, though, so Nikes are good."

"Let me loosen up my gun and put on a marshal vest," Bob said. "If he's a big-time dealer he might not be happy about unexpected drop-ins."

They stopped at the end of the street and Bob stepped around behind the truck, popped the back lid, dug in his gear bag and got out two blue bulletproof vests that said POLICE in tall white letters and under that, in smaller letters, U.S. MARSHAL. Lucas pulled off his sport coat, took his ID out of the jacket pocket and put it in the hip pocket of his jeans.

They got the vests on, turned the truck, rolled back up the street and Lucas swerved out toward the canal and then back toward Elliot's gate. He stopped with the grille two inches from the gate, the back of the truck blocking six feet of the street. He and Bob popped their doors, stood on the front bumper, climbed on the hood one at a time, and dropped down over the fence.

Five seconds later, they were on either side of the front door, a yellow-painted slab of wood that did not look kickable. Lucas pushed the doorbell and they heard the sound of the bell through sets of louvered windows to the sides of the door. Bob knocked—pounded—twice and then moved closer to the windows and shouted, "U.S. Marshals!"

A man's voice: "Hold on. I'm comin'."

Lucas and Bob pulled their pistols and a second later the door cracked open on a chain that looked like it should have been used to pull logs out of the forest. Elliot's face appeared above the chain. He looked at the vests and asked, "ID?"

Lucas pulled out his ID and flipped it open. Elliot squinted at it, then at Lucas's face, and then at Bob's, and said, "Gotta close the door to get the chain off."

He stepped out of sight and pushed the door most of the way closed. He did something inside, Lucas thought, then the chain rattled off its hooks and Elliot opened the door. He was a large man, brawny, with both muscle and a heavy layer of fat. Blond, blue eyes, broad nose, heavy lips. He was wearing a pink golf shirt, khaki shorts, and sandals.

"What d'you want?"

"This is more of an interview than anything," Lucas said. "We need to talk."

Elliot took a step, as if to come out, but Bob put up a finger on his non-gun hand and said, "Inside."

Elliot backed away and they followed him inside. The house was neatly kept, sparely furnished with a motley collection of chairs and tables. A two-drawer couch table sat to the right of the door, and when they were fully inside, Lucas put his gun away, reached out, and pulled open the closest drawer on the table. Elliot said, "Hey!" but Lucas pulled anyway, and sitting inside, on a copy of *Guns & Ammo* magazine, was a blue-black .45 auto.

Bob glanced at it and said, "Oh. My. God. A felon with a gun."

"This is a bad neighborhood," Elliot said.

"And you're one of the baddest neighbors in it," Bob said.

Elliot: "Not by a long way, buddy."

Lucas could see a kitchen at the back of the house with a break-fast bar and three stools. "Talk in the kitchen," he said. He lifted the .45 out of drawer, popped the magazine, jacked the slide and a round flipped out, onto the ragged blue carpet. Lucas bent over, picked up the .45 round, shucked all the others out of the magazine and dropped them in the drawer and pushed it shut.

Elliot, backing toward the kitchen, watched him working with the gun. Bob pointed Elliot at one stool, and sat beside him, with Lucas sitting across the breakfast bar, the .45 still in his hand. He took a few seconds to disassemble the gun, then reached back and placed the pieces on the stove.

That done, he said, "Now. Bob and I have been running around town stepping on toes."

"I hadn't heard that," Elliot said.

"Well, we have been. We've been specifically looking for guys like you, out on parole, or guys we can get for three-strikes of-fenses. For example, if we were to pull your house apart here, and find a joint . . . well, a joint is a federal offense, even if they don't believe it here in Miami-Dade."

"I know that, which is why you wouldn't find a joint in here," Elliot said.

"Okay. But you know, the damnedest things turn up with a thorough search, stuff that you might not even think is illegal, but it is," Lucas said. "I mean, that .45, in the hands of a convicted felon out on parole . . . But we don't want to go there. Instead, we want to bribe you. Don't ever tell anyone I said that."

"What do you got to bribe me with?"

"We'll get to that. We want the name of the guys who shot three members of the Coast Guard this summer up in Fort Lauderdale."

Elliot looked from Lucas to Bob, his unnaturally pale brow wrinkled, and he asked, "Why would I know that?"

"We heard you dope importer guys down here cut a deal with some Jersey goombahs not to fuck with them when they dropped a load of heroin off the beach," Lucas said. "A deal got cut, the dope was dropped, and that led to the shooting. That's why."

"I'm not . . . uh . . . Man, why would I even talk with you?"

Bob said, "Because you're on parole. We weren't even in the house for five seconds before we found that .45. Your parole officer would send you back to prison for that. Find a joint or a bag of heroin, same thing. Drunk driving, drug paraphernalia, domestic abuse . . . almost anything and you go back inside. No trial, no problem, you're gone."

"I needed the gun for self-protection but there ain't any drugs. Does it look like there's a woman in here that I'd be abusin'?" It didn't; there was one La-Z-Boy chair pointed at an oversized television in the living room. "If I was gonna . . ."

Lucas interrupted: "What we're offering is a deal that would terminate your parole. You'd be done with it. If you got caught with a little dope, you couldn't automatically be sent back to prison. The government would have to go through the whole bail bond, trial, and conviction route to put you back inside. How much would that be worth to you?"

Elliot stared at Lucas with watery blue eyes too small for his face, his heavy head bobbing a bit, and then he muttered, "Something."

Bob: "Something?"

Elliot walked out of the kitchen and in a circle around the living room; as he was doing that, a gray tiger-striped cat came out of the back of the house and meowed at him. He picked up the cat and draped it across his shoulders, where it settled in and looked at Lucas with yellow eyes.

Elliot said, "Look. I might be able to help out here. I'm not sure; I'd have to make some calls. But I think so. I won't give you shit until I talk to somebody who could help on the parole."

"You got a cell phone number?" Lucas asked.

Of course he did, several of them, he was a drug dealer; but he didn't say that. He said, "I guess."

"Give me the number and I'll set you up with one of the top assistants at the U.S. Attorney's Office here in Miami. She makes the offer and you either believe her or you don't."

Elliot stared at Lucas for a moment, and then said, "Really?"

"Yeah. Really."

Elliot pulled at his heavy bottom lip, peeled the cat off, took it to the front door, let it out, came back, and said, "I'll talk to her. When?"

"This afternoon, probably. Tomorrow morning if one of you can't make it. You might want to take your attorney along."

Elliot snorted. "He's a good criminal attorney, but if I took him along on this deal, he'll sell me out in a New York minute. I'd probably get shot on the courthouse steps. Nope. I'll talk to her by myself. I'll want some paper with some signatures on it. And I can make it this afternoon."

LUCAS CALLED ELSIE M. Sweat at the Miami U.S. Attorney's Office, got her out of a meeting, and asked about an appointment for Elliot. She'd see him, she said, at 4:40. "I'll pull his file, see what's what. He didn't kill anyone?"

"No, straight drug bust," Lucas said. "You know what the deal is, he thinks he can help."

"All right. That's 4:40," Sweat said. "If he's not outside my door at 4:40, I'll be gone at 4:41."

"Heavy date?"

"I just need some goddamn sleep," she said. "4:40."

She rang off, and Lucas turned to Elliot, who said, "I heard. I'll be there at four o'clock, outside her door. If I'm not there, I'm dead."

ELLIOT WALKED WITH them out to the gate, to take the chain off. Lucas gave him his card with his cell phone number, said, "Call me," backed the truck away from the fence, held up a hand to Elliot, and he and Bob started out through the winding streets.

Bob: "Now what?"

"If Elliot has a deal by five o'clock, he might have something for us tonight," Lucas said. "Why don't we go back to the hotel, check in with Weaver, see what's happening with the hairdressers? Take a nap, get something to eat, check with Elliot later on."

"Okay with me," Bob said. And: "I'm worried about all the cooperation we've been getting. Everybody stepped right up, said, 'Glad to help out.' That's not right."

"Don't look a gift horse in the mouth," Lucas said. "The hairdressers, they might give us something, but then we'll have to connect a lot of dots to get from guys seen on a boat days before the shooting, to proving they were the same guys who did it. Or even that it's the same boat. Everybody else, we blackmailed them and still haven't gotten a name or anything solid."

"You're not even a little spooked? By the cooperation?"

"Maybe a little," Lucas conceded.

Bob yawned and said, "I could use a nap. Miami is a crappy place to drive around. I like it better out in the countryside and there isn't any here."

ELLIOT WATCHED THE marshals leave from behind his window blinds. When he was sure they were gone, he went into the kitchen, rummaged around in the back of a silverware drawer, and took out four burner phones. One of them had never been used to make a call—but it had an encrypted vault on it, with a list of private phone numbers.

He opened the vault, found the number he was looking for, and used another of his phones to make the call.

"Yeah?"

"Yes, sir, this is a big blond guy you met last year over on the beach," Elliot said. "I made a delivery for you folks from some Latino friends of mine and picked up some money. You asked me about the blue ribbons in my hair."

"I remember. You said they were there because rednecks would give you a hard time about them, which was an excuse for you to beat the shit out of them."

"That's me. You gave me your phone number and said to call if I ever had some news you could use," Elliot said. "Well, I do. Maybe. Or maybe you know somebody who can use it. A couple of U.S. Marshals were here. They wanted a name from me. Somebody in the Mafia."

"You didn't give them one?"

"No, but they offered me a hell of a deal. I'm taking the deal. Now I need to come up with a name. You got one?"

"Let me call you back," Jack Cattaneo said. "I gotta talk to a guy."

CATTANEO TALKED TO Behan one minute later. "You're not gonna believe this. We're not gonna have to jump though our asses to set up those guys. They set themselves up."

"That's nice," Behan said. "Come over and tell me about it."

LUCAS AND BOB found Weaver sitting in the conference room with Taylor, the Coast Guard cop. Weaver looked up when Bob and Lucas arrived, and said, "We've got people all over South Florida, chasing down those girls . . ." He glanced at Taylor, caught something in her expression, and amended, ". . . women. And we've approved four dive boats to look for the drugs."

"We got a lower response on the dive boats than we anticipated," Taylor said. She brushed her hair back in frustration. "One of our officers in Fort Lauderdale asked some of the divers why that was. He was told the chance of recovery was too low, the cost of going after it was too high, and because the drug runners might cut off your head if they caught you doing it. The guys out there now are doing it for the adventure, more than anything else. I kinda don't think they'll last long, once the novelty wears off."

"Fifty thousand dollars ain't what it used to be," Bob said. "Sounds like a lot, but after taxes . . ."

"I'll tell you something else," Taylor said. "There are a lot of guns on the boats that are out there. Perfectly legal, of course. If some Mafias show up and try to push them off they could get a boat full of bullets. I don't know what I think about that."

"Even with all that, we're moving better than we were a week ago," Weaver said, to Lucas and Bob. "I appreciate what you guys have done. I'm kinda surprised you didn't go after these girls, these women, yourselves."

"You're better equipped to handle it," Lucas said. "We've got another thing going."

He told them about Magnus Elliot. "He knows something. At least, he thinks he knows something. If he does, we could get a name. We could even get it this afternoon."

"That would be off-the-scale good," Weaver said. "That'd be better than finding the dope."

"Let us know what happens with the hairdressers," Lucas said. "We'll be up in our rooms doing more research, checking with some of the Miami narcs. And we're waiting for Elliot to make his deal with the U.S. attorney."

"Anything big happens, I'll call," Weaver said.

OUT IN THE hall, Bob said, "I thought we were going to take naps."

"That's what I'm gonna do," Lucas said. "I just wasn't going to admit it."

"Ah. Good work. I knew there was a reason I partnered up with you," Bob said. "I'll call you about 5:30. If Elliot hasn't gotten back to us, we could go get some lobster."

LUCAS TOOK A short nap, then read through the new reports coming from Weaver's agents. He found little that was interesting. Bob called a few minutes after five, said, "I couldn't stand staring at the ceiling anymore. Let's go eat."

They were at the Rendezvous, chicken tenders and sea bass, when Magnus Elliot called. They were sitting far enough from the next set of diners that Lucas put the phone on the speaker so Bob could hear what was said, and they both hovered over it. "Okay, we got a deal," Elliot said.

"What do we get?"

"The one goddamn thing I got," Elliot said. "A name and a location. Donald Romano. He lives in Coral Gables, but he's got a lights warehouse store down in Florida City—he sells lights to building contractors down here, and dope up in New York."

"Spell his name," Lucas said. "Where's Coral Gables . . . and Florida City?"

Elliot spelled Romano, and said, "Coral Gables is a town that's like hung on the side of Miami. Upper-level money. Florida City is south of Miami, right by the top of the Keys, probably one of the poorest towns in the state. The lights store is called Larry and Kay's Contractor Lighting Warehouse. I think Larry and Kay are his daughter and son-in-law."

Bob: "Wait a minute. Romano sells lights? And dope?"

"Yeah. The way I hear it, the lighting business is his money laundry," Elliot explained. "He's got cash businesses in New York and New Jersey, loan sharking and dope. He buys lights from the manufacturers and sells them at a twenty-five percent markup to condo developers. He kicks the whole markup back, under the table, in cash, so he breaks even on the sale of the lights. But: the contractors now have the dirty cash, and he has a check from the contractors that he puts in the bank, reports the markup as profit on the lights, pays his taxes, and the money is clean. So I'm told."

"Are all the developers crooks?" Bob asked.

"Yeah, most of them," Elliot said. "They get those lights at wholesale and a nice pile of invisible cash to tuck in their pockets, tax-free. I mean one good-sized condo project, you're talking millions of dollars in lighting. And guano in kickbacks."

"Guano is bat shit," Bob said.

"Local idiom," Elliot said. "You know, guano-this, guano-that. It usually means 'a lot.'" He considered for a moment, then said, "Of course, it can also mean 'not a lot.' It depends."

"Who told you all this?" Lucas asked.

"A Mexican friend who's dealt with him. Romano used to buy his dope from the Mexicans and ship it north, but now he's gone outside, I guess to some Colombian newcomers. The Mexicans are fairly pissed about that," Elliot said.

"And your Mexican friend thinks Romano was on the boat, or he knows who was?" Lucas asked.

"Well, the dope ain't coming from them, the Mexicans. The Mexicans say that a big load of dope hit Staten Island right after that shooting this summer," Elliot said. "My friend said that their New York marketing guys say their whole sales strategy took a hit."

Bob: "The Mexicans have a sales strategy? They got marketing guys?"

"Well . . . yeah. How'd you think all this got done? It's a business, like Facebook. Just a different addiction."

"Did you know all this when we talked, or did you get it from your Mexican friend this afternoon?" Lucas asked.

"I knew some of it . . . and I made a call and got the rest. Romano's name."

"What else?" Lucas asked.

"Nothing else, except that attorney lady is a bitch on wheels. I wanted to smack her."

"Not a good idea," Lucas said.

"Yeah, I got that," Elliot said. "This better pan out, man. I'm taking a major chance here."

THEY GOT OFF the phone and Lucas called Weaver: "We're at dinner, down the street. We need to talk to you."

"I'm sitting here watching classic football from 2003 on You-Tube, I'd hate to stop doing that for some horseshit law enforcement issue," Weaver said.

"See you in a half hour," Lucas said.

WEAVER GOT SERIOUS in a hurry, when Lucas gave him the name.

The online FBI files identified Donald Romano as an old-line organized crime stalwart about a decade past his use-by date.

"He's been hanging around forever, never important enough to get shot. He did a couple of short pieces in New Jersey for loan sharking and related assaults. Pretty amazing, when you think about it," Weaver said, dragging his finger down the computer screen as he read the files; his finger left a trail like a garden slug's. "They don't allow payday loan shops in Jersey, so if they didn't have loan sharks, you probably couldn't get a loan . . . and he had a couple of small garbage- and trash-hauling companies that supposedly were connected to one of the New York Mafia families, but that was years ago. Decades, actually."

"Nothing about drugs?"

"No, but loan sharks aren't usually fussy about where their money comes from," Weaver said. "Maybe he saw an opening—or maybe he's the South Florida manager for one of the New York distribution systems. He's got to have a significant distribution system if there's as much heroin coming in as we think."

"Why didn't your Mafia guys know about him?" Lucas asked.

Weaver shook his head. "Don't know. I've never heard of him myself, and I thought I'd at least heard about most Mafia groups. Listen, I need to think about this overnight and I need to talk to the OC guy down at the Angelus. He'll know stuff about Romano that's not in the files. I'm going to call all my people tonight and at the morning meeting, we won't say anything—we'll just send the non-FBI people on their way and then have another meet here in my room."

"Worried about a leak?"

"No . . . but I want to talk about this only with people I've got a solid grip on. No Coast Guard, no local cops. FBI only. And you marshals."

THE GENERAL MEETING went as usual the next morning. There'd been no finds with the few dive boats out on the Atlantic and the agent at the Angelus Hotel was still compiling faces. His girlfriend, Weaver said, had picked up a jewelry shoot for *Town & Country* magazine and was pleased with the FBI.

"We've got two more dive-boat volunteers, but one will probably drop out," Taylor, the Coast Guard cop, reported.

All but two of the hairdressers had been tracked down and interviewed, and three had agreed to look at photo boards. One of the agents said, "They won't see anything. That woman that Lucas interviewed, Alicia Snow, called a couple of the girls to tell them that we'd be coming to see them. Those girls called around and they managed to scare the crap out of each other. Mafia shooters coming through their windows at midnight with silencers, that kind of movie."

"What about the girl who disappeared?" Lucas asked. "Patty Pittman?"

"She has disappeared and I believe she's probably dead," the agent said. He nodded at Weaver. "Dale's got the full report. We didn't get back from Islamorada until after midnight last night, I gave it to him this morning. We talked to Pittman's mother, who doesn't want to believe it, but . . . she's dead. Pittman had four credit cards, none are being used. Her telephone is gone. There's money in her bank accounts, it's still there. Here's the thing—she talked to her mother about the guys on the Mako. She wondered if they might have been the ones who did the shooting. She was wondering if she should call the police. She didn't, as far as her mother knows, but she disappeared within a couple of days of the two of them talking about the shootings."

"She could have identified the guys," Lucas said. "Then she did something stupid, like talk to one of them about it and they killed her."

"That's what I believe," the agent said. "Maybe she was involved with one of the guys, couldn't believe he could really do something like that, the murders, so she talked to him . . . and, she's a naïve twenty-year-old hairdresser and he's a fucking animal."

"She was a pretty girl," another agent said, and several of the agents nodded.

The agents agreed that they'd be taking around iPads with photo displays to show to the women who'd agreed to look at the mug shots, and they'd be looking for the last two. The two were not missing, they'd simply moved to different parts of Florida, out of reach on a day's notice.

WHEN THE MEETING ended, the two non-FBI members went on their way. A half hour later, the FBI agents, with Lucas and Bob, met in Weaver's room, dragging chairs around and sitting on his bed.

There was one new face, Jason Tennan, the agent working at the Angelus Hotel. He was a tall man with curly brown hair, freckles over a short pug nose, square jaw, tall and thin with bony shoulders. He was wearing a white shirt and a black bolo tie with a silver-and-turquoise slide.

"I don't want anyone to think that there's anything . . . wrong . . . with the other team members," Weaver said to the group. "But they won't be involved with the next issue we'll be dealing with, and, well, I'm more comfortable with an all-FBI meeting. Plus the marshals."

He turned to Lucas and said, "Tell them. I haven't."

"We've got a name," Lucas said.

That created a stir, and Weaver opened a file and took out a photograph, and handed it to Tennan. Tennan looked at it and said, "Yeah, I know him, Don Romano. He used to live in Perth Amboy, but he moved out when the Hispanics got too thick in there. He's been down here in Florida for quite a while—years—but his name is still on some business licenses up in Jersey and on Staten Island. He's never been one of the big dogs, but he's always been around. Maybe he's still around because he was never one of the big dogs. He's old, by the way. Must be in his late seventies by now. Might be eighty."

"Exactly what kind of asshole are we dealing with?" Bob asked.

"Routine asshole," Tennan said. "He did loan sharking for years, had a couple of leg-breakers on staff. He worked through bartenders in northern Jersey, and across the water on Staten Island. He owned a couple of dry cleaners in Jersey, probably as money laundries."

"How about drugs?" Lucas asked.

Tennan scratched his neck, then said, "Don was always sort of a smart guy. He stayed away from the high-profile stuff. I doubt he had any kind of moral problem with drugs, he just didn't want the attention from the DEA and the local cops. But there's one thing . . ."

Bob: "Like what?"

"Guns. There's a rumor, only a rumor, that if you know the right guys, you can buy a decent handgun and they're coming out of Romano's loan-sharking operation. You know, a bartender is maybe the connection between a guy who needs a loan and one of Romano's loan managers. The same system can get you a gun."

Weaver asked, "Is there money in that? Guns?"

"Oh, yeah. Not millions, but a steady income stream. There are guns all over the confederate states, which means a lot of them get stolen," Tennan said. "And as they say, shit slides to the coast, which means Florida. Buy guns cheap here, sell them up north. In Philly, you could get a grand for a good Ruger semiauto, stolen down here and sold for a hundred bucks. All those northern states are tough on handguns, like they are on payday loans, which spells 'opportunity' for the mob boys. It's like cigarette smuggling, but with bullets."

"A thousand percent is an attractive markup," Bob said.

Tennan said, "And it creates more need for a money laundry down here, if your man's right about the warehouse."

Lucas said, "The gun distribution system might work for drugs, if the bartenders were willing to get into it."

"I'm sure some would be," Tennan said. "You don't see a lot of rich bartenders walking around."

Lucas: "You know anything about Romano's son-in-law?"

Tennan shook his head: "Not much. Name is Larry Bianchi. He's good-looking. That I know. The story is, Romano's daughter met him in high school, he started banging her, they got married maybe because they had to, Don being Don. He basically runs errands for his father-in-law. He and the daughter have a couple of kids. Actually, it might be four or five."

Bob: "You know anything about the lights warehouse? That operation?"

The agent was shaking his head. "Don't know about that. Basically, Don's supposed to be retired. He's fallen off our radar the last few years. Didn't have a rep for killing people. Breaking elbows, cutting off thumbs, maybe, but not killing them. And only when he felt he needed to make an example."

"Nice," Lucas said.

Weaver said, "We need to know what he's doing, we need surveillance. We need to find a reason to punch into that warehouse. I looked up the place on Google Maps, the satellite view. It's across the street from a Quality Inn. I've talked to a fixer up in Washington and she'll get us rooms on the second floor, looking across the street. From what I can tell from the satellite photos, we should be able to see all the entrances to the warehouse."

"I hope she didn't reserve the rooms for the FBI," Lucas said.

Weaver was moderately insulted: "Of course not. We reserved them for members of an Everglades National Park research team." He glanced around the room at the suits and ties: "The surveillance team is gonna need jeans. Plaid shirts. We'll check in this afternoon."

"What are we looking for exactly?" one of the agents asked.

"We'd like to figure out what's going on in there. Are they peddling drugs? Are they collecting guns? Are they really selling lights? What? If we see anything that looks even a little bit illegal, we get a warrant and a SWAT team out of Miami and we hit the place and we take it apart."

The agents exchanged glances among each other, and then one of them said, "It's something. I mean, thank God, it's something."

THEY SPENT AN hour sorting out assignments. When they were set, they had two agents for each of two rooms, with somebody watching the Romano building all the time. Weaver would have another room for himself. Weaver asked Bob and Lucas if they wanted to take part in the surveillance—"It's working off your tip," Weaver said—and after a bit of discussion, they signed up. They'd begin checking in that afternoon, as soon as everyone had their plaid shirts.

As the meeting broke up, Lucas said to Tennan, "Interesting necktie. Haven't seen a bolo in a while."

"Yeah, well, with my girlfriend in the modeling business, I'm now fashion-forward," Tennan said.

"Really . . ." Lucas looked more closely at the tie. It appeared to be an antique. He said, "I once told my wife if she ever found me wearing a bolo tie, she should shoot me in the head."

"Maybe you're not fashion-forward," Tennan suggested.

"I normally am," Lucas said, slightly annoyed by the suggestion that he wasn't. "But you know, I run to Italian wool and British leather."

"Those were good, back when *Esquire* magazine mattered," Tennan said. "Still are, for older guys. If I were you . . ." He reached out and poked Lucas on the left nipple. "I'd look into a more square-cut, American look. Shoulders. A faint hint of cowboy. No cowboy boots, of course, that takes it too far. If you buy a bolo, get a good one. Antique Navajo, that's what you're looking for. There's a place in Santa Fe called Shiprock Gallery. They got the real stuff."

ON THE WAY back to their rooms, Bob said, "You look troubled."

"What do you know about bolo ties?" Lucas asked.

"Not a fuckin' thing," Bob said. "Not only that, I plan to keep it that way."

"Jesus . . . I mean, what if they're coming back?" Lucas was appalled.

"Raiding a Mafia nest doesn't bother you, but you're troubled by a bolo tie?"

"When you put it like that, I sound stupid," Lucas said.

"There you go," Bob said.

TWELVE

JACK CATTANEO WALKED OVER to the ice cream stand, got a strawberry cone, and sat on a bench next to Behan, who said, "The marshals took the bait, but they're not going straight in. They got rooms at a motel across the street from Romano's place. It looks like they're planning to watch him for a while."

"Why?"

Behan ran his free hand through his hair; he was dressed all in white, white golf slacks and a loose, long-sleeved white linen shirt. "I talked to Jimmy and he thinks they probably want to spot Romano doing something flaky, so they can kick the door. Anyway, they're in there and the brothers got an eye on them."

"An eye on them? From where?"

Behan chuckled. "They checked into the same fuckin' hotel. They'll be watching twenty-four-seven, and when the marshals make their move, they'll be right behind them. We want to catch them right at Romano's door, or inside, if they kick it."

"Hope it's not getting too complicated," Cattaneo said. He sniffed once: something fishy in the air, beyond the usual salt from the ocean; somebody frying up a salmon somewhere. Whatever it was, it didn't go with the ice cream. "Too many moving parts. A straight ambush would be more certain, make it look like a fucked-up robbery."

"Nobody would believe that. And we'd lose Romano—the misdirection and the benefits up north."

"I'm still nervous."

"That's what we pay you for—but this doesn't have anything to do with us," Behan said. "If the brothers fuck it up, they can't put a finger on us. Jimmy hired them by remote control, and we don't know nuttin' about nuttin'."

"What about the pipe?"

"Jimmy got one back from where we dumped them, cleaned it up, and put it in a dumpster out back behind Romano's shop. The garbage pickup was yesterday, so we got a week," Behan said. "The question is, how long do we have to wait? I don't think it'll be long . . . If Romano doesn't give them a reason, the marshals'll think of some way they can mess with him. The way these two guys operate, they'll frame something up if they have to."

"You trust this Elliot guy?" Cattaneo asked.

"No. He'll go away," Behan said. He took a lick from his cone, a rum-raisin, and said, "Which brings me to an uncomfortable subject. Your friend Alicia."

"Ah, shit." Cattaneo took a lick of ice cream. "She's a nice girl. I was afraid you'd want her to go away."

"Jack, c'mon," Behan said. "You know the score. She could have put a finger on all of us."

Cattaneo stopped licking: "What do you mean, 'Could have'? Is she . . ."

"She's gone. We didn't feel like we could wait. I sent Jimmy over there. Gotta say, though, she had a convenient apartment, right across from the 'glades."

"Ah, Jesus. Really? I feel terrible now."

"You'll get over it. You must've had some idea that something would have to happen after she called you."

"Yeah, but . . . I woulda liked to've got a last piece of ass."

"I know, but . . ." Their cones had paper wrappers at the bottom and Behan peeled his off, popped the remnant of the cone into his mouth, chewed a few times, said, "Good," and, "The real problem's gonna be the pipes. When the marshals go away, there's gonna be a lot more attention down here. I'm told the pipes are good forever, but Jaquell told us that the ones she recovered were already getting silted over. Another six months, we might not be able to find them, even with the lights."

"I've been thinking about that. I've got a partial solution if Jaquell is up for it."

"What is it?"

"Slow boats," Cattaneo said. "Sailboats, two of them. Small, maybe thirty-six-footers, something like that. Under sail in the night. Two, three knots, Jaquell rolls off the back in the dark, gets picked up two hours later by the second boat. The second boat has its sails up, but we're also running on the engine. We rig a trailing hook off a heavy line, we drag the line past her, she slides down the line to the hook, hooks up the lift bag, and then rides the lift bag into the boat. That's gonna slow the boat, pull it off course. As soon as it slows, we hit the engine, keep it going straight. With a little practice down in the Keys, we should be able to work out a smooth pickup with nobody even noticing a hitch, even if they're looking."

Behan thought about it, then said, "Could work. How much for the boats?"

"Old boats, maybe from the nineties, decent shape . . . thirty grand each."

"And if we get jumped by the Coast Guard again? Can't run."

"We never take the pipes out of the lift bag," Cattaneo said. "When the bag comes over the side, we put in some more weight. Anchor, whatever. We watch the radar, if we see anything coming at us, we drop the bag back over the side. We get the exact GPS coordinates, down to the foot, come back and pick it up later. Wouldn't be so hard to find the second time, if we've got a lift bag and five pipes inside of it."

"Huh. All right. That's the best idea I've heard," Behan said.

"If Jaquell goes for it. She was skizzed out about the Coast Guard guys. If she's decided to get lost in the Bahamas, we won't be able to dig her out. I've tried calling her, but her phone's been turned off."

"Well, we'll see. You look for a boat, maybe do a dry run. No big hurry. A month or two is fine. Let things quiet down. And maybe . . . Do you even know how to sail?"

"Sure. I mean, some, but Jaquell's good at it," Cattaneo said. "I can take some lessons if I need to. How hard can it be, some of the assholes you see on sailboats? Otherwise, we use the engines, then it's just a powerboat."

Behan slapped Cattaneo on the knee, stood up, stretched, yawned, and said, "I'll talk to Dougie about it. If he green-lights it, you handle it. I'll call when something happens with the marshals. Sorry about that last piece of ass. Plenty of choice girls hanging around at the Angelus, though. Stop up, I'll introduce you."

"Yeah. All I need is a good brisk case of the clap."

"Not with these girls." Behan was insulted by the idea. "These girls are certified. Go to the doctor all the time."

"I'll check them out. When are you going up there again?"

"Dougie's coming down in a couple of days, he's staying there, we can hook up then. Tell Belinda it's purely business. And you know, she doesn't see eye-to-eye with Dougie. She thinks he's a criminal."

"That's true. Okay. I'll take a look. Something . . . brunette, maybe. Brown eyes. Gotta have an ass on her."

"We can do that." Behan chuckled and looked up at the sky. "Great night, huh? This is the best time of year down here. Maybe we ought to ditch the condos and buy houses. Golf course somewhere."

"I was thinking along the same lines—give Belinda a real studio."

Behan laughed again: "Fuckin' Belinda. If I had her talent, I never would have started killing people."

Cattaneo said, "It mystifies me, man, the whole art thing. But she does good. I'll take the cash."

"Hey: check you later."

They slapped hands and ambled off in their separate directions. Cattaneo glanced back once, shook his head. The whole white-on-white outfit, ruined by the sandals worn over the white athletic socks. Pathetic.

THIRTEEN

BOB AND LUCAS got off the Ronald Reagan Turnpike at a Barnes & Noble bookstore and spent a hundred and nineteen dollars on books and magazines. They'd refused to share rooms, which annoyed Weaver until Lucas said, "Hey, the Marshals Service will cover it." They got side-by-sides with a connecting door and Bob knocked on his side until Lucas opened his side, and Bob said, "I don't even know why we're here. Why do we need seven guys to watch one building?"

"We're here out of politeness," Lucas said. "Weaver will let us watch for a couple of days, then if nothing comes up, we'll make something up and the SWAT team kicks the door down."

"Two days in this room will anesthetize me," Bob said. "I got a pink bedspread, for Christ's sake."

"Well, whatever you do, keep an eye on your gear bag. If a cleaning lady sees that M4, she'll call the FBI."

"Can't leave it in the truck," Bob said. "If we go out, I'll leave it with one of the other teams."

"Good."

Bob: "So . . . you wanna watch a movie tonight? I been looking at the TV lineup."

"Like what?"

"There's a Sandra Bullock comedy about the FBI . . ."

ROMANO'S WAREHOUSE WAS directly across the street, a single-story white concrete block building with angle parking for eight cars in the front, and a dumpster on a mostly unused dirt parking space in the back. The parking lots were empty when they checked into the motel and stayed that way. That night, no lights showed in the two side windows they could see and no light splashed out the front windows onto the parking lot. A single pole light lit the back parking lot.

THE SURVEILLANCE DIDN'T take two days; it took barely two hours.

They were semi-watching Bob's choice, *Miss Congeniality*, in Lucas's room, when Weaver called.

"You see the van and the SUV?"

"No. We're watching a movie."

"Well, look out the window. A van just pulled up with an SUV behind it. We're taking pictures from Carl's room."

They stepped over to Bob's room, which was dark, and looked through the carefully arranged gap in the curtains that covered the outside window. A white van was backed up to what Lucas thought must be the warehouse's front door, and light was coming out of the warehouse windows. A black SUV sat sideways in the parking lot, on the other side of the van.

"You running the plates?" Lucas asked Weaver.

"Of course. The van's from Jersey, the Benz is from here."

"How many guys?"

"Three—two in the van, one in the Benz. We got full facials on all of them, we're sending them up to Tennan to see if he recognizes them. We think the guy in the SUV is Romano's son-in-law, Larry Bianchi. I'll call you back if anything happens. I'm going back to the glasses."

Lucas and Bob stood in the dark watching as two men from the van took a half dozen large white boxes out of the truck and stacked them on the blacktop. Then they crawled into the van, and a moment later, reappeared pushing a flat, four-foot-long black box, which they carried into the building.

A few minutes after that, a third man walked out of the building to the Benz, opened the back, did something on the floor of the vehicle, looked around, then lifted out a black box identical to the box from the van. It appeared to be made out of metal or black-painted wood, and was heavy.

The man carried it to the van, staggering a bit, climbed into the back of the van, did something out of sight that took two or three minutes. Then he backed out of the van, made a "c'mon" wave at the other two, who began piling the stacked white boxes back into the van.

Weaver called, stressed. "They're moving something. They're hiding it under the white boxes."

"I think so," Lucas said. "The black boxes were the same size and shape. I think they might fit below the floor of the van, out of sight. The first box is still in the warehouse, so . . ."

"I'm sending both teams after the van," Weaver said. "You guys will stay here and I'll be here, to watch for any more activity."

Bob: "Well, shit . . ."

"I know, I know, but you really want to be part of a tag team?" Weaver asked. "It might run all night. Hell, it might run to New Jersey."

"What are you planning to do?"

"Don't know yet. We haven't gotten in touch with Tennan . . ."

Bob, looking out through the gap in the curtains, said, "They're leaving."

THE LIGHTS IN the building went out and the two vehicles pulled away. Nobody else showed up. Weaver called and said, "They're in the surveillance box, they're headed up the turnpike."

"Keep us up to date," Lucas said. "The way they put that black box in the van and then covered it with those lighting fixture boxes, or whatever they were, makes me think the box is important. Could be dope."

"Exactly," Weaver said. "I want to watch the building overnight, if you guys would be willing to take a couple of shifts . . ."

They agreed that Weaver would take the first three hours, Lucas would pick it up from one to four a.m., and Bob would take it from four until seven.

"We've still got twenty-five minutes on the movie," Bob said, when Weaver rang off. They watched the movie to the end and a few minutes of a sports talk show, and then Bob went back to his room to catch some sleep. Lucas was a night owl and spent an hour reading a Lee Child thriller.

Weaver called Lucas at 11:30 and said, "We're gonna grab the truck the first time it stops. Tennan identified both the driver and the passenger. The driver is on probation in Jersey and didn't bother to get permission to travel, so we can take both him and his passenger and search the truck. The passenger is a leg-breaker from Staten Island. Depending on what we take out of the truck, we'll see if it's enough to get a warrant for the warehouse. We've got an overnight judge ready to sign it, depending."

"Am I still staying up?"

"Yeah. We need to watch. I'll call if we get any changes, but if you could still go on at one o'clock, that'd be great."

"Go to bed now, you need the sleep," Lucas said. "I'm up anyway."

"Thanks, man," Weaver said. "Oh. I called the rest of the task force down from Broward, we're staking out Romano's house and his son-in-law's place, just in case."

AT MIDNIGHT, WEAVER called back, sounding stunned. "I no more got to sleep than I got woke back up. The van stopped at a Pizza Hut at a service plaza on the Florida Turnpike and we grabbed the guys and the van. The black box was hidden in a slot under the floor of the van. We opened the box and it's full of handguns, a hundred and twenty of them."

"Whoa. No problems?"

"We're not sure. One guy was driving and I guess the other one was sleeping in the back. When we boxed them in, the driver was yelling something to the guy in the back and he wouldn't unlock the van until our guys threatened to break the windows and drag him out. That took two or three minutes—and we couldn't see what the guy in back was doing. He could have made a call."

"Damnit. Now what?"

"We're getting a warrant now and we'll hit the warehouse to-morrow morning as soon as it gets light," Weaver said.

"Stay on schedule for now?"

"Yeah, I really need to get some sleep. I'm so goddamned tired, I'm stumbling around. I need to be sane when we hit the place."

WEAVER DIDN'T GET any sleep. He called back a minute later and said, "Romano's moving. So's Bianchi, the son-in-law. Something happened. Both houses went dark around 11:30, and then ten min-utes ago, the lights came on in what we think was Romano's bed-room and then in Bianchi's. We think Romano called him. Now both of them are in their cars, headed our way. They'll be twenty minutes or so, if they're coming to us."

"The guy in the van made a call," Lucas said.

"That's what we think. We've got the warrant and if they walk into that store, we'll hit them one minute later. Stay out of sight until then."

"Okay. We'll see you in the lobby. Ten minutes."

LUCAS ROUSTED BOB and washed his face and put on jeans, a can-vas shirt, and cross-training shoes, then took another few seconds to brush his teeth. Bob was dressed and he'd thrown his gear bag on the bed. He pulled out a bulletproof vest and tossed it to Lucas, and put on his own, then pulled out his M4.

Lucas asked, "Think we'll need that?"

"Better to have it and not need it . . ."

"Right." Lucas checked his Walther, reseated it in his cross-draw holster on his left hip. He checked his watch: time to move.

"Rock 'n' roll," he said.

"You sleepy?" Bob asked.

"Tired, but not sleepy," Lucas said. "You okay?"

"I'm fine. Let's watch out for these FBI turkeys, the ones tracking Romano and Bianchi. They'll have guns and they'll be running toward us. And it's dark outside."

Lucas took a last look out the window: "Not too dark. Lots of lights around."

Bob said, "Get the handset. Let's go."

WEAVER WAS WAITING in the lobby, cocked his head at Bob's M4 but didn't say anything. A young woman who was standing behind the check-in desk said to Weaver, "I'm going to hide in the office now."

Weaver nodded and put his handset to his ear and asked, "Where now?" He listened, then turned to Lucas and Bob and said, "Three minutes. You guys wait here. I'll run over and squat down behind that palm where I can see Romano coming in."

He pointed kitty-corner across the street at a clump of palms from where he'd be looking at the front of Romano's store. "Our guys will track Romano until he turns the corner. Bianchi right now is about a minute behind him. When Bianchi turns the corner, our guys will pull into the lot behind the store. There's a door back there and we'll put a car bumper right up against it so it can't be opened. There are no windows back there. When I see Romano and Bianchi are inside, I'll call you and you come running. As soon as the team leaders out in back see you moving, they'll go around both sides of the store, around to the front and we'll all get to the front door at the same time. One of the guys has a sledge if we need it . . ."

Weaver was cranked, talking a hundred miles an hour, the words tumbling out like pebbles. Bob said, "That's fine, man, but you've got to cool down a little. Take it easy. You don't want to have a heart attack."

Weaver looked at him. Nodded and said, "I forgot you guys do this all the time . . . I'll try to slow it down."

But he glanced at his watch and then said, "I gotta go, I gotta go," and he pushed through the door and scurried across the street to the clump of palms and disappeared.

Bob, peering out through the glass doors, said, "This is gonna be hairy. Too many guys with guns and no time to think about it."

Lucas said, "Yeah. At least we're going out first, so everybody knows where we are."

They waited, and Lucas said, "Getting tight."

As they waited, a Latino man with a pencil-thin mustache, wearing a yellow Hawaiian shirt walked around the corner, saw Bob's rifle, did a double take, said, "Oh, man," and Lucas said, "Sir, if you could go back to your room for a minute?"

The man read POLICE and U.S. MARSHAL on their vests and said, "You got it," and disappeared.

Bob grinned and said, "Didn't take him long to make up his mind."

From the office, the counter woman called, "Is it over yet?"

Lucas called back, "Not quite, but we're close," and to Bob, "Fifteen seconds? Something like that."

Twenty seconds later, Bob said, "Here they come."

◆◆◆

A BLACK SUV pulled into the parking lot across the street and an elderly man got out and went to the front of the store. Less than a minute later, another SUV, identical to the first, pulled into the parking lot and a younger man got out and went to the door. Ten seconds later, four more cars crawled around the corner and bumped over the curb into the lot at the back of the store. One man jumped out of one of the cars and motioned another car forward until the bumper nearly touched the back of the building, a door that Lucas and Bob couldn't see.

Lucas's handset burped: Weaver said, "Go."

Lucas and Bob went out the door, walking fast, Lucas in the lead, to Bob's left, headed straight across the street.

WEAVER SHOUTED "GO" into his handset and saw Lucas and Bob burst through the motel door into the street. He turned to look for his FBI teams rounding the corner of the building, then looked back at Lucas and Bob. They'd crossed the street and were into the parking lot when two more men ran out of the motel behind them and both raised guns that Weaver recognized as old MAC-10 submachine guns.

Astonished by their sudden appearance, he saw them lift the guns toward Lucas and Bob and he screamed something he didn't recognize himself, maybe an Indian war cry, and lifted his own Sig at the two men and began firing at them and saw them falter and Lucas and Bob went down and Weaver kept pulling the trigger on the Sig until it went dry and the two men were still up but staggering as a storm of gunfire erupted from behind the store and the two men twisted, turned, and went down. Somebody was shouting, "Stop, stop . . ." and Weaver realized it was him.

LUCAS AND BOB crossed the street at a run and then heard a man scream and Lucas half-turned and there was an explosion of gunfire, coming from behind them, Lucas thought, and he was thumped hard in the back and he went down on his stomach, skidding hard on the blacktop, stripping skin off his knees and elbows and one hand, his gun hand; he'd lost the handset he'd held in the other hand and he struggled to get turned around, and he looked back and saw the man with the Hawaiian shirt staggering, apparently hit by gunfire; and another man behind him, also in a Hawaiian shirt, with a long gun in his hand and he was trying to fire back at the feds who'd come down the side of the building. Still turning, confused, trying to get around, Lucas saw Weaver in the shadow of the palm tree firing a pistol at the two men and then the men were both down and Lucas thought, *What the fuck?*, and looked to his right.

And saw Bob unmoving on the ground.

Gun in hand, he crawled toward Bob and saw Weaver running toward them and he heard glass breaking, a lot of glass, more shouting. He got to Bob, who was lying on his side, facing away from him, and as he rolled him over he saw that Bob had been hit in the head and neck.

"No, Jesus . . ."

Another FBI man was sprawled at the side of the store, an agent standing over him with a gun in his hand. Weaver ran across the street, paused at the downed FBI man, said something to him and then ran toward Lucas and Bob, shouting, "Calling 911!"

When he came up, he looked down at them, then looked desperately back at the side where the other man was lying, and then down at Lucas and then over at the two men in Hawaiian shirts, dead on the ground, and then back to Lucas and he said, "I think, I think . . ."

He didn't say what he thought, but Lucas knew what it was.

"Ah, Jesus, he can't be." Lucas plucked at Bob's body, trying to get an arm under his head, to help him breathe if there was breath left in him, but there wasn't.

Weaver was saying, "C'mon, man, are you okay? Are . . . Jesus, you're hit in the back, are you okay?"

Lucas felt no pain, he was staring down at Bob, but Bob had left the building, and Lucas knew it. "Bob! Bob!"

Weaver was pulling at him. "Are you okay . . . Are you okay?"

Lucas rose to his knees and Weaver was shouting at him, "Let's get the vest off . . ."

Lucas let them pull the vest off; his back hurt, but not like it would with a gunshot wound. Weaver shouted, "You're okay, you're fine, you got hit but the vest took it . . ."

Lucas looked up at Weaver, who'd lost it: every word came out as a shout, almost a scream.

Lucas grabbed one of his arms and pulled himself up, said, "Easy, man. Easy."

He looked down at Bob. His friend lay on the crumbling blacktop, his M4 pinned under his body, a pool of blood under his head, a gaping wound above his half-open eyes that were staring up at the overcast sky, at nothing at all.

CHAPTER

FOURTEEN

LUCAS HEARD, DIMLY, somewhere else, "Fire! There's a fire! Fire! Hey!"

He tried to step away from Weaver, but his knees were shaking, and Weaver held on to him, and Lucas sank back on the blacktop next to Bob's body, head down, arms wrapped around his knees, stunned, unable to think, unable to speak.

He didn't know how long he was there, but it was a while. FBI agents came by from time to time to touch him on the shoulder, and he nodded, numbly. He looked up, blank-eyed, when two fire trucks and then an ambulance came careening into the street.

The paramedics checked the wounded agent, then lifted him onto a gurney, slammed him into the back of the ambulance and it was gone, lights flashing, siren screaming, curling around the fire-trucks. Firemen ran into the motel and Lucas could see flames behind one of the windows on the second floor. His room? Bob's? He didn't know.

More sirens, more cops, more shouting, but he couldn't shake the darkness that gripped him.

Eventually, Weaver came over and crouched next to him and

said, "Lucas, you gotta move. The crime-scene people have work to do."

Lucas reached over and touched the unbloodied side of Bob's face, already going cold, then Weaver took him by the arm and led him across the street to the motel, where he put Lucas on a couch in the lobby with a couple of FBI agents. "There was a fire upstairs, one room . . . It's out. We think it might be connected to those two shooters," Weaver said.

Lucas nodded, unresisting, sat on the couch for a half hour, frozen up, other cops looking but not talking, and finally he groaned and pulled his cell phone from his pocket and called Weather.

"What happened! Lucas, is that you?" Fear in her voice: midnight in the Central time zone; she woke at six o'clock on days she'd be in the operating room, midnight was far too late for a call.

"Bob was killed."

Silence, then a hushed, "Lucas, what . . ."

"Bob is dead. Some guys shot him."

"Oh, my God, Lucas . . . Lucas, are you okay?"

"I guess . . . I'm not hurt. Jesus, what am I going to tell Rae? What am I going to tell her?"

"Lucas, don't call her. Let somebody else do it. Call her after she knows . . ."

"That'll make it worse," Lucas said.

"No, no, it won't," Weather said. "Believe me. Please. Let somebody else notify her."

"He has a girlfriend. They were thinking about getting married."

"Oh, no . . ."

◆◆◆

THEY TALKED FOR another half hour, Lucas slowly unfreezing. He got up, still talking, wandering through the motel's first floor. He could smell smoke and something else burnt, and people were leaving the hotel carrying suitcases and bags. When he looked out the door toward the Romano building, he could see the black nylon shroud covering Bob's body, and then, on one trip through the lobby, he looked out the door and the body was gone.

He said good-bye to Weather, went out into the street. There were twenty uniformed cops from three different jurisdictions, state, county, and local, plus the FBI agents. He found Weaver, and the other man lifted a hand and came over and took Lucas's elbow: "You're back."

"Some," Lucas said. "What the fuck happened?"

"Still don't know," Weaver said. "I was over in my palm tree getting ready to rush the door when you guys got across the street and my guys were coming around from the back of the building, and these two guys . . . fuckin' assassins . . . came walking out of the motel in those Hawaiian shirts and they had machine guns and they were tracking you and Bob and I yelled at them and they turned and they started shooting and I started shooting and then the guys from the back of the building got into it and we shot the shit out of them. Too late for Bob, he went down right away, but the guy on the left, my left, I think he was supposed to take you down and I got lucky and hit him and then everybody opened up . . . It was a war out here. Their guns: they had these old MAC-10s with thirty-round mags and they kept pulling the triggers, even while they were going down. I can't believe you were only hit once. I think they were watching you two . . . you and Bob, and didn't know about the rest of us. They were in the motel, their room was set on fire with gasoline, like on that boat, the Mako. We're in there now, trying to figure it out, who they are and where they came from. Neither one was carrying an ID."

"They're not Romano's guys?"

"Romano said he never saw them before. I almost believe him, but then . . . we were going through the place, we found that black box, it was empty, but there was a floor safe with maybe a half-million dollars in it, all small bills, wadded up . . . and some more money in back we haven't counted yet, but a lot. We've got their computers, it looks like they've got their books on them. Anyway, I told the guys to check the dumpster in the back and they found what I gotta believe is one of the containers from the heroin pickup off the coast."

"What?"

"Yeah. Like the Coast Guard guy said, a pipe a couple of feet long, fourteen inches in diameter. It's got a five-pound scuba weight attached with a hose clamp. Black PVC pipe."

"So we got them."

Weaver looked away. "Romano said he never saw that pipe, either. Bianchi says the same thing and they actually seemed kinda . . . confused. We put the pipe in front of Bianchi and he said he had no idea what it was and he looked like he really didn't. The thing is, finding that pipe was awful convenient. They should have gotten rid of it months ago. Should have thrown it out the car window into a ditch, or into the ocean, not dropped it in a dumpster behind their store."

"I gotta think about it," Lucas said. "Where are Romano and Bianchi now?"

"Still inside. They'll be here for a while and then we'll transport them up to the federal lockup . . . You want to talk to them?"

"I want to think first," Lucas said. "But yeah—I want to talk to them. I gotta make a phone call first."

LUCAS WALKED PAST the spot where Bob had been lying, blood on the blacktop looking now like a routine oil spot. He continued to the motel, asked the clerk if people were barred from the second floor, and was told that they weren't, that the fire had been smoky, but was confined to a single room.

"There's a lot of FBI up there, and the firemen, it'll be noisy . . ."

"That's okay . . ."

He went up to his room, which was undisturbed except for the stink of the smoke. He lay on the bed and called Russell Forte, his boss in Washington.

Forte picked up and said, "If you're calling before daylight, it's gotta be really bad or really good."

"It's really bad," Lucas said. "Bob got shot and killed this morning."

"Holy shit! Holy shit! Lucas! What happened?"

Lucas told him about the stakeout—at one point, Forte said, "Hang on a minute," and then Lucas heard him talking to a woman, and Forte came back and said, "My wife wanted to know what was going on . . ."

The woman called from the background, "I'm so sorry, Lucas." She started to cry.

Forte said, "Keep talking."

Lucas told him about the progress of the investigation, about the arrest of Romano, Bianchi, and the gun smugglers, and the recovery of the dope can. When he ran down, Forte said, "Okay. Listen, we've got a guy somewhere around Justice who does notifications and I hear he's good at it. I'll have him get to Rae. Didn't Bob have a fiancée?"

"A girlfriend. I think Rae should go talk to her. That would be best."

"We'll check with Rae about it," Forte said. "What are you going to do?"

"I need to figure out what happened here. Everybody's confused. If Weaver hadn't been hidden in that bush, I'd be dead right now. The rest of the FBI guys . . . I mean, they did good, and one of them got shot for his trouble. We don't know what the fuck happened. I need to find that out."

"Okay. Whatever you need," Forte said.

"Russell—don't let Rae come out here. She's gonna want to come right out, but I don't want her here. She couldn't do any good."

"Well, I don't know if . . ."

"Russell—keep her out. I'm telling you, keep her out."

LUCAS STOOD IN an icy shower for five minutes, letting the water stream through his hair and down his body, a shock that brought him back to earth. He had a hand-sized red spot below his left shoulder blade that would turn into an ugly bruise, and that was it.

He toweled off, got some extra-large Band-Aids from his Dopp kit, smeared disinfectant on his knees and elbows and covered the scrapes. That done, he lay on his bed in his underwear, arm over his eyes, and tried to focus on what had happened.

Kept flashing back to the moment Bob went down. He hadn't seen it, he was already on his stomach and turning, had seen the two shooters dancing in the street, thrashed by FBI bullets. Where the hell had they come from?

Flashed back to the bullet thumping into his back. Got up, found the vest, got a knife from his gear bag, and worked the slug out of the layers of Kevlar, rolled it around in the palm of his hand. Nine-millimeter. He put the slug on the TV stand, dropped back on the bed.

He should be dead. He was hardly injured, but he should be as dead as Bob.

Flashed again to the shooting, to the blacktop, felt the blacktop slicing through his knees and elbows . . . turned to see Bob.

Have to get away from this . . .

He got dressed, went downstairs to the lobby where the desk clerk was sitting with a state trooper. Lucas identified himself to the trooper and then asked the clerk, "The two men who were killed . . . how long were they in their rooms?"

"They checked in a little while after you did. They didn't have reservations . . ."

"Did they have credit cards?"

"Oh, sure, we don't allow people to check in without them. The FBI has the card numbers."

Lucas nodded: "Thanks."

◆◆◆

He walked across the street to the Romano building, spotted one of the task force's senior agents and asked about Weaver.

"He's inside, talking to Don Romano."

Lucas went into the building. A small lobby sat behind the front doors, and a waist-high counter was barely large enough to accommodate two customers at a time. There was no place to sit, and Lucas realized that while the building was a large one, most of the business must have been done in the back. A square-jawed, dark-haired FBI agent named Parker was standing watch behind the counter. He nodded at Lucas, tilted his head toward a door that led into the back. "Dale's in back. We're all screwed up about Bob and Harry."

"How's Harry?"

"Shot went right through his gut, side to side, clipped his pelvis, missed his spine," Parker said. "We were all putting on our vests before we hit the door, but most of us didn't have them on when the shooting started. Anyway, he's a mess. They're saying he'll make it, but he's hurt bad."

"I'm sorry," Lucas said, and he was. He was haunted by the idea that he'd somehow screwed up, though he wasn't yet sure how he might have done that. He remembered Bob talking about how they were getting too much cooperation, it wasn't quite right . . .

He walked around the counter and went through the door into the large back room. An eight-foot-long wooden dining table sat in the middle of a wide-open space, with a half dozen comfortable leather chairs around it. A pool-table light hung over it; farther back in the room was an actual pool table, with another pool table light. The concrete block walls were covered with metal racks, and the racks were heavily stocked with white boxes of light fixtures.

Weaver, three other FBI agents, and a Miami-Dade cop were sitting around the table, peering at an elderly man dressed in slacks and a purple velour sweatshirt. He was short, thin, balding, big-eared, big-nosed, and loose-lipped, with wild white eyebrows like old people get. He had deep frown gouges on either side of his mouth.

Romano saw Lucas and asked Weaver, "Who's this guy?"

Weaver turned, stood, and walked over. "You're moving."

"Yeah."

"A mess. We're trying to figure it out," Weaver said.

"Yeah. Hey: you saved my life, man," Lucas said. He tapped Weaver on the back. "Thank you."

"But I lost Bob. If I'd shot . . ."

"You did good. From where you were? You did amazing," Lucas said. He looked over at the old man. "This is Romano?"

"Yeah, but . . . God help me, I'm thinking he wasn't involved," he said quietly, so Romano couldn't hear him. "The guns were his . . ."

"I'd like to talk to him."

"Sure . . ."

Lucas went over and got a chair and the old man peered at him for a moment, then said, "What?"

"Your shooters killed a good friend of mine," Lucas said.

Romano blew through his loose lips, making a farting sound. "I keep telling everyone, I don't know what the fuck happened out there. I'm in here going to work—"

Lucas: "At midnight?"

"We're early risers," Romano said. He was irritated by the comment. "Why would I have two guys hiding in a motel with guns? If I was worried about somebody kicking in the doors, they'd be in here. Bring in a couple of cots, they could sleep here, protect the place . . ."

Lucas watched his face. Romano took it, staring back, his eyes cold and black. Then Lucas asked Weaver, "Will everybody excuse me if I ask a non-fact-based question?"

"Go ahead," Weaver said.

Lucas looked down at Romano and asked, "What do you think is going on?"

Romano weighed Lucas for another moment or two, then jabbed a hitchhiker's thumb at Weaver and said, "This guy tells me the two assholes you guys killed are hired shooters. They're known."

"Known to you?"

"Fuck no. This guy told me," Romano said, tipping his head toward Weaver. "Anyway, you and the guy who got killed, we heard about you from old friends, out of the business now. You're going around town kicking over trash cans and somebody might have gotten worried that you were getting somewhere on the Coast Guard murders. So, they chumped you. They got somebody to point you at me, because of the rumors about my previous occupations, which are completely false, by the way. You come running down here and the idea was, you'd kick the front door open and they'd wipe you out, and then all the cops would come and they'd find that black thing in my dumpster . . . You were chumped and you're still being chumped."

Lucas closed his eyes and squeezed the bridge of his nose, then looked at Weaver and asked, "You got time for a walk around the block?"

"I do," Weaver said. To the agents at the table, he said, "Keep him talking."

LUCAS AND WEAVER went outside. A fire truck was still there, now spraying water on the blacktop at the side of the Romano building, and Lucas realized they were washing away the blood left behind by Bob and the wounded FBI agent. He turned the other direction, down the street, and said, "Listen, Dale. Romano said what I was thinking. Whoever the Coast Guard killers are, they spotted Bob and me, and followed us. They checked into the motel right behind us and waited for us to hit Romano. They thought it'd just be me and Bob. And they torched the room on the way out because they thought that would get rid of their DNA. I bet they were wearing gloves when they went down."

"Yeah, they were. We might have still gotten some DNA, fire doesn't always wipe it out anymore . . . but that's irrelevant now."

"What Romano said . . . you've identified them?" Lucas asked.

"Yes. We printed them, they popped right up."

"Do they hook up with Romano somehow?"

"No. They were basically for hire, whatever you needed done," Weaver said. "They collected on debts, protected dealers, they were suspected in a couple of gang killings."

"Then I think Romano nailed it. We were chumped. We've got to get up to Miami and knock down Magnus Elliot's door, and the sooner the better. He's the guy who set us up."

"I'll get a SWAT team, but you and I have to stay here. Or I do, anyway, I'll see what the guys from the Miami office have to say. They'll want everyone who fired a gun to be here while they work out the sequence of events."

"That's fine, send the SWAT team, but I don't think we'll really need them. Elliot may not have known what he was doing, or maybe he did. Either way, he's now a liability to whoever set us up. He's probably dead. If he isn't, he soon will be, so we gotta move. If he's not dead, he's squeezable."

"Miami-Dade can have somebody there in five minutes. I'll make a call . . ."

He walked away to make the call, and as Lucas looked after him, he thought, *I should have done this earlier, I shouldn't have frozen up . . .*

LUCAS WALKED THROUGH the mess around Romano's building, the fire trucks, the cops, the smell of water and smoke, the constant chatter of cops talking and shouting, radios scratching out more talk. He thought about finding the motel desk clerk again, but when he went to look for her, she'd been taken somewhere else to be interviewed. He went back to the street, saw Weaver talking to one of the task force agents and went that way.

Weaver saw him coming and said, "Miami-Dade will have somebody there right now. I've called the overnight judge for a new warrant."

"I'm going up there," Lucas said. "If your guys need me . . . tell them I left without permission. Or whatever, but I'm going. I never did fire a weapon, so . . ."

He stepped away but Weaver hooked his arm and held on.

"Nope. Not by yourself." He looked around the parking lot and shouted, "Parker! Parker!"

The young agent hurried toward them and Weaver said to Lucas, "Parker was on the far side of the building, he never fired his weapon. The Miami office guys will be pissed if he leaves, but he wasn't involved."

Parker came up and Weaver told him, "Get the bus keys from Andy and take Lucas up to Miami, where he tells you to go. Then both of you get back here soon as you can depending . . . on what happens there. Parker—lights and siren the whole way."

Weaver turned back to Lucas: "It's the only vehicle we have with lights and siren. Take off."

FIFTEEN

PARKER WAS A steady driver, even in the gargantuan Suburban, but had never driven a cop car. Halfway to Miami, pushing an elderly Buick down the highway, he said, "I've never run a car with lights and siren going. It's weird. Some of the cars scatter in front of you, some never see you at all. The ones that don't see you, shouldn't be on the road. There are some other ones that are just friggin' ignoring me."

Lucas said, "Yeah." Not up for idle conversation.

"I'm sorry about Bob. You okay?"

"No, I'm not," Lucas said. "I can't get it out of my head. I'm fucked up here."

After a long silence, Parker asked, "Are you sure you should be doing this? We could get a couple of guys from downtown . . ."

"I'm sure," Lucas said. "I need to find out what happened. Did Elliot see us coming? Were we set up right from the start? Were we set up at all . . . No, we were set up. No question. I need to know how Elliot was involved. If he was . . ."

◈◈◈

AS THEY GOT off the expressway and headed east, Lucas took a call from Washington, from Russell Forte: "Lucas, I got a plane ticket down there, I'll see you this afternoon. Are you still at that TRYP place?"

"Yeah, we never checked out. Why are you coming?"

"To see about Bob, for one thing. And to see about you. I need to talk to you about what you're doing and what you're planning to do. I've got a guy picking me up at Fort Lauderdale, I should be at your hotel by three o'clock."

"I don't know what I'm going to do. Right now I'm headed north with one of the task force agents to see if we can find the guy who put us on Romano."

"I can hear the siren . . ."

Lucas told Forte about the emerging theory that they'd all been chumped, that Bob and Lucas were set up to be killed on Romano's doorstep.

"And we don't know who'd do that?"

"If we knew that, we'd know who the drug runners are and who killed the Coast Guardsmen," Lucas said. "Who benefits from Romano going down? Whoever set us up were tracking Bob and I, and they didn't expect the FBI teams to be there. If it had gone as they expected, Bob and I would be dead and Romano would be toast."

"This Elliot guy—don't get hurt, man. I'm fairly screwed up myself," Forte said. "Bob was one of my favorite people of all time."

"Have you talked to Rae?"

"Somebody's doing that now. I expect she'll be calling you," Forte said.

"Ah, Jesus."

THEY WERE HALFWAY across Miami when Rae called. Lucas looked at his phone, didn't want to answer it, but he did: "Rae."

"Lucas. I needed to tell you, I talked to Russell. This wasn't your fault and I don't blame you in any way, shape, or form."

"Ah, jeez, Rae . . ."

Lucas let her go, his eyes closed, as she began to cry. When she could speak again, she said, "Russell said you were there with a whole bunch of feds, so this wasn't some crazy Davenport cowboy thing." She said something else, but Lucas couldn't make it out as her voice squeaked higher as she began to cry again. "I should have been there, if I'd been there he wouldn't be dead . . ."

Lucas said, "Rae, your being here wouldn't have changed anything except you might be dead yourself. The shooters came out from behind us and started spraying bullets. We were set up. We didn't have a clue. If one of the feds hadn't see them come through the motel door with guns and hadn't yelled at them and opened up . . . I'd be dead, too. I never even saw the fuckers until they were down."

"Was Bob . . ."

"Ah . . . Goddamnit, this is hard, Rae. We never saw it coming. Bob was here and then he was gone, no pain, no fear, no warning. He was hit twice . . . Listen, I'm not going to talk about this anymore. I'm trying to run down the guy who set us up."

"Get them! Get them, Lucas!" she said. And then, "Oh, my God, I got a call coming in from Shirl. The service must've notified her. Hang on, I'm going to her call for a minute . . ."

She went away and a moment later, was back: "Lucas, I need to talk to you some more, but right now Shirl needs me . . ."

"Call me later in the day," Lucas said. "I'll have more about the guy we're looking for."

"What are you going to do?"

"I don't know—maybe kill his ass," Lucas said.

"Lucas . . . Lucas, just take him," Rae said. "Take him and squeeze him. Now I gotta go, I gotta go."

She was gone.

Parker, who'd heard Lucas's side of the conversation, said, "Let's not kill his ass, okay? Let's have a nice professional arrest and slam his ass in jail."

"We'll do what we gotta," Lucas said. Then, after another moment, "Yeah, we're not going to kill him. We won't have to. He's already dead."

"Excuse me?"

Lucas shook his head.

THE CITY WAS as quiet as it ever got, three o'clock in the morning, the night people sliding along, big coupes with gray primer on their fenders and doors, long-haired guys looking sideways out the windows as they jumped the traffic lights . . .

When they got to Elliot's house, two Miami-Dade cop cars and a van were parked at the fence, and five cops were standing in the yard, all of them vested and helmeted. They were part of a SWAT squad, the leader told Lucas. "What are we doing here? We understand he's involved in a shooting . . ."

Lucas gave him a quick recap of the shootout. The cops had heard various versions of the shootout and as he and Parker filled in the details, the cops all shaking their heads, the leader asked, "If this Bob was your partner, what are you doing here? I mean . . ."

"I know what you mean," Lucas said. "I've got the background on Elliot and we didn't have time to fool around. Have you knocked?"

"Yeah, we knocked, no sign of life. We're told there might be a warrant, but we don't know about that."

"I think we're good. You guys got a ram? This place is a fort, you're gonna need one."

"Yeah, but I'd like to know for sure that we got a warrant."

Lucas told the cop who Weaver was, then called him, leaving his phone on the speaker function, and Weaver said, "Yes. We have a warrant. Under the circumstances, you can go in right now. Knock the door down."

"You got it," the cop said.

BOTH THE FRONT and back doors had steel cores. The doorframes were made of steel bolted to the concrete block walls. After a few attacks on the two doors, the cops knocked out a window, and the least senior cop crawled into the house and unlocked a door from the inside.

On a fast walk-through, they found nothing except a couple of large cockroaches sitting on the kitchen table and then scuttling out of sight. The house was silent: the television was off, so was the air conditioner and all the lights, until the cops turned them on. There were two clean dishes in the sink.

"There was an alarm, but it was turned off," the SWAT leader said.

"Because the guys who took him out of here didn't know how to set it," Parker said.

The bedroom closets were full of clothes, as was a bedroom bureau. The bathroom showed a razor, toothbrush, toothpaste, and shaving cream on a counter next to a sink, and a drawer, partly opened, revealed a half-empty Dopp kit inside. The bureau had a jewelry tray that contained a couple of rings, a diamond earring, two gold bracelets, and a gold Rolex. Two suitcases and a duffel bag were piled atop one another, in a hallway closet, under a line of jackets.

After walking through, Lucas stopped at the table next to the front door and pulled open the drawer. The .45 was there, reassembled and loaded. Parker looked at it, and at Lucas, and asked, "What do you think?"

"What I thought in the car. He's gone. If he'd walked away on his own, he would have taken some of his stuff. I don't know how much that Rolex is worth, but I'd guess between ten and twenty thousand, maybe more."

"So you think he's . . ."

"Dead."

The SWAT squad leader came into the living room from the back. He'd taken off his helmet to reveal a shaved head, and from the shine off his scalp, one that was mostly bald before he got it shaved, Lucas thought.

"We might have found a fake wall," he said. Lucas trailed him back to a small bedroom, now full of exercise equipment—a stationary bike in front of a wall-mounted TV, a weight rack with weights. One of the SWAT cops pointed at a bookcase. "I work construction on weekends. That bookcase ain't right. From the side, it's fourteen inches deep, but he's got nothing in it but CDs and Blu-Rays and they barely fit."

"How does it move?"

"Can't see anything. Maybe it just pulls straight out, but I can't get it to move. There might be a stopper or something."

"What would happen if you hit it with your ram?" Lucas asked.

"It's just veneer over chipboard," the construction cop said. "It'd fall apart."

"Then hit it."

One of the cops went back outside to get the ram and the construction cop began unloading the shelves of the CDs and Blu-Rays. He was on his knees unloading the bottom shelf and he said, "Up . . . here it is."

The team leaders asked, "What?"

The construction cop lay on the floor, looking up at the bottom of the next-to-the-bottom shelf. "Some kind of pin . . . We need a screwdriver. A big one."

"Saw a screwdriver in the utility room, there's some tools," another cop said.

Lucas walked around a corner to the utility room, saw a nylon tool bag, found a half dozen screwdrivers, shouted back, "Phillips or flat-blade?"

The construction cop yelled back, "Phillips."

Lucas carried the screwdriver back as a cop was arriving with the ram. Lucas handed the screwdriver to the cop on the floor, who did something under the shelf, grunting, and then said, "It's coming out."

He threw a wooden peg out, then said, "There's a hook behind it . . . Okay. It oughta move."

The team leader and another cop got on opposite sides of the bookcase and pulled it loose. There was a six-inch deep space behind it, with a half dozen shelves. Three of the shelves were empty; the two top shelves held a half dozen plastic bags filled with a pale brownish heroin, and two bags of cocaine. The third one down held bundles of cash.

"You're right, he's dead," the lead cop said. "He sure as shit wouldn't leave all that cash behind, not to speak of all the dope."

"Dead, or spending the night with his girlfriend," another cop said. "Or running for his life."

Lucas nodded: "We need to put out an urgent bulletin on him. If he's not dead yet, he's going to be. Though I think he's probably dead. Goddamnit, I need that guy."

Lucas sat in the truck, phoned Weaver and told him what they'd found. "There must be two kilos of heroin in there, maybe a half kilo of coke. That could mean he was working with our Coast Guard killers the whole time. Bob and I talked to a guy who said Elliot was close to the top distribution level here, that he's got quite a few dealers working for him who are selling on a semi-wholesale level. Or maybe this was Elliot's inventory and it all comes from the Mexican side, like he said it did."

"Okay. Well, we'll get that bulletin out on him, make it a big deal. We'll find him if he's still walking around South Florida."

The situation at Romano's shop was slowly being cleaned up and Romano and Bianchi had been shipped to the Miami federal lockup on gun charges. Bob's body was at the medical examiner's and the wounded federal agent was still in surgery at Jackson Memorial Hospital.

"Why don't you head back to Lauderdale? We'll bring your car and stuff from the motel . . . we got car keys from Bob," Weaver said. "The shooting team still wants to talk with you about what you saw."

PARKER CAME BACK to the truck, got in the driver's seat and said, "Headed for Lauderdale. Think I ought to use the lights and siren?"

"Lights, no siren," Lucas said. "Goddamn thing is too loud."

They drove out to I-95, in silence, reflections from the lightbar ticking off the hood. After they turned up the expressway, Parker said, "I have a comment, but I don't want to annoy you after . . . what happened."

"Go ahead."

"I've never been on a raid like that one at Elliot's. Finding all that heroin. That was cool. I liked it."

"You've got the stress gene," Lucas said. "Are you out of Washington, or local?"

"Washington."

"Get some ride-alongs with the Washington cops. Your guys can fix it. Get armored up and go with them. It'll pay you back forever."

"I'm gonna do that," Parker said.

After another stretch of silence, Parker asked, "How did Elliot know to set you up?"

"Ah, Bob and I were going around town . . ." Lucas began, but then he trailed away.

"What?" Parker asked.

"Shut up for a minute," Lucas said. He looked out the window, not seeing the concrete landscape sliding by. He and Bob had only touched Elliot once. Somebody must have gotten to him between the time they talked and Elliot went to the Miami attorney's office. Had Elliot already known a name, and called that guy? Or had Lucas and Bob been tracked into Elliot's place?

Lucas tapped his knuckles against the car's window for a moment, then muttered: "They must have been tracking us. Me and Bob. We never saw them."

"What?"

"They were . . ."

"How would they even know who you were?" Parker asked. "They could pick you up at the hotel, but how did they know what you looked like? I mean, they could look you up on the internet, I guess, but how'd they even know what your names *were*? It's not like we posted them . . ."

"We talked to quite a few dealers down here, but . . ." He rubbed his forehead with his fingertips.

"What?"

"Most of them, we didn't really introduce ourselves," Lucas said. "There was an old guy we talked to down in Miami, in Coconut Grove, but he's not connected to the Mafia guys in any way that we know about and he's retired. Elliot never saw us again."

Thinking about it some more, then, "Oh. Shit. Parker, we gotta get west. We gotta get to a place called Sunrise. A city. You know where that is?"

"My telephone would know . . ."

A HALF HOUR later, Lucas and Parker took the elevator to Alicia Snow's floor at her Sunrise condo, looking out over the Everglades. Snow had taken a card from Lucas and in chatting with her, Bob had mentioned where they were staying. At her apartment, they knocked, but got no answer. Lucas went through his phone book, found the number for her cell phone and got nothing but dead air.

"Meredith what's-her-name, Duffy," Lucas said to Parker. "She's here, down the way . . ."

They walked down to Duffy's apartment, pounded on the door. A light came on, and then Duffy's voice, from behind the door: "Who is it?"

"Davenport, the U.S. Marshal you spoke to at your shop."

The door opened a crack, and Duffy, dressed in a black tank top and leggings, looked out at them, the chain still on the door. When she recognized Lucas, she said, "Let me get the chain," and closed the door and took it off and opened the door and asked, "What happened?"

"Do you know where Alicia is?"

She put a hand to her throat. "Oh, God. Is she gone? Did somebody hurt her?"

"She's not in her apartment," Lucas said.

"She didn't go to work yesterday," Duffy said. "She called in sick, she told Maria that she had the flu and needed to take some time off . . ."

"Who's Maria?" Lucas asked.

"She runs the salon. I went by last night after work to see if Alicia wanted to go out for a drink, but Maria said she called yesterday morning and canceled her appointments and said she'd be back when she got better. She never said anything to me. I knocked on her door last night but nobody answered . . ."

"When we talked to you the first time, you said you didn't know who might have dated the guys on that fishing boat," Lucas said. "I don't think you were telling the truth, that you were trying to protect Alicia. Was I right? Was she dating somebody on the boat?"

Duffy hesitated, then said, "Yes. I think she was. I'm not sure. She told me she was seeing a guy, but he was married and she didn't want to talk about it. And she didn't. I don't even know why I think it might have been one of the guys from the boat, but, the night of that class party, on the party boat, I know she went down to a Miami Beach hotel with some of the other girls and I think they were meeting those guys. I think she hooked up with somebody that night, because she didn't come home."

"You don't know the name of the guy she hooked up with?"

"No, she didn't talk about it." She paused, and then said, "You know what I think? I think the guy had money, whoever he is, and she hoped something might happen with him. But I think the guy was just getting laid."

Lucas pushed her, and she started to cry, but insisted she didn't know anything else.

Lucas asked Duffy to sit on her couch, and he took Parker outside, out of earshot, and said, "Call Weaver. We need a search warrant for Snow's apartment. Quick as he can get it. Tell them it's a life endangerment situation, she could be hurt or injured in the apartment, but we also need to cover everything else. We want to go through everything in the apartment."

"You think . . ."

"She's gone. They're cleaning up. Everybody who might know something, that we touched: they're cleaning up."

LUCAS CALLED WEAVER and they agreed that he and Parker could enter the apartment on grounds that Snow might be inside, injured and unable to respond to their knock, but they wouldn't be allowed to search the apartment until they had a warrant. Duffy didn't have a key, but knew where the manager lived. The manager had a key, opened the door. The apartment was as empty, and as undisturbed, as Magnus Elliot's house.

"It's gonna be a couple more hours to get the warrant, it looks like," Parker said. "What do you want to do?"

Lucas looked at his watch. 5:45. "I want you to stay here with Meredith. Make sure she's not . . . interfered with. I need the car keys."

Parker handed over the keys. "Where are you going?"

"I don't know. Someplace quiet," Lucas said. "I'll be back for the search. Call me."

Lucas went down to the truck, got in, wandered around, eventually crossed what looked like a major street, Sunrise Boulevard, and took it east. Thinking about Bob. A few hours earlier, feet up, laughing at *Miss Congeniality*; now Bob was gone, on a slab at the medical examiner's office, to be cut open and . . .

He kept driving, eventually arrived at Fort Lauderdale Beach. He hardly realized what it was, when he got there; it took a moment. He turned north, parked, walked out on the sand, took his shoes off, and sat down.

The sun came up over the Atlantic; and Bob was still gone. As Lucas was sitting there, he saw two muggers walking down the beach at him. He slipped his Walther out of its holster, and let it rest against his thigh.

He looked at the muggers and said, "Hey, guys."

Lucas spent another week in Miami. Russell Forte stayed for three days, representing the Marshals Service. Lucas talked to Romano and Bianchi before they bailed out, and the old man sensed that Lucas believed them about the setup, which didn't help them on the gun or money laundering charges that the feds had come up with. The old man refused to say much while he was sitting in an interview room, but he told Lucas, "I'll be out of here tomorrow. You meet me on the way out. On the steps."

Lucas and two FBI agents interviewed Meredith Duffy, Alicia Snow's friend from the boat. She was frightened to death. She would, she said, go home to Georgia until it was all done with. She was willing to look at mug shots, and she did, but failed to identify any of the men on the boat, for sure, but ticked one face with her index finger.

"This guy, maybe. Not for sure. I couldn't really . . . but I think he might have been the boat driver."

Weaver, who was leaning over her shoulder looking at the computer screen, said, "John Cattaneo. Once known as 'Black Jack.' Huh. He's from New Jersey. Did time for ag assault, that was a while back, nothing since . . ."

ON THE STEPS of the federal courthouse, after he and his son-in-law had made bail, Don Romano told his attorney and son-in-law to walk off a way, and when they were alone, said to Lucas, "Ask your Mafia experts about the Newark group. Doug Sansone. He's the motherfucker who did this to all of us. The FBI thinks me'n some friends had a little thing going over in Perth Amboy and up on Staten Island. I'm not saying yes or no, one way or the other, but . . . that fuckin' Sansone wants all of that. They do dope, the Newark guys. A lot of it. Not weed, the hard stuff. They're the ones you want, not me."

"Doug Sansone," Lucas repeated. "How do we know you're not putting us on somebody you don't like, just to get us off your back?"

"Don't like? I hate that motherfucker," Romano said. "Listen, if those shooters only wanted to kill you, they could have knocked on your motel room door and said, 'room service.' You open the door, they're standing there with a gun aimed at your chest and they pull the trigger. You got no chance. They didn't do that. They waited until you were headed for my place. They wanted to take both of us down, to get rid of you and to hook me up for murder. They wanted somebody for the FBI to blame. I mean . . ."

"What?"

"The fuckin' can that the dope supposedly came in. I threw it in my dumpster? Do I look like a moron? No—it was somebody who wanted to get rid of me almost as bad as they wanted to get rid of you. There's only one guy who fits the bill: Dougie Sansone."

"I'll think about that," Lucas said.

Romano tapped him on the chest, "He's an evil one. Evil. He'd kill you for a dime and the people he works with are just as bad. Evil motherfuckers."

"You ever hear of a John Cattaneo?"

"Jack? Sure. If you're looking at him, you're looking in the right place. He's one of Sansone's men now. Maybe . . . two steps down, but it's a big operation, so he's a heavy. There's another guy they work with . . . mmm . . . Jimmy. He kills people. That's what he does. Or he fixes it."

"That's it? That's everything?"

"What the fuck you want? You want me to go arrest them myself? What I told you, that's a big thing. I ain't wrong about this, either. That fuckin' Sansone. For him, killing those Coast Guard guys would be like stepping on bugs. He wouldn't even think about it afterward. Probably went out for a Starbucks latte."

He started away, then turned and said, "I'd tell you I'm sorry about your friend being killed, but I didn't know him, so I guess I'm not. My attorney told me about you. You personally. I don't want to be on your bad side. You want to get even? Kill that motherfuckin' Sansone."

TENNAN, THE MAFIA expert, told Lucas that most of what Romano said was probably right, that the Newark organization was moving south on Staten Island, pushing Romano's loan organization out of the best bars where they did their loan sharking business.

And, he said, the Newark group was rumored to have gotten into the drug distribution after the new boss, Douglas Sansone, pulled together the fragments of older organized crime groups that had gone out of business.

"What are you going to do about it?" Weaver asked Lucas.

"Dunno. Give me some time." Lucas thought about it for a day, then got back to Weaver and said, "I'm going home."

"You're jumping ship?"

"I'll be in touch. I need to think about this Sansone guy, this John Cattaneo. I need to talk more with Tennan. I need to go to a funeral in Louisiana. I need to read a lot of your organized crime files. You and I . . . we need to put a surveillance team on this Cattaneo, figure out who's who in the Sansone group," Lucas said. "I'll be back. I'll be talking to you. A lot. Count on it."

JANUARY

CHAPTER

SIXTEEN

BRILL'S DELI WAS a good one, smelling of fatty meat, crusty bread, mustard, and pickles in vinegar. Sixteen feet of wall space was dedicated to coolers filled with Coke and Pepsi and beer and root beer and ginger beer and near-beer and lemonade, limeade, and sports drinks. The Mexican tile floor was cracked and worn, the tabletops scarred from three decades of use. The place even had a sandwich man named Lou.

Jack Cattaneo wandered in at one o'clock on a bright afternoon in mid-January and immediately spotted the cool dude and dudette sitting at a table across from his regular booth, which was empty. Dude and dudette were his private terms for middle-aged people who were trying too hard to stay young, and these two were trying hard. You saw a lot of that on the Beach, right up to ninety-year-old women still getting work done on their turkey necks.

These two had been in a couple of days before, new customers, he thought, though they'd been sitting on the other side of the room the first time he'd seen them. He'd noticed them because they'd seemed to be arguing, the dudette all over the dude's act.

And they were hard to miss, a biracial couple in an old people's deli on Miami Beach.

The dude had not overly clean blond hair falling down to his shoulders. A lazy look seemed permanently fixed to his face, behind multicolored dime-store sunglasses; he had earrings in both ears, fake diamonds that would make an NBA player go over and slap his face. He was wearing a T-shirt, gym shorts that looked like they'd been stolen from a high school locker, and flip-flops, though the predicted high temperature that day was only in the low seventies. He had an earphone plugged into an ear, the other end plugged into what must have been an iPhone Zero. He was listening to music, and tapped his thumb with the beat as he argued with the woman.

The dudette was exactly his opposite: a tall, lithe black woman with close-cropped hair, high cheekbones, and a sexy scar running slantwise across her forehead; maybe, Cattaneo thought, from a knife, or possibly a church key. She had bloody-red nails that looked like the claws on a cheetah, and wore a blue Nike running suit that fit her like a glove. The front zipper was down to a point about two inches above her navel. No bra, and the jacket's contents were worth looking at. The front of the suit said YALE, and Cattaneo thought, "Yeah, right."

He smiled to himself: what it actually said was YA—cleavage— LE. Most guys wouldn't make the jump.

Cattaneo got his usual, a corned beef sandwich with red onions and Russian hot mustard, fries, and a bottle of Peroni, and carried them back to his booth, where he poured ketchup into the fries cup and went to work on the sandwich and beer and half-listened to the dude and dudette quarrel.

The woman was saying, "Yeah, that worked, didn't it? We're lucky we made it out of the state."

The dude half-whined, "Shut up. I was trying."

"Try harder. I don't want to be selling retail. And I won't be waitin' two years if you get hooked again."

"Why not sell? Get a job at the Gap, or whatever. You're good at it. They like your looks. Get a few bucks, get me back on my feet."

"You could get on your feet if you'd get off your fuckin' back. How many dive shops you hit today? One? None?"

"Two. They didn't need anybody."

THEY CONTINUED TO argue, but now Cattaneo checked them out. The dude was wearing a faded yellow T-shirt that showed a grinning skull wearing a dive mask and a snorkel. He swallowed some sandwich, leaned out of the booth and said, "I couldn't help hearing what you said. You're a diver?"

The blond dude looked him over, then said, "Maybe," which Cattaneo could have predicted he'd say. "What's it to you?"

Cattaneo shrugged. "I heard a bunch of divers were down here trying to find that Coast Guard treasure. Thought maybe you were one of them."

The blond seemed to focus. "Coast Guard treasure? What Coast Guard treasure?"

"The Coast Guard has a fifty-thousand-dollar reward . . ."

"Oh," the woman said to the blond, "that dope thing."

"Yeah, we know all about that," the blond said to Cattaneo. "You'd have to be a major dumbass to think that shit's still out there. That's long gone."

Cattaneo's eyebrows went up. "Yeah? How'd that happen? The Coast Guard's all over it."

The blond tapped the tabletop with his knuckles. "I read about it. The Mexicans dumped that shit off a freighter into a hundred and fifty feet of water. They knew exactly where it was."

"But the Coast Guard . . ."

"The Coasties got no idea, except maybe a general area. That's what the newspaper said. So what'd the dopers do? Easy. They drove by in some boat maybe a mile farther out from where the Coast Guard is watching, in the middle of the night. They put a diver over the side with a good DPV, maybe . . . a Yamaha or something like it, and a lift bag. He rode the DPV over to where the dope is, towed it back to the pickup spot, hung out twenty feet down until the boat came back, surfaced, and there you are. I don't know how much was down there, but the paper said millions. It's gone now, man. Long gone."

"What's a DPV?"

"Diver propulsion vehicle? Like a torpedo that you hold on to and steer?"

The chick said to the dude, "Whyn't you get a ride on a boat, go look for it? If there are boats out looking for it, they'd take an extra diver if it don't cost them anything. What'd they have to do, give you free air? We could use fifty K."

"'Cause it's not there," the dude said. "That's why. Because if you cut up fifty K ten ways, it's five K for risking your neck, because that shit'll be down deep. Then the IRS wants its taxes. And maybe the Mexicans would make an example out of you; I don't need that kinda trouble."

"I think it was Colombians," Cattaneo said.

The dude shrugged. "Same thing."

"If you say so," Cattaneo said. "I don't know anything about diving. You a pro?"

The dude shrugged again. "Yeah. I worked out in California for a few years. Cold water out there. Hot women, though. Thought I might find a spot down here."

"He had to leave because he was screwing his Hollywood clients," the woman said. "And I don't mean out of money. He finally screwed the wrong housewife."

Another shrug. Shrugging was apparently his lifestyle, Cattaneo decided, a guy who tended not to be concerned. The dude said, "It was sorta worth it."

"Unless you need to go back to LA someday and you can't," the woman said.

Cattaneo smiled, showing yellowed fang teeth. "You piss off somebody?"

"A cop," the blond said, head bobbing as he remembered. "He had like this primo old lady. Like a starlet."

"A starlet whose time had expired. And not just a cop," the woman said. "The head of LA vice."

Cattaneo: "Whoops."

"How was I supposed to know that?" the blond asked.

"He had to go back to Iowa," the woman said to Cattaneo. Back to the dude: "That sure didn't work out, huh?"

"You can always walk," the blond told her.

"I would if I didn't feel sorry for your hopeless ass," the woman said. "I walk and you're on the street. I wouldn't forgive myself for . . . several hours."

"Where you livin' now?" Cattaneo asked.

"Got a place up in Hollywood," the dude said.

"What are you doing way down here?"

"Seeing the sights," the woman said, too quickly.

"Tell you what," Cattaneo said. "Give me your name and address and phone number. I know a guy in the dive business, he might be able to throw something your way. He's up in Broward, not too far from you."

"Don't have the gear anymore," the dude said.

"Give the man your number," the woman said. "We can figure out the equipment."

Now the guy made an effort to look hard at Cattaneo, but it fizzled: "You the man? Because I had some trouble with the man."

Cattaneo grinned and took a bite of his sandwich and chewed, while he looked from the blond to the woman and back to the poor henpecked sonofabitch. The woman leaned across the table to the blond, and said, heavy whiskey gravel in her voice, "In three weeks, we won't have enough cash to fuckin' eat. Give the man your fuckin' phone number."

THE CANTANKEROUS PAIR finished before Cattaneo, and when they got up to leave, the woman leaned over the booth table to give him a shot right straight down to her belly button, and said, "Thank you very much, sir. If your friend needs somebody, Willy can work really hard. And we need the money."

"See what I can do," Cattaneo said, trying not to look sideways under the gap between her breasts and the jacket, and failing. "Maybe it'll work out for everybody."

◆◆◆

HE WATCHED THEM out of the deli onto the sidewalk. The guy wanted to go south, but the woman wanted to go north. The blond finally gave in and trailed her along the sidewalk to the north and out of sight. Cattaneo went back to the remnants of his sandwich and thought about a slice of lemon cheesecake. He oughta watch his weight, but . . . cheesecake. It is, as a man once said, what it is.

And the diver . . . they badly needed a diver of the right type, and the dude had that look. Their previous diver had apparently been freaked out by the shooting on the Mako. They took their eyes off Jaquell for one minute and she disappeared into the Bahamas. Cattaneo and a couple of other guys went to look for her, but it was hopeless. So no luck there, not for the home team. Of course, he thought, *she* lucked out.

He went for the cheesecake and another bottle of Peroni. Five minutes later, he'd tipped the bottle up for a final mouthful, when a man walked in, looked slowly around the place, caught Cattaneo's eyes, held them, then moved on to Lou, the sandwich maker.

The man was wearing a cotton sport coat, seriously wrinkled in the back, golf slacks over a small potbelly, and brown shoes a few shades too yellow. His face was pitted with some kind of disease scars that Cattaneo didn't want to know about. He and Lou talked for a moment, and then they both looked at Cattaneo.

Cattaneo thought: Cop.

The cop walked over toward him and Cattaneo told himself to relax; no reason a cop should be talking to him.

The cop said, "Barry Cohen, Miami Beach police. You were talking to a blond guy and a tall black woman?"

"Yeah, they left ten minutes ago. I didn't know them, they were just sitting at that table"—he nodded at the table—"and we had a couple of words. What'd they do?"

"You see which way they went?"

"Yeah, they went out on the sidewalk and turned that way." He pointed south. "That's the last I saw of them. What'd they do?"

The cop ignored the question again and asked, "What did they have to say for themselves?"

"They said they were looking for work. I think they might have come on a bus. They might have been walking, something one of them said . . . mmm, the blond guy said his feet hurt."

"You didn't know them?" Cohen asked.

"No. I did see them here a couple of days ago, though. What'd they do?"

"They're thieves, we think. Working around here. We're trying to catch up with them. You didn't give them access to a car or . . ."

"Man, I talked to them for five minutes, max. I come here every day for lunch—I live three blocks from here," Cattaneo said. "If they're thieves, I want them caught. This neighborhood is going to shit. Never saw them before two days ago . . . Lou probably knows them better than I do. I didn't give them access to anyone."

The cop nodded and said, "Okay. If you see them again, call 911. My name again is Barry Cohen, Miami Beach. Tell the 911 operator to call me."

"I'll do that," Cattaneo said. "I hate fuckin' thieves."

The cop said, "Headed south?"

"Yeah. Ten minutes ago."

♦♦♦

THE COP LEFT, headed south, and Cattaneo got up and stepped over to Lou. "You know what those guys did? The blond and the black chick?"

"Yeah. Somebody must've told Cohen that they were in here. Cohen says they were over at the Rue Rouge yesterday. The black girl got talking to the valet and pulled him away from his board and they think the guy lifted some car keys. Somebody did, anyway. They took the car, a Porsche Cayenne, one of those remote-entry things, and the car had the owner's registration. They drove over to the owner's house, used the keys to get in and ripped off a few thousand bucks worth of electronics and some other shit. Silverware, a statue, some suits and shoes, some tools from the garage. Chain saw. They would have got more but there was a security system on a one-minute delay so they only got about two minutes' worth of stuff. When the security company called the guy at the Rue Rouge, halfway through his lunch, he went running out to get his car and it was gone. They found it under I-95 with the wheels gone."

"So they got some used electronics and some wheels?"

"I guess. Expensive wheels, though."

Cattaneo briefly thought about climbing on Lou about pointing him out to the cop, for talking to the dude and dudette. After a moment's consideration, he didn't, because (a) Lou thought he was an upright citizen so why wouldn't he point him out, and (b) he liked the corned beef sandwiches and didn't want Lou hockin' a loogy in there.

"Hate thieves," Cattaneo said to Lou. "They make it so hard for the rest of us."

◈ ◈ ◈

BY THE TIME Cattaneo left the deli, the blond and the chick were looking out the rear window of their ten-year-old Subaru Outback. They saw the cop leave, and then, a couple of minutes later, Cattaneo. The blond took a burner phone from his pocket and punched in a number.

"Davenport . . ."

"Yeah, this is Virgil. I'm with Rae. We talked to Cattaneo. We got a bite. Cohen was just in there, laying out our bona fides."

"Excellent. Now we wait. The apartment's good?"

"We're gonna fire up some weed tonight, to give it that necessary *je ne sais quoi,*" Virgil said.

"Hey: no inhaling . . . and what's with the Latin and fuckin' French?"

"I'm a high-quality cop," Virgil said.

When he got off the phone, Rae said, "It's bona-FEE-days, dumbass. FEE-days does not rhyme with 'fries.'"

"Maybe not in Rome, but it does in Miami Beach," Virgil said. "Let's get on home."

SEVENTEEN

AFTER THE SHOOTING in Florida City, and a series of conversations with Romano and Bianchi, Weaver had set up a surveillance net in South Florida, focusing on known associates of Douglas Sansone.

One of them, James (Jimmy) Parisi, had been identified as a killer, suspected of five murders in New York and New Jersey, carried out with semiautomatic .22 rifles; but he was good, and had never been indicted for any of them. The feds thought he might have been on the boat when the Coast Guardsmen were murdered, not because they had hard information, but simply because of his proclivities.

Six more men were identified as working for Sansone in South Florida, and rumor had it that they had a connection with Mexican heroin importers, but that the Mexicans had begun shifting their support to Hispanic dealers in New Jersey, overlapping Sansone's territory. Sansone, the rumors went, had looked for an alternate source of heroin, and had found one. Heroin was again flowing into Staten Island needles.

✦✦✦

In mid-November, a week after Bob's funeral in Louisiana—where Rae had told Lucas in no uncertain terms that she was on this case now, so Lucas could just shut up about it, and so Lucas did and started thinking—Lucas had traveled to Washington to meet with Weaver, who'd come up from Florida, and two contacts high in the FBI, Deputy Director Louis Mallard and an influential senior agent named Jane Chase.

Weaver was impressed: as they walked together down the hallway to the first of the meetings, he'd said in a hushed tone, "Jesus Christ, I didn't know you were friends with these people. Mallard is like the Archangel Gabriel, right up there next to God."

"He's no kind of angel, I can promise you that," Lucas said.

They met in Mallard's office, a cluttered double cubicle with piles of books and paper on every flat surface. As they talked, Chase wandered around the office, peering at the piles, occasionally muttering, "No way," or "Gimme a break," until Mallard told her to shut up and sit down.

"What do we know about this Sansone guy? Know for sure?" Mallard asked Weaver.

Weaver said, "For sure? He owns a chain of donut shops."

"Donut shops?"

"Mama Ferrari's Donuts. Ten shops. The OC unit did some checks on his income taxes, and they tell me he's the most successful donut seller in New Jersey," Weaver said. "People come in the door at the donut shops and pay with small bills. Mama Ferrari discourages credit cards—if you pay in cash, you get an extra donut, supposed to offset credit card fees. That means they have large amounts of small greasy bills . . ."

"A laundry," Chase said.

"That's what OC says," Weaver said. "On the other hand, they sent one of their Jersey people out to buy a box of donuts, to see if the shops were legit, and word came back that they're damn good donuts."

"How sure are you that Sansone's group is behind the Coast Guard shootings?" Chase asked.

"Eighty-six percent," Weaver said. "We started watching those guys down in Miami, best we could without a full surveillance team, and they're not doing much. They seem to be . . . waiting. For something. They can't go after the dope with the Coast Guard sitting out there, checking every boat."

WITH THREE DEAD Coast Guardsmen, a dead marshal, and a badly wounded FBI agent who might never fully recover from his wounds, neither Mallard nor Chase had needed much persuading. They'd approved a working group, to be run by the New York AIC out of Manhattan and Weaver out of South Florida, with the objective of identifying and then taking down the entire Sansone operation.

Walking out of the meeting, Weaver said, "I thought I was fucked. Now, I'm sorta a semi–big shot. I mean, I called Louis, Louis, instead of 'sir.'"

"You called him 'sir' about twenty times," Lucas said.

"Yeah, but I also called him Louis."

"That's great," Lucas said. "You can write it down in your diary."

Working with Chase and the Manhattan agent in charge, Weaver had put together a working group of carefully chosen surveillance specialists who were told the assignment required the deepest secrecy: they were to be ghosts.

Sansone was not to know that he'd come under any special scrutiny. Stalking them with extreme care through November and December, the group identified more Sansone operators in the Newark area and on Staten Island, with associates as far north as Boston and Bangor, Maine. The South Florida group was believed to be coordinating narcotics purchases for distribution in the Northeast.

By the third week of November, Lucas had returned to Minnesota and a day later drove to Virgil Flowers's girlfriend's farm, where Virgil lived, to recruit him for the working group. Frankie, Virgil's girlfriend, had sat in on the talk, sleeping twins on her lap.

"I'm not complaining, Lucas, but every time I see you, you're pulling poor Virgil in over his head," Frankie said. She was a striking woman, as blond as Virgil, short, busty, wickedly intelligent. She and Lucas tended to knock sparks off each other; Lucas liked her a lot.

"You should look a little closer. Virgil doesn't tend to get pulled unless he wants to go," Lucas said.

"What are we talking about this time?" Frankie asked.

"Can I talk?" Virgil asked.

Frankie turned her head to him and said, "No. Think of me as your agent."

"Virgil would technically be part of an interagency federal task force working out of Fort Lauderdale," Lucas said. "Nobody would know about him except me and Rae and one other marshal and a couple of FBI agents."

"Man, I'm not a diver," Virgil interjected. "I only took lessons because I couldn't afford to fish all day. Since I was off the boat in the afternoons, I got certified. In a week. In a swimming pool, mostly, with two open water dives. I dove a few more times, rental equipment, but I'm not competent. I'm a tourist."

"We can fix that," Lucas said. "You're almost as athletic and smart as I am . . ."

"That's what everybody says," Virgil agreed.

". . . Best of all, you've got that hair and that natural, built-in stoner look," Lucas continued. "By the time we send you down there, in a month or two, you'll be the best diver in the United States. Thirty, maybe forty days of training."

"Seriously, no way that could happen, that I'd get that good."

"Okay, I exaggerate," Lucas said. "But you'll be very, very good."

"But . . ."

Lucas turned and gazed out the living room window, over the November fields at the back of the house. They showed a bit of snow from an early storm, a hint of the coming Minnesota winter. He turned back to Virgil and said, "I talked to the people at the Marshals Service and they understand that you've got a family and kids. You could take Frankie and the kids with you. You'll get an Airbnb house, I don't know about the view. You'd leave here around the first of December . . ."

"But . . ."

". . . and fly to the Big Island. Of Hawaii."

Frankie said, "Wait! The Big Island? With the kids? Instead of December and January in Minnesota? Can Virgil's mom come to help with the babies and Sam?"

Sam was her youngest child by another father. He hopped in front of Lucas with wide eyes. "I wanna surf!"

Lucas smiled. "We're talking about a four-bedroom house. Should be room for everybody."

IT HADN'T ALL gone as smoothly as Lucas had suggested it might, but Virgil had never believed that it would. He spent parts of thirty-five days and twenty-four nights in the water, trained by two ex-SEALs who did contract work for the Marshals Service. When Virgil asked why they didn't send the SEALs on the Florida deal, Lucas said, "Look at them."

They looked more like cops than cops: they looked like cops in movies. Virgil said, "Okay."

When he was finished with the dive training, Virgil flew back to Minnesota, and a day later, made a trip to the Iowa State Prison at Fort Dodge for a late-night visit. He wore a ski mask as he toured the cells, the cafeteria, the workshops, making photos and movies with his cell phone. The Hawaii house had been rented for two months, and Frankie, Virgil's mother, and the kids would stay on until the rent ran out at the end of January.

THE SOUTH FLORIDA task force under Weaver had spotted Michael Behan and Jack Cattaneo as the key members of Sansone's South Florida organization and began tracking them, identifying two other men, named Regio and Lange, as other major members of the group. Jimmy Parisi, the killer, spent most of his days sleeping, and most of his nights with hookers, putting cocaine up his nose and running over curbs with his tricked-out Jeep. He didn't seem to supervise anything, but was available for any needed murders.

The feds decided that Virgil should approach Cattaneo, since he reliably ate at the same deli three or four times a week.

ON JANUARY 20, a Monday, Virgil and Rae moved into a shitty apartment in a shitty pink building on Hollywood Boulevard in the city of Hollywood. On their first night there, they'd no more than closed the door when a high-polished brown cockroach the size of a baby's shoe scuttled out from under a bed and disappeared into a closet.

"I'll take the other bedroom," Rae said.

She was back in ten seconds: "Nope. I'm taking the cockroach room."

Virgil looked in the bedroom she'd just left: "That one's worse?"

"That one smells like a man's been sleeping in there. If you know what I mean," Rae said.

"I don't know what you mean," Virgil said.

Rae made the universal jerking-off motion, pumping with her right fist, and Virgil said, "Aw, Jesus. You know what? Let's go get some plastic bedcovers and wrap the beds. And some bug spray. And a gallon of air freshener."

"Good. And new sheets and pillows and pillowcases. We'll just sleep on top of everything. It'll still look shitty."

"Deal."

"The guy who rented this for us—I wonder what he was thinking?"

"He was going for authenticity, I guess." Authenticity. Virgil scanned the fully furnished living room, with the nicotine-colored walls and overhead lights with 40-watt bulbs and a seasoning of dead moths, and asked, "What do you think? Should we wrap the sofa?"

Rae looked at the seven-foot green sofa, crouched against the wall like an overgrown fungus. "I don't think that color is the natural one. I mean, how could it be? And those brown spots . . ."

"I'll wrap it. We'll throw a blanket over the plastic. That'll still look authentic."

"You think the Marshals Service would buy us a new TV?"

They both looked at the eighteen-inch TV sitting on a window ledge. Virgil scratched his chin and said, "Lucas told me that they were picking up a bunch of electronics that we supposedly stole from some guy. I'll tell them to make sure there's a better TV in it. We'll leave this on the floor."

"More authenticity. I've never seen an eighteen-inch flat panel before. Must have been a special order."

THEY WENT OUT to a Home Depot and a Bed Bath & Beyond, wrapped the beds and then covered them with sheets and new pillows, threw all the old bed stuff in the cockroach closet. They covered the couch with a fuzzy blue blanket that began to pill as soon as they sat on it. They hosed the closet down with the bug spray and the rest of the place with lilac-scented air freshener.

A plastic tablecloth covered the square kitchen table, a dozen plastic glasses, four cups and plates in a package, along with a box of stainless-steel flatware, completed the move.

"Just like home," Rae said, pleased, looking at the line of red plastic tumblers next to the rust-stained sink. "All we need now is to throw a rubber on the bedroom floor."

That night, Lucas showed up with an FBI agent and a van.

"Place stinks," Lucas said. "Smells like a funeral home."

"The floral spray," Rae said. "It's the Fred's Mortuary scent."

THEY MOVED IN a bigger TV along with two used laptops and a printer, stereo speakers and a turntable, two pawn-quality electric guitars, a Korg electric piano with three inoperable keys, a bronze statue of a little boy peeing with a small gauge brass pipe bent and dangling from the bottom of the statue—"The kid's supposed to pee vodka," Lucas said. There was a lot of other crap, including a tool chest, bottles of high-end liquor, a load of men's size 46-short suits with a bunch of Hermès neckties, and four Porsche wheels, all with a newly stolen vibe.

Rae picked up an unopened bottle of Don Julio Real tequila and said, "Oooh. Somebody's got good taste."

THE NEXT DAY, Virgil and Rae made their first visit to Brill's, where they spotted Cattaneo. Cattaneo didn't go to Brill's the next day, but he did on the third day, when they talked.

Cattaneo didn't call that night, but they hadn't expected him to: he'd be doing research.

At nine o'clock, in the light of a flickering neon sign, Virgil and

Rae walked down the street to the Ouroboros Bar and Grill, went inside, and looked around. Virgil said, "The guy in the black T-shirt."

Rae: "I think so."

They sat at the bar, Virgil got a Budweiser and Rae went with a Tequila Sunset and they made eye contact with the guy in the black T-shirt a few times, and then Virgil slid off his barstool and wandered over to the guy and asked, "How ya doin'?"

"Doin' fine. Nice-lookin' lady you got there."

"She's good. Listen, we just come down from Iowa . . ."

"Where in Iowa?"

Pause. "Fort Dodge?"

"I come from Waterloo, originally," the guy said.

"Yeah? I've gone through there, on my way from Vinton out to Sturgis."

"Sturgis. I wanna go. Bad. I been to Daytona about a hundred times. What's your ride?"

"At the time, an old Harley softtail . . ."

They talked bikes for a couple of minutes, then Virgil sat down and said, "I've been looking for somebody who can hook me up."

"With what?"

"A little weed. I don't want to break any laws or anything. You looked like a rider, I thought you might know somebody."

Rae came over and sat down and asked, "You the guy?"

"I don't sell anything except auto parts . . ."

"Really? We got four wheels we might want to get rid of, off a Porsche."

They talked some more and the guy asked how much weed they wanted and they talked about an ounce. The man, whose name was Roy, told them to sit still for a few minutes. He went out the back door and came back six or seven minutes later with another man, who said his name was Richard. Richard, who looked more like a shoe salesman than even the narcs did, slid a baggie across the table to them.

"Two hundred."

"Whoa."

Richard smiled: "It's top-grade Chemdawg. My sources say this particular batch . . ." He tapped the baggie. ". . . has a THC level of thirty-one percent. It's like a cross between Thai and Nepalese and it will float your ass to Oz."

"Well, shit, gotta have it," Virgil said.

He looked at Rae, who opened her clutch, took out a roll of twenties and counted out ten of them. Richard took the cash and said, "Nice doing business with you."

"You got an empty baggie on you?"

"Yeah?"

"I thought we'd maybe throw an eighth to Roy. For hookin' us up," Virgil said.

Roy said, "I knew you were a stand-up guy, soon as I saw you."

Roy got his cut and Virgil tucked the baggie away. They talked about the local altered-consciousness scene over a couple more beers and Richard spoke earnestly about his paddleball game. Before they broke up, Richard gave Virgil a half pack of orange Zig-Zags, and they all parted friends.

CATTANEO CALLED THE next morning. "I might have found something for you," he said. "There's a couple of guys who'd like to come over and talk to you. About diving."

"Well . . . I'm here," Virgil said, and from behind him, Rae shouted, "He wants the job."

"Be twenty minutes or so," Cattaneo said. "Half hour."

VIRGIL CALLED LUCAS, who said, "We'll be across the street."

"Be careful. They might already be out there, watching to see if anybody comes in."

"We're careful," Lucas said. The "we" were Lucas and Andres Devlin, another marshal, who'd been recommended by Rae. She'd told Lucas, "Devlin's a tough guy. Smart. He reads nonfiction books with world maps in them. I know because I looked."

WHEN LUCAS RANG off, Virgil got out the Zig-Zags and rolled a slender joint, fired it up, inhaled, and passed it to Rae. "This is so fuckin' illegal," she said, taking a toke.

"Like traffic-ticket illegal," Virgil said. "Don't tell me you don't speed. Blow some of that smoke into my hair."

When they'd given the room and themselves the necessary ripeness, Virgil shredded the joint and flushed it, all except the last quarter inch. That, he fired up again, snuffed it between his thumb and forefinger, said, "Ouch," and put the roach for safekeeping on a Dos Equis bottlecap and put the bottlecap on a windowsill, where it might be seen.

Twenty-five minutes after Cattaneo called, Lucas called and said, "We've got two guys coming down the sidewalk. They're Sansone people, a step down from Cattaneo. Names are Matt Lange and Marc Regio. They're looking at addresses."

◆◆◆

VIRGIL GOT A beer from the refrigerator, took a swig, swished it around his mouth, swallowed and poured most of the rest of it down the sink, sat on the couch and put the bottle on the floor by his feet. Rae shoved her .40-caliber Glock under a pillow at the opposite end of the couch, turned the TV to a *SpongeBob SquarePants* rerun, and then laid back on the gun pillow and put her bare feet on Virgil's leg, flashing her bloody-red toenails.

She asked, "What do you think?"

"You could scale palm trees with those nails," Virgil said. 'They're perfect."

The two guys knocked, and after some shouting around, Virgil answered the door. "You Jack's friends?"

"We are," said the bigger of the two big guys. He waved his hand in front of his face. "Jesus Christ, I'm getting a contact high."

"That's from the previous occupants," Rae called, a barefaced lie told without shame.

"Yeah," said the smaller of the two guys. He said his name was Marc, the bigger guy was named Matt. Matt was carrying a plastic-backed notebook.

Rae asked, "You guys got last names?"

Marc said, "Regio," and nodded at Matt: "And Lange."

They looked like they shopped in the same menswear boutique: Regio wore a burnt orange Tiger Woods golf shirt, beige no-iron slacks with an Indian-weave belt, cordovan loafers, and a beige linen sport coat. Lange went with stretch jeans, a button-up Tommy Bahama short-sleeve shirt worn loose, and boating shoes. They both were fleshy-faced and sunburnt.

They checked the apartment and the four Porsche wheels lined up along one wall, but didn't mention them. Lange looked at Virgil and asked, "What kind of diving you done?"

"All kinds, but mostly divemaster stuff. I made sure nobody drowned. Some instruction in night diving and navigation. I worked off a dive boat taking guys out to the Channel Islands." When the two looked blank, he added, "You know. LA."

"You ever do any recovery?"

"Some. I mean, a boat would sink out there about once a week, sometimes they wanted to get the fishing gear off it, or personal stuff. Four rods and reels, for those movie guys, that could be five or six grand. I did that a few times, but I gotta tell you, I don't do ships. I don't do anything with an overhead. That scares me."

"What's an overhead?" Lange asked.

"Caves. Old shipwrecks or boats where you go inside. Stuff where you can't get straight back to the surface. I don't do that shit," Virgil said.

"He's a little claustrophobic," Rae said. "Lock him in a closet and he cries like a baby. Tries to kick the door down."

The two men looked from Virgil to Rae and back again, and then Lange asked, "How often does that happen to you? You get locked in a closet?"

Virgil, sullen, said, "Once."

Rae said, "Twice."

After thinking about that for a moment, Regio asked, "What's the deepest you ever been?"

"I once did a bounce to four hundred on Trimix, with a client who wanted to look at a sunken boat. I won't be doing that again. That's just fucked up."

"A bounce is where you go down and bounce off the bottom and come right back up?" Lange asked.

"Yeah. We were only down there for a couple of minutes, so he could take some pictures. I got a bunch of certifications, but I'm not a real happy tech diver, if you know what I mean."

"How about a hundred and fifty, hundred and sixty?" Regio asked.

"Do that in my sleep," Virgil said.

Regio and Lange glanced at each other, then Lange said, "You didn't mention to Jack you'd done two in that Iowa state prison."

Now Rae and Virgil looked at each other, and Rae said, "Ah, shit."

Virgil said, "He didn't ask."

The two men peered at Virgil and Regio said, "You're Willy." He turned to Rae: "What's your name?"

"Ally."

"As in alley cat?"

"I guess."

Back to Virgil: "You said you did night diving?"

"All the time. Like I said, that's one of the specialties I used to train people in. Night diving and nav."

Lange said, "Huh."

Rae said to Virgil, "Willy, I need to consult with you. In the bathroom." And to Regio and Lange: "We'll be right back."

In the bathroom, she said, "The Marc guy's got a gun."

"Yeah, I saw."

"I think this is where we tell them we've figured them out."

"Okay."

◆◆◆

Back out in the living room, Rae sprawled on the couch, her head on the gun pillow. Virgil sat at the other end, Rae's feet on his leg, her red nails like a spray of blood. Virgil picked up the beer, finished it, and said, "Look. You guys . . . you fuckers are the guys who dropped the dope off the coast. You're looking for somebody to get it for you."

"That against your principles?" Regio asked.

"I'll tell you what's against my principles," Virgil said. "Getting caught or doing it for free. Or getting shot when the job's done, to clean up loose ends."

Regio stared at him for a moment, then looked quickly around the room and came back to Virgil and said, "What we're thinking is, that shit is out there, and we think we know where and how to get it."

"Aw, man, if that's all it is, I told Jack it's long gone," Virgil said. "If you're not the original guys . . . then the original guys, the guys who dumped it, have been all over it by now."

"Let us worry about that," Regio said. "You worry about this. If you think you can get to it, using one of these DPV things you told Jack about, we'll give you . . . seven thousand, five hundred dollars for every can you bring back with you. Give it to you in cash. Every night. There are almost a hundred cans still out there; that's almost three-quarters of a million to you. In cash. If you recover at least ninety of them, we'll top off your take for an ice-cold million dollars."

Rae said, "You *are* those guys. The originals."

Neither Regio nor Lange looked at her: they were focused on Virgil, who seemed to be thinking. Then Virgil asked, "When?"

"We were told you need some gear."

"Yeah. Like all of it. I got nothing left. There's a big scuba place out west of here. They'd have most of it," Virgil said.

"You know about GPS?" Regio asked.

"Sure. Used it all the time on the boats."

"Then, how about we go shopping? Now," Lange said.

Virgil looked at Rae, who said, "He might be a little stoned."

"We noticed."

"Shit, I'm fine," Virgil said. He looked at Regio and Lange. "I got to dig out my certification cards. That'll take one minute. You need to tell me what I'll be doing. How deep I'm going, and how far I'm going to have to motor."

"We can do that right now," Lange said. He held up the notebook he was carrying. "I made some sketches based on what we know."

They sat at the apartment's shaky kitchen table and Lange opened the notebook and said, "This is all based on our first diver. She's not with us any longer—she went back home."

"What was her problem?" Rae asked.

"Not relevant to you," Regio said.

"Let us decide that," Rae said.

Regio and Lange looked at her, then Lange tipped his head and said, "She was . . . worried about, mmm, the police. The Coast Guard. We thought we were good with her, but she took off and we can't reach her now."

"That's it?" Rae asked. "She split?"

"That's it, really," Lange said. "She was good at what she was doing, and I guess she sorta freaked out."

They sat and looked at each other for a moment, then Virgil

asked, "Are you guys really good at this? What you're doing? Or are you a bunch of fuck-ups?"

"We're good," Regio said. "We're about the best. Our problem with Jaquell—she's the diver—was a one-time thing. She opted out, and we're good with that. But we need a diver. We're hoping you're it."

Lange held up the notebook. "You want to see this, or not?"

Rae looked at Virgil and asked, "What do you think?"

Virgil bobbed his head. "Okay. Let's take a look."

LANGE HAD DRAWN a series of simple sketches on notebook paper. The containers holding the dope were a hundred and fifty feet down on a reef that paralleled the coastline north of Fort Lauderdale. He said they had GPS coordinates for each end of the drop string. Each container weighed about twenty-eight pounds and was a hair less than twenty inches long—fifty centimeters. They had custom lift and cargo bags, designed to take five or six containers at a time. Each lift bag could lift a maximum of two hundred pounds.

"You talked to Jack about using one of the DPV things from a mile out," Lange said, tapping his sketch. "We won't have to do a whole mile. A half mile would be good enough, because the containers, the cans, are right on the east edge of where the Coast Guard is searching. A half mile further out, they wouldn't pay us any attention. Jack's run up there a half dozen times in his sailboat, never got a look."

Virgil said, "Let me get *my* notebook."

He went into the bedroom and came back with a spiral notebook jammed with loose pages. He got out dive tables and sat at the table peering at them, yanking on an earlobe as he did it, twisting one of the fake diamonds. He borrowed Lange's pencil and made a couple of calculations, then said, "We'd need a twin set—double tanks. Gonna need a good scooter. Gonna be expensive."

"You can do it?"

"I can do it, if you can do your part. My part isn't that hard; yours is the part that scares me."

"We can do our part. We've been in the business for a long time," Regio said. He looked between Rae and Virgil with a tight smile, and added, "Since our folks left the old country . . . like a hundred years ago."

Rae said, "Oh. Okay."

Virgil thought about that, looked at Rae, who nodded, and he said, "If we're going shopping, I gotta get my certifications."

"We can wait."

Virgil went back to the bedroom and returned with a cloth satchel, pawed through it, and came out with a drop-down plastic card file meant for the credit card–addicted, and dangled it up for Regio and Lange. "There you go. Twelve certs."

"Let's rock," Regio said.

OUT THE DOOR, the three of them; Rae stayed behind. Regio was driving a Lexus SUV, Virgil got in the back and Regio said, "Safety belt."

On the way west to Scuba City, Lange asked, "How was Fort Dodge?"

"Oh, you know. Not bad," Virgil said. "A little primitive, there were like three guys in a cell. Nobody hassled you too much; mostly just chickenshit. Food was okay. Didn't have to blow anyone, it wasn't that kind of place. I mean, it was Iowa."

"I can deal with chickenshit," Regio said. "I'll tell you what, though. You want to stay away from New York. I got a friend . . ."

They talked prisons for a while, and both Lange and Regio seemed conversant with prison conditions in the Northeast, including one called the James T. Vaughn Correctional Center in Delaware, which Virgil thought was a funny name. He goofed on it for a while, in a mildly stoned way, until Regio told him to shut up. "There ain't nothing funny about Jimmy Vaughn."

Virgil, in the backseat, leaned forward and said to Regio, who was driving, "I couldn't help noticing that your fine ride here has inferior wheels. I got four Porsche wheels and the tires are right next to new. N-Specs. They'd really cheer up this, uh, you know, Toyota . . ."

Made Lange laugh. "Toyota."

Regio: "Fuck you. Lexus. Best car I ever owned."

Virgil, stoner: "You own this car?"

"Of course I own it. What'd you think?"

"I thought maybe it was your wife's."

Made Lange laugh again.

SCUBA CITY HAD everything they needed except the diver propulsion vehicle—DPV—and there was a decent tech shop in back. Virgil produced his certification cards and chatted with the salesclerk about their requirements. Regio listened in, while Lange strolled around the place looking at the gear. In the car, Virgil had asked what the budget was, and Lange had said, "There isn't one. Get what you need."

"That DPV gonna cost six or seven grand . . ."

"Get what you need."

"Like Christmas . . ."

"Don't need to buy the lift bags. We got those, big ones, custom, cost a goddamn fortune," Lange said. "And we've got a top-of-the-line GPS watch. Don't need to buy one of those, either."

SINCE PRICE WAS not a problem, Virgil bought a Halcyon backplate and wing, on which the store's shop would mount twin steel scuba tanks nominally holding a hundred cubic feet of air each, depending on pressure.

When the salesclerk had gone to look something up, Lange said, "Our first diver had something different. Like a life vest, sorta . . ."

"She was diving single tanks, right?"

"Yeah. We could get her right on top of the drop."

"So she had a standard BC—buoyancy compensator. I need more air because we're a lot further out. Easier to mount twin tanks on a backplate. The wing is the equivalent of her BC."

"Okay."

VIRGIL ASKED THE clerk about tank pressure, and she said, "We do standard fills at three thousand psi."

Virgil said, "I'm going deep and cold. These are new tanks and perfect. You think your guy could bump that to thirty-three hundred?"

"I could ask him," she said.

THEY BOUGHT THE necessary valves for the two tanks, one left- and one right-handed, the manifold that joined them, harnesses and miscellaneous attachment rings for the plate, a wrench kit that would handle all the various nuts that held things together. They added an "octopus," which included a breathing mouthpiece and hoses to inflate and deflate the wing, a very expensive Perdix dive computer with an effective electronic compass and two Bluetooth transmitters that would read the tank pressures, a seven-millimeter wet suit, full-length dive skins for warmer water, two short, tight Speedo swimsuits, goggles, fins, snorkel, three flashlights, a titanium line cutter, and, because Virgil once needed them and didn't have them, a pair of wire cutters.

Lange had been looking at dive knives, but Virgil told him he really wouldn't have a use for one. Lange was disappointed, so Virgil got the largest, most expensive titanium knife he could find. "In case you run into a barracuda," Lange said.

"In case I walk by a pawn shop," Virgil said.

The store could deliver a top-of-the-line Genesis DPV in two days for $8,000.

REGIO SAID THAT was "fine," and at the end, he went out to the truck, came back with a briefcase, and gave the saleswoman $13,000 in hundred-dollar bills and $460 in twenties. She looked at the money with something like hunger, and then at Regio, Lange, and Virgil with something like doubt, but said nothing. She took the bills, said, "Give me a few minutes," went into a back room and came back in a few minutes with a smile on her face. "We're good," she said. She gave Regio $6.50 in change. "Where are you guys diving?"

"We're actually exporting this stuff to a rich guy who's got this private island over in the Bahamas," Virgil said. "You ought to see his boat. It's basically a *ship*."

"So it's not for you?"

"I wish," Virgil said. "He told me to get the best. We're the same size, so I can buy it for him, but I'm going to be wearing junk when I give him his lessons."

They agreed to pick up the two tanks, banded together, filled and certified, when they got the Genesis.

Out in the car, Lange said to Virgil, "Good story about the rich guy in the Bahamas. You're kind of a natural con man."

"I try. Listen . . . what you said back in the apartment, about your folks coming from the old country. Are you guys in the Mafia?" Virgil asked.

Regio laughed, and then asked, "What makes you think that?"

"What you said. And you both look sort of Italian, and your name is Regio, which sounds sort of Italian . . ."

Lange: "So what?"

"I dunno," Virgil said. "I was wondering, if you're Italian, why don't you have Italian names? Marc and Matt don't sound like, you know . . ."

Regio turned to look at Virgil: "My great-grandfather got to

New York a hundred and twenty years ago. Nobody's been back to Italy since then. So what the fuck do you think they'd name me—Pinocchio?"

"Just wondering," Virgil said. "No offense."

LANGE AND REGIO helped carry the dive gear up to the apartment, where they were met by a stoned Rae who was watching a jewelry sale on QVC.

"Fuckin' place doesn't look like it'd have cable," Regio said.

"It doesn't," Rae said. "This is over-the-air."

Regio blinked. "You gotta be shittin' me."

THEY AGREED THAT Regio and Lange wouldn't have to go along when Virgil picked up the DPV and the tanks. "Three days from now, we want to see you on Key Largo at a place called Sunrise Dive," Lange said. "We'll be riffin' on your Bahamas rich-man story. We're going to put you with a dive instructor to evaluate your . . . abilities. We'll tell her that story about you being hired by the rich guy to teach him how to be a pro diver."

"A test," Virgil said.

"Damn straight," Regio said. "Don't even think about hocking that gear and running back to Iowa. We *got* guys in Iowa."

Rae handed Virgil a joint and he took a long pull at it, wrenched his face into a model of stoned sincerity, and let some smoke roll out of his lungs. "You said a million bucks. I'd kill your mother for a million bucks. Both your mothers."

Rae said, "Shit, we'd kill Willy's mother for a million bucks, the racist old bitch."

Lange said, "We'll see you in Key Largo. We'll call you tomorrow with the time."

"If you've got this other diver, the one who's gonna test me, then why me?" Virgil asked.

"She's not with us. She's somebody we checked on, a dive instructor. Jack talked to her to see if she could do this kind of evaluation. She could. But watch your mouth when you're around her."

"Three days," Rae said. And: "Listen . . . you guys wanna get high?"

Regio put up a hand: "I'm a Scotch guy. I don't even like the smell of that shit. Smells like wet burning leaves back in Jersey."

WHEN REGIO AND Lange had gone, Virgil called Lucas: "We got the real deal, man. These are the dope guys. I don't know if they were involved in killing the Coast Guardsmen, but they could have been. Put them in the right clothes and they fit the descriptions."

"Good work. When you were in the scuba place we put a locator on their Lexus. We'd be following them right now, except they drove up the block, did a U-turn, and are sitting on the street watching your door."

"Don't let them see you. This'll be tricky enough without them smelling something wrong."

"We're cool."

"I know that *you* are. I'm worried about *me*."

EIGHTEEN

FOR THE NEXT two days, Virgil and Rae walked and drove around Hollywood and Fort Lauderdale, and went shopping at a downscale mall where Rae bought high-heeled sandals and Virgil got a T-shirt that showed a picture of a guitar with a caption that said, OLD MUSICIANS NEVER DIE, THEY JUST DECOMPOSE.

Late on the second day, Virgil picked up the Genesis DPV and the freshly filled tanks at Scuba City, and spent the evening rigging the backplate and wing so he'd be ready to dive. The day after that, with Rae driving the old Subaru, they headed south through the concrete canyons of Miami to the Florida Keys.

"I hope this piece of junk makes it that far," Rae said. "We're at 240,000 miles."

"I've been told that everything mechanical was rehabbed," Virgil said. "Shouldn't be a problem."

"Speaking of problems, did you bring your nine-millimeter problem solver?"

"I don't much believe in pistols," Virgil said.

"Lucas told me that," Rae said. "Besides, it's only Mafia killers we're dealing with."

The back of the Outback was stuffed with the scuba gear and a plastic suitcase with a change of clothing for both of them, in case they wound up staying overnight. As they went through Florida City, Rae slowed, searching roadside signs, and then pointed out the motel where Bob was killed.

"Best friend I ever had, or ever will have," Rae said.

"Sounds like a hell of a guy," Virgil said. "Lucas has lost a couple of friends, but he was really shook up by Bob. His wife was worried that he was falling into a clinical depression. He's had that trouble in the past."

"Not good," Rae said.

"Figuring out what we'd do about Bob, that pulled him out of it, I guess," Virgil said. "The last time I talked to his wife, she said he was back on solid ground."

"I'm not there yet," Rae said.

South of Florida City, they ran through scrubland, then onto causeways through mangrove swamps and eventually off the two-lane highway and onto four lanes into the town of Key Largo. They passed the entrance to John Pennekamp Coral Reef State Park, went on a few more minutes, and turned left at a sign that led down a coral road to Sunrise Scuba.

"One o'clock, right on time," Rae said. "Wonder if Matt and Marc are here . . ."

Regio and Lange pulled in two minutes later, as Virgil was looking around the scuba center's layout. The Sunrise consisted of a compact red-tile-roofed, white-painted concrete block building, a small parking lot surrounded by five-foot palms, an oversized swimming pool with a diving board at one end. Two tiger-striped cats, one gray, one red, lazed on the sidewalk outside the building's front door.

"Talked to anyone yet?" Regio asked.

"Just got here," Virgil said.

Lange: "The instructor's name is Julie Andrews. Not *the* Julie Andrews."

"Right."

INSIDE THE BUILDING they were met by a balding man with a hat line across his forehead—stark white on top, burned below—and heavy chest and shoulders. He checked the four of them and decided to talk to Lange: "You're the Willy Carter party?"

Lange poked a finger at Virgil: "He's Willy."

The man turned and shouted, "Julie, they're here."

A woman walked out of a back room, fiftyish, short, stocky, with cropped blond hair. She was wearing knee-length shorts and a coral-colored knit shirt with a Sunrise Scuba logo. She scanned the four of them and asked, "Carter?"

"That's me," Virgil said, half-raising a hand.

She looked him over—T-shirt, cargo shorts, worn tennis shoes, hair on his shoulders—and asked, "What's with . . ." She waved a hand at Lange, Regio, and Rae.

Virgil looked at Lange and said, "I thought you explained all of this?"

"The basics," Lange said. "Told them that we wanted to check your qualifications."

Virgil turned back to Andrews. "Here's the thing. I'm supposed to train this rich guy in the Bahamas. He wants to be sure I can do it, because he doesn't want to drown."

"Why didn't he hire us?" the bald man asked. "We can go to the Bahamas."

"'Cause he's my uncle," Virgil said. "My mom suggested that I could train him. He's skeptical. These two guys . . ." he tipped his head at Lange and Regio, ". . . are supposed to check out you, before you're checking out me."

"Seems a weird way to go about it," Andrews said.

"Well, it is," Virgil agreed. "I had a little legal trouble in Montana and my mom wants to get me away from my friends up there. She got Jerry to hire me."

"Jerry?"

"Uncle Jerry."

"What do Matt and Marc do . . ."

"They're, uh, Uncle Jerry's . . . uh . . ."

"Security team," Rae said. "Part of it, anyway."

Andrews looked at Regio and Lange and said, "Okay. I'll buy that. Still seems strange."

"You don't have to jump through your ass trying to figure out who we work for and why, you just gotta take Willy down to the bottom of the ocean and come back up and tell us if he's a bullshitter," Regio said, in a voice that approximated a snarl. "That's all. That's why we're renting your whole boat and your whole day and night."

The bald man said, "We don't take American Express."

Regio said, "We're paying cash. Up front."

The bald man, quickly: "Let me welcome you to Sunrise Scuba."

◆◆◆

REGIO PUT A thin stack of fifty-dollar bills on the counter and said to Virgil, "We've got rooms across the highway. Got one for you and Ally, since you'll be out after dark. No point in going back tonight."

Neither Regio nor Lange wanted to go on a boat ride. Rae inquired about things to do on Key Largo. After a few suggestions from Andrews, she decided that if the local Publix market was a high point, she might as well get some sun.

Sunrise Scuba ran a 36-foot dive boat good for twelve divers; they powered out of the marina at two o'clock, headed to the reefs that paralleled the Key Largo coastline. The water was smooth and warm, crossed by a dozen other boats leaving long, streaming white wakes behind.

"Picked the perfect day for this," Andrews said. The bald man, who was driving the boat, and whose name was Rolf, said, "We got a cold front coming, two days out. Looks like a rough one. That would have made things interesting."

"I'm happy with smooth," Rae said. "Catch a few rays . . . You guys brought some beer and sandwiches, right?"

"Do I look like a teetotaler?" Rolf asked.

VIRGIL WOULD DIVE his twinset all day, while Andrews dove smaller aluminum eighties.

"I'm here to work you out, not lift weights," she said to Virgil. "I gotta say, I got my doubts about you."

Rae: "So—how many college courses you took in customer service skills?"

Rae watched as Virgil suited up. "Like the Speedo, sweetheart," Rae said.

"So do I, actually," Virgil said, as he pulled the dive skins up his legs. "I almost bought one of the slingshots, but, you know, I'm kinda body-shy."

"Right," Rae said. To Andrews: "Willy's the least body-shy man you ever met. Not that he necessarily has anything to brag about."

Virgil: "Hey!"

"I didn't need to know any of that," Andrews said. She watched as Virgil set up his equipment. He'd drilled with equipment setup every morning for a month and could do it with his eyes closed, with his toes.

When he was ready, she asked, "Well, at least you checked your pressures first thing. I look for that. When do you start getting narced?"

Virgil said, "At about a hundred and ten, I'm aware it's in the background. At a hundred and thirty I'm there, but not a problem. I can do a hundred and fifty or a hundred and sixty and get the work done, but I'm narcing. Much deeper than that, I definitely need Trimix if I'm going to get anything done. I've been to two hundred and ten on air, but I was goofier than a shithouse mouse."

"As long as you know."

When they were both ready to go, Andrews said, "You lead,"

and Virgil slapped one hand over his mask and mouthpiece and stepped over the side into the warm green water.

"WHAT WAS ALL that about?" Rae asked Rolf, after Virgil and Andrews had gone under. "The narc thing."

"Nitrogen narcosis. You soak up too much nitrogen, you start getting high. If you don't know how to handle it, you can die. You ever had nitrous oxide at the dentist's? To relax you?"

"No, but I done whippits at the grocery store."

"Then you've been narced, or something close to it."

THE DAY WAS brilliantly, almost blindingly blue, with a mild breeze—almost nothing, but tasting of salt and smelling of seaweed—and some negligible current. As the boat swung gently on its hook, Rae got her sun and Rolf worked his iPad, complaining every once in a while about the weak-ass cell phone service. Virgil and Andrews surfaced after forty-five minutes, sat and talked in scuba code for a while, then they went down again.

When they came up the second time, they stopped for dinner and to watch the sun drop closer to the palms on Key Largo. After they'd shed their gear, Rae asked Andrews, "Well? What do you think?"

"He's not terrible," she said.

Rolf said to Virgil: "Jesus. You must be good. That's her second highest rating after, 'He's okay.'"

Virgil asked, "Am I still in the running for 'okay'?"

"We'll see after the night navigation," Andrews said.

◆◆◆

WITH THE SUN on the horizon, Andrews put on a fresh tank and they went down a third time; when they resurfaced, in total darkness, Rae asked, "Well?"

"He's okay," Andrews said.

"Yes!"

"But maybe a little reckless. I'm going to have to say that when we talk to your . . . supervisors."

"Why reckless?" Rolf asked.

"He cut his lights and did a blackout figure-eight around the tits. Stuck a light on his tanks so I could follow him."

"Yeah, that's . . . not totally recommended," Rolf said. He asked Virgil, "You hit anything?"

"Not a thing," Virgil said. "But I'm the tiniest bit tired. I haven't done this for a while and I got some leg cramps. Hurt like hell. But the Genesis—I love the Genesis more than sex. I mean, except with sex with Ally, when she does that reverse cowgirl thing . . ."

"Shut up," Rae said. "Let's get back."

REGIO AND LANGE were waiting at the marina as Rolf eased the boat into its slip. Andrews gave her report: "He's as good as they come. But reckless."

She told them about the figure-eight navigation in the dark. "You won't want to do that with Jerry," Regio told Virgil. "He drowns, I'm out of a job."

"There's always room for a rent-a-goon in Vegas," Virgil said.

"That's really funny," Regio said, with a snake-like stare.

Across the street at Morgan's Inn, Lange patted Virgil on the back. "That was everything we needed to know, pal. Including the figure-eight. She seemed damn impressed."

"Like I told you, I can dive," Virgil said. "I don't do overheads, but I'll do anything else you got."

"So when are we doing it?" Rae asked.

"We're thinking tomorrow night, at least for a trial run," Regio said. "It's supposed to be quiet water out there. Like Rolf was saying, there's a cold front coming, and it'll get rougher when that goes through."

"Bring the cash," Virgil said. "Lots of cash."

Regio smiled. "We will do that. And we've got a few things for you to look at."

Inside their room, they had two oval-shaped lift bags of two hundred pounds lift capacity each, two black torpedo-shaped mesh bags to hold the drug containers, and two pen-sized waterproof LED flashlights with sliding hoods.

"You need to figure out how to hook all this up to your equipment," Lange said. "When it's time to pick you up, you'll be right on the surface and you hit us with a hooded flashlight. It's bright, but with the hood pushed out, nobody will see it but us. We'll drift up to you, you hook the ladder, you get out of your plate and wing and we'll pull it aboard with the tanks. You come up the ladder, we'll help you if you need it. Then we'll all be there for the lift bag, if it's got anything in it."

"That's a lot of weight," Virgil said. "The gear weighs close to a hundred pounds by itself, and that's before the lift bags, and there'll be drag from the boat."

"We'll have three guys on board to do the lifting."

"Plus me," Rae said.

"Plus Ally," Lange said.

Virgil said, "Okay. That should work."

Regio handed Virgil a thick gray watch and a thin white booklet: "This is your GPS watch. Good to three hundred feet, already been tested. You need to figure it out with the instruction book. We'll give you the exact GPS coordinates for the pickup spot."

Rae: "And you've got all these numbers, this GPS shit, figured out?"

"Down to a couple of yards," Regio said. "The last thing we need is to have Willy pick up a million bucks' worth of dope and then not be able to find him."

Rae to Virgil: "You know how to read all this shit?"

"Sure. Can't drive a boat without it," Virgil said.

She shook her head. "I dunno. You can't make change for a one."

Virgil asked Regio, "Once I'm in the zone, how do I find the shit? If the Coast Guard couldn't find it in six months . . ."

"We'll explain that to you when we're on the boat. You just figure out the watch."

When Virgil and Rae were alone in the motel room, Rae put a finger to her lips and moved close to Virgil's ear. "They rented the room. Might be listening."

Virgil nodded and said, aloud, "Let's get showers and change clothes and see if we can sneak away from those motherfuckers and get something to eat. I'll break some goodies out of the car."

"There's that shrimp place . . . we could walk there in five minutes."

"Let's go."

✦✦✦

THEY PUT ON cotton jackets and were out the door in twenty min-utes, walking slow. Halfway to the shrimp restaurant, with no sign of either Regio or Lange, Virgil pulled Rae into the parking lot next to a plumber's shop and fired up a joint and handed it to her. "This is our excuse for stopping, if anyone's watching," he whis-pered. He got on his phone and called Lucas. "We're doing it to-morrow. Are you set?"

Lucas: "We've been ready for a week. I'm not getting cold feet, exactly, but they're getting cool. Are you sure you're up for this?"

"I am. The biggest problem would be if they decide to take what I find and kill me," Virgil said. "When I surface, I'll be more or less helpless. Rae will be on the boat, she made that clear, and she'll have that little nine stuck inside the bottom of her leggings. If anything funny starts, we'll have that."

"If you want to back away, nobody would blame you," Lucas said. "The people who know about it figure you for balls like wa-termelons. I know better, but I'm a little worried."

"Hey. I'm good. Watch for a tail when we split up tomorrow."

"We are. Haven't seen anyone watching you other than Regio and Lange. We've seen Cattaneo on a sailboat in Hollywood, we think that might be where you're going."

"That sounds right. Sailboat will be moving slow, which is nor-mal. In the dark, nobody would see me going over the side, or coming back on. So . . ."

"Easy does it," Lucas said.

"Are you still in Hollywood? You personally? Right now?"

"No. We're across the highway from you," Lucas said. "Your two guys walked out three or four minutes before you. It looks like they're headed for the same place you are. There's not much else up there."

"They might have been listening to us; they rented the room, there could be a bug, so . . . don't call."

VIRGIL HANDED THE phone back to Rae, who turned it off and dropped it in her jacket pocket. Virgil took a joint from her and said, "Sweet authenticity."

Virgil took a drag, blew the smoke into Rae's hair and passed it. She took a drag, blew the smoke into Virgil's hair. They did that one more time each, then dropped the joint and Virgil smashed it into the gravel.

Regio and Lange were sitting in a two-person booth when they arrived at the shrimp place. Virgil lifted a hand when he saw them, and drifted over. "Place is a little sketchy."

Regio laughed and said, "So you fit right in."

Lange sniffed: "You gotta go easy with the weed, man. You gotta be straight tomorrow."

"I don't touch it before a dive," Virgil said. Rae had taken another booth. Virgil ambled away from the two men, sat down. They ate a couple of pounds of shrimp and drank four margaritas between them, and wandered out the door while Regio and Lange were still eating.

"If they didn't buy that," Virgil said, "we're cooked. Because we shoulda gotten an Academy Award."

◆◆◆

BACK AT THE motel room, Virgil looked at the king-sized bed and whispered, "I can take the floor if that would make you happier."

"You're going to need your sleep for tomorrow night," Rae whispered back. "I don't figure you'll be coming on to me at this point and rape doesn't seem to be your style."

"You're right and you're right. Not that you don't have a nice . . . mmm . . ."

Rae rolled her eyes. "We won't be spooning, either."

"Of course not," Virgil said.

Which didn't mean he wouldn't wake up a few times with spontaneous erections; he'd been away from Frankie for two weeks and he could feel the heat coming off Rae's body. The second time, he heard Rae quietly laugh, but then they both went back to sleep. They woke together in the morning and Rae stretched and said, "See? No harm, no foul."

She was wearing black dancer's leggings and a half top, which revealed much of her personal terrain.

Virgil grumbled, "Fuckin' Bob must've been a fuckin' saint, to be traveling around with you and nothing's going on."

"No, he wasn't. We were like brother and sister, sorta."

"Well, I'm not your brother. I'm committed. Got new twins. Got an old lady I'm in love with. But Jesus, Rae, you . . ."

"Hush up."

THEY MET REGIO and Lange in the parking lot and Lange said, "We'll come by your place this afternoon and pick you up. What time?"

"Depends on how far we have to drive to get to the boat, and how far the boat is from the drop spot. I'll let you figure that out," Virgil said. "We don't want to go out too late—we need to get out there after dark, but not way dark, just dark enough that nobody will see me going over the side. It'd be good if there were still some boats on the water. Their screws will confuse Coast Guard sonar, if there is any sonar watching the dive zone."

"Gets dark around six . . ."

"Sundown is a few minutes before six o'clock," Virgil said. "I looked it up. Let's say we want to be cruising past the drop-off spot between six-thirty and seven."

Regio nodded: "We'll pick you up at four o'clock. Be ready."

"We'll stop and refill my tanks on the way back to the apartment," Virgil said. "I want to get a nap if I can, before we go out."

"We're on. For sure. The thing you gotta do, is figure how to rig up all that gear so you don't get all tangled up in it. That was a problem . . . in the past."

FROM THE CAR, Virgil called Lucas and filled him in. "If we're going past the drop-off at six-thirty, and they're picking us up at four, that means the boat's got to be close. You've still got the tracker on their Lexus?"

"We do. We're watching them now."

"If they find it, I could be fucked," Virgil said.

"They won't find it. I can guarantee that."

"And what do you do if they show up with a different vehicle? One you can't track?"

"We're talking about that," Lucas said.

On the way north, off the Keys and headed for the scuba center, Rae said, "I'm starting to pucker."

"I didn't think good-looking women had anything to pucker."

"You'd be wrong about that," Rae said. "The thing is, I sorta like the feeling."

Virgil glanced at her, smiled: "So do I. So does Lucas."

"So did Bob," Rae said.

NINETEEN

MICHAEL BEHAN, JACK Cattaneo, Marc Regio, and Matt Lange met at Behan's waterfront condo and Behan opened with, "This Willy guy—he can do it?"

"That's what the diver chick said," Lange said.

"And you think he's legit?"

"I do," Regio said. "Matt's a little nervous about him."

Cattaneo asked, "Why?"

"Can't really tell you why," Lange said. "You've talked to him, Jack. He comes across as this stoner, lazy do-nothing slacker, but then, all of a sudden, he seems a little too . . . smart. A little too driven. He opens his mouth and all this technical stuff comes out."

"But only about diving," Regio said.

Lange: "That's true. Only about diving. He seems to have trouble with his cell phone."

Behan and Cattaneo looked at Lange for a couple beats, then Cattaneo asked, "You nervous enough to pull the plug?"

"If it was a small deal, I might pull it. But the guy's a hell of a diver, and . . . I don't know. This chick he's with, she's no kind of cop, I promise you that. She's right out of the ghetto. So . . ."

Behan considered that, turning to look out the oceanside windows, scratched his ass once, turned back, and said, "That shit's already been down there way too long. Could be silting over, could be gone. That'd be a hell of a hit. Other than you being nervous, he looks good?"

Lange nodded.

Behan looked at Cattaneo. "Jack?"

"I say we go with him. There's enough shit down there to make everybody in the organization a rich man. And I'll be on the boat. That's what I think: I'm sure enough that I'll be on the boat."

"The least we can do is fuck him out of his money," Regio said.

Behan smiled and said, "I like the way you think. But. If he brings up anything, it's not going to be much. How many can he handle at a time? Three? Four? Even with the lift bags, I can't see him doing more than that. Underwater? Swimming a half mile? So if he brings up anything, we pay him. Because we'll need him for the other tubes. This is a long-term operation. Might be the first of a bunch of operations."

"Jaquell brought up six in one load," Lange said.

"Because she knew exactly where they were, to the foot, and she was going straight up and down. She had it easy. Doing what we're talking about . . . using this DPV thing from a half mile away, maybe she could do it, maybe not, but she wouldn't be bringing up six," Cattaneo said.

"Okay. So we pay him," Regio said.

"Which brings up another problem," Cattaneo said. "Say he brings up three tubes, and we pay him what? More than twenty grand in cash? If they're the kind of people we think they are, ten grand goes up their noses the first night, and then they start splashing money around town. He could get noticed."

"This chick, Ally, seems to be the brains of their operation," Regio said. "She has Willy under her thumb. We'll have a conversation with her. Make the point that if his behavior pulls in any cops, his next dive will be in the Everglades."

Behan said, "Jack: the boat's ready?"

"It's perfect. Our vulnerable spot would be if the Coast Guard jumped us exactly during the pickup. That won't happen, because we'd see them coming on the radar. If we see them coming, we slow down, they board us, we drift until they're gone and we go on to the pickup," Cattaneo said. "If they board us and tell us to follow them into port, we leave Willy in the ocean. He sinks the cans, marks the exact GPS coordinates and then uses this DPV thing to pull him to the beach and we pick him up there."

"He knows this is the plan?"

"Not yet. We'll explain it to him tomorrow," Cattaneo said. "When he's on the boat."

"What if they board after the pickup? Coming into the marina?" Behan asked.

"That's trickier," Cattaneo said, "But it won't be like the last time. There's a bow stateroom, one narrow bed, and we've filled it up with dive gear, tools, a bicycle, like we're using it for storage. The bed's on an eighteen-inch platform, screwed to the hull, with a hollow space underneath. When the tubes come over the side, we run them to the bow, stick them under the bed. When they're all in there, we screw the platform back down. We've rehearsed it: we can get the bed screwed down and the junk tossed in the cabin in four or five minutes. If we have five more minutes, all the scuba gear will be stowed on top of it. But I don't think any of this will be necessary. I've gone up to Boca Raton a half dozen times since Christmas and nobody ever looked at me. Whoever heard of a drug runner in a slow boat?"

Behan looked out at the ocean for a while, then turned, spread his arms, and said, "Let's do it, guys. I don't believe it'll ever get better than this."

ANDRES DEVLIN WAS such an average-looking black man that he might not be noticed at a Klan meeting. He was five-eleven with close-cropped hair, was wearing a dark blue T-shirt, black jeans, Nikes, and a Knicks ball cap. One distinctive feature, not visible from the front, was a thin scar that crossed his back at the level of the shirt collar, the product of RPG shrapnel that he'd picked up in Syria.

He sat next to Lucas in the rented Volvo and said, "I couldn't do what Virgil's doing. You know what happens when I get in a swimming pool? I sink. I'm told I'm too dense to float."

"Some fat does help, I've heard," Lucas said. "The only pools I get in have ice on the top."

"Never understood hockey," Devlin said. "You gotta be born further north than I was."

Devlin was from Normal, Illinois, and had gone to college at Purdue. Purdue had a hockey club, rather than a full-blown team, he said, and he'd never gone to a game. "You gotta drive all over the countryside to see them play. I'd rather watch wrestling."

"You have low taste in sports," Lucas said. "Though I have a friend who was a big-time college wrestler at Minnesota. And of course, Bob . . ."

"Yeah. Bob." They thought about Bob for a moment.

They'd been tracking the Mafia guys for more than a month, along with two selected FBI agents, and were running out of conversational gambits. On this day, Lucas had opened the talk with a couple of minutes of vulgar, detailed speculation about why Devlin wasn't all over Rae, since they were both marshals and stationed at the same facility, and Devlin had asked, "Why should I be? Because we're both black?"

"Because she's . . . Rae," Lucas said. "You even look at her?"

"Fuck you. Of course I looked at her and she's definitely Rae," Devlin said. "But, you know, I have a taste for those Mississippi blondes."

"Blondes are good," Lucas said. "You get their clothes off and they look really, really naked. Of course, the way young women get around with their razors these days . . ."

"You think black women don't shave a little off the top?"

"I don't really . . . um . . ."

Devlin snorted and said, "I'm just fucking with you, man. But Rae . . . Rae's out of my league. I got a degree in mechanical engineering, for Christ's sake. I fix old motorboats and Hammond organs. She's about art and literature and all that."

"Offer to change her oil," Lucas said. "Even artists need regular maintenance."

DEVLIN SAT UP. "Here we go."

Lucas got on a handset and said, "We've got Lange and Regio."

"We see them. We'll wait for Cattaneo."

The three were walking out of Behan's condo. Lucas and Devlin were two blocks away, watching.

"Want to go after them?" Devlin asked.

Lucas considered it, then got back on the handset to the FBI agents in a second car, who were two blocks on the other side of the condo. "Let them go. Track them on the slates."

"You sure, boss man?" the surveillance agent asked.

"Yes. Give them at least five minutes before you pull out. If anyone is watching their backs, that'll be enough of an interval. We'll pick them up later."

Devlin was typing on an iPad, noting the time and character of the surveillance for a later formal report, along with Lucas's decision not to try a close tail.

Lucas was looking at an iPad-type device that showed Regio's Lexus on one screen, and Cattaneo's on another. "I think they're all headed back to their apartments. We'll pick them up at Virgil's place in . . . two hours."

Devlin made a note on his draft of the day's activities.

RAE WAS STARTING to freak, pacing around the apartment. "I could do a joint for real," she said.

Virgil was working out the various tethers for the scuba gear. He would keep the lift and cargo bags rolled and tied to his backplate until he needed them; that was simple enough. Less simple would be attaching tethers once the cargo bags were full of dope canisters, and he was towing the bags while trying to control the DPV, which would be on a different set of tethers. If he had trouble untangling things, working with flashlights in pitch blackness a hundred and fifty feet down, then he had serious trouble.

So he was carefully packing the tethers, as though he were packing a parachute, taking his time with it. To Rae, he said, "If it'd help, go for it. More authenticity for the goon squad."

"Ah, it wouldn't help," she said. Then, after a minute, "What's it like down there, in the night? When you get way down?"

Virgil sat back on his heels, the tethers still in his hands. "Way down isn't much different than being fifteen feet down, after dark, except for getting narced," Virgil said. "It's like instrument flying through clouds in a plane. You have instruments, you believe them, even if your mind tells you they're wrong. I'll stay on the surface after I jump off the boat and navigate over to the GPS spot they give me. When I'm there, I'll go straight down. Coming back, I'll have to go through a decompression regime. I'll be dragging lift bags, and moving slow, coming back up to the pickup spot at an angle, to decompress. I'll be looking at my dive computer the whole way. It'll tell me how deep I need to stay, each step, to decompress."

"The thought scares the heck out of me," Rae said. "I've jumped out of airplanes, but I wouldn't do this . . ."

"It's actually kind of restful when you get used to it. Peaceful."

"Yeah. Like being dead." Rae looked at her watch. "Two o'clock. You almost done there?"

"I *am* done. All I'm missing is the information they'll give us on the boat." He stood up and looked at the litter of gear on the floor. "Let's bag it. I need that nap."

Virgil got an hour. He got up and they dressed, Rae in a long-sleeved black cotton top, black jeans, a little loose down the legs, and Salomon trail runners. She pulled an elastic ankle support over her right ankle, and slipped a nine-millimeter Sig 938 under the elastic band and jumped up and down a few times to make sure it was secure.

"Doesn't even feel like much," she said. "Not gonna be a fast-draw, though."

"Don't bump into anything and make a clank sound," Virgil said.

LANGE AND REGIO showed up early, wearing head-to-toe nylon sailing pants and shirts, and helped carry the gear down to a different vehicle, a Suburban. After they'd loaded the scuba equipment, Virgil climbed into the backseat and said, "New wheels, huh? I'd like to get me one of these. Travel all over the country, you could sleep in the back, you know, at the Walmarts, never have to pay a motel bill . . ."

"You bring us enough of that stuff up, you won't have to worry about paying for motels," Regio said over his shoulder.

Rae: "That's what I'm talking about. Hot showers, big TV, king-sized bed."

Lange: "Mini-bar . . ."

"Oh, yeah."

LUCAS AND DEVLIN watched them loading the Suburban, and Devlin said, "Man, I hope they don't do anything tricky. Wonder why they changed cars? Christ, without the tracker . . . They could spot us if they start dragging us through the back streets."

"Might be something simple—all that scuba gear plus four people. Maybe the Lexus is a little tight."

Lucas got on the handset to tell the feds about the change in vehicles. The feds had tracked Cattaneo first to his condo, and then, a half hour later, to his sailboat at an Intracoastal marina south of Hollywood. He was getting ready to move it, they said. Lucas had called them in, to help track Regio and Lange. "We'll try to get you in front of them until we figure out where they're going," he told them. "If they're headed toward the boat, we'll back way off."

"Got it."

The Suburban's turn signal came on and the truck made a U-turn and headed toward Lucas and Devlin. They both ducked down and a minute later the Suburban went past, and after another hundred yards, made a left turn.

"Shit, they're going to drag us through the neighborhoods," Devlin said. Lucas, at the wheel, got the Pathfinder going and followed, but instead of making the left turn, looked down the street and saw the Suburban make the next right, to run parallel to Lucas and Devlin, but one street over.

"That's what they're doing," Lucas said. He got on the handset. "They're looking for a tail, gotta be careful, guys. They're one street north of Hollywood, headed east, get out in front if you can."

They hardly saw the Suburban over the next fifteen minutes, but it gradually became clear that they were getting closer and closer to Cattaneo's sailboat. "Gotta be the boat," the feds called. "Usual spots?"

"Usual spots, let's go, don't try to track them anymore. We gotta get there first."

◆◆◆

AFTER DRAGGING DOWN narrow streets and through yellow lights, Virgil said, "I think we're clean, guys."

Regio grunted and said, "Looks like."

He nevertheless continued a back-street route down to the Intracoastal, where they parked a couple of hundred feet from Cattaneo's chunky white sailboat. Virgil carried the tanks and Regio and Lange carried the two gear bags down to the boat.

"Right on time," Cattaneo said. He checked Virgil: "You ready, Willy?"

"That's why I'm here," Virgil said. "We got things to talk about. I need GPS numbers, coordinates, I need to know what tricky thing I've got to do to find the cans."

"We got time to talk," Cattaneo said. "Get everything down below and out of sight. I want to be the only one visible as we're going out through the cut."

"Got two hours before it gets dark," Virgil said.

"Going to take a while to get there at four knots," Cattaneo said. "We've got this nailed down. Don't worry about it."

Rae to Virgil: "You know when I said I was getting puckered up? I'll tell you what, cracker: right now, I couldn't poop poppy seeds."

FROM ACROSS THE Intracoastal, Lucas, Devlin, and the FBI team watched the boat from a condo parking lot. "They're doing it," Devlin said. "It's all going down."

CHAPTER

TWENTY

LANGE STAYED IN the cockpit with Cattaneo as they cast off, then eased the boat into the Intracoastal and motored north toward the Port Everglades cut into the Atlantic. The boat rode slowly and smoothly with a southerly breeze not strong enough to create even a light chop on the waterway.

Virgil could talk to Cattaneo through the open hatchway and as they passed under a bridge, asked, "When do we get there?"

"Around six-thirty," he said. "We've got to go through one drawbridge and then I'll give the wheel to Matt and we'll talk."

"We're going to motor the whole way?"

"Yes."

Rae was poking around the interior of the cabin and said, "This is really neat. I've never been on, like, a yacht. It's like an RV, but way better."

"Until you get in rough water," Regio said. "It's quiet today, so that's not a problem. But if you start getting queasy . . . If you have to hurl, do it in the sink, or over the side."

◈◈◈

THEY HAD TO wait a few minutes at a drawbridge, then Cattaneo steered it through, gave the wheel to Lange, and dropped down into the cabin. The cabin was fifteen feet long, with two parallel benches, each six feet long, facing each other and covered with beige Naugahyde cushions. The deck was wood strip, the walls were white fiberglass.

"Everybody sit down," Cattaneo said. "Now, Willy. The cans will be in a straight line on the bottom, the line's only about a half mile long. They were dropped out of a chute over the side of a moving reefer ship that had stopped at Port Everglades and was heading north to Norfolk."

Virgil: "They stopped? Wasn't that a big risk?"

"No. The ship was carrying bananas inside containers in a temperature-controlled hold. Our stuff was in a little access hatch under the floor of the hold, between the floor and the hull. There was a stack of Jersey-bound containers sitting on top of it. Too much for the inspectors to move without it being a major pain in the ass. Once the Florida containers were pulled out, and the ship was underway again, the containers were moved and our stuff pulled out from below and loaded into the chute."

Virgil: "Cool."

"We have an exact GPS location for both the beginning and end of the string. Our first diver had no problem finding the cans, but then, we were able to drop her right on top of them. You're going to have to get there yourself."

"I can do that. I'm surprised the Coast Guard didn't find them, though."

"The Coast Guard was mostly looking in the wrong place. The string is right on the edge of where they were searching and they are very hard to see, unless you have one of these." He held up what looked like an oversized remote control for a television, except that it had no visible buttons and did have three rubber arm straps and a parachute-cord hand-loop.

"You turn this on by slamming the wand forward." He snapped the wand forward in his hand and a red LED light blinked at the top; the blinks continued for ten seconds or so, then turned off. "It's transmitting a low-frequency sound—most people can't hear it—that will be picked up by the cans. That will turn on bright white LEDs on the outside of the cans. They'll blink for a minute or so, then turn off. You'll need another shake to turn them on again. Our first diver had no trouble seeing the LEDs, but then, that was a long time ago. There may be more silt on them now."

He handed the wand to Virgil: it weighed perhaps two pounds, and had three rubber straps meant to snap around a forearm or ankle, as well as another hand tether in case it was dropped.

"High-tech," Virgil said. "Must have cost a fortune." He snapped the wand forward, and the red indicator light started blinking.

"All of this—the scuba gear, the high-tech, even this boat—it's all chump change compared to what's down there on the bottom," Cattaneo said. "Oh. I need to show you this."

He walked to the end of the cabin, opened a refrigerator, and pulled out a package of frozen green peas. The package had been opened and resealed. He pulled open a resealing strip, and extracted three bricks of cash, fifty-dollar bills. "Forty grand. We wanted to be sure we had enough to cover your bill. This is your money, right here and now—or right after you get back to the boat."

Rae: "Makes my little heart go pitter-patter."

LANGE CALLED DOWN, "We're coming in to Port Everglades."

"I'm going back up, y'all stay down until we're out on the ocean," Cattaneo said.

"Y'all," Rae said.

"My family came from southern Italy," Cattaneo said, as he climbed the ladder to the cockpit.

THEY COULDN'T SEE much through the cabin's narrow portholes, but did see the lights of the buildings at Port Everglades as they made the turn into the Atlantic. Shortly after the turn, they began rolling, only slightly, and then, after ten minutes, they came around to the north again, and the boat settled down.

Cattaneo, at the wheel, called down to Virgil, "We're almost exactly an hour and a half out. Anytime you think you want to get into your wet suit . . ."

"I'll do that when we're twenty minutes out," Virgil said. "Be too hot before that."

"Whatever you say. I want you guys to stay below for another half hour or so, until we get away from Port Everglades and farther out. Then you can all come up."

✦✦✦

A HALF HOUR later, the sun was sinking below the coastal condos, and Virgil, Rae, Regio, and Lange went up on top to sit in the cockpit with Cattaneo. "Pretty," Rae said. "The lights."

"I was never much for the water until I got this boat," Cattaneo said. "I'm still not much for sailing—too fussy for me. But I like the quiet. On the other boat, the Mako, you always had engine noise. This boat's got a power plant about the size of my lawnmower, so . . . it's peaceful. You can think out here. My wife likes it."

Thirty minutes later, in near darkness, Cattaneo said, "Okay, Willy, you said twenty minutes to get loaded up. We're thirty minutes out. Anytime you want to get started . . . you don't want to be late."

THEY'D STOWED THE gear in a front cabin, and Regio and Lange went below with Virgil to pull it out, while Rae stayed on top with Cattaneo.

Virgil got into his Speedo, then the wet suit, which was tight as a full-body girdle, as it should be. With the suit on, he put his dive computer on his right wrist and the GPS watch on the left. Two separate packs of lift and cargo bags, rolled tight, were fixed to his backplate with fat rubber binders. The locator wand went on his right forearm above the dive computer. Flashlights and a Trilobite cutter were fastened to D rings on the plate and the dive knife that Lange had insisted he buy went on his left thigh. Regio and Lange carried his plate and tanks out to the deck, while Virgil followed with his mask and fins.

Rae asked, "You okay, babe?" She clutched Virgil's upper arm and squeezed.

"Yup. I'm good."

Cattaneo said, "We're twelve minutes out. When we get close I'm going to back off the engines. I'll kill them one second before you go overboard and restart about three or four seconds later. Nobody'll pick that up, even if they're listening for us. I'll do something like that when we pick you up. You don't have to worry about the prop."

"Sounds good. I'll have the lift bag neutrally buoyant, and a twenty-foot line tied to my waist belt. As soon as I'm aboard, grab the line and pull it in. Stay off the engine. We don't want to put a lot of stress on the bags and we don't want them windmilling."

"Got it," Cattaneo said.

Regio to Rae: "I'm starting to pucker up myself. This nighttime shit is getting real."

Virgil turned on his air, and with Lange's help, pulled on the backplate and wing with the tanks. He loosened the shoulder straps a bit, checked to make sure he could reach over his shoulder to both valve knobs, tightened the waist and crotch straps, pumped some air into the wing, stuck the mouthpiece in his mouth, and took a few breaths, then pulled it and said, "We're good to go."

"Three minutes," Cattaneo said, looking at the screen on his navigation station. "We're right on line."

Virgil went through a last rapid check of all the equipment, and when Cattaneo said, "One minute," Rae stepped up to Virgil and kissed him on the mouth: "You be cool, babe."

"Yeah, yeah, yeah . . ."

✦✦✦

AT THIRTY SECONDS, Regio and Lange helped Virgil up on the rail on the eastern side of the boat and held him there, looking out at the ocean and away from the beach. Virgil could see lights of boats well ahead, and well behind them, but only three or four, total. Not much close-by traffic after dark . . .

Cattaneo: "Ten seconds. I'm going to cut the engine in eight, seven, six, five, four, three, two, it's off."

Holding the Genesis DPV in his hands, like an extra-long submarine sandwich, Virgil tucked his chin and stepped over the side and into the dark water. The boat slipped silently away, and Virgil bobbed on the surface like a cork. A moment later, the boat's engine fired, and Rae called quietly, "Careful, babe."

Virgil checked the gear again. Everything seemed good and tight, and he looked at his dive computer, on which he'd gone to the compass screen. They'd put him in the water at a point where he had to navigate directly west to the dive location. He steadied his arm as he rode up and down in the low rollers, picked out a brightly lit condo on the coast that was due west, turned on the Genesis.

At what he and Julie Andrews, the Sunrise Scuba instructor, had figured was about two hundred feet per minute, Virgil settled in to drive, the Genesis just below the surface, his head just above. The prop of the Genesis wanted to pull him off line, so he had to continually correct, but it wasn't a problem, as long as he could see the condo.

Ten minutes. Eleven. Twelve. He cut the DPV's engine, gave

the wing a shot of air to lift him a bit higher, and looked around. No boats nearby.

He checked the GPS watch, did some numbers in his head. He was a bit north of where he needed to be and still a couple of hundred feet east. He powered up the Genesis, counting to himself, then cut the engine. According to the GPS watch, he was within fifteen meters of his precise drop spot. The coastal lights were brilliant to the west. He could see nothing either north or south, although he could see what he thought were freighter lights well to the east.

He kicked to the exact drop spot, aware that the GPS was probably not as precise as he was trying to be. When he got there, he took a minute to relax and recalculate. The heroin cans should be almost straight beneath him. If there were no current, he'd be dropping about a hundred feet north of the south end of the drop string. No GPS underwater, so he had to hope he was close.

When he was cool, he checked the binders on the lift bags, then began releasing air from his wing. He dropped slowly at first, and then more quickly. He put quick shots of air into the wing to slow the descent, watching his dive computer as he dropped. He could feel no current, but then, he wouldn't feel much, because he was fundamentally part of it.

He dropped past a hundred feet and a hundred and ten, where he often began to feel the first soft effects of nitrogen narcosis. He felt fine, nothing unusual. At a hundred and thirty, he began to feel it, a hint of light-headedness. A moment later, he slowed his descent and hovered, pulled a flashlight and pointed it down, dropped a bit, dropped a bit more, and the muddy bottom showed up as a near-featureless gray plain beneath him. He dropped until he was at the bottom, then hovered again. He put the flashlight away, brought up his arm with the attached magic wand, and snapped it forward. No red light.

Thinking: *Shit.*

Shook it harder, the red LED blinked at him and he turned to scan his surroundings. To his left, he saw a tiny light. He went that way, the light growing brighter as he approached. Then he saw another light, and a third.

He reached the first light, swept his gloved hand over it, stirring up sediment, but revealing the black plastic can sitting on the ocean floor. The can had two plastic straps around it: one held a diver's weight tight to the can, while the other held a square box, which powered a band of brilliant LED lights.

All right . . . Enough junk to kill a hundred junkies, but still, a thrill to find it, a feeling of accomplishment, there in the dark at the bottom of the Atlantic Ocean . . .

He stripped one of the lift bags from his plate, separated the actual lifting bag from the cargo bag, and stuffed the first of the cans in the cargo bag. He gave the lift bag a shot of air, and it rose gently above him, held down by the weight of the cargo bag. He dragged the bag to the second can, retrieved it, saw two more lights beyond it. He gave the lift bag another shot of air, retrieved the third and fourth cans, and saw two more. Another shot of the air to the lift bag, lightening the load he had to move himself.

He was working his way to the south end of the drop string. When he'd retrieved the fifth can, he saw two more, but the cargo bag would only take one. The lift bag was now straining hard toward the surface, held down by the weight of the loaded cargo bag.

He began to untie the second lift bag roll, but he fumbled it, and fumbled it again—and recognized the fumbles. He checked the computer: he'd been down for sixteen minutes and was getting narced. What to do: he thought it over, the thoughts coming slowly, like the water drops on a turned-off shower head. A bit cloudy, he decided, but no more than that. He did a number puzzle: $(1 + 2) \times 3$. Answer, nine. Or is it seven? No, nine. The brackets made the difference. Sometimes, his mental puzzles didn't have them, sometimes they did. With brackets, the answer was definitely nine. Okay. Took eight seconds, but that wasn't too bad.

He grabbed the seventh can, stuffed it in the second lift bag, saw no more. Looked at his compass, headed north, finning, staying in touch with the bottom, the Genesis dangling from its tethers. Shook the magic wand. No lights. Farther north. Shook it again, and saw lights to his right. The cans were right there, in a string, twenty or thirty feet apart, and he stuffed the eighth, ninth, tenth, and eleventh cans.

$(1 + 2) \times 3$. What? Nine? Maybe twenty seconds this time. He checked his down-time. He'd been on the bottom for almost twenty-five minutes. Time to go.

The lift bags were like hot-air balloons, with the cargo bags hanging below. As with hot-air balloons, the bottom end of the lift bag was open, to allow air to be shot inside. When filled with air, the bags would begin to rise, lifting the cargo bags, like the baskets below a hot-air balloon.

Virgil gave the lift bags a shot of air, until they began to gently ascend, lifting the cargo bags off the bottom. He held on to their tethers, and let them pull him. They rose easily, and then more quickly. There were air-release valves operated by cables on each of the bags, and he released some air to slow the ascent.

At sixty feet, he stopped, waited more or less a minute, to

decompress, until his computer told him he could continue up. His brain was clearing now, $(1 + 2) \times 3$ took only a second.

Instead of ascending directly, he started a diagonal ascent to the east, using the Genesis and towing the bags, which would allow him to move toward the pickup point, and, at the same time, hit his decompression targets—a minute at fifty feet, three minutes at forty, a bit longer each ten feet or so.

The computer knew . . .

Something bumped his leg, hard; he tensed. Dolphin? Shark? Ray?

No. The cargo bags, twisting beside him. The lift bags were a problem. The bottom openings were small, but he couldn't pull them so hard that they flattened and dumped air. If they did that, the cargo bags would be a three-hundred-pound anchor pulling him down.

He experimented, watching them in the wide-beam flashlight, decided he could safely tow them at about fifty feet a minute. At that rate, it would take him almost an hour to get back to the pickup point. He had enough air, and he needed to stay under a little more than fifty minutes to decompress, at a variety of different levels, slowly ascending. Nothing to do but take care, watch the computer, switch every half minute or so between the decompression numbers and the compass . . . slow and easy was the path of righteousness.

TETHERED TO THE Genesis, he floated at a slow swimming speed through the dark, nothing but himself, the glow of the computer and the hum of the Genesis to prove he was alive.

At the estimated pickup, he checked the computer for his decompression status, was told that he was good to surface. He did, checked the GPS watch, found he was a few hundred feet off. He carefully made his way toward the pickup spot, much slower now, the top of the lift bags just kissing the surface. When he was at the pickup spot, he hung there, watching far-off boat lights, and one fast-moving vessel that passed him well toward the brilliantly lit coast.

He had thirty minutes to wait; he did it on the surface, sitting wrapped in the wing almost like a rocking chair. His body was still cool from the deep dive, but getting warmer. Ten minutes before the pickup, he started looking for lights toward the north. At five minutes, he saw the first of the lights, then picked up another. A bright light winked at him, as agreed.

He took the hooded flashlight from its case and shined it toward the boat. The sailboat made a small correction, until it looked like it would run over him.

Virgil thought: This was too fuckin' easy. He pulled off his fins and let them dangle from his hand.

The boat slowed until it was barely moving, but Virgil could still hear the prop. Somebody on board shone the light on the boarding ladder and the prop noise stopped and Virgil caught the barely moving ladder with one hand and held up the fins with the other, and yelled, "Fins!"

The fins were taken and he unbuckled from the backplate and he shouted, "Don't dump the lift bags, don't dump the bags," and the vest and tanks were pulled over the rail and on board, Regio, Lange, and Rae all lifting. He started climbing the ladder; both arms were grabbed and he was hauled unceremoniously over the side like a large rubber billfish, and dumped butt-first on the deck.

He could hear Cattaneo chanting, "Get the lines, get the lines," and then Regio, "I got 'em, I got 'em," and the two orange lift bags came over the side, and then, with Regio and Lange and Rae all lifting, straining, the cargo bags came over the rail, one at a time, and Cattaneo was calling, "We good? I'm firing it up," and Regio calling back, "We're good, let's move," and then Lange, "Man! We are way more than good! *Way* more than good."

Virgil pulled off his face mask as the engine started, and then Cattaneo was standing over him. "Willy! Willy! You're a rich man, Willy. You're a rich man!"

Virgil said, "What?"

Rae squatted next to him and put her arm around his neck and she said, "I knew you were good, but I didn't think you were *this* good!"

REGIO AND LANGE had disassembled the bed in the forward cabin and now they stashed the eleven cans under it, and screwed the mattress support back down. A variety of gear, including a bicycle, went on top of the platform, and then the scuba gear was piled around it, neatly done, as if it had been there for a while.

Virgil went down to a cabin, stripped off the wet suit and bathing suit, dried himself with towels, and his hair with a hair dryer, and dressed in his street clothes. Rae smoothed his hair with her hands so it didn't have that tangled fresh-out-of-the-ocean look.

The wet suit was squeezed and wiped dry with paper towels;

the towels were wadded around a bolt and dropped over the side. The wet suit was draped over the bicycle in the forward cabin; the bathing suit and towels went in the clothes dryer.

When it was all done, Virgil came back up on deck. Cattaneo, at the wheel, said, "We'll give you that package of peas when we get back."

"Hope you've done this right," Rae said. "Hope there are no cops on the dock."

"That's not a likelihood at all," Cattaneo said. "We've got a man watching the dock from a condo parking lot across the water, haven't heard a peep."

Regio asked, "You talked to the guy yet?"

"Not yet. Not calling until we get inside the port. I don't want any calls from my phone coming out of the Coast Guard search area."

They were an hour and a half getting back to the Port Everglades cut, taking it easy; Lange broke out a Whole Foods salad and a bundle of chicken-salad sandwiches, and beer; Cattaneo turned down the beer in case they were boarded by the Coast Guard, but they made the food and beer cans prominent on the dining table: party boat, coming back from Boca Raton.

"We need to talk about something," Cattaneo said to Virgil and Rae. "You guys don't seem like the type that might have a lot of cash around—the kind of cash we're talking about here."

"We do all right from time to time," Rae said.

Lange: "This is more than all right."

Cattaneo: "Way more than all right. What we're trying to say is, don't go flashing that cash all over town. Most people buy stuff with bank loans and credit cards and so on. If you go into a car dealer and try to buy a car with thirty thousand in cash, they'll call the cops. They're going to be thinking 'dope money.' You want to buy a little toot, or a little weed, cash is fine—but don't go buying a kilo or something. Keep it small."

"I need some more shoes," Rae said.

"Shoes are fine. Couple dresses, no problem. You want to buy a car, you take the cash out to Vegas, tell the car dealer that you hit a number. They'll take the cash, but you might have to fill out some forms and pay taxes on it. Be better to buy used, a private sale, but, you know, what happens in Vegas . . ."

Virgil said, "I love that place. I once took two thousand golf balls out of a pond out there. Did I ever tell you about that?"

Rae said, "Ah, for Christ's sake, Willy, don't tell that story . . ."

Instead of telling that story, Virgil told the others about the dive, and that he thought he'd cleared out the south end of the string. "With eleven cans, you should be able to map out where the new south end is. The cans were maybe twenty feet apart. We'll need new GPS numbers for the next drop."

"Got it all on my laptop at home," Cattaneo said. "I'll figure it out tonight. Goddamnit, Willy, you really don't appreciate what you've done here. I'm so fuckin' excited, I mean, this is *large*."

COMING INTO PORT Everglades, Cattaneo made a call, which was picked up instantly. He said one word, "Eleven," and clicked off. At the dock, they spent a half hour tying up and cleaning up the boat, bagging trash. Cattaneo told them to leave the trash on board, "I'm going to need it later."

As they were about done, a tall, heavyset man came walking

down the dock under the overhead lights. Cattaneo looked up, surprised, and said, "Hey, man."

The tall man looked at Virgil and said, "You must be Willy."

Virgil nodded and said, "Yup." He recognized Behan from surveillance photos.

He asked, "You get your peas yet?"

Virgil held up the pea package full of cash and said, "Right here."

The man handed him an envelope. "No way we thought you'd get eleven, so the pea package is a little short. This is the rest of it. Another forty grand; a bit more than that, actually."

Virgil took the money then passed it all to Rae, who said to the tall man, "You are a class act. We thank you a whole fuckin' lot."

"There's much more where that came from," the tall man said. "If this works out as well as we think it should, you might have a permanent gig down here."

TWENTY-ONE

VIRGIL HAD TWO phones, the iPhone Zero that Cattaneo had seen in the deli, and his real phone, which he'd left in the apartment, taped under the refrigerator. He retrieved it as soon as they were back, went in the bathroom with Rae, shut the door, put the phone on speaker and called Lucas.

"Brought up eleven. We were told they were about ten kilos each, so that's what? More than three million, I think. It was still on the boat when we left and it looked like everybody was taking off. Like they were planning to keep it on the boat until they were sure they could move it."

"We saw you all leave and nobody's been back to the boat," Lucas said. "We've got a couple of FBI agents in an apartment across the waterway from the boat, they'll be watching twenty-four-seven until they move the shit, and then we'll track it."

"Word gets around a condo, you know, if they've got somebody in there," Rae said.

"Female agents. They've got actual jobs in a restaurant on Collins Avenue, different shifts."

"That's good, but listen," Rae said. "Cattaneo let slip that there was somebody watching the boat from a parking lot across the water. I hope they didn't see you guys when you were over there."

"Ah, boy! We didn't see anybody. I'll warn our people, see if we can spot the guy. Nobody said anything to you?"

"No, but it's something to worry about," Virgil said. "The guy who came down to the boat was Behan. You see that?"

"Yes. We thought it was him," Lucas said. "That's good. That's confident. No way Behan would have showed up if they'd spotted us watching."

"All right," Rae said. "By the way, we're going to spend some of this money in case they're watching us full-time."

"Go ahead, spend it all if you want. Andres and I are in the back of the Pathfinder, a block or so away. About the time you were dropped off, a Jeep pulled over and nobody got out. It's just sitting there. So . . . we don't know if it's a problem, but it could be."

"Won't be going out tomorrow," Virgil said. "The cold front's already in Palm Beach, it's going to be rough out there for the next two or three days. They don't want to lose their most valuable employee."

"Okay. Listen, we want to get together tomorrow, if we can," Lucas said. "I'll figure out a spot to meet, probably at a motel somewhere. We're going to put an FBI countersurveillance team on you tomorrow morning, whatever's a good starting time. Ten o'clock?"

"That'd be okay," Virgil said.

"When we're sure nobody's following you, I'll call with an address for the meet. Figure out somewhere to go where we could spot anyone on your back."

Rae: "I told them I wanted to buy some shoes and so on. I'm thinking we head down to the Bal Harbour Shops. It's like north of Miami Beach."

"That should be fine," Lucas said. "Give us some time to spot them, if they're out there. Watch this Jeep, though. Red Jeep, across the street, halfway down the block."

WHEN THEY RANG off, Virgil said, "Let's get cleaned up and head down to Ouroboros. Spend some money."

"Soon as I get the salt off me. You want tough ghetto chick or cheap slut?"

"Slut's always appealing," Virgil said. "Haven't seen that look so much."

"You got it," Rae said. She stepped closer and whispered, "You gonna have to carry the gun, because I won't have a place."

"It's a very small gun," Virgil whispered back.

"Outfit I'm gonna wear, I couldn't hide a paper clip."

SHE WAS RIGHT. She showered, wrapped a towel around herself, and headed to her bedroom. Virgil showered, got dressed in the bathroom, and when he emerged, Rae was waiting in a streaky short romper the color of walnut wood, excessively but not quite obscenely low cut, and strappy low heels. "How do I look?"

"I won't say, because I could be arrested," Virgil said. "We might have to shoot our way out of the bar."

"You are such a gentleman," Rae said.

VIRGIL HID HIS phone again, and they fired up a little more weed before they headed out the door. They spotted the red Jeep, still parked down the block, paid no attention to it, and walked on to the Ouroboros bar. Inside, Roy, the biker, was in his booth, back to the door, poking at a laptop.

He brightened when he saw them, said, "Hey, people," and pointed at the seat opposite him. "Jeez, Ally, you look like a movie star."

"Keep talkin' like that and it could get you somewhere," Rae said, as she slid into the booth.

Virgil ordered beers for the three of them and Rae leaned across the table and asked, quietly, "I don't suppose Richard could get us couple of eight-balls?"

"He maybe could," Roy said, dropping his voice. "You guys sell your house or something?"

"Nope. Sold some wheels, though."

"Let me make a call."

ROY MADE HIS call and the three of them were drinking beer when a guy in a flannel shirt too warm for the night sidled through the door and up to the bar and ordered a beer.

The conversation rolled along and the guy at the bar glanced at them from time to time, seriously uninterested in them, way *too* uninterested in them, and Rae nudged Virgil with an elbow and Virgil nodded. Richard showed up and slid in next to Roy, leaned across the table, mentioned a price, and said, "Two eight-balls."

Virgil glanced around the place, pulled a sheaf of bills from his pocket, made a big deal of hiding it and secretly counting it out, folded the cash in tight thirds and passed it across the table. Richard said, "Skinx." He reached out to shake hands and left the eights-balls in Virgil's palm.

Virgil said, "Party time," and Rae said to Virgil, "Give him a couple more bills. Birthday gift for Roy."

Roy said, "Thanks again." And to Richard, "I'll take it in weed."

They sat and talked through two more beers; between the first and second, the flannel shirt guy finished his beer and left. When Virgil and Rae left, Rae stepped close to Virgil as they went through the door and asked, "You think he was smart enough to know a drug deal when he saw one?"

Virgil looked up the street: the red Jeep was gone.

"I believe he was. We've sold ourselves solid. At least for a while."

THE NEXT MORNING, with a fat envelope of cash, they headed south to the Bal Harbour Shops. An FBI countersurveillance team tracked them and saw no one watching. Once inside the shopping mall, Rae hit a series of stores selling Italian shoes, pulling chunks of cash from her purse, collecting shopping bags from high-priced brands.

Virgil bought expensive shorts and boating shoes, and loose long-sleeved shirts with sleeves that could be rolled up; he found a men's room, stepped into a toilet booth and changed. He threw his old shorts and T-shirt into the trash and when he emerged from the men's room, Rae said, "My, my. You look like you own a banana plantation. Except for the sunglasses. The sunglasses look like they came from a Dollar Store sales bin."

"I need some blades," Virgil said, and they found some, with opaque gold lenses that wrapped nearly around to his ears.

Virgil shopped and enjoyed watching Rae shop, and watched

for watchers, spotting no one. Lucas called and said, "You're clean. We're right across Collins Avenue at the St. Regis."

"See you in ten minutes. Maybe . . . twenty. Rae's found a La Perla lingerie shop."

"Ah, Jesus, we've got everybody here waiting . . ."

"Hell hath no fury like a woman yanked out of La Perla . . ."

VIRGIL FINALLY EXTRACTED Rae from La Perla and they crossed Collins Avenue to the hotel, took the elevator up to an ocean-view room, and found it populated with Weaver and three more FBI agents, plus Lucas and Andres Devlin. Devlin gave Rae a hug and said, "I've been told about La Perla, if you're modeling . . ."

"In your dreams," Rae said, but she liked the hug.

Lucas to Virgil: "You've finally perfected your dirtbag look. The earrings are amazing; the sunglasses are even better."

"Happy you approve," Virgil said, taking off the glasses. "Where are we on this thing and why are we all in this room?"

Weaver, with a cell phone in his hand: "They're moving the heroin off the boat. They've got one of those aluminum pull carts, they put all eleven heroin cans in the cart and covered it with a tarp and garbage bags. They're pulling it up to the parking lot right now. We're all over them."

"What's the plan for that?" Rae asked.

"We believe they'll transport it up to New Jersey in a hearse . . . We're not sure about the details, but we're sure about the hearse. We think they paid some guy to have his mother taken to a funeral home and embalmed and then taken up to New Jersey for burial."

Rae: "They bought a body?"

"Exactly. The old woman was at the medical examiner's, she was going to be cremated and, you know, disposed of, however they do it here. Cattaneo gave her son a couple hundred bucks to transfer her to the funeral home."

"Sounds like an upright guy, the son does," Virgil said. "But a hearse?"

"It's a big vehicle with a lot of good hiding places and it's got a coffin with a body in it," Weaver said. "Not even cops are going to mess with a body, if there's a fender-bender or something."

"You know when they're leaving?" Virgil asked.

"No. We're watching, we assume it'll be soon, but it'll probably take two days to get it up to New Jersey," Weaver said. "We won't let them keep the dope, but we want to get it as close to Sansone as we can. We want him looking at it, if that's possible."

"Wait a minute, wait a minute." Virgil shook his head. "Man, that's a problem. That's not the way it's supposed to go . . ."

"Virgil's right," Lucas said. "I'll tell you what. I never was a narc, but I knew all the narcs in Minnesota, and if you think Sansone's going to drive over to some motel to look at that heroin, you're dreaming. He knows what heroin looks like. When that heroin comes in, he'll be skiing in New Hampshire. There's only one thing about the dope that Sansone is going to be connected to, and that's the money that comes from it."

"That's not the plan . . ." the agent began.

"Then we need a new plan," Lucas snapped.

"Yeah, you do," Virgil said. "I thought this was settled. You're all worried I'm going to drown, but I've got all kinds of bailouts for that—I could swim to shore if I needed to. You fuck up in New York, and Rae and I are in trouble. They'll kill us, or try to."

Rae: "You really can't hit them first down here, either, because that word will instantly get back north and Sansone's people will dump the dope and scatter."

Lucas said to Virgil, "We'll get a new plan. If I have to, I'll drag Louis Mallard's ass down here to explain it to these boys."

Weaver put up his hands: "Okay, okay. No need to do that. New plan, then. We don't have much time, but we'll work something out."

"I'll tell you what we work out—we follow the money," Virgil said. "Sansone won't look at the heroin, but he sure as shit will look at the money coming back."

"I gotta talk to the Manhattan AIC," Weaver said. "We're getting pressure to keep the dope off the street."

"I'll give you some help with that, talking with the AIC," Lucas said to Weaver.

"Lucas, goddamnit . . ."

VIRGIL SAID TO Lucas, momentarily cutting out the feds, but loud enough for them to hear, "I'm counting on you, man. You got to get us out. Don't let these fools go after the dope and leave me in the water."

"I'll take care of it. If I have to yank you out and leave the FBI standing there in New York with their dicks in their hands, I'll do it."

Weaver said, "Hey, that's not . . ."

Virgil interrupted: "But I come back to the other question: why are Rae and I standing here with you?"

Lucas said, "We need to know where you're at. Where your head's at. The thought of that dive scares the crap out of most of us. You won't be diving today or tomorrow, but how about the day after tomorrow? Weather is supposed to be better . . ."

Virgil shook his head: "Cattaneo said we wouldn't be going back out for two or three days. As far as my head is concerned, it's not hard diving, as long as you're not scared of the dark."

"Or sharks," an agent said.

"Sharks aren't a problem," Virgil said. "I'm more worried about losing my dive computer and getting disoriented. But it's a solid computer, so that's unlikely. These guys are so greedy that as long as I keep pulling up the junk, they're happy to keep me working."

"You're good with making more dives?" Lucas asked.

"I'm fine with it," Virgil said. "My bigger worry is that the Coast Guard gets onto us, and they shoot first and ask questions later . . . that wouldn't be good."

One of the agents said, "We're monitoring them. If they look like they might be about to intercept you, we'll call them off. We're set to do that."

"But they're not in on the action? Not yet?" Rae asked.

"Not yet," Weaver said. "We're still holding this close. We'll have to do some PR work with them when the arrests happen, but . . . that's the way it is, for now."

Lucas asked Virgil, "Do you need anything from us?"

Virgil looked at Rae, who shrugged. Virgil said, "Yeah. Stay away from us. We're solid with these guys. We're out there embarrassing ourselves . . . did a drug deal last night, bought some cocaine for the benefit of that flannel shirt guy, if he's actually working with them. We're over at those shops, Rae's spending money like water."

"That guy last night, he's not much of a threat," Lucas said. "He does work with them, but he's casual labor. If you're sure you're good, we'll stay away."

Rae nodded: "Virgil can't carry, but I can. If worse comes to worse, I've got that Sig on my ankle."

Lucas rubbed his face, then said to Virgil and Rae, "Okay. We keep going. When we hit Sansone, you bail out. That's all we're looking for right now."

"OKAY. NOW, MY other big problem," Virgil said. "I can't carry my phone. Two phones would be suspicious, especially for a dirtbag like me. If they shake me down and want to look at my incoming and outgoing calls and numbers, I can't say no. Neither can Rae. So I'm carrying that burner. If you need to make an emergency call on our carry phones, you've got to be set up to fake a spam call—car insurance, like that, in case they're right on top of us."

Weaver said, "We can do that."

"Call me on my real phone when you get it figured out. Like tonight," Virgil said. "And you can't hit Sansone or Sansone's people without warning us off. If you hit Sansone when I'm twenty feet down, they'll shoot me in the head when I come back up. I need to know when you're going to move. If you can't reach me, or I can't talk, you've got to be ready to back off. Because I'll tell you what—when you hit Sansone, every member of their organization will know about it in five minutes and somebody will call down here and Behan will get rid of Rae and me. He'll get rid of us even if they think we're okay, like they got rid of that Magnus guy, and the woman that Lucas interviewed, whatever her name was. As a precaution. Cleaning up potential problems."

One of the agents said, "I don't know—I still think if we can get that dope close to Sansone . . ."

"Fuck you, man," Virgil said.

Lucas: "Easy."

"Big flashy drug bust that everybody in New York knows about in one minute? And the guys down here know one minute later? Can't do that," Rae said. "Everybody has to go down at the same time, both here and New York. That can't happen if me and Virgil are on a boat."

Virgil asked, "You want us to poke Cattaneo or Regio or Lange, to see if we can find out who shot the Coast Guard guys?"

"Not unless you can do it with some care . . . get them bragging about it or something. Don't risk anything to do that," Weaver said.

One of the other agents said, "Listen, you guys: we've got Behan, Cattaneo, Regio, Lange, and a half dozen other associates in the bag, for the heroin operation. Those guys are toast, you don't have to do anything more. An identification of the shooters would be a bonus, but, you know, it'll be the difference between thirty years in prison, and life without parole. For guys in their forties, like these guys, not too large a difference. We don't want you guys taking unwarranted risks and getting killed, trying to pay for the difference between thirty years and life."

"Gotcha," Virgil said. "That's good."

THEY TALKED FOR a few more minutes, Virgil describing the dive and process of recovering the dope. "When we hit them, we need to recover that wand thing that operates the LED lights," Virgil said. "With that, we can get most of the rest of the heroin. Without it, it'll stay on the bottom."

"Not the worst place for it," Weaver said.

"Except you'd probably have the Colombians up here looking for it, with new wands and machine guns, even if you take down Sansone," Virgil said.

"There's that," Weaver conceded. "We'll go after the wand."

THE MEETING WAS over in half an hour and Virgil and Rae were back out the door and across the street. "That was unnecessary," Virgil said. "The whole meeting was a waste of time, except for making sure that they pull us out before they hit anyone. Even that, we could have done on the phone."

"I dunno," Rae said. "Did you notice that one agent who didn't say anything? The guy with the striped tie?"

"Yeah?"

"I think he might have been a shrink, the way he was watching you talk. Lucas was telling the truth, when he said they were worried about where your head's at. They really don't know anything about diving. They're thinking about diving in movies, all those sharks and the enemy guys cutting air hoses."

"A shrink? Really?"

"I think so."

"Hmm. Like I told them, I'm more worried about coming up and finding somebody's pointing a gun at my head," Virgil said. "But then, I've got you to take care of me."

"I will," Rae said.

"I believe you," Virgil said. "So—you got enough shoes?"

Rae snorted: "I'll never have enough shoes. This is not an act, the shoe thing. I can't afford a private jet, but with the right shoes, nobody'll know that."

"All right. I've got the energy for a couple more stores, but first, we gotta find a place to get a sandwich."

They didn't find a sandwich, but they did find a sushi shop, and as Virgil was dunking a chunk of raw tuna into a cup of wasabi, Rae said, "You sounded . . . smart . . . up there. In the meeting. Like a smart cop. With a hard nose. Giving shit to the feds."

"Why not? I am smart," Virgil said.

"You hide it well. Even when it's just you and me."

Virgil tried the shrimp: "Jesus, this stuff is good. Don't much get good sushi in the rural Midwest." He chewed for a moment and then said, "You know about the tall poppy syndrome?"

"Mmm, no. Does it have something to do with heroin poppies?"

"Any poppies, I guess. You hear about it mostly in Australia and Canada, but Minnesota's almost Canada anyway—same people settled both places. Anyway, the tall poppy syndrome refers to the idea that the tall poppies in a field will get their tops cut off to make everything neat and equal. When it comes to a culture, it means that people who let their light shine will eventually get dragged down, and a lot of people will enjoy seeing that happen. If you're in a tall poppy culture, it's all right to be smart, but you can't *act* smart. You can't show it."

"That sounds like girls in eighth grade: 'You think you're so smart?' That kind of thing."

"Exactly," Virgil said. "If you grow up in Minnesota, you develop this cover. You know, you do well, but, 'I'm an ordinary guy who got lucky, that's all, I really like standing around on the street corner when it's ten below zero having long conversations about the Vikings.' Eventually, it becomes reflexive. You really sort of become that. The guy who likes to hang out on street corners, bullshitting. You don't let the smart out."

"Not exactly New York or LA," Rae said. "In those places, they can't wait to let you know how smart they are."

"Different culture. That's why we're going to fuck Behan and his crew. They're from New York. They look at us—we're from Iowa, for Christ's sake—and they can't imagine that we're anything but a lazy motherfucker and his ghetto girl. They're too smart to make a mistake about it."

"But they are."

"And we're gonna fuck 'em because of it," Virgil said; a happy guy. He looked down at Rae's plate. "Say, you want that octopus?"

CHAPTER

TWENTY-TWO

BEHAN, CATTANEO, LANGE, and Regio gathered at Behan's condo to celebrate: a hundred and ten kilos of heroin, worth something in the neighborhood of three and a half million dollars wholesale in New York, had come out of the ocean and were safely packed away in a high-security storage unit in Hallandale.

"We're taking it north tomorrow," Behan said.

The four of them were standing around with crystal whiskey glasses in their hands, all of them drinking scotch, except Behan, who had a bottle of water; all of them in sport coats and dress shirts and loafers. Behan's low-rent designers had just installed ten of the world's most famous black-and-white photographs down a long hallway, and they all pretended to be interested in them, though Behan couldn't remember the photographers' names. "Sandy and Steph are driving, they're pulling the old lady out of the funeral home tonight."

"That's, what, a day and a half up 95?" Regio asked. He sniffed: the place smelled of lemon Pledge, and he was mildly allergic to it.

"Something like that," Behan said. "I've never driven straight through myself. I'm told it's eighteen or nineteen hours, going with the flow of the traffic. The storage place opens at six, they figure to be on the road before six-thirty, about the time it starts getting light. They wanna beat the rush out of town. They'll drive until it gets dark, then do the rest of it the day after tomorrow."

"I'll be happy when New York gets it and we're not responsible anymore," Cattaneo said. "I'll tell you, when Willy came up with eleven cans, I was so excited I almost shit myself."

Behan turned his eyes on Lange: "What do you think, Matthew? You still worried about Willy's credentials?"

"Less than I was, but . . ."

"But what?"

"We're gonna get a test when the shit gets to New York. If Dougie's standing there looking at all those bags and a hundred feds come crashing through the doors, well . . . it could be Willy."

"Doug won't get anywhere close to it," Behan said. "It'll go straight out to the A level, a kilo or two at a time and they'll be the ones who have hands on."

"Okay," Lange said. "But if it does get hit, we'll need a closer look at Willy. I-I-I guess I don't think it'll happen. After the other night, I think Willy and Ally are on the level. I'm just sayin', if that cargo does get hit, we'll need to take a real close look. Because, let's face it, we all know each other, we're all watertight. If there's a leak . . ."

"'Nuff said," said Behan. "You're right. If the hearse gets hit, anywhere along the line, we'll look to Willy."

"Willy's okay," Cattaneo said. "He's in as deep as we are, now . . ."

Behan was watching him closely, and Cattaneo faltered, then asked, "What?"

"An odd thing happened yesterday," Behan said, "which is why I brought up the whole subject."

He pointed at Regio. "You told me that you stopped by their place yesterday around what, three o'clock, to tell them to ease off the dope? And they just got back from Bal Harbour?"

"Yeah, our guy saw them in a Hollywood bar the night before, a block down the street from their apartment. A Willy-style shithole called Ouroboros. They bought some cocaine from a dealer named Richard. He's a well-known dealer, been around for a while. Not a cop."

"So that looks good, that's what we expected," Behan said. "Then we thought they'd probably go out and shoot up some of the cash."

"Yeah," Regio said. "They did. Like I told you, it looked like they hit every shoe store in Bal Harbour Shops. Ally must have had ten bags stacked up in that apartment. Willy bought a pair of crocodile cowboy boots, which I didn't even know they sold over there. Is that bad?"

"No, but a curious thing. Jack, you know Lauren Hopps, right?"

"Sure, I know Lauren."

"Who's Lauren Hopps?" Lange asked.

"Nice lady, smart, she's with the Beach guys," Behan said. "I knew her up in New York, she's down here now, she supervises the girls working the South Beach. Anyway, she was up at the St. Regis Hotel yesterday for a late lunch, and as she was going in, she sees this FBI guy, Weaver, go by with what looked like a bunch of feds, on their way out of the hotel. Weaver was the task force guy up in Lauderdale, he was down at Romano's place in that fight. So Lauren thinks I might be interested, because she kinda knows what we do, and she gives me a call."

Regio: "Yeah? Does that mean something?"

"The St. Regis is right across the street from the Bal Harbour Shops. I mean *right* across the street. A one-minute walk. The feds would have been at the St. Regis at the same time as Willy and the hand-jive were supposedly shopping."

Lange said, "Oh, shit."

Behan shrugged. "Doesn't necessarily mean anything, but it's a curious coincidence. The Bal Harbour Shops are where I would have guessed those two would go. The feds? I don't know about the feds, why the whole bunch of them would be at the St. Regis."

They stood in silence for a moment, and then Cattaneo said, "You're letting the shit go north?"

"Yeah, but I don't want Willy back in the water until we find out what happens up there."

"Can't go back in anyway, not for a couple more days," Cattaneo said. "Jesus, I'd hate to lose that shit. Three and a half bucks."

"Only a small slice of what's down there," Behan said.

"Yeah, but . . ."

"Have you told Dougie about this?" Cattaneo asked.

"Of course. He told me to make the call, and I did."

They stood around, not talking, nipping at the whiskey, until Behan said, "So, we'll see. I thanked Lauren for the information, told her I knew some guys who might want to tap into her highest-end girls. If any of you guys are inclined, I'm buying."

Lange and Regio shook their heads; faithful married men. Cattaneo said, "Well, if you're buying. I hear they got some wild women down there."

"That's what I hear," Behan said. "Feel free."

TWENTY-THREE

Lucas and Devlin watched the heroin leave downtown Hallandale and head out to I-95, tagged by a half dozen FBI surveillance teams in Toyotas. The teams were rarely in sight of the target hearse, except at exits. The hearse cruised north at five miles an hour above the speed limit, which was about ten miles an hour slower than the traffic; that might normally make a state trooper suspicious, but not with a hearse.

"We still going to New York?" Devlin asked, as he and Lucas headed back to the hotel.

"Washington first," Lucas said. "I need to talk to some people. I don't like the way these guys want to go for the easy kill."

"I don't really think . . ."

"Oh, they will. They'll say they're not gonna do it, but something will come up in New York and they'll get anxious and they'll pull the trigger," Lucas said. "They'll probably be careful about not dropping Virgil and Rae in hot water, but they'll miss Sansone."

"They'll still get everybody down here."

"They won't cut the head off the snake," Lucas said.

"What's in Washington?" Devlin asked.

"An old FBI friend named Louis Mallard. He's a deputy director, he's already involved with the task force. I'll squeeze him—get
him to tell Weaver and the boys in New York that if they fuck
up and jump too soon, they'll all wind up in a field office in West
Jesus, Idaho."

"Think that'll work?"

"Yeah, if Louis will do it. There's also a Florida senator I might
talk to . . . that I might refer Louis to, if the going gets tough. Louis
is very politically aware."

"Is this gonna ruin my career?" Devlin asked.

"No, you're too obscure to ruin. Get a few more years under
your belt and a little more status, get closer to a pension, then
you'll be worth ruining. Ruining you now would be like shooting
a squirrel and mounting its head. Nobody would be impressed."

"Thank you."

"Always happy to advise young people," Lucas said.

AFTER A FINAL meeting with Weaver and his team, Lucas called
Senator Christopher Colles and was told by the woman who an-
swered the phone that Colles was about to get on an airplane to
Miami. "Ask the senator to call me as soon as he's on the ground.
He'll know what it's about. I'll need about ten or fifteen minutes of
his time."

"I will tell him you called—and you'll be at this number?"

"Yes, but I'm leaving Miami myself at three o'clock, flying to
Washington. If we cross in the airport, we could talk face-to-face."

"I'll alert him to that possibility," the woman said. "When will
you be at the airport?"

"At one o'clock."

"That could work. I'll tell him."

LUCAS AND DEVLIN were walking into MIA when Colles called: "We're taxiing to the terminal now. There's a Cuban restaurant called La Carreta. I'll meet you there."

Both Lucas and Devlin had TSA passes and approval to fly with their weapons. They printed tickets and badged themselves through security, and were at La Carreta in twenty. Lucas spotted Colles with a redheaded woman at a corner table.

Colles looked like a movie version of a senator: tall, ruddy face, big white teeth, carefully groomed gray hair. He stood to shake hands with Lucas and Devlin, nodded to the woman, and said, "This is Andrea Thompson, my PA. She knows more about everything than I do, so she'll be sitting in. She's the one you talked to this morning . . ."

Thompson was in her late thirties or early forties, pretty enough, but with the tough demeanor of somebody who'd fought the DC wars for a decade or two. She nodded at Lucas and the two marshals took their seats. Lucas looked around: the nearest customers were two tables away, two Hispanic women, both looking at phones, and his back would be to them.

Lucas leaned into the table, and said, "Here is where we're at."

And he told them. When he finished, Colles said, quietly, "Then we're about to bring the sonsofbitches down."

"Yes. There's a problem, though. The FBI guys have been working this case since last summer and now we've got a lot of these Mafia guys in our sights. I'm afraid they'll jump too fast and we'll miss the top people—the top people in New York and New Jersey."

Thompson: "What should they be doing? The FBI?"

"They're following the heroin instead of following the money. They want to grab the guys handling the dope, but the top people won't get close to it—what they will get close to is the money. We have to let Sansone's men deliver the heroin to their distributors and watch the cash come back. We need to grab one of those distributors, turn him, have him pass his cash to Sansone."

"Is that likely?" Colles asked.

"Probably, if we pick the right guy," Lucas said. "We've been researching them for more than a month, we know who most of them are. We'll pick a guy who'll be looking at three strikes, life in prison, and offer him witness protection and a clean bill of health if he turns."

"How will you work the money? Mark the bills or something?" Thompson asked.

Devlin chipped in: "They won't mark the bills, they'll xerox them. There won't be any markings on the cash, but we'll have every single serial number on a stack of used bills of all different denominations. That way, it's undetectable."

"What do you want from us?" Colles asked.

"I'm on my way to Washington to talk to a deputy director at the FBI. I'm going to ask him to have a come-to-Jesus talk with his boys. He'll probably agree to do it, but if I recommend that he speak to a U.S. senator about it . . . then our chances are even better."

"If you insist on doing it your way, isn't there a possibility that the heroin will make it into circulation?" Colles asked.

Lucas nodded. "Yes. A hundred and ten kilos, that's almost two hundred and fifty pounds, is on its way north. They'll probably cut it with fentanyl to give it more kick and a higher price, and some junkies could die. On the other hand, there's a hundred tons of heroin coming in from Mexico alone, every year. Literally, a hundred tons. This is a lot of dope in one batch, but on the national scale, it's a drop in the bucket. If we put a whole Mafia gang in prison, that sends a message. To everyone."

Colles thought about that, peering at Lucas and Devlin, then leaned back, picked up the briefcase he'd put at the side of the chair, looked down at his plate and the half-eaten enchilada on it. "Tell your FBI guy to call me. I'll encourage him to go for the whole enchilada."

Lucas nodded: "Thank you."

LUCAS AND DEVLIN left MIA on the three o'clock flight and got to Louis Mallard's house in Georgetown at seven o'clock, and inside, found Mallard waiting with Jane Chase. Lucas introduced Chase and Mallard to Devlin. Chase said, "You're going to be fucking with the FBI again."

"Only with your complete cooperation," Lucas said.

"Yeah, that's likely," Chase said.

"Let's hear it," Mallard said. He was in his early sixties, approaching the end of his career; he was a solidly built man, a lifelong bachelor the love of whose life had been a woman agent shot down and killed in St. Louis. "Anybody need a drink? No? Then . . ."

Lucas gave him the same pitch he'd given to Colles, and when he was done, Mallard got up and wandered around his living room, looking at the watercolor landscapes that lined the walls. Chase said to his back, "Louis: we really need to leave the decision up to the New York AIC. He's on the ground there . . ."

"He'll want the sure arrest and a big pile of heroin to show to the newsies," Lucas said. "A one-day PR victory that'll get his face on TV and nobody'll remember next month. We need him to hear from you guys. That we want the whole bunch of those assholes, not the distribution."

"Let me sleep on it," Mallard said.

Lucas shot him an annoyed look, exhaled impatiently. "You may be getting a call from Senator Colles, from Florida, you know, the guy who runs the Homeland Security Committee," Lucas said. "He's the guy who brought me down to Florida. He's taken an interest."

Mallard smiled, but wasn't amused. "You sandbagged me, didn't you, you motherfucker?"

"Louis . . ."

"I told you, Louis," Chase said. "I said Davenport wasn't going to come plead with you, that there was going to be a rock inside the request."

"Yes, you did, and I would have been a little disappointed if there wasn't a rock." To Lucas: "Where are you guys staying?"

"The Watergate."

"I used to have an apartment there," Mallard said. "They allow dogs."

"That's great, Louis," Lucas said. "But what are you going to do?"

"I'll talk to Colles and then to you tomorrow morning . . . probably not much before noon. Are you going on to New York?"

"Yeah. Early train, unless you need us here to answer questions."

"I don't think so. Your argument's clear enough. Talk to you tomorrow."

CHASE GOT UP and walked to a liquor sideboard, as if she'd done it before, glanced back at Mallard, and asked, "Tequila?"

"A small one, I think. Lucas? Andres?"

Lucas shook his head and a second later, Devlin did the same.

As Chase poured the liquor, she said to Lucas, "I'm not pissed off at you anymore, Lucas. Don't trust you to do the right thing, but I never did trust you all that much."

Lucas said, "I try to do the *right* thing. Not always the court thing."

"We're supposed to be a country of laws," Chase said.

"And what we are now is a country of special interests and influence," Lucas said.

"Don't argue with him," Mallard said to Chase.

"You're taking his side?"

"Only because he's right," Mallard said, taking the short glass of straight tequila from Chase. "Though I still resent being clubbed like a baby seal."

"Odd how you get clubbed like a baby seal and you still manage to become the most important professional cop in the United States," Lucas said.

ON MALLARD'S PORCH, waiting for an Uber, Devlin said, "Well, that went well. We sandbagged one of the most influential guys in the Justice Department and you get in a fight with Jane Chase, who looks to me like a big-time nut-crusher who might be banging the most important guy. I'm thinking of crawling under my bed and not coming out until it's all over with."

"A little secret, Andres. When we—Bob and Rae and I—fuck with the FBI, there's a little thrill that goes around the Marshals Service," Lucas said. A bug that was circling the porch light collided with his forehead, and he brushed it away. "People know about it. If you'd planned to transfer to the FBI, that wouldn't help. But if you plan to stay in the Marshals Service . . . people will speak well of you. The director will know your name and might even ask about your kids, even if you don't have any."

"All right." Devlin hitched up his pants. "Though my long-term plan is to spend five more years in the service, get a solid vesting in the retirement plan, learn everything I can about how cops and prosecutors work, then go to law school and become a defense attorney working the federal courts and get really fuckin' rich."

"Good plan. In the meantime, you want the people in the service to speak your name in awe."

"Do they speak *your* name in awe?"

"I expect they do," Lucas said. "Especially since the people who work with me fly business class and stay in separate rooms, usually in suites."

"That's awesome, all right," Devlin said. "Though, I have to say, I never heard of you until Rae pulled me in on this."

THEY WERE OVERNIGHT at the Watergate and took the early train into Manhattan's Penn Station and caught a taxi to the Grand

Hyatt above Grand Central Station. On the way, Lucas took a call from Mallard, who said, "You get your way."

"I hope you were sweetly persuasive."

"No more than a gentle whisper in the AIC's ear," Mallard said. "A virtual zephyr."

Manhattan always smelled like week-old sour buttered popcorn to Lucas, but he usually visited in late spring or early autumn; on this day in January, with the temperature hovering around twenty, it smelled like week-old sour cold-buttered ice.

Lucas and Devlin grabbed sandwiches at the Hyatt's deli and took the elevator to the twelfth floor to meet with the Manhattan assistant agent in charge, whose name was Loren Duke. Weaver and two other supervising agents were waiting with Duke. The room was small and stuffy, and one of the agents stood next to a drawn window shade, peering past the shade as if he might actually see something important on the street below. Weaver looked like he was suffering intense gas pains.

Duke: "I'm here for the AIC. He hates you two, by the way. You sicced Louis Mallard on him and the conversation was not a pleasant one. Ten or twenty kilos will probably make it on the street because of you guys and I'd be surprised if a couple people didn't die from it."

"Nobody's forcing anyone to shoot up that stuff. If they do and die, well, tough shit, what did they expect?" Lucas said. "The important thing is, we're following the money. That's what we're doing, right?"

"If we can spot the prime distributors before they spot us," Duke said.

"They better not spot you," Lucas said, "or Mallard will rip your AIC a new one. Mallard's got some exposure here, too. He's the one who approved the whole task force."

"We have some damn good FBI surveillance guys down in Florida," Devlin chipped in. "They could handle that. Are your people less good?"

"Our people are good," Duke snapped. "None better. But we're doing this the hard way, and we're putting some of our people at risk."

"Sort of like the junkies. This is what they signed up for," Lucas snapped back. "So—since we're going after the money, what's the plan?"

"We're watching the hearse. It'll be coming in . . ." Duke looked at his watch. ". . . what, two, three hours from now."

The agent who wasn't looking out the window said, "They're still south on I-95, not in any big hurry. Slow lane only. We expect they'll take the 440, the Outerbridge Crossing, onto Staten Island. Or they could go on further north on 95 and take 278 onto the island, because most of Sansone's assets are in Port Richmond, which is way up at the north end of the island."

Lucas: "I thought Sansone was out of the Newark area . . ."

"He is, but they won't take the heroin to his house," Duke said, with a hint of sarcasm. "If they did, we'd be all over them."

"Is Sansone in town? Right now?"

"Yes. He has an office in the back of one of his donut shops in Newark. So: what are you two planning to do?"

"We want to hook up with your Staten Island task force. You identify the distributors. We'll pick out the one most likely to take a deal, and approach him."

"You're welcome to ride along," Duke said. "Even though the AIC is grinding his teeth to a very fine powder. Keep in mind that our people know what they're doing: don't get in their way."

"How do we hook up?" Lucas asked.

"Go downstairs to Grand Central, get on the 4 subway to Bowling Green, which will get you to a quick walk to the Staten Island Ferry. You can't see exactly where you want to go when you come out of the Bowling Green station, so use your phone maps. We'll have somebody meet you on the Staten Island side."

"I'm heading back to Florida," Weaver said. "We need some further discussion here. Doesn't involve you guys."

"That sounds unpleasant," Lucas said.

"Could have done without the call from Mallard," Weaver said. "May all the saints bless his slightly soiled soul."

DUKE WAS RIGHT about getting lost coming out of the Bowling Green station, and they did resort to Google phone maps, although Devlin thought it unmanly. Lucas sat inside for the twenty-five-minute trip, having ridden the ferry with all of his children at one time or another. He could see small, mean snow pellets whipping across the harbor, but Devlin had never been, and went outside to look at the shrinking Manhattan skyline and then the Statue of Liberty, which, to Lucas, always looked smaller and greener than it should. After taking iPhone pictures of Liberty, Devlin came back inside, his face as rigid as a chunk of ebony, and said, "It's colder than Prancer's dick out there."

"I think Prancer's a girl," Lucas said.

"No fuckin' way," Devlin said. He went to Google on his

iPhone, and a minute later said, "Damn! *All* of Santa's reindeer are girls. Even Rudolph."

AN AGENT NAMED Dillon Koch picked them up at the Staten Island terminal in a Chevy Equinox, a small gray SUV picked, Koch said, for its anonymity. "You look at it, and you don't see it," he said.

Koch himself was a small gray man, balding, bespectacled, dressed in a dark blue parka, a blue oxford cloth shirt, and black jeans, as unnoticeable as the Equinox. A member of the FBI's Special Surveillance Group, he mostly worked street surveillance for the antiterrorism squad in Washington, now temporarily forwarded to the Sansone task force.

"Where are we going?" Lucas asked.

"The Hilton. We've got a big business suite," Koch said. "Some of the agents are staying there, at the Hilton, some are next door at the Hampton Inn. They divided us up so . . . there wouldn't be so many FBI-looking people at the same hotel."

"How many agents are working this deal?" Devlin asked from the backseat.

"I'm not sure exactly, but I'd guess a dozen or so, here on the island, most of them SSG singles in a bunch of different rented Camrys and Civics and these Equinoxes. We're not tailing the hearse directly, it's all indirect, and we're watching the tracker you guys planted on it. It's on the island, by the way. They're headed for the Clean N Go car wash up in Port Richmond. We've got a truck a half block away, parked on the street, with a good view of the entrance and exit. They're spotting and filming people as they come and go."

"Hope to Christ nobody is spotting and filming the truck," Lucas said.

"Naw, it looks exactly like a Penske rental," Koch said. "The way it's positioned . . . you'd have to see it to understand it, I guess. They have a good view of the Clean N Go, but from the Clean N Go, you have to look between a couple of evergreen trees to see it, and then you only see the top of it. The top is where our guys are at, but you'd never know it from the outside. Looks like an ordinary moving truck."

"Any way we can watch?" Devlin asked.

"Not directly. You can't go to the truck," Koch said. "But you can see what their cameras are seeing, from the task force suite."

"How far is the hotel from the car wash?"

"Ten, twelve minutes. Three or four miles. The word from the top is, we don't want anything to give us away. Everybody stays back, except for us surveillance guys. We're online with the mob specialists in Washington, they'll call out Sansone's people when they go through the car wash . . . assuming that any of them go through the car wash, and we're not barking up the entirely wrong tree."

"We're not," Lucas said. "When will the hearse get there?"

"About now," Koch said. He pointed out a large beige building on the street ahead. "That's the Hilton. We'll be there in two minutes."

THE TASK FORCE suite was on the hotel's top floor, behind double doors. A sign sat on a tripod by the door, and said, PRIVATE MEETING—BENELUX INSURANCE CORPORATION. Inside, three men and four women sat at two boardroom-style tables, looking at computer screens, or chatting; one of them was reading a copy of the *Times*. Two cartons of pastries sat on a side table, with some dry-looking Saran-wrapped sandwiches; a Yeti cooler held soft drinks and single-serving bottles of orange juice.

Another man and a woman were at a window, looking out over Staten Island. Everybody paused to look at Lucas, Devlin, and Koch; then the people at computers went back to the computers, or chatting, while the two at the window walked over to the newcomers.

The woman was tall, wearing a dark green suit that matched her eyes, and reddish hair. She stuck out a large, square hand to Lucas and said, "I'm Kate Orish, I'm running the room here." She nodded at the man, "Dick Kerry is my second."

Lucas introduced himself and Devlin, then asked, "Where's the hearse?"

"Looking for surveillance. We were worried that they might be going somewhere we didn't know about, but then we realized they were running a countersurveillance pattern. They're still doing that, weaving through the streets, but they're getting closer and closer to the car wash. Don't worry, they haven't seen us."

"Any idea about their schedule? How soon they'll be moving the dope?"

"The car wash has a garage on the back part of the lot. We think that's where they'll park the hearse. But they've got a body on board, and we think they'll want to get rid of it as soon as they can. We think that the prime distributors will start coming by today. It's likely that each of the prime guys will be cutting the heroin on his own, rather than somebody trying to cut it all at once, because they all know their own markets. Some will want to cut with fentanyl, some might cut with baking powder, some might move the pure stuff on to lower levels. We don't know how they do it in this operation."

"Here we go," said one of the women looking at computers. "The hearse is making a move toward the car wash."

Lucas looked over her shoulder, to what looked like a Google map; the map was actually following the tracker on the hearse. Lucas asked, "Where's the car wash?"

She tapped the screen: "Here. He's five blocks away."

They watched as the hearse made another quick turn, and another, and then the woman said, "They'll drive right past our truck."

They watched the tracker, then switched to a new computer screen, with a male operator, as the hearse popped up on the camera view of the car wash. After pausing at the cross street, the hearse crossed it, pulled into the driveway at the car wash, and drove toward the garage, where an overhead door opened as it approached. As soon as the hearse was inside, the door came down.

"There are two people in the garage, besides the hearse drivers," Orish said. "Neither one is a prime distributor. Those guys haven't shown up yet."

Nothing moved for a half hour, when an access door opened, and a man came out, followed by the two drivers who Lucas had seen in Hallandale. They walked across the driveway and into the main car wash building, and out of sight. "That's our guys," Lucas said. "They looked happy enough."

"They're probably looking for an envelope full of cash," Kerry said. "I expect they'll be filling out their income tax forms later today, reporting the payment."

"Probably," Devlin said. "Getting that Social Security deducted."

✦✦✦

TEN MINUTES LATER, the hearse drivers came out of the car wash building, walked back into the garage. The overhead door went up, the hearse backed out, and rolled out of the car wash. Lucas watched on the mapping computer as it headed south on the island, then east, and finally stopped. "Funeral home," the computer operator said. "They're dumping the body."

"The heroin is in the garage," Orish said. "This is good. This is good."

Nothing was moving at the garage and a half hour after the hearse arrived at the funeral home, it set off again.

"You know what?" Orish said, after watching the tracker for a while. "I think they're coming here. Either here or over at the Hampton Inn."

"They'll probably stay overnight and then head back to Florida," Devlin said. "By the time they get back, they'll have another load."

"I'm hoping we'll only do this once," Orish said.

"We're all hoping that. We've got a couple of people undercover, risking their necks with every load," Lucas said.

Orish: "Then let's get it right the first time."

TWENTY-FOUR

Behan called Cattaneo and asked, "What do you think?"

"It's still a little rough, but we're going out. Willy's okay with it—he wants the cash."

"Talked to Dougie," Behan said. "The hearse is in the garage."

"Excellent," Cattaneo said. "Though that sounds like a euphemism for a guy who has trouble getting it up, finally getting a hit of Viagra."

"What?"

"Never mind," Cattaneo said. Behan thought he had a good Irish sense of humor, but he didn't. When he got off the phone, Cattaneo wandered into the living room where Belinda was looking at three different shades of blue acrylic paint and said, "That fuckin' Behan can be a moron."

"Don't let him hear you saying that," his wife said. "Are you going out for sure?"

"Almost for sure. I mean, we're going out, but we actually have to get out there before we decide to dive."

Cattaneo called Virgil and asked, "You all set?"

"How's the water?"

"I'm looking out my window. I'm not seeing whitecaps, but it's rolling some."

"I don't want to go over the side if the boat's gonna come down on me and crack my head like a fuckin' walnut," Virgil said.

"We gotta be careful, but it's not all that bad—we'll know more when we get out there, and if you think it's too rough, we'll come back. It's your call."

"'Kay. I've made a couple changes in the rigging, nothing major. When do you pick us up?"

"Same time as last time?" Cattaneo said.

"See you at the boat."

A half hour before Regio was to pick them up, Virgil helped Rae fix her Sig 928 to her leg, just above the anklebone, with a piece of black gaffer tape. He first folded a piece of the tape back on itself, as a handle, that Rae could jerk free of her leg with her left hand, while she pulled the gun with her right. The first time out, they'd fixed the gun to her leg with an ankle compression wrap, but Rae said it hadn't been secure enough, and she'd had to sneak quick readjustments on the boat.

With the gun firmly in place, she jogged up and down the apartment a few times and said, "Much better."

Regio showed up at 3:30, and the three of them carried the scuba gear to the Lexus, did the back-street crawl to check for tails. When he was satisfied, Regio took them to the boat, where Cattaneo and Lange were ready to cast off. Both Cattaneo and Lange were wearing light foul-weather suits. The sky was mostly cloudy, the leftovers from the cold front.

"We need rain suits?" Virgil asked. "If it's that rough . . ."

"Just in case," Cattaneo said. "If we really need them, you won't be diving."

"Not much air," Virgil said, putting a hand up into the breeze, and looking up into the sky.

"We'll see when we get outside," Cattaneo said.

THEY MADE THE run to the Port Everglades cut, went through, past a rusting inbound Panamanian freighter, and out on the ocean. When they turned north, into the wind, they got some rock and roll, but nothing serious.

"What do you think?" Cattaneo shouted down the hatch.

"If it doesn't get any worse than this, I'm okay with it!" Virgil shouted back.

"Good man!"

AS DARKNESS FELL over the boat, Virgil suited up, checked and rechecked all the gear, went topside to look at the water. The rollers were perhaps two feet high, but showing no foam. "Looks okay, but I'm still worried about getting hit . . ."

"We'll do it a little different this time," Cattaneo said. "There's nobody out here, so when I'm coming up to your light, I'll stay well off to your left as you're looking at me. I'll kill the engine a couple of boat lengths farther out. By the time I get to you, we ought to be dead in the water."

"But still riding up and down," Virgil said.

"Yeah, but you won't have any momentum to deal with. Shed

your gear, stay well back, and we'll pull it over the side. Then we'll take the lift bags and you can stay off to the side, finning, until you're ready to grab the boarding ladder. We'll take the fins when you're ready, and once you get your feet on the ladder, you're good. We'll help you up."

Virgil nodded: "That should work. I mean, this really isn't much, the rollers."

Cattaneo said, "Better get your tanks on; we're ten minutes out."

Nine minutes and forty seconds later, Virgil took the big step into the water, got oriented as the sound of the boat faded away, and started toward the line of heroin cans.

RAE WATCHED VIRGIL disappear over the side, then said to Cattaneo, "I'm gonna go lay down. Call me when you turn around."

"You want somebody to lay down with?" Regio asked, showing some teeth.

"Okay, you win the day's lame asshole award," Rae said. "I don't need some wannabe Tony Soprano climbing on me. I *could* use a little sniff of cocaine, if you happen to have some in your pocket."

Cattaneo: "We don't carry drugs. Or even use them, really."

Made Rae laugh: "You don't carry drugs? You mean, except for a hundred kilos of pure white boy?"

"Pure white boy. Sounds like a right-wing campaign slogan," Lange said.

"Get your sleep," Cattaneo said. "Gonna roll some. If you think you're gonna hurl, try not to do it on the bed."

✦✦✦

RAE STRETCHED OUT in the middle berth, tried to ignore the boat's motion, and dozed; at some point, she woke, and felt somebody had peeked through the door, checking on her, but the door was closed and the cabin dark when she sat up. The Sig was cold against her leg, and might have been visible while she was asleep, but the room was dark, gun was dark, her leg was dark, and the gaffer tape was black, so, she thought, she was okay.

She straightened herself up, checked the gun, which was solid, left the cabin and climbed the stairs—Cattaneo called it a ladder—into the cockpit. A light mist, little more than a fog, was falling on the boat, dampening her face.

"How are we doing?" she asked.

"We'll make the turn in a couple of minutes," Cattaneo said. "Sit down and enjoy the night. There's a poncho in the locker just below the ladder."

She went back down the stairs and got it, pulled it on—a piece of plastic with a head hole and a hood—climbed back up the stairs and sat next to Regio. They made the turn, and off to the west, the oceanside condos had an eerie glow in the mist.

"Where are you from, Ally?" Cattaneo asked. "I mean, originally."

"New Orleans."

"New Orleans. Only been there a couple of times," Cattaneo said. "Gotta tell you, I don't understand the charm, though I had some shrimp thing that was good. My wife knew about it."

"Well, it's got beat up the last few years," Rae said. "Still like it, though. They do got good food there. Good weed, good music."

"Huh. Used to be a big Mafia town," Regio said. "Long time ago, not much going on there now. All those ratshit gangbangers selling eight-balls and killing each other. Used to have some nice casinos, nice ladies."

"You mean whores?" Rae asked.

"That's ungenerous," Cattaneo said.

"Ungenerous, but right," Lange said. "I once spent a week down there and some of those women were flat nasty. I talked to one who had a scar that started between her tits and went all the way down to her pussy. Straight line. Some guys get off on that, I guess. Nasty."

"If you didn't get off on it, how do you know it went all the way down to her pussy?" Regio asked.

"She told us."

"She told you?" Rae asked. "Just like that? 'Yeah, I got a scar that goes from my tits all the way down to my pussy'?"

"Look. I was in a titty bar with this dufus motherfucker from Queens whose old lady would never let him go to one, so we got to New Orleans and he had to go. Anyway, she was hustling drinks and she was wearing a bikini and dufus saw this scar and asked her where it stopped."

"And she told you?"

"Yeah. I don't think he was the first guy who asked," Lange said.

THEY RODE ALONG on that thought for a while, until Rae asked, "How much longer?"

Cattaneo looked at his watch. "Forty minutes."

"You really gonna pay me'n Willy a million dollars?"

"If Willy keeps bringing up the goods, damn straight. There

may be a lot more than that. This was only the first load coming up the coast. We might get them to dump it further north next time, but Willy's skills are exactly what we've been looking for. I like the way this boy works."

"What happened to your first diver?"

"She decided she didn't want to do it anymore. She was from the Bahamas and she said she was going to go back and visit her mama after . . . the problem we had. But she didn't do that. When we went to pick her up again, no diver, and no mama."

"Jaquell was a nervous one," Regio said. "We're better off with Willy. And Ally."

AFTER SOME SILENCE, Rae asked, "You the fools that shot those Coast Guard sailors last summer?"

Lange glanced at Regio, which was as good as a "Yes, he did it," but Cattaneo said, "We really don't talk about that kind of thing. It's impolite. We don't mess with the Coast Guard."

"So it was somebody else who shot them?"

Regio was staring at her, his rattlesnake stare, but Rae had been stared at by worse people when she hadn't had a gun taped to her ankle.

"We don't talk about those things," Cattaneo repeated. He smiled at her. "So, you know . . . shut the fuck up. Please?"

VIRGIL WAS FLOATING on the surface. They spotted him a couple of hundred feet out, off to their left, and Cattaneo cut the motor and they glided on forward, slowing as they went, and then Lange threw Virgil a line. Virgil pulled himself up to the boat, which, as Cattaneo had said, was dead in the water. Virgil stayed five feet away, shed his backplate and tanks, passed them up to Regio and Lange. The lift bag line went next, up to Regio, and Virgil said, "Didn't do so good this time, but I got five. We got a problem."

"Five is good, five is fine," Cattaneo called down to him.

When the orange lift bag, followed by the cargo bag, were pulled over the side of the boat, Virgil passed up his fins, then hooked his bare feet in the stainless steel boarding ladder, rode up and down a couple of times, then stood up on the bottom rung. Lange and Regio got him under the arms and helped him onto the boat. As soon as he was on, Cattaneo kicked the engine over.

"Get the shit below," Cattaneo said. "And Willy—five is great. We owe you thirty-seven-five. What's the problem?"

Virgil shook the water off his back and legs and asked Rae, "How're we doing, Ally?"

"Two more dives, I'm thinking Porsche, sweet pea," and she again kissed him on the lips.

Virgil sat in the cockpit and looked up at Cattaneo, brushed his hair back, and said, "The ship that dumped the cans wasn't running exactly parallel to the outer reefs . . . it was sliding off to the east, into deeper water. The south end of the dump was in a hundred and forty to a hundred and fifty feet. Today I was down at a hundred and sixty-six. By the end of the dump, it could be close to two hundred feet, or two-ten. That's getting . . . risky. I'll need more bottom time to collect the cans and I'll need more decompression time coming back up."

"But you can do it?"

"I guess. Depending on how deep it gets—it's impossible to

know, depending on where the ship went. I might need to go to Trimix instead of straight air. I don't know about sources for it here in Lauderdale. I'm sure there must be some."

Cattaneo said, "Hold on to the wheel for a minute. You don't have to steer, just hold on."

Virgil did that and Cattaneo went below and returned with a plastic briefcase and took out an iPad.

"Aqua Map," he said.

He called up a chart of the ocean north of Port Everglades, touched the screen, said, "Here's the drop site. Did you check the compass heading for the drops?"

"About five degrees off north. That's probably not exact, but it'll be close."

Cattaneo fiddled with the chart for a moment, then said, "Damnit. You're right. The north end of the site will be close to two hundred—a hundred and ninety to two hundred."

Rae said, "Time to bail?"

Virgil rubbed his eyes and said, "Ah, I can do it. I can't stay down as long without going to Trimix, though."

Cattaneo said, "Tell you what. I'll throw in an extra thousand dollars for the deep dives. Don't cheat me, I'm going to look at whatever depths you get to, but below a hundred and seventy-five, I'll throw in the extra grand."

Virgil nodded: "Okay. What's the weather tomorrow?"

Cattaneo said, "Gonna be smooth as a baby's butt."

THE REST OF the run back to the boat slip was routine. On the way, Virgil told them about the dive: "I'm not sure, but I think I might be done with the south end. There was more silt stirring around tonight, I might have missed some stuff, so I'm not positive."

"Don't worry about it—we'll worry after we know what is down there. Go north. You're the dive boss," Cattaneo said.

At the slip, Virgil, now dressed in street clothes, helped pile the scuba gear into Regio's Lexus, and Regio drove them back to the apartment. "Tomorrow at the same time?" Regio asked, as they carried the gear up to the apartment.

"Yeah. I'll call around, see what I can find out about Trimix. I don't really need it at two hundred, unless I need to stay down."

"You gotta get into the computer age, Willy," Regio said. "I'll get back to my place and check dive shops. I can call you tonight with a Trimix shop."

"That'd be awesome," Virgil said.

Regio said to Rae, "Don't talk him out of it. Eight thousand five hundred dollars per can. If he gets eleven cans like he did the first night, that's a hair less than a hundred grand."

"It's ninety-three five, which is a couple of hairs less than a hundred grand," Rae said. "And we don't get nothin' if he's dead."

"Neither will we," Regio said. He turned to Virgil: "You're doing good, Willy. Gotta keep it up."

CHAPTER

TWENTY-FIVE

STATEN ISLAND:

They'd waited a long time in the FBI suite on Staten Island, but as Cattaneo's boat was pushing out of the Atlantic through the entrance to Port Everglades, the surveillance guys in the truck called and said, "Look at this, look at this."

A Chrysler sedan rolled past the truck, paused at the cross street, and then rolled into the car wash parking lot. The overhead door on the garage went up and the Chrysler went inside. The door came down and one of the computer operators was already running the license tag.

"This is one of the prime dealers," she said. "Jerry Poole, AKA the Hat. He wears hats."

"What's his file look like?" Lucas asked. He'd been sitting on a couch, reading a battered *New Yorker*, and came to look at the computer screen.

"He's bad. Bad enough? Maybe," Kate Orish said.

"If he's only a 'maybe,' then let's wait," Lucas said. "Can we track him?"

"We can. I seriously doubt that he'll put anything on the street tonight. He'll want to get it cut, talk to his people . . ."

"Are we covering his phone?"

"One of them: but he has another and we don't know what it is. He mostly talks to his wife on the iPhone."

"Damnit. Stay on him, and let's wait."

"Your call," Orish said. "For now, anyway."

"There's still somebody in the garage. You can see the light under the doors. There are more people on the way," Devlin said.

RAE CALLED. "WE'RE back at the apartment," she said. "Virgil brought up another five cans. You'll have to talk to the surveillance guys to find out where they went. But: Regio shot the Coast Guardsmen. He didn't admit it, but he did. Cattaneo was on the boat and I think Lange was there, too."

She told him about the short conversation on the boat, and how Cattaneo had cut it off.

"Don't push it," Lucas said. "We don't want them pissed or suspicious."

"They're too greedy to suspect anything. We're going back out tomorrow night, unless you say otherwise. They're pushing Virgil."

"Watch your phones. We've got people picking up the dope now. You get the red flag, you bail, okay?"

"Got it."

After a brief silence, Lucas added, "Tomorrow could be the last dive. I think we'll be grabbing them tomorrow, probably tomorrow night. Watch the street tomorrow, and when you see them coming to pick you up, call me. I may tell you to bail right then."

✤✤✤

ANOTHER CAR PULLED into the car wash, which was now dark. The car disappeared into the garage, as the others had, and when the computer operator ran the New Jersey license tag, it came back with Salas Zamora, a street dealer with a half dozen low-level drug busts.

"He's moving up, but he's not the one you want," Orish said. "We've been here all day. I'll give it another hour, and then I'm going to bed. I'd suggest you do the same—if anything really good-looking comes up, the night shift will give us a call."

"What about the guys in the truck?" Lucas asked.

"We've got another shift coming in for them, too. They'll drive out a way, drop the day shift and load the night shift, and go back. While they're making the trade, we've got a car that'll park in their space to keep it open."

"You know what I want to do?" Lucas asked. "I want to see where the garage guys go, when they close down. Could I get a surveillance car around front, somebody to give me a ride?"

Orish said, "Sure. What are you thinking?"

"Unless they're passing out kilos of heroin on credit, those prime dealers are handing over cash when they pick up the dope. In my experience, credit is unlikely, though I don't have that much experience with dope."

"I think you're right," said one of the feds. "I used to be a cop in Boston and worked narcotics for a while. Credit was nonexistent on the street and rare higher up. They might not be collecting money from everyone, but I bet they're collecting from most of them. From the new guys, anyway."

As they were talking, Zamora left, and Orish called for a sur-veillance car to pick up Lucas. Lucas asked Devlin to hang at the task force suite, watching incoming cars, then hurried down through the lobby and caught a tan Camry. The driver, whose name was Rob Blake, said, "We'll wait completely out of sight until they move. There are Cokes in the cooler in back."

They drove over to the street where the surveillance truck was parked, found a dark space under a tree, well back, and pulled in.

Devlin called a while later: "We got another customer. Black Jeep."

He called again, one minute later: "He's not a customer, the Jeep guy. I think he's a night guard. He left his Jeep outside, by the car wash, and he went in the garage."

And ten minutes later, "Okay, the inside man is leaving. He's got a shoulder bag. Driving a black Audi A5. He's in the car, he's heading north."

The Camry was already creeping out of its parking spot, took it easy going down to the corner. They peeked, then turned and fol-lowed the Audi. The driver was good, gauging traffic lights, hang-ing back behind other cars. "The thing about Camry headlights," he said, "is they're like everybody's headlights. You get some of those German cars, they're distinctive. That Audi will have a line of LEDs, really bright white, you see them in your rearview mir-ror, you don't forget them."

Orish called Blake: "Where are you?"

"Heading south on 440 toward 278. Hang on a minute, we'll be coming up to the junction . . ."

"He's getting off," Lucas said.

Blake went back to the phone: "He's heading west on 278. We've got another junction coming up, hang on . . . no, he's staying on 278, we could be headed for Jersey."

"That would be interesting," Orish said. "I'm hanging on here: call me when you know where he's going."

THEY STAYED WITH the Audi as it crossed the Goethals Bridge and then went north into the town of Elizabeth, through a few back streets—they almost lost him there, but Blake picked up his taillights after an anxious two minutes—and watched from a distance as he pulled into a parking space outside a small, dimly lit building. From two blocks back, they watched the Audi driver get out of the car, knock on the front door of the small building, and then disappear inside.

"Let's cruise the building," Lucas said.

They did that: the sign above the building's door said GOOD-WIN'S LOCK AND SAFE with a subscript that added, WE'LL TAKE CARE WHEN YOU CAN'T.

They continued on, two streets, did a U-turn, parked at the corner. The Audi driver was inside for five minutes, then reappeared, carrying his shoulder bag in one hand. "Follow, or let him go?" Blake asked.

"Let him go."

Two minutes later, one of the lights in the locksmith shop went out and a man stepped outside, turned to pull the door shut, and locked it. For a moment, the low interior light shone on his face, and Blake, watching with binoculars, said, "Well, I'll be blowed."

"What?"

"That's Sansone," Blake said. "He's carrying a brown grocery bag. That gives me a little woody."

"Not interested in your woody, but I'm interested in that bag . . ."

"You want to grab him?"

"Ah . . ." Sansone walked fifty feet down the street, got into a Mercedes SUV. "I don't know," Lucas said. "That's probably the cash, but if it isn't . . . damnit."

He called Orish and told her about it. "I'd let it go," she said. "There'll be a lot more where that's at. I don't think these guys are picking up ten kilos at a time, but even if they were, there's still a lot in that garage. I say we watch for exactly the right guy tomorrow, turn him, then hit Sansone for the marked money. If we do both things, he'll have no way out."

Lucas thought it over, then said, "Okay. We're heading back."

AT THE HILTON, the day shift feds had left and the night shift had taken over.

Lucas, Devlin, and Orish lingered, talking, watching the cameras. A half hour passed, and Orish finally said, "I'm going."

To the senior agent on the night shift, she said, "If anything moves, anything, you get me out of bed. I'll have my phone on the pillow next to my ear. *Anything.*"

After she had gone out the door, Devlin and Lucas waited another two minutes, then went down to their own rooms. "This is going to work," Devlin said. "If we can get the right guy, we'll have the whole operation pinned, from Lauderdale to New York."

"Sleep," Lucas said.

◆◆◆

LUCAS SPENT TEN minutes talking on the phone with Weather, climbed into bed, and slept—but not well. He was tense, and even though he was asleep, the stress kept him close to the surface. Though he didn't sleep well, he slept long enough. He'd expected a call in the night, or early in the morning, but his phone alarm went off at seven o'clock, and he rolled out, undisturbed by the FBI watchers. He called Devlin, who was also up, and they agreed to catch a fast breakfast before heading back up to the task force suite.

Devlin hadn't slept well, either, and they ate the same way they'd slept: in a hurry. Up in the task force suite, Orish and her second, Dick Kerry, were drinking coffee and cruising the various computers. The day shift was back again, along with fresh boxes of pastry and a couple of gallons of coffee. Short stacks of the *New York Times* and the *Wall Street Journal* sat next to the donuts. When Lucas and Devlin arrived, Orish nodded and said, "The going's slow."

There'd been no movement overnight. The day shift was back in the truck and the cameras were focused on the car wash.

"What happened to the Hat?" Devlin asked Orish.

"He owns an apartment house over on the east side, six apartments. He went in, and that's the last we've seen of him. He could be in any of the apartments and we haven't seen anybody arriving who might be carrying off the heroin. Makes a raid tough."

"He's probably cutting it," Devlin said.

"Or he sleeps late," Kerry said.

One of the computer operators said, "The hearse is moving."

Orish and Kerry went to the windows and looked out. "There

it goes," Orish said, looking down at the hotel driveway. "Probably back to Florida for the second load."

"We need to keep close track of it," Lucas said. "I mean, what if the dope is still in the hearse, and they did the whole car wash thing to make sure they were clean?"

Orish and Kerry glanced at each other, and then Kerry said, "Unlikely."

"Yeah, I know," Lucas said. "But I'd sure hate to lose track of the dope . . ."

Orish said to the computer operator, "If that hearse slows down for more than a traffic light, I want to know about it. I want a car on it until it's well out of town. Not where it could be seen, but where it could catch up in a minute or so, if the hearse starts to wander."

"Got it," the computer operator said.

They stood around, watching the arrowhead that represented the hearse crawling across Staten Island. It was approaching water when the computer operator who was monitoring the surveillance camera called, "We got another one."

THEY WENT TO the surveillance screen and watched a Cadillac SUV disappear into the garage. The plate went to a Cheri Malone; she showed no criminal record at all.

"I'd call that a possibility," Orish said, looking at the photo on Malone's driver's license. She was a hard-faced fifty and held a New York real estate license. "What do you think, Lucas?"

"Don't know. Like you said, a possibility. If she's never been in-side, the prospect might frighten her. On the other hand, she's not likely to draw a lot of time . . . clean record, she might even claim to be doing a favor for a friend."

The Cadillac backed out of the garage after a two-minute stay and rolled away.

The hearse had crossed into New Jersey and had turned south on I-95.

Twenty minutes later a pickup truck drove into the garage. "Paul Curry," Orish said. Wrinkles appeared on her forehead. "I know that name. I think he might be . . ."

A computer operator said, "He might be the one. He's been inside four times, twice for dope, once for ag assault, once for criminal sexual assault. He's fifty-two, one more big bust and he goes away forever."

"Anything on his family?" Kerry asked.

The operator rattled some keys and then said, "Married, two children in their twenties."

"The problem is, if he flips on Sansone, Sansone's people could take it out on his family, even if Curry and his wife are in witness protection," Devlin said. "Of course, being an asshole, maybe he wouldn't care."

"But he's another possible," Lucas said. "Let's start digging on him. Find out where he's going, where he has the dope."

"Crank up an entry team?" Orish asked.

"Not yet," Lucas said. "Let's just track him."

They tracked him to a neighborhood called New Dorp, south and east of the car wash.

"We got another one. They're starting to come in," the surveillance operator said.

They went to look: a black five-liter Mustang. The tag went out to a Kent Pruitt, and when they looked, they found a complicated rap sheet that involved drug sales, burglaries both alleged and proven, and three alleged sexual assaults, a guilty plea on one with the other two nol-prossed. "Prosecutor traded a guilty plea for the nol-prosses," Kerry said.

They all read through the rap sheet and Lucas pointed at the bottom of the computer screen: "Look at this. He was a witness in a rape trial. Actually, if I'm reading this right, it looks like he was a victim of a rapist, while he was in prison. He will *not* want to go back. If we hit him for anything heavy, like possession of a kilo of heroin, he'll be going back forever."

"Attention, people," Orish said to the group, clapping her hands twice. "We've got a live one. We need everything we can get on this Pruitt. We need to move three cars and box him, don't lose him. He could be our man."

THE SURVEILLANCE TEAMS tracked Pruitt to a house that was owned by a Kills Realty, which apparently specialized in rental management. The trackers watched, but Pruitt didn't immediately reemerge.

Orish wanted to watch for more prime distributors and Lucas agreed with that, but suggested that she was unlikely to find some-body better than Pruitt. "Devlin and I will pick him up," Lucas said. "You need to have someone good at interrogation, I think in Manhattan—and we don't take that ferry over there, we drive him. We don't want anyone to see his face after we have him in a car."

"We feel one of our teams would be better," Orish said.

Lucas shook his head. "Look. You guys do a mountain of research and you're really good at that, but you do two kinds of arrests. One is, you send in a SWAT team, knock down all the doors, and pile on top of people; the other is more like a party. You all show up wearing your FBI vests and you seize all the file cabinets. And that's fine, you do it well. Us marshals arrest individual fugitives. That's what this is going to be: we can't have any excitement at all. Devlin and I will sort of amble up to him and ask for a light and tell him he's under arrest and if he resists we'll beat the shit out of him, in a hurry. Mug him. That's what *we* do. That's what we need in this situation."

"If it goes wrong?"

"That's where you come in. We'll want surveillance watching us with some of your people ready to jump, if it all goes to hell. But it won't. We'll take him, and nobody will know except us chickens."

"I'll talk with the AIC," Orish said. "We need to clear it."

"Clear it, then. Tell the AIC to have a chat with Louis Mallard before he makes a decision," Lucas said. "By the way, we're going to need a warrant to go into Pruitt's house after we crack him, and we'll need at least some surveillance all day today. We need to know how many people are in the house, whether there are any children, whether there's a back way out, and all that."

"All day? When are you planning to take him?" Kerry asked.

"Tonight, after dark. We really don't want people looking at us. People of the drug-buying variety. They can smell a cop at a hundred yards."

"Let me talk with the AIC," Orish repeated.

"Fine. In the meantime, let's get the guy who brought us in here yesterday—Koch? I want to go down and take a look at Pruitt's place, and the neighborhood."

ORISH WENT OFF somewhere to consult with the Manhattan agent in charge while Lucas and Devlin took the elevator down to the lobby, where they met Dillon Koch. "I have the address," Koch said. "It's a neighborhood called Westerleigh. Wester-lay or Wester-lee, I don't know if I'm pronouncing it right. It's eight or ten minutes from here."

The cold hit them when they left the building—something in the low twenties, Lucas thought, and windy. Little mean snaps of snow, more pellet than flake, stung their faces.

Devlin kept his head down into the wind, and Lucas said, "Not something you get much of in Louisiana, huh? The cold."

"Not like this. But this isn't terrible."

Lucas disagreed: "It's on the edge of terrible and would be even in Minnesota."

WESTERLEIGH TURNED OUT to be an older neighborhood, mostly prewar and World War II–era two-story houses, painted in pastel shades, and remodeled and remodeled over again. They sat on heavily patched blacktopped streets with mature trees and on-street parking everywhere. Narrow driveways separated the houses, reaching back to single-car garages. Lawns were short and narrow with spotty, dirty snow. The neighborhood reminded Lucas of any number of neighborhoods in the Twin Cities, not far from his own.

Pruitt lived in an old gray house with red shutters and a heavily scarred maple tree on the front boulevard; as with most houses on the street, a tight driveway led to a small garage. Pruitt's Mustang sat in the driveway next to the house.

"Gonna be hard to keep too close an eye on this place," Lucas said, as they cruised the house. "Narrow street, if anyone sits in a car too long, the neighbors will spot them."

Koch pointed at a Chevy van a block up the street. "That's ours. One guy, he's now in the back."

The sign on the side of the van said DAVE'S REMODELING AND RE- PAIR, with a New York phone number beneath it. "Only problem is that it's a Manhattan number," Koch said. "That might raise an eyebrow, if anybody really paid attention."

"Somebody watching the back?" Lucas asked.

"Yes. Same deal. Parked van."

Satisfied with the watch, and the neighborhood, they went back to the Hilton and up to the task force suite, where Orish told him, "It's your bust. We'll do the backup. Nobody's come or gone from the place except Pruitt. He's there now."

"We saw his car," Lucas said, as he peeled off his overcoat. "Do we know any more about him?"

"No. Nobody really pays any attention to him. He has a day job with—guess who?"

"Sansone?"

"There you go—he's supposedly a baker at one of the donut shops. That's probably a cover. He's still on parole, he reports in to his PO once a month, clean reports so far. He originally got a job as a house cleaner after he got out of Greene Correctional Facility."

There were several online photos, both from Pruitt's arrest

records and prison days, and from his driver's licenses. He was a thin man of medium height, going bald, dark questioning eyes, large nose, and large ears.

"Not a real good-looking guy," Devlin said. "He looks . . . seedy."

"He's a drug dealer," Kerry said. "He's not a dumb guy—he scores relatively high on the tests they did in prison. He reads well, he took online accounting courses when he was inside."

THREE MORE PRIME distributors came into the car wash, spaced almost exactly an hour apart. "It's like they don't want the dealers to see each other," Orish said. "Suppose it's some kind of security thing?"

Lucas didn't know. None of the dealers looked better than Pruitt.

RAE CALLED AT 3:20 and said, quickly and quietly, "Our ride is here. Are we still on?"

"Yeah. We have a target, but we won't be going after him for another two hours. Watch your phone . . ."

"Take it easy, Lucas. These guys will kill you."

"You do the same, Rae. Easy does it."

THE LEAD SURVEILLANCE car, watching Pruitt, called at 5:15, just as it was getting dark, to say that Pruitt was moving.

"You going?" Orish asked.

"We're going," Lucas said, pulling on his overcoat. "We'll call when we've got him. Keep a van close, but out of sight."

Lucas and Devlin stopped at their rooms long enough to retrieve lightweight bulletproof vests, then went down to find Dillon Koch waiting for them. They briefed him on the pickup—"We'll spot his car and wait for him there, then move him to a van for transport"—and they headed south. The cars covering Pruitt said he'd gone to a Vietnamese restaurant called Loan's on the southeast side of the island. Loan's was in a strip mall and they found Pruitt's black Mustang at the edge of a nearly full parking lot.

"What do you think?" Devlin asked.

"Lot of windows looking out at the car," Lucas said.

"If he unloads the shit here . . . and we grab him later . . . we got nothin'," Devlin said.

"He won't unload a kilo here. This is only his first stop of the night. He'll have more to spread around."

THEY MOVED A half block away to watch the restaurant, and Pruitt showed five minutes later.

"He didn't eat," Lucas said. "He's unloading the junk."

Pruitt opened the trunk of the Mustang, did something inside, and carrying a paper sack, climbed into the driver's seat, sat there for a full three minutes, then pulled out of the lot, heading farther south. They crept along behind, turning down side streets and then making immediate U-turns to get back behind the Mustang.

Pruitt's next stop was in a neighborhood called Eltingville, according to Koch's iPad, at a tiny yellow house with a tiny attic sticking up like a cheese wedge. There were three cars parked on the street near the front of the house and Pruitt parked down two houses, got out, carrying the brown paper shopping sack.

"This is it," Lucas said to Koch. "As soon as he gets inside, put us right on the other side of his car, then watch and get ready to call the van."

Koch dropped them and accelerated away while Lucas and Devlin walked up a driveway and waited behind a thin hedge at the corner of the house that was hiding them. A few minutes later, Pruitt, still carrying the paper sack, sauntered down the sidewalk toward the car. He used a key fob to unlock the car, and as he turned to step off the curb to go around the back of his car to the driver's side, Lucas and Devlin bounded out of the dark and were on him.

Pruitt turned, brought up a hand; Lucas batted it aside and said, "U.S. Marshals. You're under arrest. Open the car and get in the back."

"Fuck you . . ."

Lucas hit him in the solar plexus, the blow blunted by Pruitt's leather jacket, but the smaller man bent over and Lucas slapped him hard on the side of the head.

Pruitt dropped the sack he was carrying and the keys. Lucas looked around for interference, saw none, then led the stunned man to the passenger-side door, did a quick search, found no weapon. As Devlin held the front seatback forward, Lucas pushed Pruitt facedown in the tight backseat.

When he was in, Devlin crawled into the front seat, backward, looking over the seat facing Pruitt, and Lucas picked up the sack and the keys and walked around and got in the driver's seat. Devlin said to Pruitt, "I've got a sap in my hand. If you fight me, I'll break your skull. Do you understand me?"

Pruitt muttered, "Lawyer."

Devlin: "We'll get you one. Don't fight us, or I'll crack you like a fuckin' lightbulb."

Lucas started the car and eased it down the street. Devlin had Pruitt by the hair with one hand, and with the other, groped through Pruitt's jacket and came up with a cell phone.

Lucas's phone rang and Koch said, "Straight ahead three blocks. I'll give you a left turn signal when I see you coming. Follow me, it's about two more blocks."

Pruitt began kicking and Devlin said, "Hey, hey!" And then *whack*. Pruitt stopped fighting.

"Only hurt him enough," Lucas said, for Pruitt's benefit. "We don't want him paralyzed or anything. If you can help it."

Devlin: "I hate fuckin' dope dealers. I'm gonna hit him some more . . ."

Pruitt stayed quiet.

Lucas spotted Koch's turn signal, flashed the headlights, and Koch led them around a corner and down two blocks, into an alley space between a pizza parlor and a dark commercial building of some kind. A van was waiting and when Lucas pulled up beside it, a side door slid back and two large FBI agents climbed out. Devlin got out of the Mustang, pulled the front seat forward, and he and the two agents yanked Pruitt out of the back of the Mustang and half-carried, half-dragged him to the van, where they cuffed him to a steel ring welded to the floor.

One of the agents said, "Call Orish. We'll see you—or not— over in Manhattan."

"Check him for weapons or another cell phone," Lucas said. "We didn't have a lot of time back there."

"Do that."

A minute later, the van was gone.

DEVLIN GOT BACK in the Mustang and Lucas pulled deeper into the alley, found the interior lights, looked in the paper bag and found a thick stack of currency, mostly twenties and fifties. "I need to take a look in the trunk before we go," he said. "Pray for heroin."

"I want to look, too," Devlin said. He stepped down toward the street. "What happened to Koch?"

"Kept going," Lucas said. "Surveillance guys don't like to be seen."

They popped the trunk, found a leather satchel, and opened it. Inside were a dozen plastic bags of heroin, ranging from a few ounces to perhaps a pound. They transferred the satchel to the backseat and Lucas called Orish.

"We got him. We got money and we got the heroin. A lot of heroin."

"I talked to our pickup guys in the van and the surveillance cars. They think you got away clean."

"Okay. Now it's up to you guys: break him, and we'll sweep up the whole organization tomorrow."

LUCAS TALKED TO Virgil. "How'd the dive go?"

"Routine. Five cans. We've really got it down, now. I'm going deeper, though. I'll be okay tomorrow, maybe one more day, but after that, I'll be getting uncomfortable. We'll see."

"We'd all be happier if you didn't die," Lucas said.

"Me, too," Virgil said.

TWENTY-SIX

PRUITT DIDN'T BREAK.

The agents in the pickup van reported that he said nothing but the word *lawyer*.

He was held overnight in the isolation section of the Manhattan federal lockup. Since he'd asked for a lawyer, the feds couldn't press him with questions, but they could *talk* around him.

"This poor chump thinks some of his Mafia buddies are going to bail his ass out. Not gonna happen. Sansone takes care of one person: Sansone. This genius is going to prison forever to protect him. Forever, and man, that's a long time. With as much dope as he had on him . . . you think they'll send him out to ADX Florence? These are the guys who shot those Coast Guardsmen and murdered the marshal . . ."

Didn't work. Pruitt continued to say "lawyer" for a while, then put his head down and went to sleep. The door to his cell was opened every ten minutes or so during the night, then slammed shut, waking him, but he still refused to say a word.

"He's asked for a lawyer by name," Orish told Lucas. "A drug lawyer, well known for his connections. About two minutes after he leaves Pruitt in the lockup, Sansone's going to get a phone call."

"You can still hold him for another couple of days," Devlin said.

"Yes, but that's the limit. Then we'll have to call his lawyer. Bottom line is, we've got today and tomorrow to turn somebody and arrest Sansone. If you've got any ideas . . ."

Lucas said, "I've been running through the notes, diving into backgrounds. I'm thinking we go after Paul Curry. He's been inside four times; another conviction and he's done. He gets life. One other interesting thing—he apparently has had problems with the Aryan Brotherhood, but the Brotherhood wasn't strong where he spent his time and he had enough Mafia buddies to protect him."

"What got the Brotherhood on him?"

"He apparently talked to the prison guards about a Brotherhood member who shanked another convict, a friend of his. A couple of Brotherhood guys went off to Southport."

"The New York supermax."

"Yeah. Curry has more than one reason to stay outside. And he's got the wife and kids . . ."

Kerry, Orish's second, said, "We gotta do something, quick, and he sounds as good as any of them. You want to take a shot at picking him up in daylight hours?"

"I'd rather not . . . he'll be harder to tail without him spotting us," Lucas said. "He makes a phone call, we're screwed. Most of his dealers will be working at night, in the clubs, he'll be making the most stops then."

"Be a long day, not doing anything," Orish said.

Lucas looked at his watch: "Seven hours. Okay. Let's think

about doing something in daylight. Let's put a full crew on him now. That dope he picked up, that must be at his house, right?"

"As far as we know . . ."

ORISH GOT THAT started, and Lucas called Virgil: "You're either going to have to make one more dive, or figure out a reason not to, something that won't make Behan and Cattaneo suspicious."

He explained what had happened—that Pruitt refused to deal—and Virgil said, "Listen, these guys are loosening up around Rae. They're talking to her more while I'm in the water. We ought to go out, see if there's anything more we can get from them before it all comes down."

"Don't interrogate them," Lucas said. "You gotta be super-careful. We're right there at the climax of this whole thing. We'll have people waiting for you when you get back to the dock. I'll call Weaver."

"We're okay. I gotta go get some air right now, fill my tanks. I'll talk to Rae. If anything changes, for Christ sake, call us. Don't let the feds hang us up."

"I'm all over them," Lucas said.

HOLLYWOOD:

Virgil and Rae were driving north to a shop in Deerfield Beach to get the scuba tanks refilled. As they loaded the car, he and Rae talked over the call from Lucas, and Virgil asked, "What do you think?"

"I don't know. We've got one guy in a cell who isn't talking, so they're going to go after another guy. Will they be missed? That's the question," Rae said. "These guys aren't stupid. I mean, Regio isn't the brightest bulb on the porch, but we have to be careful around Lange and Cattaneo. Cattaneo especially—he talks softly, but I have a feeling that he might be the meanest of the bunch."

"What about Behan?" Virgil asked.

"Another smart guy," Rae said. "There's some stress between him and Cattaneo. I don't know where that's coming from, but it's there. It comes out every once in a while, when he's talking to Lange and Regio."

"Maybe Cattaneo is looking for a promotion and Behan's in the way?"

"Could be. I don't know."

"We could bail on tonight's dive," Virgil said. He slammed the back hatch on the car.

"You worried about it?" Rae asked.

"Not about the dive. I'm worried about something leaking out of New York. Or, if they spot somebody following us down here."

"Everybody's backed off . . ." Rae said.

"So they tell us. But you know the FBI. The office competition to be the hero."

"Your call," Rae said. "With all the gear you carry, you could probably slip a revolver inside your wet suit without them spotting it."

"Nah. If we think I might need a pistol, we'd be better off bailing."

"Your call," she said again.

"Let's go get the air," Virgil said, walking around to the passenger side. "We've still got some time to decide."

◆◆◆

ON THE WAY north, Virgil said, "Something I need to talk to you about."

"Talk."

"About Bob."

"Oh, jeez, Virgil, I'm not . . ."

Virgil interrupted: "Your pal Lucas is a killer. He's also a good friend of mine, but we don't do things the same way. I don't like it when people get hurt, even assholes. I know you were tight with Bob and now we're beginning to see the guys who got him killed. Who hired the killers. Cattaneo, probably, or Behan."

"You don't want me killing them."

"That's right. You marshals . . . I mean, some of you guys . . ."

"I've shot three people," Rae said. "Only when I thought they were going to shoot me or another marshal. I'm not looking for personal revenge. I'm happy to get them into court."

Virgil nodded: "That's what I do. Get them into court. Lucas doesn't always do that. He does it most of the time, but if the guy is bad enough, or the woman, for that matter, he'll flat-out kill them."

"I know that. That's not me, so don't sweat it."

"Good. I don't want to climb on the boat and find myself standing in a pool of blood." After a moment, he added, "Especially if it's *your* blood. If you *gotta* pull a trigger, do it."

A FEW MORE miles and Rae said, "Last night you were talking about Trimix. I don't have a tight hold on how that works."

"Regular air has two main gases, oxygen and nitrogen. When you dive deep, nitrogen can cause some problems . . ."

"You get high."

"Yeah, that's one thing. And the deeper you go, the worse the nitrogen narcosis gets. I start feeling it at about a hundred and thirty, and I'm definitely there at one-fifty, if I stay long enough. At two hundred, I'll be narced. It's like smoking weed and then trying to walk down a curb, like that. Not gonna kill me, but I'll be high. I can handle it, I've been there a dozen times. Trimix replaces some of the nitrogen with helium, but filling the tanks with Trimix takes more time than we've got right now. Most places, it'll take a few hours. There's a heat problem . . . never mind. So, if I gotta do it, I'll do it on straight air. If the line of cans takes me too deep to-night, I'll say fuck it and come back up. I won't go deeper than one-ninety."

"This bothers me."

"I'm more bothered about you up on top, looking at three to one. About the assholes down here being tipped by the Jersey assholes after the FBI assholes screw it up."

"I'm thinking about that," Rae said.

REGIO AND LANGE watched them leave the apartment.

They were sitting a block down Hollywood Boulevard and followed the battered Subaru, two blocks back, until Willy and Ally turned up I-95, headed north. Regio did a U-turn and they drove back to the apartment.

Lange had started to annoy the others with his suspicions about Willy, and Behan and Cattaneo had told them to take a closer look.

Regio had spent time as a thief before he became organized, and he slipped the crappy apartment's crappy lock with a pocketknife.

They spent fifteen minutes methodically going through the place. "Why does Willy have all these suits?" Regio asked, after a couple of minutes of looking around.

"Not his," Lange said. "Look at the sizes on them. I think they stole them, Jack said something about it."

"Who would they even fit?" Regio asked, holding up a sport coat.

"I don't know, man. Tweedledum, maybe. Humpty Dumpty."

"Why would they have all this weird shit?" Regio asked. "What's this rug? It's two feet wide with a big fuckin' hole in it."

"Practice putting carpet. They must've hit a golfer," Lange said. "They got all this shit because they're stupid burglars. They went into a place, the alarm went off, they grabbed everything they could in two minutes and ran. I did that myself, when I was about fourteen. They're like a lot of dopers, they never grew up. We oughta mention that to Jack."

In the fifteen minutes of searching, they found nothing that seemed out of place. They did find a much-folded snapshot of Ally in a tiny pink bra and even tinier pink thong. "She's a hooker, or was one," Regio said. "Look at this."

"Got the body from hell," Lange said. "I'd take a piece of that. You know, if my wife would let me."

"Wonder where the cash is?" Regio asked, peering around, as though the cash might jump out from behind a curtain.

"They take it with them. Would you leave a hundred grand in this place, with nobody to watch it? I'll bet you a thousand dollars that they have those cheap nylon money belts and keep the cash around their waists. They're not going to leave it sitting around."

Regio opened a closet door, sniffed, said, "Jesus Christ, it smells like they're shittin' in the closet." He closed the door again.

Lange lifted the edge of a blanket that covered the couch. "Gun," he said.

Regio went over to look: a Smith and Wesson snub-nosed .38 that might have been manufactured in the 1930s, rust on the cylinder and barrel, chipped grips. "Junk. They must've found it laying on the sidewalk," Regio said. He pushed the thumbpiece to release the cylinder, looked at the ammunition. "The ammo looks older than the gun. Anyway . . . put it back."

"WHAT DO YOU think?" Lange asked when they got to the end of the search.

"I don't know. I swear to God, Ally's a ghetto chick. And Willy isn't a cop," Regio said. "One thing about cops, even undercover cops, is that they've got this edge, they're like . . . authoritarian. Willy couldn't give orders to a ham sandwich. But . . ."

"But what?"

"Sansone's boy is in the wind. Or somebody grabbed him. Some shit could be coming down. These two are loose ends."

"Be nuts to do anything about it," Lange said. "Give them plane tickets to Idaho, tell them to lay low. We're gonna need Willy."

"Could do that," Regio said. "But then . . . they'd always be out there."

Lange said, "Not my problem. Or maybe it is, but I'm not going to do anything about it. I like the guy. I like Ally, as far as that goes."

"It's up to the boss man," Regio said. "Whatever he decides."

"Well . . . I dunno. Killing them . . . it's bad business. Bad *for* business. Jimmy killed those two chicks and that Elliot guy, and man, word gets around. I think a lot of guys were . . . set back. I was. Didn't want to hear about it."

"Matt . . . you're a criminal," Regio said.

"I know, I know. Some people need to get put down," Lange said. "That's not always a solution—sometimes it makes everything worse."

TWENTY-SEVEN

THE SSG TEAM assigned to track Paul Curry had picked out his house in the New Dorp neighborhood. Lucas rode with a team member named Jim Ochoa to Burbank Avenue, and Ochoa pointed out a handsome redbrick corner house with a black Ford F-150 parked in the driveway.

"An apparently humble pickup truck, which you don't often see with the wise guys," Ochoa said. He spoke with a New York accent, way up in his sinuses. "You have to know your pickup trucks to understand that it's a Limited, which is the highest trim you can get in an F-150. You're looking at a seventy-five-thousand-dollar pickup truck."

"Who in the hell would spend seventy-five thousand dollars on a pickup?" Lucas asked. "For that price, you could get a nice BMW SUV."

"Which would tend to attract the eye," Ochoa said. "Nobody pays attention to a pickup, unless it has thirty-five-inch tires."

They continued down the street, past a humble Toyota Tacoma: "That's our lookout," Ochoa said, as they passed the truck. "Stuck in a taco. Don't tell anyone I called it that."

"What? Why not?"

"Sorta racist," Ochoa said. "That's the truck driven by every Mexican gardener in California, which is a lot of Mexican gardeners."

"Could be short for 'Tacoma,'" Lucas said.

"Yeah, but it ain't, at least not in California," Ochoa said. "Wanna go around the block?"

"Sure, but let's go down the side instead of the front."

They did that. A tall, heavy hedge ran down the side yard, but Lucas could see a blue crescent above the hedge and said, "Aboveground pool. Big one. Wonder if the kids are still with him? Or if there's a grandchild?"

"Could be, but we haven't seen any young people coming or going—nobody but Curry and his wife. We don't know enough about Sansone's people. Even after watching them for a month. They won't tell you this back at the task force, but Sansone was never really billed as a heavy hitter. The OC guys were kind of surprised that he could wrangle this much heroin. Anyway, that's what I'm told. Sansone's gang isn't an old-line Mafia outfit. Most of them have some college—Sansone's got a degree in finance—and you don't have to be Italian to be a boss. Curry, I don't know what kind of name that is, but it's not Italian."

"Sounds kind of British," Lucas said.

"Fuckin' British drug dealers," Ochoa said.

"Almost as bad as the fuckin' Canadians," Lucas agreed. "Scum, the whole queen ass-kissing bunch of them."

WHEN OCHOA DROPPED Lucas back at the hotel, Orish asked, "You got it figured out?"

"Grab him the first chance we get, put the screws to him. Taking Pruitt to Manhattan sucked up a lot of time—would it be possible to do the first interview with Curry here at the hotel?"

"Could blow our cover, bringing a cuffed guy through the lobby," Kerry said.

"How about some other place? A motel somewhere? How about the post office or some other federal office? We need to get a quick read on him. If he's like Pruitt and tells us to go fuck ourselves, I need to warn off Virgil and Rae. If Sansone tries to get in touch with Pruitt and can't, and starts to wonder, and then calls Curry, and can't get him, we could have a problem. They killed at least three people in South Florida just cleaning up, not counting the shooters who died, or Bob, or the Coast Guardsmen. If they decide they need to clean up Virgil and Rae . . ."

Orish scratched her forehead, wandered over to the window and looked out, thinking, then said, "Curry's at his house. Why don't I get a warrant and a couple of uniforms from National Grid Gas? And a truck. We'd need a gas truck. We'd need somebody with serious weight to get the truck, to ask for it . . ."

"That's what an AIC is for," Devlin said.

"It's an hour from Manhattan to here," Orish said. "We could do preliminary interrogation and the offer right at his house."

Devlin looked at Lucas, who said, "Six hours to dark. What would it take to organize a gas truck? Two or three hours? Let's try that. Have somebody get us the uniforms and the truck. I'd take an extra large. Devlin, what, a large?"

"Yeah. Large. Maybe we could get some kind of technical-looking tool box," Devlin said.

Orish looked at Kerry, her second, and asked, "What do you think?"

"I like it," Kerry said. "We would need to put some SSG guys right there, on the block, when Davenport and Devlin go through the front door, to make sure nobody runs out the back."

Orish said, "Let's plan on this, figure out what else we need to do. Get a satellite picture of that block up on one of our screens . . . I'll call the AIC."

AFTER SOME DISCUSSION, the Manhattan agent in charge agreed to the daylight pickup and search. Warrants had been prepared for all the homes of the identified prime distributors, and the warrant for Curry's house was printed out in a half hour.

National Grid agreed, after some persuasion, to loan a van, uniforms, and tool bags for what they were told was a surveillance operation in Pleasantville, which was in the opposite direction from Staten Island.

The AIC was getting involved: "You kick the door, or whatever you do," he said to Lucas, with the rest of the task force team listening in, "We'll put SWAT guys in a couple of the SSG cars and have them close when you kick the door. That way, if you're shot to pieces, we'll have somebody to pick up the pieces. And shoot back."

"I wouldn't want our pieces neglected," Devlin said.

Then the AIC continued, "Then we send in three nicely dressed ladies in a small SUV. They knock on the door and you let them in, like they're going to a tea party. Or a quilting bee. One's an assistant U.S. attorney, who'll help sweat Curry. The other two are search specialists. They'll have lady-style tote bags with their tools inside . . ."

Over the next two hours, details were filled in and the tension began to crank up. The gas company van arrived, the unforms were brought up. Before Lucas and Devlin had time to change, an SSG agent called to say that Curry was leaving his house in the pickup.

Orish: "Ah, no! We're ready to go."

Lucas looked at his watch: 1:20. "We've got to move on this. Virgil and Rae will be on their way to the boat before four o'clock. If I'm going to pull them, it's got to be before three."

The SSG agent called again, three minutes later, and said, "He's going to a ShopRite, a supermarket."

Lucas said, "Let's get the uniforms on." He and Devlin went into the bathroom, got out of their street clothes and into the uniforms, which fit well enough. The uniforms had leg pockets for tools, and they put their handguns inside them.

When they came out of the bathroom, Kerry said, "I'd buy it."

Orish: "Except that the uniforms have never been used and they both have creases from the packages they came in." Lucas and Devlin spent a couple minutes bending and stretching, trying to twist up the uniforms, and an agent came out of the bathroom with a damp towel and wiped them down. "Still look too clean," she said. "And you still have creases. You could spend a couple minutes crawling around the parking lot when you get outside."

Devlin said, "I put on a suit right out of the dry cleaners and five minutes later I look like I slept behind a dumpster. Now I can't uncrease my goddamn pants. Why can't they make suits out of this shit?" He pulled at his pant legs.

Lucas: "Because it's canvas. They make tents out of it. You wanna wear a tent?"

CURRY WAS INSIDE the supermarket for twenty minutes, came out pushing a cart and loaded four grocery bags into the truck, then drove to a bakery and went inside.

Lucas said to Devlin, "He's gotta be on his way home with the groceries. Let's go," and to Orish, "Tell everybody. We'll be there in fifteen minutes."

Kerry: "Good luck, guys. Careful."

IN THE ELEVATOR, they dropped two floors, the elevator stopped, and an older couple got in. As the doors closed, the woman looked at the uniforms and asked, "Is there a problem?"

"No, a routine inspection of the shutoff valves and the safety inner locks," Devlin said cheerfully. "Everything is fine."

"I didn't smell anything," the woman said.

"That's because there aren't any leaks," her husband said.

She said, "Huh," and peered at Devlin, then Lucas, as though she didn't believe a word of it.

When they were across the lobby and out the door, Devlin looked back and said, "Suspicious old bat."

"She knew we weren't quite right," Lucas said. "We got creases."

"Or, could be your haircut. Gas company plumbers don't have hundred-dollar haircuts."

◆◆◆

ON THE WAY to Curry's house in the gas company van, with Devlin driving, Lucas took a phone call: "The lawyer and the two search specialists are on the island, a few minutes behind you," Orish said. "It's coming together. Good luck and call me the minute everything is secure and I'll send them in."

Lucas clicked off and said to Devlin, "Sounds like a bad British spy movie. 'Everything is secure.' I was ripping on the British again this morning . . ."

"Could be a bad Canadian spy movie," Devlin said.

"So then we sound like anti-Canadian bigots."

"Yes. We're nervous and we're trying to be funny. Happens every time," Devlin said. He pulled out his Glock, popped the magazine, reseated it, put it back in his pocket. "Bob could be funny."

"He tried," Lucas said. "But we weren't *very* funny. Not really."

Orish called again: "Curry's in his driveway unloading the groceries."

"We're five minutes out. Call us when he's done unloading and is inside."

They were four blocks away when she called back: "He got the last load out and locked the truck. He's inside."

"We'll be there in a minute or two," Lucas said.

"I know. We've got eyes on you."

THEY PARKED DIRECTLY in front of Curry's house. The day hadn't gotten any warmer, and there was nobody on the sidewalks. Lucas looked up at the house and said, "Two doors, the inner door and the storm door. Both might be locked, so they'll get a long look at us before they unlock the storm door. The storm door will open out. Looks like there might be some ice on the top step, so watch it. I don't want you falling on your ass."

"I got it."

"Right. You Louisiana guys are like ballerinas on ice," Lucas said.

"I got it, man," Devlin said impatiently. "Let's do it."

They climbed out of the van and Devlin got a canvas tool bag out of the back; it was stuffed with newspaper to fill it out, since it was empty when delivered with the uniforms.

Lucas led the way up the steps, unsnapped the leg pocket with the gun. He glanced back, saw that Devlin had his hand in his pocket. Lucas said, "Little ice," and reached out to the doorbell and pushed it three times, hard. They could hear it ringing inside.

Ten seconds later, Devlin muttered, "Looking at us out the window."

Then the door lock rattled and Lucas said, "I'm gonna punch it."

A fleshy middle-aged blond woman looked out through the storm door's window, frowned, fumbled with the lock and handle on the storm door and said, "Gas company?"

Lucas had his hand on the handle of the storm door, yanked it open, pulling her off balance, said, "U.S. Marshals," and pushed past her and through her, knocking her back into the house and as he went by, the woman screamed, "Cops!"

LUCAS BURST DOWN a short entry hall and into the home's living room, where two elderly people were watching television, an old man from a wheelchair and an elderly woman from an overstuffed green couch; both of their mouths were hanging open. Through a hallway off the living room, he could see Curry standing in front of a refrigerator with a twelve-pack of Pepsi-Cola in his hands. Lucas ran straight on through, toward Curry, heard two doors slam behind him, the storm door and the inner door, heard Devlin shouting something at somebody, not him.

Ahead, Curry leaped sideways and out of sight and Lucas pulled his weapon in case Curry was going for one, but one second later, as he charged into the kitchen, he found Curry trying to get out a back door, rattling a heavy deadbolt lock, and Lucas shouted, "Stop! Stop!"

Curry looked wildly back into the muzzle of Lucas's gun and put up his hands. "Okay. Okay!"

Devlin, in the front room, was shouting, "Show me your hands, your hands . . ."

A screeching sound ripped through the house and Lucas waved his gun at Curry and shouted, "Keep your hands up . . . Keep them up and get in the living room, get in the living room!"

There was another screeching sound and a woman shouted, "Get away from her, get away from Mom."

As Lucas pushed Curry down the short hallway to the living room, a bird—he thought a chicken, large and white with a flash of yellow, but flying—dove straight at his head. He flinched, turned, the bird flapped around the kitchen and came back on a second pass, and Lucas pushed Curry harder into the living room and found Devlin pointing his weapon at the two women, the younger one standing in front of the older one, and Devlin shouted at Lucas, "Gun! The old lady's got a gun in the couch!"

The bird hit Lucas on the back of the head, and he felt a claw scrape across his scalp. Lucas pushed Curry hard between the shoulder blades farther into the living room and the bird ricocheted around the room, brushing both the younger woman and Devlin's shoulders before going after the old man in the wheelchair, who swung a cane at the bird and called, "Get away, get away, you shitass."

Devlin shoved the younger woman into the lap of the man in the wheelchair and snatched the old lady by her blouse off the couch; a gun skittered out of her hidden left hand and fell on the floor. Lucas kicked it like a soccer ball down the hallway to the kitchen. As he turned back, he realized for the first time that a dog was barking at them, crazy, excited, and maybe panicked barking, and he looked down and saw a dachshund dancing around Curry's feet.

"Everybody shut up!" Lucas shouted. "Somebody get the goddamned bird."

The younger woman shouted, "Stay away from my bird! You motherfucker, stay away . . ."

The bird came after Lucas again and he swatted at it with his gun, smacked it hard, two or three small feathers flying. The bird crashed into a wall and fell flapping to the floor, and the woman came at Lucas with her fingernails. She had to pass Devlin, who stuck out a foot, tripped her, and she went down in a pile, landing on the dog, which squealed and ran under a chair.

In a moment of stunned silence, Lucas said, loudly, but not shouting, "You're all under arrest. Everybody except the old guy." He pointed at the elderly man, who shrugged.

Curry said, "We want a lawyer."

"You've got one coming," Lucas said. "Right now, you've got the chance to commit several more felonies. You want to do it, it's up to you. If you don't want to do that, sit down."

The younger woman crawled to the couch, used it to push herself up. She began to cry and the older woman patted her vaguely on the back and stuck her hand down between the couch cushions behind her.

Lucas moved quickly to stand over her, his pistol next to her nose. "Is that another gun?"

She said, "It's my Kleenex pack." She dug deeper, and came up with a Kleenex purse pack and began excavating a tissue.

The bird was up, but not flying; it walked around the room with an occasional, questioning squawk, avoiding Lucas. Lucas asked the younger woman, "Could you put the chicken somewhere? With the dog? Stick them in a bedroom?"

She was still crying and gathered up the bird and said to the dog, "Come on, Noodles." The dog wandered after her, and Lucas followed her down the hall and watched as she put the bird in a bedroom with the dog. He pointed her back to the couch, and Curry asked, "What's this all about?"

"It's about a life sentence," Devlin said. "Without parole. And this lady? This your mother?"

Curry glanced at the old lady and said, "Mother-in-law."

"It's about her going for a gun, which is aggravated assault on a federal officer which is about six to eight years, minimum. And this lady"—he pointed at the younger woman—"went after a federal marshal with her fingernails. That's assault, that's a couple of years."

Lucas ran his fingers through his hair, across his burning scalp, came away with blood. "As for that fuckin' chicken, I'm gonna wring its neck . . ."

"That's a very valuable sulphur cockatoo," the younger woman said. She sat on the couch next to the old woman. "That's no kind of chicken."

"What the fuck do you want?" Curry asked.

Devlin looked at Lucas, who shrugged and said, "Sansone. We want Sansone. We've got a lawyer coming to explain all of that to you, your options."

"I want an attorney," Curry said. "I'm not answering any questions, I want a lawyer, I haven't done anything wrong."

Lucas: "Really? You already unload all that heroin?"

Curry opened his mouth to answer, then slammed it shut, and the younger woman sobbed, "Oh, no."

"We're not going to ask any questions. Not without you saying okay," Lucas said. "What we're going to do is, you're going to listen to a lawyer talk. Then, you're all four going to the Manhattan federal lockup. If you're not interested in talking to us, we'll hold you for seventy-two hours and then we'll give you any lawyer you want or call in a federal public defender."

"If I talk to you, Sansone will have me killed," Curry said.

"Sansone will be in prison and you won't be," Lucas said. "You and your family will be in witness protection. Nobody in witness protection has ever been killed."

Devlin asked Lucas, "You want to call Orish?"

LUCAS CALLED, TOLD her what had happened, and she said, "Good. Expect company in three or four minutes. They're close."

Lucas passed the word to Devlin, then went into the kitchen, got a kitchen chair, brought it back to the living room and told Curry to sit. He did. Five minutes later, the doorbell rang, and Devlin let three women inside, all in dresses and high heels, all carrying tote bags with brightly colored designs.

One of them, a tall, fortyish woman with salt-and pepper hair, gunmetal rimmed glasses, skinny like a runner, said to Lucas, "I'm Ann Wright with the U.S. Attorney's Office. We need to speak privately for a moment."

"In the kitchen."

One of the other women said, "Jill and I need a place to change. We're not doing this in heels."

Devlin pointed down the hall toward the bedrooms, but said, "Don't go through the door on the left. There's a chicken in there that already attacked Davenport and drew some blood."

"Fuckin' cockatoo," said the old man.

TWENTY-EIGHT

Lucas and Ann Wright went into the kitchen and shut the door behind them. Wright took a black spiral notebook and a pen out of her bag, opened it on the kitchen counter and said, "All right. We'll begin the search as soon as Jill and Ivy change clothes. Tell me what happened here. Was there any resistance?"

Lucas filled her in on the entry, the old lady with the gun, the younger woman with the fingernails. Wright wrote it down in what appeared to be excellent shorthand.

"But she didn't actually get to you? With her nails?"

"No, she fell on her dachshund."

"Dachshund," she said, and made a note. "Then . . ."

"There was this bird . . ." Lucas stepped to the kitchen counter and ripped a paper towel off a roll hung next to the sink, wiped through his hair and showed her the spots of blood. He told her about the attack.

"There was no evidence, though, that the Currys were directing the attack?"

Lucas suspected sarcasm, but Wright showed innocent brown

eyes and no sign of a smile. "Well, no, but it's obviously a danger-ous bird, a sulphurous cockatoo, as I understand it."

She finished with, "You saw no sign of the heroin?"

"Not yet, but we haven't looked for it."

LUCAS GLANCED AT his watch as Wright led the way back to the front room: three o'clock, and they hadn't started yet with Curry. Too late to call Virgil and tell him to bail.

"Too late," he said, aloud.

Wright turned: "What?"

He shook his head, but Devlin looked at him and said, "Fuck me."

IN THE LIVING room, the four inhabitants of the house were seated in a line, like a jury. Devlin introduced them, pointing at them one at a time. "Paul Curry on the end, and then Sophia Curry, Paul's wife, and Sophia's mother and father, David Bruno and Carol Bruno."

Wright, standing in front of them with a clutch of paper, peeled off a piece of it and handed it to Paul Curry. "You are under arrest. This is a search warrant for your house. We are searching for her-oin and money, currency. These two women . . ." she turned and nodded at the two search specialists, ". . . are going to tear this house apart looking for the heroin and the currency. I mean that literally. They have tools with them, wrecking bars and so on. They'll take apart furniture, pull up baseboards, clean out closets, and so on. If you wish to concede the presence of the heroin and the currency, that won't be necessary."

Paul Curry held up a finger and said, "I . . ."

"Let me finish," Wright interrupted. "You've been under surveillance for several days. We have high-resolution movies of you picking up the heroin at the Clean N Go car wash and making contact with your dealers on the street. You are a criminal, Mr. Curry, and your past history makes you liable for a life sentence in prison, if we find as much as an ounce of heroin in this house. And you *will* get life in prison, without the possibility of parole, I can promise that."

She continued: "But we're prepared to offer you a deal. In return for your testimony against Douglas Sansone and for surrendering the heroin and the currency, we will place you and your family in the U.S. Marshals Service's witness protection program. No one who ever entered in the program, who has followed the rules of the program, has ever been traced and killed by his former colleagues. You will be safe."

"Not in New York. You wouldn't let us live in New York," Sophia Curry blurted.

"I don't know the details of the Marshals Service's protection program, but I will tell you, there are some nice places outside of New York," Wright said. "I actually come from one of them—Charleston, South Carolina. Charleston is far, far better than any prison in the federal prison system."

Paul Curry asked, "How soon do we have to decide?"

"Right away, today, this afternoon," Wright said. "There are several parts of this investigation already in motion. The South Florida gang is being rounded up as we speak. We have already arrested Kent Pruitt and he is currently being protected in our Manhattan lockup. Despite Mr. Pruitt's arrest, we'd also like your cooperation. With more than one of the top dealers testifying against Sansone, we will cinch his conviction."

Lucas smiled; she lied well.

"I want to talk this over with a lawyer," Curry said. "See what he says about the deal."

"I'm afraid that won't be possible," Wright said. "You'll notice that I'm not asking you any questions, because you already asked the marshals for a lawyer and so I'm not permitted to question you. And I won't. I'm telling you things and making an offer. If you decline my offer, the four of you will be taken to the federal lockup, held for seventy-two hours, beginning with your arrest, and then allowed to speak to a lawyer. The deal, however, will have been withdrawn—and I don't care how good your lawyer is, Mr. Curry, you will be going to life in prison. Because we have got you."

"Jesus Christ," the old man blurted.

"You can talk about it, and you can ask me questions," Wright said. "Don't take too long. This is a complicated process and we don't have a lot of time."

THE CURRYS AND Brunos sat and looked at each other, and then David Bruno said to his son-in-law, "Paul, take the deal. You been talking about retiring to Florida. Tell them you'll take the deal if they'll send you somewhere warm."

"What about the kids?" Sophia Curry asked. "What if they go after the kids?"

David Bruno waved her off: "That's against the rules, honey. Nobody goes after nobody's kids. That'd be a nightmare all the way around. That'd set off fights that would never end. And they won't come after me'n Carol, because that's another nightmare."

"Sansone's not like the old guys, Dad," Paul Curry said. "He doesn't respect anything."

"Sansone goes to prison, with most of his outfit, you'll be an old, old man by the time he gets out, if he ever does," Bruno said. "I'll be dead. He won't have an outfit anymore, he'll be an old has-been. He's what, forty-something?" He tilted his head up to Wright. "If all this comes true, you get Sansone on dope . . ."

"Not just dope," Wright said. "We're going after him for numerous murders in Florida. If he doesn't get the death penalty, he'll be gone forever."

"There, that's it," Bruno said to Paul Curry. He looked around. "You sell this place—you don't let these assholes wreck it—and you buy a place wherever they hide you, somewhere warm . . . take it easy."

"We'd be poor," Sophia said.

"There's some money floating around the family," Bruno said. "You won't be poor."

All of them, including Wright, Devlin, and Lucas, looked at the old man. Paul Curry's forehead wrinkled and he said, "What? You've got money?"

Bruno used the end of his cane to wave at Wright and the others: "These are cops. We'll talk about it some other time."

Curry stared at him, then buried his face in his hands, stayed that way, then rubbed his face, looked up and said, "Deal."

Lucas: "Where's the dope?"

"What's left of it is on the shelf in the kitchen closet. The money's there, too."

One of the search specialists said, "We got it." They'd pulled on blue vinyl gloves and now they headed into the kitchen, trailed by Wright.

A HALF HOUR passed as the searchers uncovered and documented the heroin and the cash. Wright, still in her dress and heels, went out to the SUV and returned with a box containing a small copy machine, on which one of the searchers and Devlin began copying the currency. The currency was wrapped with rubber bands, most hundred-dollar bills with some fifties and twenties, in five-thousand-dollar stacks. Wright asked Curry, "How much do you get for a kilo? You personally?"

"I get forty, more or less. Doug sells it to me for thirty. So I get to keep ten. By the time it gets to the small guys, they're getting a hundred and fifty a gram, so that's . . . what? A hundred and fifty K for a kilo on the street? But it's gone through three more people by then."

"Nice little profit all around," Devlin said.

"Nobody's getting rich except maybe Doug. We got a lot of expenses and we don't get loads like these every day. I'm lucky to clear two hundred K in a year of work. In New York, that's nothing," Curry said. He looked at Devlin and the search specialist at work with the copy machine. "Why are they xeroxing all that cash? Why are they doing it here?"

"Because you're going to deliver it to the guys at the car wash and get another brick of dope," Lucas said.

"What?"

✦✦✦

WRIGHT EXPLAINED IT: Curry was going to get in his pickup and drive up to the car wash and buy another brick of heroin, his usual order, and deliver whatever money he needed to cover it. That money would be delivered to Sansone and then Sansone would be picked up with the cash in his pocket and would go to prison.

"We need to tie him to the dope, and the dope ties him to the murders."

"Those guys in the garage . . . they're sorta my friends," Curry said.

Wright nodded and said, "I know." She smiled at him. "Tough shit."

Sophia Curry began crying and then Carol Bruno. They cried for a while and the copy machine kept grinding away in the background.

CURRY SAID HE couldn't show up with a pile of cash and check out with a kilo of heroin. He had to call ahead to see if it was even available.

"Then call," Lucas said.

Curry said he had to use a burner phone that he kept hidden in his truck. If the people in the garage got a call from an unrecognized number, they simply wouldn't answer. Lucas sent him out to get it, warning that the house was surrounded by FBI agents, and that if he tried to run, he wouldn't get a block. Curry nodded miserably and went to the truck to get the phone. When he was back,

Lucas, Wright, and Curry talked about what he'd say. When everyone was satisfied, Curry punched in the number, which was picked up on the second ring.

"Clean N Go."

Curry said, "Hey, man. This is me."

"Hey, you. How's things?"

"Need to get a rapid wash. Got really dirty last night. What's the situation there?"

"Not too busy. Which wash?"

"I'm thinking the gold."

"Gold, it is. When you coming?"

"Five o'clock?"

"Make it five-thirty. We got a little line-up."

"See you then," Curry said, and he punched off. To Wright and Lucas: "It's done."

LUCAS WANTED TO drive along with one of the SSG members while Curry delivered the cash to the car wash, and left with another bag of heroin. He took a few minutes to change out of the gas company uniform and back into his suit and overcoat, and after Wright issued a series of warnings and threats to Paul Curry, they left the house in the dark. Lucas drove the gas van around the block, where he transferred to the SSG RAV4, and then he and the SSG agent dropped in behind Curry, two blocks back.

The drop was routine: Curry drove into the car wash garage, and ten minutes later, backed out, and drove back toward his house.

"He could have said anything in there," the SSG driver said. "He could have called anyone."

"Yeah, but we were afraid to wire him up, and we didn't have a wire anyway," Lucas said. "At this point, I'm willing to believe he's come over."

"I hope."

Lucas was dropped at the gas van, which he drove back to Curry's. The pickup was already parked in the driveway.

IN THE HOUSE, Curry was telling Wright about the currency delivery and the purchase of the new bag of heroin, which lay on the living room table.

Lucas: "Did it go right?"

Curry said, "Yeah, just like every day. They were surprised that I got rid of a whole kilo last night. I said there was some hunger out there, that the new bag wouldn't hold me more than a few days. They said more was on the way."

Wright said, "We have a couple of SUVs coming by to transport the four of you to Manhattan . . ."

"All four? Do we all have to go?" Sophia wailed.

Her mother said, "Shut up."

Wright: "For seventy-two hours. Then we can arrange for everybody but Paul to be released on their own recognizance. When you get back here, you might want to talk to a Realtor. Sansone won't know for a while that Paul has agreed to cooperate with us, but . . . you might want to get started on that."

Sophia started crying again and Wright went into the kitchen to call her boss at the U.S. Attorney's Office. When she'd finished, she came back through the living room, put on her coat, and gathered up her briefcase. On the way out, she touched Lucas's arm and said, quietly, "We're very pleased. And by the way, that's a great suit, but your tie's a little crooked." She straightened his tie, said, "There," patted him on the chest, and went out the door.

Devlin said, "Wow."

Lucas: "Happens all the time."

The old man said, "You're fulla shit," but then he cackled and shook his head. "Fuckin' women."

As they waited for the transport vans, Carol Bruno asked, "How come you were in such a big hurry? We shoulda been able to talk to a lawyer before we decided what to do."

Lucas said, "This . . . investigation . . . has a lot of moving parts. The FBI's organized crime guys told us if we let you talk to one of your regular lawyers, that guy would run outside and call up Sansone and everybody else he could think of, and warn them off."

Paul Curry asked, "Didn't you say you'd arrested Kent Pruitt?"

"Yeah. He's already over in Manhattan."

"Did you let him make a call to Sansone?"

Lucas felt a chill of apprehension: "No. Should we have?"

"I want credit if I tell you about this."

"You'll get it," Lucas said.

"Well, if Kent didn't make a call . . . then Sansone knows. We all call in, we all have our times. When I'm working, when I'm moving a big load, I call between five and six. I even got an alarm set on my phone. If I get picked up by the cops, I don't make a call and a bunch of shit starts happening. For one thing, nobody knows me until it all gets straightened out. Until somebody talks to me, to see why I didn't call. A lawyer starts looking for me. If Kent didn't make a call, you're fucked: Sansone knows."

Lucas looked at his watch. Ten minutes to six. Virgil was certainly on the boat, maybe already in the water. If Sansone was looking for Pruitt, if he realized that one of his top salesmen had gone missing and if he had called Behan in Miami Beach . . . then Virgil and Rae could be in trouble.

Lucas turned to Devlin: "We want Curry on the phone to Sansone, right now. Everything is okay, everything is perfect." He headed for the door.

"Where are you going?" Devlin called.

"Gotta make a car insurance call . . ."

Lucas jogged out to the van, got his pack, retrieved the burner phone, and punched in the number for Rae's phone, feeling the sweat start on the back of his neck.

But Rae answered on the third ring.

Lucas put a big smile on his face, because a big fake smile turns your voice into a salesman's, and said, "We're calling to alert you to an opportunity to insure your car against . . ."

At the word *insure*, Rae said, "Fuck you," and hung up.

Lucas sat back. She was on the boat, she was with Cattaneo and the other hoods, and couldn't talk.

And she was alive.

TWENTY-NINE

Virgil and Rae helped carry the scuba gear down to the boat. The water was dead quiet, dark and smooth as oil; a man in a sleeveless white shirt went by in a rowing shell, the only one they'd seen on the Intracoastal.

When the last of the gear was stowed, Virgil and Rae went to the bow of the boat while Cattaneo was doing an engine check, and Rae slipped an arm around Virgil's waist and muttered, "Are you okay with this? We could be pushing our luck."

They'd talked earlier with Lucas and knew that an arrest had been made but without a deal and another one was imminent. Sooner or later, the word would get out.

"I don't think we have anything to worry about until I get back on the boat," Virgil said. "They want the shit too bad. The danger point will be when I'm in the water and they've got a hold on the lift bag. If they want to get rid of me, that's the time."

"I'll be ready for that," Rae said.

Cattaneo called, "We're set. Marc, you want to cast us off?"

✦ ✦ ✦

THE NIGHT WAS cloudy but windless, and warm enough, in the sixties. There were lights already showing in the marina, and Virgil could hear somebody playing Dave Alvin and Jimmie Dale Gilmore's "Downey to Lubbock." A woman laughed off in that direction, like a woman might do when she has a martini in her hand and a friendly hand on her ass.

As the boat edged out into the Intracoastal, Virgil and Rae made their way back to the cockpit. "Should be a good night for diving," Cattaneo said. "About as flat as it ever gets out there."

"Looks fine," Virgil said. "I think we got this figured out."

"You oughta look into investments," Cattaneo said. "Fidelity, Vanguard. Get some mutual funds so you'll have some money coming in, when you get to your old age."

Virgil cocked his head. "What the fuck are you talking about, Jack? You think I'm gonna get to old age?"

Cattaneo thought about it, then said, "Okay, forget it. But. Let's try to stay alive for a while, okay? Don't take any chances down there, we're doing too good to lose you. And maybe you don't make it to actual old age, but with the cash we're gonna give you, you could have a hell of a good time before then."

"Weed, women, and song," Lange said.

Virgil: "I try to stay away from song. When I try to sing, I sound like a frog."

THEY PUSHED OUT of Port Everglades into the Atlantic and made the turn north. Nice night, their forward motion creating a soft salt breeze in their faces. Regio and Lange were sitting on the deck, knees up, watching the shore lights; farther out, a freighter was headed west in toward the cut. Virgil, Rae, and Cattaneo were in the cockpit, and Cattaneo asked, "How'd you two get together, anyway? You're not what I'd think of as an obvious match-up."

Rae said, "I was hurtin' in Vegas. I had a hotel job there, cleaning rooms. Temporary thing. They said I stole some stuff from a room, which was a lie, and I got fired. Once you get fired from a Vegas hotel for room theft, you're shit out of luck. They put your name around and nobody will touch you: they're like running you out of town.

"Anyway," she continued, "I was walking around looking in store windows, hoping I might see a 'Help Wanted' sign—this was just before Christmas, four years ago—and I'm walking around, and there's Willy outside a Dollar Store, ringing a bell, with a red pot, raising money for the Salvation Army."

Cattaneo laughed, looked at Virgil: "You were working for the Salvation Army? Bullshit."

"That's what I said, soon as I saw him," Rae said. "He had this sneaky look around his eyes. I backed off and watched him and when the traffic died off, he took the pot and the pot stand and his bell and he went around the building and got in the Subaru. I knocked on the window and when he lowered it, I said, 'Can I have some of that money?' That's how it started."

"Where you get the bell and pot?" Cattaneo asked.

"Found them," Virgil said.

Cattaneo and Rae said, simultaneously, "Right."

"How much were you taking out?" Cattaneo asked.

"Good day, worked all day, could be four hundred dollars,"

Virgil said. "Best day was almost five hundred. Somebody put in three fifties."

"Why weren't you diving?" Cattaneo asked.

"Because they pay you shit," Virgil said. "Dive operators act like you ought to be paying them, because you get to dive. That's what they say: 'Hey, we're giving you the chance of doing what you love.' Yeah, well, I love eating, too. No way in hell you can stay alive in California on a hundred bucks a day, three days a week."

THEY TALKED ABOUT the cost of living for a while, California versus Florida versus New York versus Iowa—"Really low in Iowa, especially out in the countryside. I really liked that place, except their prison sorta sucked."

"That was a burglary deal, right?" Cattaneo asked.

"I don't talk about that shit," Virgil said.

"But Ally stuck with you?"

"She didn't so much stick with me as look me up afterward," Virgil said.

"I was working at a Gap in St. Louis. There's another crap job for you," Rae said.

They talked off and on about crap jobs, and Regio and Lange chipped in, and then Cattaneo said, "We're thirty minutes out, Willy."

"Back to the salt mines," Virgil said.

VIRGIL GOT SUITED up, did a last check on his tanks, dive computer, weights, and the Genesis DPV, flicked all three flashlights on and off, made sure the two lift bags were correctly positioned, put on his mask and fins, sucked air through his regulator, and a little after six o'clock, right hand pinning his mouthpiece and mask to his face, took the long step into the Atlantic Ocean. When he heard the boat engine start, he oriented himself toward the west, and turned the Genesis on.

ON HIS LAST dive, he'd seen one more can of heroin that he didn't think he had time to get to, but as he ascended, he used the Genesis to pull him over to the brilliant white LEDs, and then went as straight up as he could, pausing for decompression stops, and then all the way to the surface, where he checked the GPS watch and noted the reading.

On this trip, he steered directly west from the drop point, surfaced, made his way to the noted GPS coordinates. Boat lights were approaching from the north, appeared to be a bit off to the west of him, but coming fast, and he vented air from his wing and dropped straight down.

He got lucky. Visibility had improved overnight, and when he activated the light wand at a hundred and thirty feet, he immediately saw LEDs of two cans to the south, and another to the north. He had the southern cans bagged in the first minute on the bottom and could still see the glow from the can to the north. That gave him a solid compass heading for the line of cans, and he picked up the northern can a minute later and could see another beyond that.

He was moving quickly, and slightly lower, now down to a hundred and seventy feet, getting narced, six cans bagged, when his leg was snagged and he was yanked off-line. He would have lost the Genesis if it hadn't been tethered to his backplate. He struggled against the opposing pulls on his leg and from the Genesis, managed to drag in the machine and turn it off.

He swiveled, gathered himself, let his heartbeat slow, and then used his most powerful flashlight to look at his right leg and fin. He was tangled in a coil of half-inch-wide plastic strap, the kind used to secure boxes for shipping. It rose in a snarl off the bottom, a tangle the size of a government desk. He pulled at it, and found it securely fastened to a lump of something on the bottom. There were a half dozen bright-colored fishing lures hung up in it and tangles of line. What the lump was, he couldn't tell—maybe concrete, or something metal. Junk, covered with mud.

He'd trained for this. The first rule: stop and think. He did that, then tried to slowly unwrap the tangle from his leg; that didn't work so well, as the Genesis had pulled the tangling plastic strips into a knot. Moving in slow motion, he took his wire cutter from its pocket on the backplate harness and started cutting.

The stuff was tough, but his wire cutter clipped through it easily enough. He made a half dozen cuts, dropping the scrap pieces to the bottom, and then kicked free. His leg stung, and he took a moment to look at it. He'd cut himself and was bleeding, a trickle of blood from his calf, black in the LED light of his flashlight. He pulled the leg of his wet suit around to one side, so an undamaged section of the suit would cover the cut in his leg; the bleeding seemed to stop.

To the north, he could see the LED lights of another can, and he got himself away from the tangle of plastic straps, turned on the Genesis, and went after it. He fitted six cans in the first cargo bag and had five in the second, when his computer told him that his time was up. His bottom time had been shorter because of nitrogen build-up from the day before, but he'd done good.

He shot squirts of air into the lift bags, and he and the bags rose slowly until the computer told him he was at the first decompression stop. He waited for a full minute, then began the diagonal run back to the pickup, struggling to keep the bags rising as slowly as possible. They wanted to circle each other, and with slightly different amounts of air in each bag, and slightly different weights, they wanted to rise at different rates. Each bag had a release valve, but releasing exactly the right amount of air from each was tricky—as they rose, the air expanded and the bags tried to drag him up.

He hovered a stop at thirty feet, where he rested. He was sucking too much air, he thought, struggling with the lift bags, although his computer said that he had plenty left. His leg itched from the cut, and from the saltwater inside the suit. A boat seemed to be coming toward him, high-speed screws, so probably shallow draft, still some distance off. A sport-fishing boat? He got the Genesis going and headed east, into the ocean, praying that the boat wasn't trolling. A big hook in the face—or in the bags, for that matter—really wasn't something he needed to deal with.

He continued pushing east until the boat was well past, then surfaced and checked the GPS. Worried about the boat, he'd overrun the pickup point, so he turned back west and steered over to it, adjusted the lift bags until they sat at the surface, then added air to his wing until his head and shoulders were above water. With nothing but low rollers, he could see red and green boat lights out across the ocean; none seemed to be coming his way. He had twenty minutes to wait. He removed the regulator mouthpiece, and settled in to do that.

◈◈◈

RAE SAT ON the deck and watched the condo lights go by on shore. A tranquil night, and beautiful, the salt air heavy and soothing in her face. The three men sat back by the cockpit talking; she couldn't quite hear what they were saying. Then Cattaneo called out to her, "Ally, we're coming up to the turn."

"All right."

Cattaneo was watching the radar for anything that might be Coast Guard. The only thing near them, as they came around, was a radar blob that was closing from the north on a line parallel to theirs, and not far away; they could clearly see the lights getting larger by the moment. When they came around in the turn and headed south, their radio burped, and a woman's voice said, "Sailboat off Deerfield turning south, this is the powercat *Uncaged* coming up on your starboard side. If you hold your course we'll stay well off to starboard."

Cattaneo got on the radio and acknowledged the other boat's call, then said, "Goddamnit, I hope Willy's keeping a good watch. They're running down the same line we are."

The boat that went by looked like a fat white wedding cake, a catamaran at least three tiers high. A man on the cat's flybridge raised a hand to them as it went by.

"Gonna get me one of those," Regio said, as he watched it go. "Fuck a condo down here. You could live on a boat like that and wouldn't cost you anything like a condo."

"That boat cost anywhere between a buck and a half and two when it was new," Cattaneo said. "You can get a damn nice condo for that price."

They were talking condo prices when Rae's phone rang: she took it out of her pocket, looked at it, frowned, and answered. A man's voice, artificially cheery: "We're calling to alert you to an opportunity to insure your car against . . ."

Rae said, "Fuck you," and punched off.

Cattaneo laughed and asked, "What was that?"

"He wanted to alert me to an opportunity," she said. She felt a chill crawl down her spine, but forced a skeptical grin. "Like Willy and his Salvation Army pot."

"Got a cousin up in Jersey doing that, phone work," Lange said, faking a shudder. "You know what they say when somebody listens to the pitch and then declines the offer? They say, 'Fuck you very much.' The guy who's listening never picks it up. They think you're saying, 'Thank you very much.'"

"Another bit of garbage information from the brain of Matthew Lange," Cattaneo said.

Rae: "I'm getting a little chilly, I think I'll get my wrap."

She went below and got a zip-up cotton sweatsuit top, carried it back up to the cockpit, handed it to Regio, and said, "Hold this, help me get it on."

He held it so she could get her arms in it, and helped tug it up over her shoulders. "Thanks." She zipped it. "How much longer?"

"Thirty minutes," Cattaneo said.

Ten minutes later, Cattaneo's phone rang. He looked at the screen and said, "Uh-oh. Trouble. It's the boss. Ally, if you want to go up on the bow or down below, this might be kinda private."

"Sure," she said. "Go ahead and not trust me."

She dropped down the ladder into the salon, then stepped into one of the cabins. Davenport's call had been an alert to warn of possible trouble. She'd gotten the sweatsuit top, and had asked Regio's help with it, so that he would have hefted it, and would know that there was nothing in the pockets. Nothing heavy, like a gun.

She had an edge now, something like fear, but maybe not quite there. Apprehension. Trepidation.

Moving quickly, tense but not in a panic, she ripped the tape from her ankle to free the Sig, made sure there was a round in the chamber, that the weapon was cocked and locked, and stuck it in her sweatsuit pocket. She moved over to the cabin door and tried to hear what was being said. The phone call was apparently over, but the three men were talking in low tones—or Cattaneo and Regio were. Lange was louder, and it sounded like he was objecting to something, his voice intense.

Trouble, all right, Rae thought.

CATTANEO CALLED HER: "Hey, Ally?"

She hesitated, then stuck her head out the cabin door. "We there?"

"Not quite, but we're getting close. Could you come up and help spot?"

"'Kay."

RAE CLIMBED UP to the cockpit and Cattaneo said, "Probably best if you're on the deck . . ."

"Gimme a flashlight, I'll flash him," she said.

Cattaneo dug around in his equipment bag, then handed her a compact Maglite.

Rae climbed up on the deck and turned, and saw Regio had a gun. "Hey. What the fuck you guys thinking about here?"

Cattaneo said, "Ally, I'm sorry, but we've had a major problem."

Rae's hand was in her pocket, gripping the Sig, flicking the safety. Regio was smiling at her, Lange had his face turned away, and Regio started to bring the gun hand up.

Rae slipped the Sig from her pocket and shot Regio twice in the heart, two flat shocking *bangs* with spark-like muzzle blasts.

She knew she hit him in the heart because Regio was only six feet away and she could almost reach out and touch him. Regio, astonished, looked down at his chest and then dropped straight into the cockpit with a butcher shop *thump*.

Rae was already pointing the pistol at Cattaneo's head and she snarled, "If Matt or you makes a single fuckin' move, I'm gonna shoot you in the fuckin' head, Jack, and I'm not going to miss, and then I'm gonna shoot Matt if I have to. I'm faster than either one of you assholes, so keep that in mind."

Lange was freaked, looking down at Regio: "What! What! You killed him!"

"That's right," Rae said. "He shoulda been quicker. But he was a dumbass, he wanted to enjoy himself, looking at me, seeing the fear." She was talking street because she wasn't yet sure she should announce herself as a marshal. If they thought she was street, they might still think they could talk their way out of their problem.

The muzzle of her Sig never moved from Cattaneo's forehead. "Now, here's what we're gonna do. I'm gonna move off to this side . . ." She tipped her head. ". . . and Matt's gonna move up the other side where he can pull Willy out of the water."

She added, "While he's doing that, this gun is pointed at your head, Jack. From this distance, I could choose which eye to shoot you in. You're the boss and you better tell your boy not to be fuckin' around, because if he fucks around, I'll deal with you first thing, and worry about him one second later. Then you both be dead. But you first, Jack."

"We can talk this out," Cattaneo said.

"Maybe we can, maybe we can't," Rae said. "Whatever happens, we gonna want more than the pea bag full of cash. We gonna want a couple of those cans that Willy's bringing up."

"Deal. Don't point the gun at me anymore."

"What, you think I'm stupid? I'm pointing at your left eyeball until I'm on that fuckin' dock."

VIRGIL SAW THEM coming. Twenty minutes earlier, the wedding cake powercat had gone by, a few hundred yards toward shore, making twenty knots. Now Cattaneo's boat was coming up, bow lights coming right at him. He flashed his light at them, got a return flash. Cattaneo cut the power and the boat glided up, barely moving when it got to him. As it came up, he saw Rae standing to one side, Lange to the other, with no sign of Regio.

Virgil swam to the boarding ladder, looked up, and said to Lange, "Gonna be heavy. Got eleven cans in the two bags."

On the first two nights, the recoveries had sparked minor celebrations. This time, Lange said nothing except "Hand me the lines."

Virgil: "Everything okay?"

Rae shouted: "Fuck no. These motherfuckers were gonna shoot us. Marc, he's dead. I'm pointing a gun at Jack. If Matt gives you any trouble at all, you yell and I shoot Jack in the fuckin' eyeball. Then I shoot Matt."

"Fuck me," Virgil said. He passed up the lines for the lift bags and Lange struggled to get them on board, and Cattaneo came hurrying to help, Rae shouting warnings at him. When the second bag went over the side, Virgil unbuckled the backplate harness and the tanks went on board, followed by his fins. He got his feet on the ladder, and Rae shouted, "Matt, you go way up on the end of the bow, away from Willy. Get up there."

Lange moved to the bow and Virgil climbed the ladder. Rae was calling him "Willy." That meant that she'd kept her fake identity, and for whatever reason, he should as well.

When Virgil was on board, Rae said to Cattaneo, "Willy gonna come over by you. Willy, get down in the cockpit, reach under that asshole's body and you find a gun. Jack, you make one fucking move toward him and I kill your sorry ass. I got my eye on you too, Matt."

Virgil carefully stepped into the cockpit and halfway down the ladder to the salon. The floor of the cockpit was awash with purple blood. He tugged Regio's legs around, picked up a bloody black Beretta 92. "Got it," he said. He leaned over the side of the boat, rinsed the blood off in the ocean, then shook the water off.

"Get up on deck," Rae said to Virgil. "Matt, you get down in the cockpit with Jack. I know you probably got a gun, but don't even think about it. Willy's not a good shot, but we can't miss and we're really worried about all this and you twitch wrong and we kill your sorry asses."

Lange said, "I don't have a gun."

Cattaneo said nothing for a moment, then, "We probably ought to get rid of Marc's body."

"Fuck that," Rae said. "We get back to the dock, me'n Willy gonna put a couple-three cans under our arms and all the cash you got and run for it. What you do then, with the rest of the shit and Marc, that's your problem. We be gone."

Cattaneo nodded once.

"I can't fuckin' believe this," Lange said. Then, to Rae, "I tried to talk them out of it."

"Don't give a wide shit," Rae said. "You still an asshole. You didn't want to shoot me, but you weren't gonna stop them."

The ride back was tense: Cattaneo kept trying to come up with alternatives to returning to the marina—he suggested a hard left turn and a trip to the Bahamas, dropping Regio over the side before they got there—but Virgil was silent and Rae wouldn't take anything but a ride back to their car.

On the way, Virgil watchfully stripped off the wet suit, the Beretta close at hand, and changed into his street clothes, and checked the cut on his calf. It was deep, and bleeding, but Cattaneo had a good first-aid kit and he smeared the cut with disinfectant and covered it with a gauze bandage, wrapped it with a couple yards of medical tape.

At the marina, with Rae's gun still pointing at Cattaneo's eye, Cattaneo made the sharp turn into the slip, and as they pulled in, a half dozen men dressed in dark clothing materialized from the moored boats around them.

Cattaneo saw them, looked to Rae. "What the fuck is this?"

Rae: "Oh, shit. Did I forget to mention that me'n Willy are U.S.

Marshals? You're under arrest for God only knows how many drug violations, and now, with Marc dead, I believe you're up for felony murder."

Cattaneo goggled at them, finally managed, "What?"

Lange, depressed, in a defeated voice: "I warned you. Way back when. I warned you something wasn't right."

Cattaneo lifted a hand at Virgil: "This moron is a marshal?"

Rae said, "We don't brag about it, but he sorta is, yeah."

Virgil said to Lange: "You want to help tie up, or you gonna stand there with your dick in your hand?" And he yelled to the agents on the dock, "This guy might have a handgun on his belt."

Four feds, three FBI and one marshal, took Cattaneo and Lange off the boat. Neither one was carrying a gun.

Virgil put an arm around Rae's waist and squeezed her tight: "You were . . . you're so fuckin' amazing."

"I was scared," she said, squeezing back. "I was so . . ."

"Fuckin' amazing," Virgil repeated.

Two more agents started pulling cans of heroin out of the lift bags. The team leader, a tall thin man with a military look to his face, wearing a flat Marine Corps utility hat, said, "We've got a problem. Somebody tipped off Behan. We kicked the door on his condo—we saw him go in and it was him—but he wasn't there. We'd never been inside and we found out he had two floors with an interior staircase between them. He went down one floor and probably out the fire stairs or something even trickier. We've got no idea when he did it, or where he went. He was there an hour ago and then gone."

"What about his phone?" Rae asked.

"His phone is sitting on the kitchen counter on the upper floor. We were watching it, of course, and it never moved."

"Damnit. He's probably the number-two guy in the whole operation, after Sansone."

"We know that . . ."

VIRGIL LOOKED AT the file of feds leading Cattaneo and Lange down the dock toward waiting SUVs. "Hey, tell your guys to hold off on Lange. We want to talk to him."

"You think he might know something?" the team leader asked.

"Maybe. I don't know if he'll talk," Virgil said. "Rae and I should give it a try, though."

The team leader called on a handset down the dock and the two feds with Lange stopped walking. Virgil and Rae hurried down the dock, trailed by the team leader. A sailboat was moored in one of the slips, its rail a couple of feet above the dock, and Virgil pushed Lange toward it and said, "Sit."

"I want a lawyer," Lange said.

Rae said, "You said you didn't want to shoot me."

Lange shrugged.

"You're down for felony murder, 'cause Regio's dead. And for me, you were gonna let it happen," Rae said. "The only way you're not going to spend the rest of your life in prison is you talk to us."

Lange shrugged again, but he didn't say no.

"Behan took off. He managed to avoid our surveillance people," Virgil said. "If you have any idea where he might be, now is the time to say something. If you have something to say about that, and it pans out, you might actually walk around free, someday. If he's gone . . . well, if he's gone, you're gone, too."

Lange bowed his head, shuffled his feet on the concrete dock, then looked up and said, "You really sucked us in."

Virgil: "You have something to say?"

"I want more witnesses to this deal. Not just you and Ally and this hat guy."

The team leader called over a couple more of his men to listen and witness; Lange wanted all their names, written down.

When that was done, Virgil said, "So . . ."

"Behan's a pilot. He's got a plane . . ."

The team leader said, "God . . . bless me."

"They were gonna use it to fly the shit up north, but every time you land a plane up there, I guess, coming out of Florida, they got a dog to sniff you . . . so, they didn't do that, but they thought about it, because he's a good pilot. His plane could fly to anywhere. It's one of those two-engine jobs, six seats in the back."

"Where does he keep it?" Virgil asked.

"Miami. I've never seen it, but I know it's down there. He's made a couple of trips when I was around. I know he's been to Venezuela."

The team leader said, "I'll make a call."

Virgil: "We need to get down there. We need to identify him, tie him down. If he gets off the coast in that plane, gets over the Bahamas, everything will get a lot tougher."

"I'll get a ride for you," the team leader said. "Our own people will be way ahead of you, though."

"We still oughta go," Rae said to Virgil.

The team leader said to Rae, "You can't. You gotta stay. You shot Regio, there's official stuff you gotta do right now."

"Man . . ."

"He's right," Virgil said. "I got this. Won't be much for us to do, anyway."

She nodded, reluctantly, and watched as Virgil rinsed off Regio's gun again, with a freshwater dockside water hose, then rinsed off the magazine and slapped it back in the gun. "Think it'll work?"

Rae shrugged and said, "What difference would it make? Lucas told me you couldn't hit the side of a barn if you were standing inside it."

"That's an unwarranted exaggeration," Virgil said.

Lange looked from Rae to Virgil and back to Rae, and said, "I argued against shooting you two, but Jack and Marc overruled me. Anyway, remember me."

"Shut up," Rae said.

THIRTY

KENT PRUITT HAD been in the Manhattan federal lockup, in solitary confinement for just short of twenty-four hours when the cell door rattled, and he got to his feet and a large marshal with a don't-fuck-with-me look stepped in and said, "Sit."

Pruitt sat. The marshal was followed by an elegant, chilly-looking woman with a brown file envelope in her hand. She had short salt-and-pepper hair, narrow steel-rimmed glasses on her nose, a gray suit, and a gold Hermès scarf around her neck—all the better to strangle her with, Pruitt thought—though the presence of a second, even larger marshal behind her made the thought go away.

"I will not ask you any questions. I'm here to present you with a further development in your situation," the woman said. She didn't bother to introduce herself, but Pruitt knew the type—a killer. "We have two undercover marshals in imminent danger of being revealed and murdered by the Sansone organization, because, we have learned, you have alerted Sansone to our surveillance. If the marshals are murdered, we will seek the death penalty for your involvement in this conspiracy."

"I want a lawyer," Pruitt said.

"You will get one, in about forty-eight more hours," the woman said. "The marshals may be killed in the next few minutes." She turned as if to leave. "If you have no further comments or suggestions, I'll be going."

Pruitt noticed that the marshal standing behind her had clenched his fists so tightly his knuckles were white. With that, and with the words "death penalty" rattling around his brain, he held up a hand and said, "Wait, wait, wait . . . How could I . . . ?"

"We've been informed that you have an emergency alert system in which you call Sansone each night while you're delivering drugs to your salespersons," the woman said. "If you don't call, the alert is automatic. So, you've alerted him . . ."

That was all true: the feds knew and he really couldn't deny it. Or he could, but it wouldn't do him any good if Sansone ordered hits against some marshals. Which Sansone would do, if he thought he could get away with it, and Pruitt suspected Sansone wouldn't lose a single minute's sleep if his old pal Kent Pruitt got the needle.

The woman continued: ". . . and that's enough to get you the death penalty as a critical accomplice in the murders of the marshals."

"What do I get if I . . . comment?" Pruitt asked.

"We won't push the charges any further than those we are already planning to file, having to do with the delivery of drugs. Unless the marshals are already dead," she said, adding elegantly, "in which case, you are, as the marshals would say, shit out of luck."

Pruitt stared up at her and saw no mercy at all in the gray eyes behind the steel rims.

"I was supposed to call between three and four o'clock today," he said. "When you picked me up yesterday, I'd already called for the day."

"So it's seven-thirty now. He's already scrambling his organization?"

Pruitt shook his head and said, "It always takes time for them to get everything going—right now, a lawyer will be looking for me. Doug won't be sure there's a problem until the lawyer gets back to him. If the lawyer doesn't come up with something in a couple of hours, three or four hours, maybe, depending . . . Sansone is gone. He might be gone already."

The woman nodded, turned, and left the cell. The marshal backed toward the door, but before he was out, he muttered, "You better hope that none of our guys been killed, or you're gonna be shit out of luck a lot sooner than the lady expects."

AS SHE WALKED down the hallway, the woman took out a cell phone and punched in a recall, which was answered on the first ring: "Davenport."

"Lucas. Pruitt was supposed to call between three and four," the woman said. "He says they'll be looking for him, but that Sansone is probably already worried and maybe worse: he could be in the wind."

"Goddamnit!"

LUCAS WAS BACK at the task force, and he relayed the information to Orish. She said, "I think we go after them all—right now."

"Where's Sansone?"

"At his house," she said. "We saw him go in, the lights are on . . . but we haven't actually seen him since he went inside."

"And you don't have a hundred percent coverage, either."

"Not in that neighborhood. It's just not possible."

"Okay. Listen, let's not hit the car wash yet," Lucas said. "Everything else, but let's not go after the guys in the garage. They've had four dealers checking in with them this afternoon—that could be eighty or a hundred grand in cash. If Sansone's in the wind, he might still try to get it. Could reel him in if he's making a run for it."

Orish nodded. "Good. We hit everything else."

"Andres and I will go with the guys who hit his house . . ."

"Better hurry, then," Orish said. "I've got a SWAT team ready to rock in a half an hour."

"Slow them down until we get there . . ."

She looked skeptical and said, "You better hurry."

THEY RAN. DILLON Koch was waiting in the surveillance car and Lucas piled into the backseat while Devlin took the front passenger seat. "Gonna be close," Koch said. "We're probably a half hour, forty minutes away, this time of night."

"Then go, go . . ."

KOCH WAS AN excellent driver and pushed his Chevrolet through the evening traffic like a slalom skier. Devlin said, "I love this shit."

After a while, Lucas relaxed and said, "Yeah, it's not bad, but it is too bad we can't drive any faster. I could skate over there faster than this."

"Christ, I'm doing ninety through New York traffic," Koch said. "Okay, New Jersey traffic now. We're lucky the state patrol isn't all over us."

"What's that funny smell?" Devlin asked.

"It's just Elizabeth."

"Elizabeth?"

"New Jersey. You wanna stop and sniff?" Koch asked.

"Keep going. Faster," Lucas said.

They were fast for the traffic, but the traffic was tough and they wove their way through a web of freeways between Staten Island and Sansone's place in South Orange. They were still a few miles out when Orish called and said, "Two things. First, we're seeing lights go on and off in the house, we're seeing shadows on the window shades. Second, SWAT is nearly ready to move. They're still doing some recon, but it's gonna be soon."

"We're five minutes out. Maybe seven minutes. Tell them to hold on . . ."

THE SWAT TEAM was staging in the parking lot at the Orange Lawn Tennis Club, five or six minutes from Sansone's home, because the parking lot wasn't visible from the surrounding streets. Koch had the address plugged into his nav system, and as they got closer, Devlin said, looking out the windows at the stately homes and lush lawns, "Jeez, this isn't exactly my idea of New Jersey."

Koch said, "Hey, not all of New Jersey is Elizabeth. There are million-dollar houses back in here. More than that, some of them."

"How do you know that?"

"Everybody in New York knows about real estate, even when it's in Jersey," Koch said. And he added, "We're there. And on time. You're welcome."

He pulled into a lane off the main street, which they followed down to the parking lot. Though it was dark, the freezing parking lot was half full. Several people with tennis bags in their hands were standing around gawking at the feds, and Koch said, "Indoor tennis, I guess."

"If there isn't, somebody's freezing his stones off," Devlin said. "It's twenty degrees out there. And windy."

With all the other vehicles in the lot, five large black SUVs dominated. A few FBI agents, bundled in olive drab uniform coats against the cold, were standing around the trucks; one was even smoking a cigarette, not often seen with FBI agents, and there was testosterone in the air, despite the presence of female agents. One of the agents walked over to their car as Lucas and Devlin got out, and asked, "Davenport? Devlin?"

"That's us," Lucas said.

"We've been waiting."

"How long?" Devlin asked.

"Maybe . . . thirty seconds? Maybe a full minute?" The guy smiled cheerfully and said, "Good to have you with us. One of you is in the four truck, the other in the five. You got armor?"

Lucas: "No."

"Then stay back until things are quiet," the fed said. "Shouldn't take more than a minute or so. We're taking the door down. People are moving inside. We want to get right on top of them."

Lucas got in the backseat of the four truck next to a woman

who was armored and helmeted, her hands linked across her stomach, her sidearm pressing into Lucas's hip. She nodded, looked at him, and said, "You're the guy who shot Elias Dunn down in Georgia."

"In a fair fight," Lucas lied.

"In his particular case, I don't much care about fair," she said. "Are you going in at Sansone's place or are you mostly a witness?"

"I always feel I can learn something useful from watching an FBI operation," Lucas said.

The agent in the front passenger seat said, "Bullshit's getting thick back there."

"I do feel he lacks sincerity," the woman said.

As she spoke, the driver said, "We're going."

And they went.

They must look like a train, Lucas thought, five heavy black cars running so fast and close through the suburban streets that they might have been on tracks. The neighborhood, already very nice, edged toward even better as they got to Sansone's street, tall houses, stone and brick with a custom look about them, set back from the street.

The driver said, "We're coming up . . ."

LUCAS HAD BEEN on a couple of raids with FBI SWAT teams, and they were good at it. Sansone's house was two stories tall, built of some kind of gray rock, with a brick driveway leading to a detached garage in back. The house was lit up—light streaming from almost every window.

The house backed up to a line of trees with another rank of

houses behind it—and the trees would have made it possible for Sansone to slip out undetected, if he had, because the houses in back and on the sides made it impossible for surveillance SSG agents to conceal themselves for any length of time.

Looking over the shoulders of the agents in the front seat of the truck, Lucas watched as the first three trucks rolled up the driveway and the SWAT team swarmed the front door with a ram. The door went down, interior light flashing across the front yard as the team piled into the house. Simultaneously, the agents in his own truck were out and sprinting up the driveway, covering a side door to the garage and a door that went out through a porch in the backyard.

Lucas walked across the lawn, Devlin at his elbow. Devlin said, "We oughta be doing this."

"They're better at it—at this kind of thing," Lucas said.

"You really think that?" Devlin was surprised.

"I do. And we do things that they can't do. Can't have a SWAT team tracking some asshole across Kansas. The FBI plays zone defense, we're man-to-man."

"Let me think about that."

The house was surprisingly quiet. Lucas and Devlin went through the front door to find the SWATs in the living room talking to a frightened, bespectacled Hispanic woman with a vacuum cleaner. She was saying, ". . . by the time they got home, they wanted every rug in the house to be clean. Really clean. I been vacuuming . . ."

The team leader asked, "They went out the back door?"

"Yes, but I seen no car go down the driveway, maybe I was in the wrong room . . ."

"When was that?"

She shrugged. "Maybe . . . one hour? Maybe less."

The team leader said to Lucas and Devlin, "Sansone and his wife are running for it."

LUCAS GRABBED DEVLIN by the elbow and pulled him to the door. "They had the housekeeper running around the house so the SSG guys would see her shadow on the drapes."

"Now what?"

"We go man-to-man." Lucas got on his cell phone, called Koch. "Where are you?"

"Out at the curb. I followed you over. What's happening?"

"We need another ride," Lucas said. He held up a hand to the SWAT team leader, saying, "We're outta here," and on the sidewalk outside the door, Devlin asked, "Where are we going?"

"When we followed the money delivery man, he went to a locksmith shop over in Elizabeth. Sansone was there to get the money. I'm hoping he went there for one last pickup . . . could be a hundred thousand dollars. Might be hard to give up, if you're about to run off somewhere. South America, Southeast Asia."

"I'll buy that," Devlin said. "We better hurry, though. He's been out for a while."

LUCAS DIDN'T KNOW exactly where the locksmith shop was, and called Orish to find out. She found the address from the SSG driver's daily log and asked, "Do we hit the car wash?"

"Is anything happening there?"

"Yes, we had that Zamora come in a while ago. Just left."

"Hold off, then. Call me if the car wash delivery guy leaves. He might, and soon."

ORISH CALLED A few minutes later, said that Kerry, her second, wanted to be at the locksmith shop. "That could be awkward," Lucas said. "Devlin and I do this a lot. If this isn't Kerry's kind of thing . . ."

"He'll be fine, he used to be SWAT, and besides, he's already on his way," Orish said. "Where do you want to meet?"

The driver had a map up on the navigation screen, and gave Orish an intersection a couple of blocks from the locksmith's. Off the freeway, they threaded their way through an older section of the city, tall narrow yellow- and blue-painted clapboard houses built directly on the front sidewalks, no lawns at all, the houses separated by narrow driveways. Cars were parked all along the street, and in the dark, and cold, they saw only one man and one woman, the man getting in a parked car, and then pulling away, the woman standing outside a closed store, hunched against the wind, smoking.

"Let's troll the shop," Lucas said. They did that, saw one dim light, but no movement in the windows.

Lucas got on the phone to Orish: "Call your SWAT team. See if there are cars in Sansone's garage."

"Back in a minute," she said.

A minute later she called back and said, "It's a three-car garage with two cars in it, and the third space is filled up with stuff—lawn mower and so on. So . . . they're on foot."

"I can promise you that they're not on foot," Lucas said. "Where's Kerry?"

"He should be at the rendezvous," she said, anxiety leaking into her voice. "I talked to him three or four minutes ago and he was close."

"We'll be there in a minute or so."

They were, and saw a deep red RAV4 sitting on the street with its windows fogged. "There they are," said Koch. "How do you want to do this?"

"We'll walk down, I think," Lucas said. "We'll call you when . . ."

His phone buzzed and he looked at the screen. Orish. "Yeah?"

"The money man is leaving the car wash. We're tracking him."

"*Do not* let him spot you," Lucas said. "Stay way back, all we need to know is that he's coming this way."

"We got it, we got it," Orish said.

"We just pulled up behind Kerry, we'll tell him," Lucas said.

LUCAS TOLD KOCH to stay in the car, while he and Devlin walked to the RAV4 and jammed themselves into the backseat. "Tell me what you want," Kerry said.

Lucas relayed Orish's call about the money man, and said, "We need to wait until he gets here. We'll catch them with the money. I think we should walk the last block or so, quieter that way."

"I know," Kerry said. "We drove one time past the shop, to get an idea of the layout."

"Good."

Orish called and Lucas touched the speaker button on the

phone. "The money's coming your way," she said. "Same route as last time."

THEY WAITED. A man walking a leashed dog went past, blowing puffs of steam into the cold air. He stooped a bit to look at the Toyota, then hurried off. Not a neighborhood where you got curious about four men sitting in a compact car at night.

"Hope he doesn't call the cops," Kerry said.

"He might," Devlin said. To Lucas: "We all know what we're doing, let's move back to the other car. It's getting stuffy with four of us in here."

TIME DRAGS WHEN you're not having fun; they took a call from the leading SSG car tracking the money man. "We're five minutes away, maybe less."

Lucas said to Koch, "Let's go, stop a block out and around the corner from the shop."

Devlin was on his phone to Kerry: "We're moving."

They were less than a minute from the locksmith's shop. When they pulled to the curb, Kerry pulled in behind. Most of the houses around them showed lights, but there was nobody on the freezing street. Lucas and Devlin walked back to Kerry's car and got in.

The SSG tracking car called: "One minute."

"Last time, the driver was only inside a few minutes," Lucas said.

Devlin: "What if he's picking up Sansone to take him to the airport?"

"Good thought. If they do that, we jam him with the SSG cars," Lucas said. To Kerry: "They're all on radios to Orish. Tell her that the SSG might have to jam them. If we have to do that, we want to do it here where they can't try to outrun us. Block them on these narrow streets."

Kerry pushed a button on his phone, and, talking fast, told Orish what they might have to do with the SSG cars and she said she'd call them. "Let me know what's happening, Christ, I wish I was there, I should be there . . ."

"You're fine," Kerry said, and she went away.

The tracking car called and said, "He's turning the corner . . ."

At the end of the next block, headlights turned the corner and crawled toward them.

"Wait, wait, wait," Lucas said.

The lights eased to a curb, several car lengths away from the front door of the locksmith's shop. After a moment, the driver got out with a package in his hand, and walked down to the shop. He was a heavyset man wearing a black knee-length overcoat.

"The money," Devlin said.

The money man walked to the front door of the shop, did something—rang a doorbell?—waited for a moment, then the door opened and he stepped inside.

"We're on," Lucas said. To the SSG driver, he said, "Call Orish, tell her to stage the other SSG people in case they try to break out."

THE HOUSES ON the locksmith's street each had a tree in the boulevard out front, and Lucas, Devlin, and Kerry crossed the street and hurried toward the shop, not quite running, staying in the gutter, which kept the line of trees between them and shop windows.

When they got close, Lucas said, "Run."

They ran, Lucas leading, to the front door, guns in hand. Without hesitating, Lucas kicked it, hard as he could, and the door shuddered in its frame, but didn't entirely give way. Lucas stepped back, kicked it again, and it gave way. He kicked it again and he heard somebody shouting inside and he turned to Kerry and shouted, "Watch the back," then he and Devlin were inside in the dim light.

They could see a man standing in a patch of light through the door of an interior room, but then, closer, the money man rose up from behind a counter, where he'd crouched when Lucas first kicked the door, and he hurled something at Lucas's head. Lucas was only six feet away, and he flinched but had no time to duck, and the object—he found out later it was a demonstration lockset—hit him on the forehead and he staggered, sent to his knees.

Devlin shouted, "Hands, hands in the air or I'll kill you!" and then he shouted at Lucas, "You okay?"

Lucas stood up and took a tentative step and said, "Hold this guy," and he ran toward the lighted door, went through, and saw Sansone at a back door, looking at him, and Lucas lifted his pistol but Sansone was gone.

Lucas went after him, saw him running down the side of the shop toward the sidewalk. He shouted, "On the ground, on the ground!" and he heard somebody else shouting and, thirty or forty feet behind Sansone, he fired his pistol into a tree. He shouted again, "Stop, on the ground!" Sansone got to the sidewalk, looked both ways, then at Lucas, and put his hands in the air.

Lucas jogged up behind him and farther down the sidewalk, in the light from a line of house windows, saw a woman running away from Kerry, the lights blinking off her tan coat like a strobe. Kerry was closing in and Lucas saw her turn and lift a hand. Kerry went a bit sideways and the woman fired a gun at him, missing, and then turned, took a few more steps, turned back toward Kerry, and Kerry went down as she fired again, *bapbapbapbap,* straight down the sidewalk.

Lucas heard Sansone scream, "Ahhh!" He went down on the sidewalk and the woman was running away again and Kerry stood, lifted his gun, and fired once and she went down.

Devlin came down the side of the house, pushing the heavyset man in front of him, looked at Sansone floundering on the sidewalk, and then down at Kerry, standing over the woman's body, and Lucas with a gun in his hand, and asked, "What happened, what happened? Were you hit?"

Lucas: "Sansone's wife tried to shoot Kerry and she missed and hit Sansone."

"What?" And, "You got blood all over your face."

From down the sidewalk, Kerry yelled, "Ambulance. Ambulance."

Lucas was on his phone to Orish: "We're at the locksmith shop. We need a meat wagon, maybe two. In a hurry."

"Mother of God! Who's hurt?"

"Sansone and his wife. His wife shot Sansone and Kerry shot her."

"Wait a minute. Say that again?"

"Call a fuckin' ambulance, we got people bleeding here!"

THE ELIZABETH COPS and two ambulances arrived in a cloud of snowflakes and the cops taped off everything in sight and the EMTs put pressure bandages on Sansone and his wife and took them away in no great hurry. A two-person crime scene crew arrived and began marking empty nine-millimeter shells on the sidewalk.

Orish pushed through a crowd of rubberneckers, followed by two other feds from the task force and two SWAT team members from the South Orange raid. Orish demanded to know what had happened and how bad the wounds were: Sansone was hit in the right leg, breaking the femur halfway between the hip and knee. Kerry had hit Sansone's wife in the butt, in and out through her pelvic bone. Neither wound was life-threatening, which pleased Orish.

The SWAT members took charge of the money man and the $118,000 in the money man's package. One oddity: there were three checks among the currency. Devlin: "There are junkies who can buy with checks?"

Orish: "This is New York, not some remote backwater."

"Actually, it's New Jersey," Devlin said.

An FBI medic put some antiseptic on Lucas's head cut and told him not to scratch it.

Kerry was walking up and down the block, breathing hard, hyped on adrenaline after being shot at and narrowly missed. As it happened, he was wearing an Apple Watch that alerted him to unusual heart behavior. An EMT with one of the ambulances took one minute to slap a heart monitor on him and sent the EKG to the local hospital, where a doc said he didn't see any problem other than overexcitement, and who should he send a bill to?

LUCAS WAS WANDERING around the crime scene trying not to scratch his scalp and to avoid the rubberneckers when Virgil called.

"We have a problem," Virgil said. "We got Cattaneo and Lange, Regio's dead, and Weaver's team is rounding up the small fry, but it turns out that Behan probably knew we were coming . . ."

He gave Lucas a quick summary of the night so far.

"Sansone called him. He had a silent alarm . . ." Lucas explained, and told him about the arrests and the shootings in New Jersey.

"Well, we don't have Behan, not yet," Virgil said. "Turns out he's a pilot and has a plane down in Miami. We're on the way . . ."

"I can hear the siren," Lucas said. "You get Behan and we'll have a clean sweep. We'll have set back New York heroin dealing by at least an hour and only cost the American taxpayers a couple of million."

"But hey, we had a good time doing it and that's what really counts," Virgil said. "And we're gonna put the Coast Guard killers away."

"Yes, we are. Call me when you've got Behan," Lucas said. "Please tell me you're not carrying a pistol."

"Can't do that," Virgil said. "I've even got seventeen bullets. I know because I counted them. Rae couldn't come, because she had to talk to the bureaucrats about shooting Regio."

"Okay, then," Lucas said. "Take care, Virgie."

MIAMI.

Rush hour was well past but traffic was still snarly as it always was in South Florida, unregimented and fast once they were on I-95 headed south. The FBI driver, whose name was George Hamm, said, "I'd like to be there when they take him, but we're gonna be late."

"How long does it take to get an airplane up in the air from an airport?" Virgil asked. "I've never been on a private flight out of a major airport."

"Me, neither," Hamm said. "I can't believe you could run in the door and drive the plane out the other side in one minute. There are millions of commercial flights in and out all the time, I expect you'd have to wait at least a little while. Maybe quite a while."

"I hope," Virgil said. "Behan would have been the guy who set up the shootings down in Florida City."

"I've been told," Hamm said. He missed an aging Saab, with Minnesota plates, barely.

VIRGIL TOOK A call from a fed at Miami International Airport. "You sure you got good information? We've gone through the fixed-base operators here and they never heard of Behan and they don't recognize a photo."

"The guy who gave it to us is looking at a murder charge and wants some consideration, so I think he's probably telling us what he thinks is the truth," Virgil said. "No guarantees."

The agent said, "There's a bunch of general aviation airports around here. We're told to try the other ones; we're gonna split up here . . . Where are you at?"

"Broward County on I-95, coming up to the Miami-Dade line . . ."

"All right, there's an Opa-locka general aviation airport, you're right on top of it. Go west on 135th Street . . . I hope we're not screwin' the pooch . . ."

"You and me both, brother," Virgil said.

Virgil rang off and Hamm pointed at the navigation screen and said, "We're two miles from 135th, that must be the airport over here, this blank spot . . . It looks big."

Virgil got back on the phone and called Weaver in the Fort Lauderdale task force suite and told him what was happening. "You need to call somebody who can hook us up with whatever cops they've got at this place . . . It's the Opa-locka airport . . . I don't know the real name . . . Hook us up with some cops and get us to a place where small planes go outta . . ."

"Don't they have to sign up with somebody to fly? The FAA or somebody, file a flight plan? There should be a computer . . ."

"Well, shit, I don't know, Dale, I'm calling you *because* I don't know. You need to call one of your feds, get them on this."

"I'll get back to you."

Hamm: "We're coming up to 135th. How do you want to do this?"

"I need my iPad so I can look at a map," Virgil said. "Unfortunately, it's in Mankato, Minnesota."

"That's probably too far to drive," Hamm said. "You can make the nav map bigger by turning the dial . . . and we're getting off."

Virgil screwed around with the dials below the nav map until he managed to enlarge it and move it over the airport. "Okay, when we get there . . . It's further away than that FBI guy made it sound, we're not right on top of it, we're a couple of miles, I think, maybe three or four . . ."

Traffic wasn't good; Hamm was snarling at the drivers in front of him, reluctant to move even for the cop lights and siren. "You motherfucker, get out of the fuckin' way . . . Get your ass . . ."

"You need to turn north on 42nd Avenue when we get there, that should take us right through the middle of the airport," Virgil said, squinting at the nav screen.

"That'll probably be tomorrow morning the way it's going, get out of the way, you cocksucker . . ."

Virgil asked, "You armed?"

"Of course."

"You ever shoot anybody?"

"No."

"Okay, let's sort of follow my lead, huh? We're a major problem for this guy. If we take him down, he's going away forever."

"Got it." He leaned on the truck's horn and didn't get off it until the car in front of them, a Prius, edged off to the right, and the woman in the driver's seat gave them the finger as they went by.

"At least another mile," Virgil said. His phone rang: Weaver.

"You there yet?" Weaver asked.

"Couple more minutes, at least."

"Okay, I called the Miami office, they've got links to everyone. There's a street . . . 42nd Avenue . . ."

"We see it on the map."

"Okay. There'll be a cop car sitting at the intersection of 42nd and Curtiss, he'll have his flashers on. He'll take you around to wherever it is that you need to go."

"Great, thanks, man."

"I've been looking at the other Miami airports, I think you've got the best chance—that's the closest general aviation airport to Broward, in Miami-Dade. Get him."

"We're there . . . well, almost," Hamm said. He edged through a red light and they were moving fast again, came up to 42nd, made the turn north into the airport.

A block up the street, they saw the flashing lights of a cop car.

"Here we go," Virgil said.

WHEN THEY PULLED up to the cop car, a heavyset flatfoot got out, chewing on a sandwich wrapped in wax paper. "You guys are looking for somebody at the airport?" he asked, still chewing.

"He could be flying out of here in a private plane, a twin-engine plane, would have been in the last little while, we don't know where to go, who to ask," Virgil said, blurting it all out in a jumble of words.

The cop swallowed and said, "Well, it'd be out of one of the four fixed-base operators, they do everything from single-seaters to jets, so . . ."

"Let's go, take us there, lights and siren," Virgil said, not quite shouting.

The cop had taken another bite of his sandwich, chewed once, swallowed, made no move to get back in his car. He said, "I could do that, but there are four of them, probably take us a half hour. Or I could call them all and that'd take two minutes and if he's out here, we could go right to it."

"We gotta hurry," Hamm said, and he *was* shouting. "Make the calls, make the calls."

The cop nodded, asked, "What's the guy's name again?" and when told, punched a number into his cell phone. "Hey, Betty, this is Gene Potts. Yeah, how ya doin'? Listen, we're looking for a guy named Behan who might have left here in the last hour or so in a twin-engine plane, don't have any further information, the FBI is looking for him . . . No. Thanks, Betty."

Hamm said, "Jesus. Jesus."

Potts punched in a new number. "Hey, Bill, this is Gene Potts. Yeah, how ya doin'? Listen, we're looking for a guy named Behan who might have come through here in the last hour or so, flying out in a twin engine . . . Yeah? Where is he? Yeah? Listen, I got the FBI here, we'll be with you in two minutes."

He hung up and said to Virgil and Hamm, "He's here, at Catskill Aviation, but he's on the way out."

"Lead the way, and fast, really fast," Virgil said. They piled into their cars and took off. Though Potts was a slow talker, he was a fast driver, and took them down the street and into a parking lot in front of a sprawling white concrete block building where a man was waiting at the front door.

Hamm jammed the car in a handicapped parking space and he

and Virgil jumped out and ran toward the man at the door, who asked, "What'd he do?"

"Drugs and murder," Virgil said. "Is he still on the ground?"

"Yeah, I think so. He left here a couple of minutes ago . . . come on this way."

The man led them across the building at a jog, and out the back, where he pointed through the dark to a plane three or four hundred yards down a taxiway, moving slowly away from them. "That's him, the white plane, the lights, see the twin engines? It's a Beechcraft King Air 250, an older one . . ."

Virgil: "Can we get out there?"

"You mean, in a car?"

"Yeah, in a car. In a car!"

The man hesitated, then pointed down the length of the long building. "I can open up that door there, and another one on the other side, we use it for limos delivering passengers . . ."

"Do it!"

Virgil and Hamm ran back to the truck and climbed inside. The building's doors were already rolling up ten seconds later when they pulled up to the first door. Virgil said, "Kill the lights, kill the lights."

Hamm did that. They drove through the building and emerged between a couple of baggage carts and out on a semicircular concrete apron attached to a taxiway. Hamm hit the gas and Virgil rolled down the windows and Hamm asked, "What are we gonna do?"

"Try to take out the tires, I guess. I hope they have air in them, hope they're not solid . . ."

"I got no idea . . . I don't know if a nine will punch holes in them anyway."

"If I can't, I'll put a few shots into the cabin," Virgil said.

"You could kill him . . ."

"I'll shoot low . . ."

"Hope to God we got the right plane."

THEY WERE GAINING on the white plane, probably a quarter-mile away when they hit the taxiway, but as they watched, the plane slowed and then made a right-angle turn.

"Shit, he's going for the runway," Hamm said.

The plane continued rolling for a few seconds, then turned again, toward them, this time.

"I'm cutting across the grass, I'll come up behind him . . . maybe I could ram him."

"Just get me up beside him . . . Don't ram him yet."

THE PLANE HESITATED on the runway, rolled forward a few feet. Then a few more feet. Behan had apparently not yet seen them. Hamm drove the car across a grass island between the taxiway and the runway, onto the runway, and as the plane began its take-off roll, Virgil saw the pilot's white face turn toward them.

He'd seen them now. Hamm swung behind the plane and floored the accelerator, and caught it, well off to the side because of the plane's low wing.

Virgil leaned out the window with Regio's Beretta and as they pulled up beside the plane, began firing at the nose gear with no apparent effect, five, ten shots, hard to hold because the car was bouncing, then the tire suddenly collapsed and the plane twisted toward them. Virgil, watching the prop, screamed, "Get away, get away!" and Hamm swung hard away.

Virgil looked back. The plane stopped beside the runway, half on, half off, and wasn't going anywhere.

Hamm cranked the truck in a circle as the plane's engines died, and brought it nose to nose with the plane. Virgil climbed out of the truck and ran around it as he saw stairs coming down from the side of the aircraft, and then Behan in the doorway.

Virgil pointed his pistol at him and shouted, "Out! Out!"

Behan squinted at him and said, "What the fuck? Willy?"

Hamm came up and shouted, "FBI! Get out of the plane! Let's see your hands."

Behan said, "Fuck you. I got no gun."

He came down the steps and marched straight at Hamm, who was closest to the door, and Hamm said, "You're under arrest for . . ."

Behan lurched forward and with a truly excellent straight right hand, hit Hamm in the nose, knocking the FBI agent down. As Hamm rolled and tried to crawl, Behan turned toward Virgil, and Virgil said, "You take another step, Mike, I swear to God I'll shoot you in the balls."

Behan put his hands up and said, "Don't do that."

Hamm staggered to his feet, hands to his face, and when Virgil asked if he was okay, said, "I think he broke my nose. I'm bleeding like a fire hose. Shoot him. C'mon, shoot him."

Behan said, "Hey! Hey!"

◆◆◆

MORE LIGHTS WERE rolling toward them, fast, including a fire engine. Potts, the cop, got there first, and when he got out of the car, Virgil said, "Put some cuffs on this guy. And we're gonna need some gauze or something for the agent here."

When things were controlled, Virgil walked away from the crowd and called Lucas.

"You get him?"

"Yeah. I had to shoot down his plane to do it, but we got him." He took a minute to tell Lucas about the chase and shooting.

"Well, good. Finally found a target big enough for you to hit," Lucas said. "Maybe the gun company will pay you for an endorsement. Anybody hurt?"

"The agent with me got punched in the nose. That's about it. Regio's dead and Lange's cooperating, so . . ."

"Clean sweep," Lucas said.

Loose ends, trials, more diving, a little sex, and the Islands . . .

Virgil gave his last GPS coordinates to the Coast Guard, along with the magic wand. The Coast Guard brought in a group of professional divers and they cleaned up the heroin cans in two days. Coast Guard officers were a little irked that they'd been cut out of the surveillance and the arrests, but they made the best of it, piling seven hundred kilos of heroin on an admiral's desk in front of the Coast Guard flag, for the reporters and photographers to gawk at. There were unconfirmed rumors from the DEA that a cartel kingpin in Colombia saw the picture and wept.

Despite the follow-the-money tactic demanded by Lucas, which was a major feature in the trials, the Manhattan agent in charge was shown, the day after the final raids, with rolled-up shirtsleeves, piling the seized heroin on a table in an FBI basement somewhere. Orish, who ran the actual operation, was allowed to hang in the background, smiling wistfully.

DOUGLAS SANSONE'S ORGANIZATION was torn to pieces by the investigation. All the major figures—with two exceptions—drew life sentences in federal prisons. The trials, held in New York, New Jersey, and South Florida, got sporadic media coverage. A small Canadian forest was cut down to create paper for the FBI press releases.

DURING THE TRIAL of Sansone, Behan, and Cattaneo—they were tried together—Cattaneo's wife, Belinda, was put on the stand by the prosecution, as a friendly witness, given immunity for information tying the three men together in a single conspiracy. When questioned about her authority to speak to the subject, she conceded that she'd had a long-standing sexual affair with Behan. The resultant shouting, Cattaneo on his feet, Behan with his head down on the table, Sansone laughing like a madman, was eventually contained by the federal marshals who worked for the court.

THE TWO EXCEPTIONS to the life sentences were Matt Lange and Sylvia Sansone. Lange got fifteen years with the possibility of parole, for his testimony about the other members of the organization. Sansone was sentenced to eight years on a charge of aggravated assault on a federal officer for shooting at Kerry during the final chase in Elizabeth, NJ. She accepted the plea and the sentence in return for the government dropping a list of additional charges that, if proven, would have added years to the sentence. Both Sansone and his wife were hit with huge fines, and the government seized, and auctioned off, their house, cars, and donut shops. A wealthy fan of Mama Ferrari's Donuts won the auction and expanded the chain down the East Coast, and became even wealthier. Damn good donuts.

PATTY PITTMAN, ALICIA Snow, and Magnus Elliot were all killed by Jimmy Parisi and a couple of assistants. One of the assistants, given a modest deal, took Miami-Dade homicide cops to an area of the Everglades where the bodies had been dumped. A body was found, but it was in an advanced state of decay, and DNA analysis proved that it was not one of the three people known to have been killed by Parisi. The body was never identified. A jury took the assistant's word for it, however, and Parisi went to prison for life without parole.

DON ROMANO AND Larry Bianchi walked. There'd been a fundamental error in the arrest—there was nothing illegal about possessing a hundred and twenty handguns in Florida. If they'd transported the guns across a state line, they would have been up to their necks in felonies. As it was, the driver of the van took some heat about leaving New York without notifying his parole officer, but given the prisoner-population problems in New York, he eventually got away with it. The legbreaker riding with him had no warrants or parole problems. Final score: Mobsters 4, Feds 0.

✦✦✦

CHRISTOPHER COLLES, THE Florida senator, held a press conference in Miami, thanking "all the federal law-enforcement agencies, including the FBI, the Marshals Service, and the Coast Guard" for breaking the Coast Guard murder case. He shook Weaver's hand on camera, and the hand of the Coast Guard district commander, but that part of the video was cut by most TV stations. After the show, Colles phoned Lucas and said, "I owe you and I pay my debts. When you need something legal that I can get you, call me."

VIRGIL TOLD LUCAS, "Rae saved my life. If she'd been a little slower, we'd both be dead. No doubt in my mind. She's the most impressive cop I've ever met."

"Present company excepted, I imagine," Lucas said.

"I don't know, Lucas. She's something else. If you need me to do this again, working with Rae, all you have to do is call me. I'm in. I love that chick."

"I'll do that," Lucas said. "I mean, you're the only cop I know who shot down an airplane with a pistol."

"Another episode in the growing legend of Virgil Flowers, Minnesota lawman," Virgil said. "I've got another question. A delicate one. Rae and I turned in all the payment money we got from Behan and Cattaneo, of course, but we used some of it to buy stuff— it was really a necessary part of the work. They would have been suspicious as hell if we hadn't. I got this pair of crocodile cowboy boots . . ."

"*Used* cowboy boots now," Lucas said. "Weaver told me you'd turned over the cash and asked what I thought about Rae's shoes. We talked to Mallard about it, he says you guys should keep what you bought. He says you can even keep the scuba gear, if you want it, in case you work for us again. He said it was necessary equipment for the charade and now it's used and surplus to requirements."

"Cool," Virgil said.

Rae said to Lucas, "I couldn't believe that thing about the shoes. I even asked, 'Am I only supposed to wear them when I'm on duty?' Weaver said, 'As a marshal, you're required to carry a pistol at all times. That means you're sort of on duty at all times. You can wear the shoes any time you feel like it.' I got a pair of Tom Ford stiletto sandals that I might have mugged somebody for, if I'd seen them on another woman."

"What'd you think about working with Virgil?"

"Virgil. If he wasn't so committed . . . but I won't go there. He might be the best cop I've ever met."

"Present company excepted, I imagine . . ."

"I'm not sure about that, Lucas, no offense," Rae said. "We were sitting in that shitty bar talking to those dopers and Virgil was so naturally comfortable with them, I had to be there to believe it. Those guys are now his best friends in Hollywood, Florida. He's apparently got this great girlfriend and everything, but he's hot. And he makes me laugh. He's got a hard nose when he needs it . . . He shot down an *airplane*. Have *you* ever shot down an airplane?"

✠ ✠ ✠

WEAVER WAS BUMMED that his face didn't feature in the FBI's video celebrations. A couple of weeks after he returned to his open-style work space in Washington's J. Edgar Hoover Building, he was staring at a screen full of memos from the U.S. Attorney's Office in Miami when Louis Mallard walked through. Mallard saw him and called out, "Hey, Dale," and swerved into Weaver's space, borrowed an unused chair from an adjacent desk, and sat and chatted about the case.

During the entire conversation it was all "Dale" and "Louis" under the eyes of twenty or thirty agents and clerical personnel. When Mallard left, he slapped Weaver on the back and said, "Terrific job, buddy. Makes me proud."

When Weaver told him about it, Lucas said, "That's Louis for you. He didn't walk through there by accident. He was looking for you. Another ally, you know, and jacking up the morale around the office, which I hear isn't so good. But he's not a phony: you're a real friend of his now."

"Yeah, I . . . Jeez, I'm getting a different kind of treatment around here," Weaver said. "When we broke the case, it was 'Great job, what we expected from you.' That was nice, but backslapped by Louis Mallard? My boss is almost afraid to talk to me. You can't know how good that feels."

VIRGIL GOT HOME to Mankato, Minnesota with the scuba gear and cowboy boots, in time for a major dump of snow. He, Frankie, his mother, the twins, Frankie's ten-year-old son, Sam, and Honus the dog were more or less home-bound for two days, which was not a hardship. Honus the dog was all over him, as was Sam, who insisted that the three of them play Nerf football in the snow. Honus won, with three interceptions and runbacks estimated at between two and three hundred yards each. During the relatively short time Virgil was gone, the twins had calmed down somewhat, and didn't bawl for more than four to six hours a day.

After an extended first night in bed, Frankie said, a soft and lazy sloe-eyed look on her face, "I gotta meet this Rae. She really got you wound up."

"Sweetheart, you do all the winding I'll ever need," Virgil said.

He got away with it. The third day he was back, he sat at his computer, peered at the empty screen for a bit, called up a blank page on Microsoft Word, and typed, "Chapter One."

Lucas was in and out of St. Paul for two weeks, tying up loose ends in South Florida and New York. When he got off the plane for the last time—or the last time before he'd be called to rehearse for the trials—he told Weather, "I need to spend time with you and the kids. When spring vacation comes up, let's write a note to the school and get an extra week off. Paris and Rome, like that. Madrid. Make one great trip out of it."

"Okay with me," Weather said. She'd done three surgeries that day, and had been busy all winter. "I could use the break. If we *can* do it, I'm up for it."

"Why couldn't we do it?" Lucas asked. "Be good for the kids' education."

"I meant, if we're *allowed* to," Weather said. "All the docs are talking about this Covid virus. I guess it's bad—it's a killer. It's apparently as infectious as the flu."

"So we get the shots . . ."

"There aren't any shots to get," she said. "I talked to an epidemiologist at the U and she says it could be as bad as the 1919 pandemic. That's hard to believe, but she's scared. *Really* scared, and she's not the scary type. She says we might have to lock down the country, ban travel."

"I guess we'll see," Lucas said. "Hell, with all the modern tech you got in the hospitals now, how bad could it get?"

JAQUELL THE DIVER fled to the Bahamas' Out Islands. With her parents and siblings and girlfriend, she spent her days fishing, diving, selling lobster to snowbirds who were too lazy to dive for their own.

She was calling herself Darshan, now, and told friends she'd decided to go by her middle name.

Out there on the islands, nobody was too concerned about what was happening in the States and Jaquell/Darshan never heard about the convictions of the Coast Guard killers. So she stayed out there, in the sun, occasionally glancing over her shoulder.

You can look for Darshan down the Exumas—an attractive, athletic woman with a tentative smile, in a size-small wet suit.

Steel drums, you know, the chicken dance. Pretty women around a fire on the beach. Like that.

AUTHOR'S NOTE

MY BROTHER-IN-LAW DAN called me up and told me that in *Golden Prey*, I'd referred to a 40mm pistol. Should have been .40 caliber. Calibers are hundredths of an inch, millimeters are . . . millimeters. A 40mm pistol would shoot a bullet about an inch and a half across. There *is* a 40mm round—it's fired from a grenade launcher, not the kind of weapon that Lucas Davenport would have tucked under his sport coat.

How do these mistakes happen? It's not usually ignorance. They arise out of all kinds of things . . . haste, changes in story, weariness, boredom, juggling too many nouns at once. In another Prey novel, I had a man click off the safety on his Glock 9mm pistol, stolen from a Minneapolis detective, before he entered a house. The 9mm was fine, except Glocks don't have safeties.

I'd originally written that the man had been carrying a Beretta, which do have safeties. Then, I made the mistake of talking to a Minneapolis detective who told me there'd been a change of policy, and they were no longer allowed to have personal carry pistols. They were required to use issue pistols, which were all Glocks. So, trying to be accurate, I changed "Beretta" to "Glock"—this was after the novel was essentially finished—and forgot that several lines above that, he'd clicked off the safety . . .

In *Winter Prey*, on the first page, I have a snowmobiling villain following a compass course of 375 degrees through a blizzard. That's tough, since compasses only have 360 degrees. It was supposed to be 275 degrees, or west, but instead, he's going northeast. I don't know how that mistake occurred, but it should have been caught by somebody, at some point. I suspect it was a pure typo.

The thing is, I know about guns and have been shooting since I was in elementary school. I know the difference between millimeters and calibers, I know Glocks don't have safeties, I know how many degrees there are on a compass.

Holding a hundred thousand words in your head, through numerous edits and rewrites, is a complicated business, and by the time you get to the end, you can barely stand to read through them again. When you're dealing with numbers, especially, they can jump up and bite you in the ass.

Now, to *Ocean Prey*. I'm a recreational diver, but the diving portrayed in this book isn't recreational, it's technical. Scuba diving is overrun with numbers, and necessarily so. It starts right with the capacity (maybe a hundred cubic feet of air) and pressures (maybe 3,000 pounds per square inch) of your scuba tanks. When you're diving, you have to know how much air you have left (numbers) and how long you've been down (numbers) and how deep you went (numbers) and how soon you can dive a second time (numbers). It's good to know at what depth you start to suffer from nitrogen narcosis (numbers) and how much weight you need to be neutrally buoyant (numbers) and how fast you can surface after you've spent time down deep, to avoid decompression sickness (numbers).

Errors often creep in with this kind of technical matter. Although I dive, I'm not really at ease with technical diving, so I searched high and low for good advice, and wound up consulting my next-door neighbor, Marcus Randolph, who is certified to do almost everything in scuba, and who has dived around much of the world. His comments caused an extensive revision of this book at literally the last moment (a Sunday, I remember it well; the manuscript was due in New York on Monday). I think we got it right; if any mistakes have crept in, they are down to me, and my efforts to simplify a highly technical and numbers-heavy subject matter. I greatly appreciate Marcus's help with the book.

However, if you are a diver, and you do find a serious error, I would ask that you write it down on a piece of scrap paper, then wad the paper up, put it in your mouth, and chew thoroughly before you swallow.

I don't want to hear about it.

I'm asking nice—don't make me come over there.